THE
BEST
THiNGS

MEL GIEDROYC has been entertaining the nation for nearly thirty years. A comedian, writer, actor and presenter, Mel is best known for her work with Sue Perkins in the double act Mel & Sue. They have presented many TV shows such as multi Bafta-winning *The Great British Bake Off* (BBC) and *Light Lunch* (Channel 4). Mel has written two non-fiction books and has appeared in sitcoms and panel shows, on radio and on the West End stage. Mel and Sue reunited in comedy drama *Hitmen* for Sky TV. Mel lives in London with her husband and two daughters.

The Best Things is Mel Giedroyc's debut novel.

MEL
GIEDROYC

THE
BEST
THINGS

H

REVIEW

First published in 2021 by Headline Review
An imprint of HEADLINE PUBLISHING GROUP

1

Cataloguing in Publication Data is available from the British Library

Hardback ISBN 978 1 4722 5621 8
Trade paperback ISBN 978 1 4722 5622 5

Typeset by EM&EN
Printed and bound in Great Britain by Clays Ltd, Elcograf S.p.A.

Headline's policy is to use papers that are natural, renewable and recyclable
products and made from wood grown in well-managed forests and other
controlled sources. The logging and manufacturing processes are expected
to conform to the environmental regulations of the country of origin.

MIX
Paper from
responsible sources
FSC® C104740

HEADLINE PUBLISHING GROUP
An Hachette UK Company
Carmelite House
50 Victoria Embankment
London EC4Y 0DZ

www.headline.co.uk
www.hachette.co.uk

For the gang

Rank squanders money; trade makes it; – and then trade purchases rank by re-gilding its splendour.

Anthony Trollope, *The Way We Live Now*

On average a horse will produce between fifteen and thirty-five pounds of manure a day. To her it felt as if all the horses of the world, from cowboy steeds roaming the plains of Texas to snooty show-jumpers lifting their tails in the Leatherhead area, were simultaneously dumping on her. While laughing at her.

She caught sight of herself, a Stig of the Dump creature reflected in the tiny window of the dark stable. Bright blue eyes piercing through a face-pack of teak-coloured horse manure. Her nails, once used to laying themselves elegantly out on a manicurist's cushion, were now worn down to the quick and wedged with grime.

She looked down at her feet. She was wearing her daughter's trainers, which were a size too small. And a pair of combat trousers that even a small marine wouldn't touch.

Soon after the Great Horse Manure Crisis of 1894, when large cities were in danger of drowning in the stuff, the *Times* newspaper predicted that, in fifty years' time, every street in England would be buried under around nine foot of manure. A hundred and twenty-five years later, here she was proving that, yes, she was eye-deep in the shit and it was way, way deeper than nine foot.

1

Ah, Leatherhead! You are the very lungs of Surrey. Regular as an oxygenated pendulum, your life-giving bellows swish in and out, out and in. For you are much like good health itself. And like health, that most precious thing, we take you for granted. Our eye does not see you. You are simply part of the rolling, verdant canvas that soothes the clutter of our daily lives. But if you were not here, Heaven forefend, what should we do then? Oh, Leatherhead, don't take away your luxuriant hills, rolling out expansively in a rich shag pile of fertile grass from the back of Cedar Vale all the way to Weybridge and thence to the horizon itself.

Sally Parker frowned, wrinkling her delicate freckled nose, and rubbed out the word 'fertile', replacing it with 'fecund'. She listened to the wellness podcast 'From Anxious to Blanxious' religiously every morning when she was on her running machine. Today's episode had advised her that writing could be a mindful and meditative antidote to life's bumpier moments. The soothing voice went on to suggest writing about the everyday things that surround us. And since Leatherhead was what surrounded her, that was what Sally decided to write about.

'"The very lungs of Surrey",' she read back to herself. 'I like "the lungs of Surrey", but "the very lungs"? Too

3

forceful. And I'm not so sure about "pendulum". Can a pendulum swish in and out? And I'm not sure about "out and in" after "in and out". It sounds immature. And who the hell says "Heaven forefend" these days? Not even my mother says that and she's eighty-three.'

And with that she screwed up the piece of paper she'd been writing on and threw it petulantly into a beige high-heeled boot beside her.

Sally Parker had a morbid fear of big social events and it was for this reason that she was crouching down low among her Kurt Geigers in the shoe section of her walk-in wardrobe. Her anxiety was on the rise today and her wardrobe was the perfect place to get away from it all, be on her own and try the art of mindful writing that the podcast suggested.

Sally knew that the staff would be taking care of everything downstairs, power walking around her house with purpose, checking off their mental spreadsheets.

Paloma, Sally's Spanish cook-cum-housekeeper, liked to draft in members of her family if the Parkers had a big do on. And this was a barbecue for seventy-five to celebrate the tenth anniversary of Frank Parker's hedge-fund management company. Two of Paloma's cousins were busy finishing off marinating the guinea fowl, lark, duck and lamb, laying out the trestle tables with white linen tablecloths outside and arranging the enormous gas-fired barbecues for Frank to take charge of as soon as he arrived home. They'd even put out his special glove – more of a medieval gauntlet really – with 'BARBECUE LIKE A BASTARD' emblazoned on it in gold. It was a gift from a client; Frank's love for a barbie was so legendary in the City that certain colleagues had been known to call him Ken.

The expansive and luxurious salad buffet was prepped – artichokes, wild rice, tiny jewels of pomegranate, butternut squash, heritage tomatoes and organic basil as far as the eye could see, all laid out in the ornamental patio area. Paloma was test-driving a new salad tonight – jackfruit couscous with a wasabi sauce. Sally thought it sounded inedible but didn't have the guts to tell her. Paloma had been with the household for nearly eleven years now, and would purse her lips into a self-pitying prune if her culinary experiments met any sign of resistance.

A big event like this also meant that Sally had to deal with the household speaking in Spanish, making her feel even further alienated and stripped of authority. She had done a Spanish course when her children were tiny, specifically to try to bridge the divide between herself and her housekeeper, but she was not the most gifted at language-learning. Even so, she'd made a stab at it that very morning.

'Er . . . Paloma . . . *por favor* . . . *el* . . . wasabi. *Es* . . . er . . . a bit . . . *piccante*? Spicy?'

Paloma shared a secret smile with her cousin. 'I sorry Miss Parker. I no understand. Spicy?'

Sally's English-rose complexion had blushed a delicate pink. Paloma blatantly understood English very well, particularly a word such as 'spicy'. In fact Paloma could probably translate the whole of the Maastricht Treaty if she was offered cash to do it. Paloma was wont to play the 'Manuel card', as Sally rather sharply explained to her husband, when she wanted to get one over her employers. And Frank's response? The same he used for most of his wife's dilemmas. He would look at her with puppy-dog eyes, full of the love that had burned since the moment he'd first set eyes on her when they were both sixteen. Then he'd say, 'Sal, babe. It's all taken care of.'

And that was Sally's life. All taken care of. What she really, *really* wanted to do was sack Paloma. Had done for six years or more. But she never seemed to find the right time, or indeed pluck up sufficient courage. And Frank just wouldn't hear of it. He and Paloma had a mutual love-in going on. Every time he was near her he'd say something cheesy in Spanglish, or break into 'Paloma Blanca' loudly. Paloma would then giggle like a school-girl. And since Frank was the one paying her wages, Sally didn't have a leg to stand on. All taken care of.

Sure, Sally loved coming down late on a Sunday morning to a huge family table already laid out with glis-tening blueberry pancakes, homemade Bircher muesli and a tall glass of freshly squeezed passion-fruit juice. Sally adored the hot coffee simmering on Paloma's spick-and-span hob. But it needled at her, made her throat dry with guilt. Sally often felt as if she were a guest living in a hotel, rather than a wife and mum running her own home.

She breathed deeply in through her nostrils, another good tip from the podcast.

'Leatherhead. You are sanctuary. Leatherhead. You are soothing yang to my anxious yin.' She shook her head, rummaging around in the pocket of a biscuit-coloured Reiss coat. 'That's another thing you can cross off your list. A writer you are not, Sally Parker. Along with painter, hostess, and, let's face it, parent. The end.'

Her hand alighted upon a little pack of Temazepam in the coat pocket. Dr Livesy had prescribed this for Sally earlier in the week. She hadn't touched any Valium for two years but just recently the stress of life had begun to weigh more heavily.

'Just in case you need to take the edge off, Sally,' Dr Livesy had said to her with a wolfish smile.

'This is just to take the edge off,' she repeated to herself in the wardrobe, 'and save the world from your appalling writing. Who do you think you are, Sally Parker?'

And with that she swallowed her little guilty pleasure. No, not a pleasure, she remonstrated with herself, it was a guilty necessity.

'Muuuuu-uuuuum!'

The familiar pipes of her daughter Mikey blasted up the stairs. It must be four o'clock already. Another day and where had it gone? Slipped off the calendar like soap, and what had she achieved? She'd walked the dogs, surfed the internet for a couple of hours and done a Body Conditioning class at the gym. Oh, and she'd spoken to her so-called great friend Francesca Daly-Jones on the phone about the upcoming Charity Ball. She was starting to question that friendship. Should the sight of a friend's name coming up on your phone make you feel itchy?

No time to analyse this now. Sally could hear the power of eleven-year-old Mikey's strong and insistent calves pumping up the stairs, two at a time. Mikey was a carbon copy of her dad – just like Frank, everything had to be done now, faster, bigger, better. Exhausting. Sally sighed to herself, stood up in the wardrobe with purpose and promptly banged her head into a hard-edged designer grip bag. It had cost £2,400 and Sally had never even used it. It was hideous, actually, a shiny maroon monstrosity with a silver key pattern all over it.

'Muuuuu-uuuuum!!' Mikey's voice had a grinding edge now.

'Mikey darling,' shouted Sally brightly, 'I'm here, I'm in the wardrobe!'

'What?' Mikey slid back the huge cream door to find her mum rubbing her head and standing among many items of clothing sheathed in polythene bags.

'What are you doing in there, Mum?'

'I was . . . er . . . actually doing something very useful.

A bit of seasonal sorting, Mikey. So. Coats here for autumn
. . . and then these ones for winter. Move over high summer
gear, and hello . . . er . . . the things with a heavier tone and
weave. As I said, it's very useful.'

Mikey folded her arms across her chest and narrowed
her lively brown eyes.

'Why?'

And there was silence. It was a very good question to
which Sally had no immediate answer. Why was she doing
this? In fact, why was she doing anything? She could feel
her heart start to beat faster and her face flush up. She was
on the outer edges of an anxiety attack. Not now. Come
on, sweet Valium. Kick in, my friend. Do your stuff. Help
me get through this.

'I mean, why isn't Paloma doing this, Mum? That's
what she's paid to do, isn't it? So that you can, you know,
do the things that you're supposed to do, like . . . like . . .'

And Mikey trailed off, stumped.

Sally smiled, breathed in and emerged from the wardrobe.

'Paloma's busy preparing Dad's special barbecue,
Mikey,' she said, tidying her expensively highlighted
honey-coloured curls and smoothing down her white
linen shirt, 'and besides, I do . . . er . . . a lot of useful
stuff like this round the house. Paloma doesn't do everything you know. She's great at helping, of course, but
she's our back-up, Mikey, our Plan B, she's there to . . .'

Mikey had already started to march off. So like Frank.
She had the attention span of a gnat. Then suddenly she
turned and was right under Sally's nose, almost giving her
a heart attack.

'Miss McBride wants to talk about my dyslexia with
you,' said Mikey in a forthright tone. 'She'll call you. And
I made twenty-eight quid seventy this lunchtime!'

Sally felt a pang of worry as her daughter told her this. Mikey's money-making had gone from the odd fifty pence in the playground to multiples of pounds these days.

'Oh Mikey, what for this time?'

'Slime.'

And she was gone. Sally took a deep breath; her heartbeat was starting to regulate. She put her slim, tanned little feet into a pair of furry white Adidas sliders, padded through the bedroom, out on to the vast gallery landing, and started to descend the wide staircase.

Her hand slid down the smooth birch banister as her white slippers sank into the thick white carpet. Everything around her was white, now she thought of it. A big white carpeted padded cell. There was a series of family photos taken in a posh studio six years ago which lined the staircase in silver frames. All of the family had been asked to wear white for the photoshoot. There was Frank in white linen looking a bit Boyzone, Stephen in white T-shirt and shorts – that was probably the last time she'd seen her son in shorts, she thought wistfully. And Cleo, Emily and Mikey in white shift dresses. How Mikey had hated that dress, even at the age of five. Sally could see her scowling as she lay on the white furry rug. Stephen looked sweet, and the right weight, Sally couldn't help noticing. There he was with his normal nine year old's body. Why did she only ever look at him now and see kilos and grams? She made a mental note to herself to try and stop doing that. True, he'd grown a lot larger lately, but he was her son and she must love him, however much of him there was.

The Parker children were in a line, facing the camera, lying on their tummies with their feet swinging up behind them. The photographer had wanted them all to grin like buffoons. He kept saying things like, 'Come on, Mum, let's see you react to your cheeky little monkeys!'

Emily, through a half-hearted grin, was looking directly into the camera with a faintly bored expression. She was Frank and Sally's niece but had lived with them since the age of one, when Sally's wayward sister Nancy had pretty much left her in a basket on their doorstep. Nancy had then disappeared to follow a new boyfriend and the promise of a sculpting career in India, and her visits in the last fifteen years had been sporadic and disruptive. Through it all, Emily remained unphased, observing everything with an inbuilt capacity to weigh it all up. Like her bedroom, her thoughts were neat, deft and ordered. She was half-Thai (her mum was something of a traveller), and this marked her out among the Parker children as the daintier, more petite of the four. She was also the brainiest by far of the Parker children. Indeed, the entire household. Sally was in awe of Emily's brain. Frank found it harder to deal with. Her cousins adored her and were thankful for the endless supply of homework she'd done for them over the years.

Sally smiled wistfully at Emily in the photos – they'd been a bit distant from each other in the last few months. She made a mental note to get closer to her niece. Maybe a little evening course together? Pottery? Fencing?

Cleo, aged eleven in the pictures and a year older than her beloved cousin, had managed to smuggle some foundation on (artfully blended even then) plus mascara, and just the slightest whiff of lip gloss. Cleo owned the camera. In every photo she gave the lens something slightly different, and in Sally's least favourite Cleo was fake-smiling with her tongue showing through parted lips. Cleo was born Instagram-ready. Sally made a mental note that she must work on Cleo and her Instagram use. She must help her find a nice wholesome hobby. What would be good for a seventeen-year-old non-reader? Floristry, perhaps? Or caving? They could go caving together, mother and daughter, that'd be fun. There must be some caves near Leatherhead, surely?

In almost every photo, Sally was widening her eyes, which to others might seem alluring, but to Sally just looked stressed. She had to face that wide-eyed look in the mirror most mornings. And Frank Parker, in every photo, looked like the cat with the cream. He'd loved every minute of that photoshoot. He loved the photographer, and the rugs, and the results. That's why so many of these damn pictures were hanging up here on the staircase.

And then of course the Daly-Joneses had gone to the exact same photographer, dressed themselves in white too and posed on that exact same furry rug, like gurning idiots, the lot of them. Sally shook her head. This happened a lot with the Daly-Joneses. When the Parkers went on safari to Namibia, the Daly-Joneses made an African trip soon after. When the Parkers had a basement cinema and gym complex built, would you believe it? Francesca announced to the Leatherhead charity ladies that builders were starting on their basement project immediately. Sally once pretended to Francesca that they were buying a giraffe, just to see if Francesca would make the call to Chessington Zoo.

Sally stepped down into the hall. Paloma's cousin Feliz was scurrying around it, wielding a mop across the nearly life-sized marble chessboard. The pawns were knee height and the rook and bishop reached Sally's chest. Frank had been given it by a client from Jeddah and it was his pride and joy. You'd need to be Geoff Capes to play with it, though. Sally thought it was hideous and ostentatious, but still organised for the entire hall floor to be chequered in black and white marble for Frank's fortieth birthday to display it on. It was, as the neighbours around Cedar Vale liked to say, a real talking point.

One day maybe all the objects around her husband would be larger than life, Sally thought ruefully. Frank would end up like one of the Borrowers, eating peas the size of space hoppers off a fork the size of a garden spade.

In this resplendent chess setting, Garry Kasparov was the only thing missing, and he'd have to be enlarged to the size of a house to play with this ghastly thing. Emily played chess on a sensibly sized board. Sally wished her son would play too. Stephen was always on that bloody PS3 or whatever it was called, for hours every day. She must get him interested in something else, something life-affirming that would help him shed weight. Hockey? Boxing? Potholing? There must be potholes near Leatherhead. She made a mental note to herself to find out.

The double front door opened to the music of the 1812 Overture – Frank had commissioned this specially from a firm in Switzerland. Sally loathed it. Every time the bell rang or the door opened there was a long and pompous refrain to remind Leatherhead that the Parker family were a cut above everyone else. It was a constant running joke with the postman.

'You could say it's a door HANDEL, Mrs Parker!' he'd been saying jauntily for the last ten years, and Sally would laugh dutifully every time.

In came Stephen, huffing and puffing as usual, chomping through a chocolate bar. Sally took it as a personal slight, every time she looked at him, that he should be overweight.

'Stephen, sweetheart,' she said gently as he loped past her in the hall, heading for the stairs up to his games console, 'didn't you find the . . . er . . . granola bites that Colette put out for you?'

On cue, Colette the Australian nanny came barging through the door carrying various PE kits and bags, Emily and Cleo in tow. Colette threw the Jeep keys down on the sideboard, which Sally had found in a Sussex furniture boutique for £10,600. It was made from hornbeam wood and imported from Serbia. It annoyed Sally that the nanny had so little respect for its flawless honey-coloured surface. Many times a day those Jeep keys clattered on to it, causing Sally to bite her tongue, on the verge of telling the nanny off but never quite plucking up the courage to do so. It often struck her that Colette, who was paid £1,100 a week plus all food, petrol, a self-contained flat upstairs and every weekend off plus four weeks' paid holiday a year, appeared to have the God-given right to throw the Jeep keys down on her beautiful Serbian sideboard.

'Emily's got a letter for you about the orchestra trip?'

Everything Colette said ended in a question mark. Sally sighed. Fifteen years of empty questions that led nowhere. Stephen started to hump his bag and himself up the stairs.

'Thank you, Colette, I'll have a look at that later. Ste, love, you know that your allotted snacks are in the green-lidded Tupperware. Aren't they, Colette? Is that up in the corner cupboard . . . or . . . ?' Colette shrugged her shoulders unhelpfully. 'Or they might be next to the dried fruits in the tin? Is that where Paloma keeps dried fruits? Dr Livesy was adamant that you stick to your calories, Ste. I know it's boring, but as your mum I can just sense that you're going to feel so much better when you start to . . . you know . . . feel a little lighter. You'll be able to really get involved with things that your friends are into, sport . . . er . . . and lots of other different—'

But Stephen's door was already shut. This was a recurring theme in Sally Parker's domestic life. Half-finished thoughts, pieces of maternal advice curtailed by a door slam, the buzz of a phone, or simply a teenage death-stare.

Luckily the Valium was starting to do its job. The edges of her sightlines were now gently fudged and her teeth felt comfortably soft in her mouth. She could handle anything. Even Colette's annoying upturned voice.

'I've got the letter for Emily's music trip right here?'

Every time Sally heard Colette's voice, a little piece of her synaptic process died. Colette questioned but didn't want answers; she just wanted enough cash to get ratted every Friday night with her mates in the Redback Bar in Epsom. Why couldn't Sally just sack her? The children were far too old for a nanny now. Sally could justify having one when Emily was deposited on their doorstep. Colette had blazed into their lives with her boundless energy and ballsy bright red hair.

'I don't know what I'd do without you, Colette!' Sally had said to her at least six times a day.

But these days Sally had a fair idea what she'd do without her. She'd get the bunting out, dance a jig with her pants down and shout at the top of her voice, 'THANK GOD THAT ABRASIVE, MATERIALIST MONEY DRAINER IS OUT OF MY LIFE!!!!'

'Thank you so much, Colette,' came out of her mouth instead, and, 'er . . . Colette? I've been thinking, wouldn't it be better for the kids if you didn't drive them to school quite so much? It's only an eight-hundred metre journey, we're trying to get Ste's weight down as you know and—'

'My knee injury is really playing up?' Colette interrupted.

'Oh Colette, I'm so sorry about that,' Sally said. 'I'd forgotten. Of course, do drive them . . . yes . . . of course you must . . .'

'And I'm not being funny, Sally? But sometimes I do worry about them walking alone to school? What with the crime rate and everything?'

Sally had no idea which particular crime rate Colette had been analysing. The only crime ever recorded in this lush, electric-gated enclave of the Leatherhead borders was the very occasional botched break-in (people's Alcatraz-level burglar alarm systems usually put paid to any felony) and somebody had once stolen a hydrangea from Jennifer Mayhew's front garden.

Emily and Cleo's faces were glued to their phones, thumbs flicking across their screens as they effortlessly weaved around the chess pieces. What endless vacuous messages, stupid emojis, pointless slang or hideous bitching were they being bombarded with now? Why wasn't Colette acting as a shield from this rubbish? Sally's brain was trying to engage and rage, but her sweet friend Valium whispered to her soothingly, 'It's good for them to be connected,' and in stereo, 'You'd be depriving them of their social lives.' So Sally smiled weakly. She made a mental note to herself to definitely sort out a rigorous phone-use rota with her children tomorrow. She added it to her list of Things to Face Up to With My Children.

The list was quite long these days. She wanted to have good constructive chats with them all about manners in general and opening up to her more. She certainly wanted to talk to Cleo about her plans for the future. Did she have any? She wasn't showing any interest in applying to university. It seemed that nothing had entered her head at school other than an encyclopaedic knowledge of every single contestant of *Love Island* past and present; if she'd shown as much interest in the Periodic Table as she had in the Fenty line of contouring brushes, she'd have been a Grade A student all the way.

Cleo had a sunny nature, was a good listener (when she wasn't making pouty faces on Instagram) and was as lazy as a street dog that likes to lie in the sun on its back and toast its hairy nether regions. Not that Cleo's nether regions were ever hairy. Many hours spent with the most sophisticated depilatory systems in the western world made sure of that.

Cleo lived by far the closest to school in her class but was always late. She had a breathtaking array of excuses at the ready as she sauntered into school with a huge smile, freshly contoured cheekbones and a swinging mane of groomed golden hair twisted up into a jaunty topknot.

'Oh, hi Miss Rafael, you look nice this morning. I like your earrings. I'm not going to lie –' many of Cleo's excuses began with the go-to phrase 'I'm not going to lie', a sure-fire sign that she was going to do exactly that – 'but I had a really difficult journey to school this morning. Some kind of blackberry bush just sprang out at me as I was walking along and scratched me. And also stained me. I had to go home and change my top. I cannot tell you how sorry I am,' and then she sat down with an earnest look on her dewy peach of a face.

If there was any iota of gossip or romance going around school, Cleo Parker would be the first to know. For her, school was as much of a reality show as anything on the telly.

'OMIGOD, AMY STRALLEN AND FLORENCIA MCGINTY FROM YEAR TEN ARE A THING!' would be treated with as much shrieking as 'SPENCER FROM *MADE IN CHELSEA*'S HAVING A BABY!'

Cleo preferred the fantasy *Love Island* version of boys to the reality of the spotty, greasy-haired pool of sixth formers around her. She'd had a little dalliance with an older driving instructor who had nice hands and beautiful olive skin, but after their first kiss in a lay-by off the Epsom ring road, he'd suggested that she might like to join him for a game of darts at the pub, and that was that. Cleo didn't do pubs. Or darts. She wanted cocktails on a rooftop bar in Botswana, like Harry and Meghan, or long barefoot walks on sandy beaches like Katy Perry and Orlando Bloom. In Cleo's head, there was somebody exotic, chisel-jawed, and probably wearing swimming trunks, who was going to whisk her off her feet, out of Leatherhead, and into Paradise itself.

And Stephen. What about the limited daily calories that Dr Livesy had set down? And his GCSEs? Which ones was he doing again? And Emily. Was she missing her mum? She hadn't seen her for two years. And what about her A-level choices? She'd mentioned wanting to do six A levels. Wasn't that too many? And Mikey. Well, Mikey was a mystery. Sally mainly wanted to know why Mikey always had such a lot of cash on her.

Yes, Sally would override Colette and her mollycoddling ways, and really get through to her children. She had given birth to three of them. Who knew them better than her, after all?

The cousins were still locked into their phones.

'Hi girls!'

Silence. Except for the tick-ticking of nails on phone screens.

'Er . . . did you have good days, girls?'

Nothing.

'I'm afraid I've had some bad news from Dr Livesy, girls. I've got a terminal illness and I've actually been given about two months to live.'

Cleo raised one threaded eyebrow in Sally's direction. Briefly. And then her head was bent to her phone again.

'Er . . . that was a joke . . .' Sally smiled.

Cleo and Emily remained enthralled by their devices, like pilgrims worshipping at a shrine.

'Oh yes,' said Emily never taking her eyes away from her screen, 'the school needs three grand for my orchestra trip to Vienna.'

'Wow,' said Sally, taken aback, 'why so much? That's an awful lot for a school trip.'

Emily shrugged her shoulders, still not looking at her aunt. 'It's an elite ten days with two of Europe's greatest living flautists. I don't have to go.'

'No way!' said Sally. 'Of course you're going! You're the best flautist in the school! It'd be my pleasure to send you to Vienna . . . for three grand.'

Silence.

'And Cleo, darling,' ventured Sally to her daughter, whose eyes were also glued to her screen, 'isn't there some sort of A-level enrichment school trip that you could go on? What are you doing – textiles, PE and psychology? Is there some textiles trip to . . . er . . . Sweden? Isn't that where they have a lot of textiles? Or perhaps to somewhere where they love PE, China maybe! Or a trip to Austria! They love their psychology in Austria.'

There was a pause.

'Nah,' was Cleo's reply.

'Oh,' said her mother.

And then the air was filled with Cleo's shrieks.

'No! *No!* NO WAY! Look at this, Em! Teddy Smith in Year Thirteen has got a tattoo of BTS actually ALL ALONG HIS BUTT CRACK! Omigod, that's the most grossest thing I've ever actually SEEN!'

And the two of them howled with laughter over the image on her screen.

Sally smiled, trying to share the girls' enjoyment.

'You don't say "most grossest", Cleo,' she endeavoured jauntily, 'that's doubling up grammatically. I forget the term for it. Is it a tautology? Anyway. "Grossest" is enough. You don't need the "most". And what is BTS?'

If Sally had bowed down and shown them her own butt crack they wouldn't have noticed, so engrossed in Teddy's were they.

'That's fricking HILARIOUS and also DISGUSTING!' shouted Cleo. 'Eeurgh, imagine the tattooist having to deal with the skids in Teddy's BUTT CRACK!'

Emily burst out laughing.

'Cleo, please!' pleaded Sally. 'Can't we talk about something other than Teddy Smith's butt crack?'

'Let's see Teddy Smith's butt crack?'

This was Colette. And then the three of them were poring over the unfortunate Teddy.

'That is lush?' said Colette. 'That is a skilful tattooist that can actually render all of BTS up a butt crack?'

'Once again,' said Sally. 'Who or what is BTS?'

Nobody was listening to her, so she turned on her heel to go.

Cleo called out to her merrily, 'Oh Mum! I'm not coming down for the barbecue. Lottie and Star are coming over, is that OK? Then we'll probably go out?'

Sally turned to face her daughter. 'Oh darling, it's Dad's special do and I know he'd love you to be part of it.'

'I'm not going to lie to you, Mum, I'd love to be there and everything. But it's, like, Friday, and I promised Lots and Star . . . and . . . you know . . .'

And she gave her mum the chocolate-brown saucer eyes.

'OK. I'll talk to Dad . . .' said Sally.

And with that, Cleo and Emily ran upstairs. Mikey crossed their paths as she came bounding down, flicking Cleo's skirt up as she went.

'TWATFACE!' shouted Cleo with laughter. 'I'm going to get you for that, douche!'

'Language, Cleo, for goodness sake . . .' begged Sally.

'Language, language! Language is a SOCIAL CON-STRUCT, Sally!' shouted Emily gleefully as the girls laughed loudly and slammed Cleo's bedroom door shut.

'Where's Dad?' said Mikey, bounding towards the front door and freedom.

'I don't—' began Sally.

'And what's this about Teddy Smith's butt crack?'

Sally shook her head, lost for words.

'I need to talk to Dad about something business related. Got to go. I might be back for the barbecue. Might not.'

And Mikey, her fingers a blur over her phone, was out.

Sally turned to Colette, who was standing with her arms folded, clearly enjoying the spectacle of Sally's parenting.

'She's eleven years old, Colette. What can she mean by "business related"?'

Sally turned towards the sitting room, which led out on to the patio where the barbecue was being prepared. The Valium armour was in place, and she talked herself up as she made the approach towards her serried ranks of staff.

'Now what's the Spanish for "goodness me but I bet that wasabi salad tastes like a sumo wrestler's jockstrap"?'

And Sally laughed to herself, before tripping lightly on the edge of a marble pawn. She coughed, trying to style it out. She was in charge after all.

2

'Jesus, FRANK!'

There was a collective uproar of alpha male laughter as Frank Parker ducked down just in time, dodging the golf ball careering towards him like a bullet. Frank Parker was not a man to be stopped by something as paltry as a speeding bullet.

He stood up, regained his composure, winked at his friends and adjusted his bollocks, housed in a £52.99 pair of Dolce & Gabbana brushed-silk Y-fronts, with a practised flick. He turned to his fellow golfers, who were standing like stags, but stags in overpriced golfing gear, against the majestic Surrey backdrop.

'All right,' Frank bellowed, 'last one to the third hole's an A-HOLE!'

And the group of friends laughed over-appreciatively, as only friends in the company of a considerably wealthier and more powerful leader are wont to do, around Leatherhead Golf Course.

'Hoydens!' sniffed a chap in a buggy who passed the braying group. 'They let any sort of riff-raff into the club these days,' he murmured.

Amerjit Singh, Frank's best friend since primary school and partner in HNB Capital Management, their hedge-fund business, was negotiating a tricky shot out of a bunker.

'Come on, Ammers, give it some BOLLOCKS!' yelled Frank, forcing Amerjit to muff the bunker shot. It filled the air briefly with sand, most of which landed squarely in the turn-ups of his slightly too-shiny grey golfing trousers (part of a £1,500 Armani suit). Amerjit was taller than Frank, slender of frame with a sensitive face, aquiline nose and eyebrows which tended to form an upturned V of worry over the bridge of his nose.

Golf was not Amerjit's strongest skill, and he did some-times wonder if this was why Frank was always so keen for him to play; Amerjit never had the will to turn Frank down when he asked. To be honest, it was impossible to turn Frank down. It was the energy of the man, the ebullient force of that character which zoned in and then pulled you, a directionless asteroid, into the tractor beams of his orbit. He had his own gravitational force, did Frank Parker.

Frank and Amerjit had first bonded at school over small collectable plastic football players found in cereal boxes. They came in the form of enlarged heads that you could stick on the end of pencils. When Frank spotted Kevin Keegan on the end of Amerjit's pencil in maths one day, he showed him his own Kenny Dalglish, and the friendship was cemented. It turned out that Amerjit had carefully collected the whole set. He had three times as many as his friend, so Frank persuaded Amerjit to bring the entire collection into school so they could sell them, and then split the profits. Amerjit pointed out that he owned most of the football players, so surely he should keep most of the money? The ten-year-old Frank thought this over, agreed, but said that the plan had been his idea, so shouldn't that be reflected in his percentage of the profits? Frank also revealed that the school's breakfast club invested in the same boxes of cereal, so if he could talk to the dinner ladies, they would have access to even more supplies of football players, thus ensuring that their own profit margins grew substantially.

Amerjit was impressed. What he was witnessing here was somebody thinking outside of the cereal box, and his ten-year-old mind was blown. He didn't know how Frank had charmed the dinner ladies, but they all knew him by name and gave him extra helpings of sponge and chocolate custard at lunchtime. It didn't take Amerjit long to come back to Frank with a handshake in the playground, on a 50/50 split of all profits. And thus, their first business was born and they became like brothers.

Amerjit had a second go at the bunker shot and failed again. Frank laughed, and sure enough, like an echo, the other men laughed after him.

'NOT AGAIN, AMMERS!' Frank guffawed. 'Another suicide in the bunker! You're as bad as bloody Adolf!'

And he clapped his old mate on the back, which made Amerjit lose his footing in the sand. The laughter this time was raucous. Frank was pleased with that quip.

'Come on, Parker, show us what you've got!'

This was the slightly reedy voice of Tim Daly-Jones, neighbour and friend of Frank. Although Frank did some-times ask himself if they would truly be friends if their wives were not. Frank popped his golf ball straight into the hole and then clapped Tim Daly-Jones on the back. Tim clenched his jaw muscles with repressed anger and forced out an over-jolly, 'Shot, Frank Parker!'

Frank was having a good day. The early September weather was clement and warmed his skin nicely; he was looking forward to the celebratory barbecue he and Amerjit were throwing at Cedar Vale that evening to celebrate ten good years as hedge-fund managers. Frank and Amerjit had started HNB with a third partner, a safe pair of hands called

Brett Grover who was HNB's business manager and shot caller. Frank's role was front-of-house schmoozer and salesman, while Amerjit was Head of Research, the backroom brains of the operation. Brett had left HNB two years ago to live on his polo ranch in Argentina, leaving Frank at the helm of HNB. There were rumours in the City that Frank had bitten off more than he could chew.

At this moment his jaws looked perfectly capable of the job, as he set about thrashing Tim Daly-Jones on the golf course. While Frank contemplated his next shot on the fairway, his thoughts turned briefly to his Sally at home, being gorgeous as always and overseeing everything for the barbecue.

He balanced himself on his feet so that his stocky legs stood about three feet apart. He'd read in a Sunday supplement that this was a good stance for a man to have in 2019. It showed the world that you were in charge. He took off his cap and ruffled his still-luxurious head of curls. A little bit grey around the wings now, but Frank liked that. He felt it gave him a statesman-like aura. It was good for business. It went with his wainscotted office in Finsbury Square in the City.

Everything about Frank looked solid. His nose was a little too solid, maybe, and he blamed the Welsh side of his family for that. His granddad Wyn, a miner, had had beautiful eyes of the clearest crystal-cut blue, and a nose like a King Edward potato. And these had travelled straight down the genetic pipes to Frank.

'Eyes for the bed. Nose for the flowerbed,' his granny Bronwen used to say of Wyn. 'Just like you, Frank.' And she'd look at him, all beady, ancient, compact and Welsh, as if that gave her the God-given right to slag him off to his face.

'Shall we sink a cheeky bever-aaage, hale fellows well met?' Dr James Livesy asked in his trademark drawl. Pronouncing the 'age' of beverage in the French way, to rhyme with 'mirage', was his latest fad. Livesy, Frank's quack and confidant for many years, liked to say things in his surgery like, 'Well, we'll ask the practice nurse to put a band-aaage on that for you, shall we?'

James Livesy ran a tanned hand through his receding mane of thick hair to reveal a large £11,000 Rolex watch on his freckled, tennis-playing wrist. His eyes were a watery green, and if you were male, his eyes were never quite capable of meeting yours, but if you were female they would flit between your eyes and your breasts. Flit, flit, flit. Eyes like an insect that hovers over water and then darts lethally with its proboscis. His chin was weak, so often a feature of those boys from minor public schools who never quite manage to get into Russell Group universities. Not to say that Livesy was lacking in brains. His brain was furtive and self-preserving, like a creature of the night.

'Right, winner pays for the bever-aaages. That's you, Parker. Mine's a foaming pint of beer-aaaage, my good sir!'

Livesy was extremely pleased with this latest wordplay and felt that it put him above his golfing peers in the badin-aaaaage stakes.

Frank Parker always ended up paying for drinks in the clubhouse. A round or two would normally set him back £100. To be fair, wherever they were, Frank Parker always ended up paying the bill. They'd all had dinner at a nice Michelin two star the week before (£3,480) in Godalming. Tim Daly-Jones had chosen some breathtakingly expensive wines. He was good at that, choosing wines that he wasn't paying for. And Amerjit had insisted on ordering the eye-wateringly expensive truffles flown in from Calabria.

'Are you trying to bankrupt our business, mate?' whispered Frank to Amerjit in the restaurant when everyone else was discussing the rugby. 'Those truffles sound bloody disgusting. What's wrong with the duck salad, it's a quarter of the price, you twat!'

Amerjit laughed at Frank behind their menus like they were schoolboys again.

'We're HNB, Frank. Just the two of us! We've got places at the table with the big boys. We're operators! Mobilisers! Galvanisers!'

'We're not in school debating club now, you ponce,' said Frank, poking his old friend in the ribs.

'Look Frank, you can't cock about with a substandard hors d'oeuvre. You've got to swim with the big fish. Not the crappy little minnows!'

'Go on then, you absolute douche, give us a try of that truffle stuff,' and Frank popped some in his mouth. Almost immediately he grimaced dramatically and had to reach for a napkin to spit it out, much to Amerjit's delight.

'That is bloody AWFUL, Ammers. It tastes like one of your worst farts.'

'My farts are like roses compared to yours,' jousted Amerjit. 'Remember that school trip to the mock-up of the trenches? You guffed so badly all day, I had to actually wear the gas mask. Remember?'

And the two of them fell about laughing at the memory. The other men looked at them bemusedly. Since the HNB boys had lost the more serious Brett Grover and had become a double-act partnership they were always joshing about, like they had a secret society all of their own.

The rich food had played havoc with Frank's colon. He'd spent most of the next day at HNB Capital Management pebble-dashing the wood-panelled loo. As he'd sat, silently howling on the big white throne, it had struck him how quickly money passes through the digestive system.

As the Golfing Pride sat in the sunny area of the clubhouse, crotches splayed in lounge chairs, Amerjit was interrupted by his rose-gold mobile phone. The fact that he hopped out of his seat as if it were a burning griddle meant only one thing – it was his wife calling. Laura Piggott liked to phone Amerjit twice a day, usually to give him a long list of terse instructions. Amerjit moved away to take the call in private, hunched over the phone like a naughty boy.

'Bloody hell,' drawled James Livesy, 'there's a man who needs to call the A-Team.'

'I don't think even Mr 'T' could save him from Laura Piggott,' quipped Frank. Everyone laughed.

'I don't think even Mrs T could have saved him from Laura Piggott,' added Tim, grinning. To absolute silence. James Livesy coughed and smirked into his ale. Tim soldiered on, determined to get a laugh like Frank just had. 'What I mean is . . . Laura Piggott probably has a lot in common with Mrs T in terms of her economic policies, both tough-ass women who've come from humble beginnings. Both—'

'Game of pool, anyone?' suggested Frank, patting Tim lightly on the shoulder like you would your nan when she's had one sherry too many. The golfers, except for Tim who sat with two cheeks aflame, roused themselves from their haunches to follow Frank to ever more competitive feats of manliness.

Stephen Parker was facing his very own feat of manliness at that precise moment, on his PS3. He, and only he, could save the great simulated city that he'd built, from alien doom and destruction. Stephen was fifteen, Frank's second child, and didn't have a competitive bone in his body. Not many bones in Stephen's body were visible, to be honest. Three years of snacking and gaming had piled on the pounds, and Stephen now had a beautifully rounded face which made him look strangely very young and very old and wise all at the same time. His dad occasionally called him 'Kim Jong-un', his mum called him 'cherubic'. Both parents knew that something had to be done about his weight, but somehow they were hoping that Colette would work the magic for them.

Frank had tried to bring out Stephen's competitive spirit through sport, but the torturous Sunday mornings at football club with his dad shouting, 'Tackle, Ste! Tackle!' or 'Do a Dalglish, son! DO A DALGLISH!' had just confused him. He had no idea what 'doing a Dalglish' actually meant, and it only made Stephen feel more like slowing down. The force of his father was enough to make him curl up like a cat in front of a fire. Too much roaring for Stephen. He was content just purring.

'Come on, Ste! Feel the fire in your belly! Remember sixty-six, Ste!' he had yelled once from the sidelines.

'How can I remember sixty-six, Dad? I wasn't born till 2004.'

'I don't remember it either, Ste. But I REMEMBER it, if you know what I mean.'

Stephen had given his father a blank look. And the relationship between father and son had maintained something of that blank look ever since.

The golfers headed to the clubhouse pool table. Frank Parker was the undisputed High Priest of Pool. Most of his teenage years had been spent in Paddy's Pool Hall in

Hayes, when he should have been poring over his GCSE textbooks. All he was interested in was watching people, sizing them up, facing them down, beating them and charming them while he did it. This he learned at Paddy's Pool Hall. Hours, days, months, aeons of time spent in his gloomily lit kingdom prowling, judging, witnessing all of humanity and working out how it ticked. He started to get quite a reputation in the Hayes/Hounslow area. Most were beaten by him, but also won over by him. He had that effect on everyone, did Frank. It was hard to begrudge him a win.

The art of conquering he learned in the pool halls, and the art of diplomacy on his Uncle Phil's market stall. Phil was a tight old bastard who'd only give Frank his wages if he managed to clear five entire boxes of fruit or veg by the end of a Saturday. It became a matter of deep personal pride to Frank that he empty those boxes. That fifteen quid would be his, whatever it took. He didn't care what the boxes contained – sprout, beetroot, parsnip or cooking apple. His mission was to sell that fruit and veg to anyone who'd fall for his spin.

'You want teeth like Marie Osmond, darling? Well, buy a beautiful pound of these Granny Smiths. Tell your dentist Frank Parker sent you!'

And Frank's customer would flash her pearly whites, reach into her purse and the deal was sealed. Frank Parker wheedled and needled, diddled and dandled, laughed and winked through many a Hayes winter.

One memorable Saturday in early February, Frank was left with a boxful of visibly mouldering Brussels sprouts. Phil looked his nephew in the eye and said,

'I'll give yer an extra five quid if you can shift those. Betcha can't.'

Frank felt something in his sap rising. He looked his Uncle Phil square in the eye and nodded at him silently.

He left the stall and proceeded to do a sort of dance around people in the High Street with his box of sprouts. He surprised people, cajoled them, flirted with them. When Frank returned to Uncle Phil's stall at five p.m., it was dark. Frank plonked the empty sprout box at his uncle's feet and gave him handfuls of coins.

'I think you'll find that's every sprout sold, Uncle Phil,' said Frank, eyes shining. 'Oh, hang on. I saved you one for your tea!'

And with a flourish he pulled a sprout from behind Phil's ear. The extra five quid was his.

The only person capable of whipping Frank at pool was, at a pinch, Amerjit, who'd spent a fair amount of his teenage years in Paddy's Pool Hall too. But unlike Frank's parents, Amerjit's had taken a very active, some might say embarrassingly over-solicitous, interest in their son's education. They were going to make damn sure that their golden boy was not going to go down the academic Swanee like that disreputable Frank Parker. They were determined that Amerjit was going to go to Cambridge. And he did. And then Princeton for his Master's.

Amerjit, with his first-class Honours in Maths and Business Master's, was still on the phone being read the riot act by his wife. Now was Frank's chance to rule the pool. James Livesy was a floppy opponent, too interested in his own drawling commentary of the game. Tim Daly-Jones was weak, still licking his wounds over the Mrs T debacle. Frank smelled dead prey. He grabbed the blue cube of cue chalk, swivelled it deftly round the top of his weapon, surveyed the group and bared his teeth delicately. A devastating Frank Parker smile.

He looked briefly at the clock. This should all be over

in twelve minutes. Just enough time to annihilate the opposition before they were due back at Cedar Vale to celebrate ten magnificent years of HNB. He didn't want to keep his adorable little wife and children waiting.

Sixteen minutes later, to the booming sounds of the 1812 Overture, the Golfing Pride marched into the hall at Cedar Vale. Frank was clearly at the end of a long and hilarious anecdote because the pack were laughing loudly and dutifully, as Frank bent down to kiss his petite wife on the lips.

'Wifey! We must have meat!'

Sally pulled her shirt sleeves down to cover her hands with her cuffs. She wished that she could think of something clever and loud to come back at Frank with. But all that she could manage was a supportive smile.

Frank held his arms out expansively like an opera singer.

'Meat and many ales! We're like huntsmen of yore, Sal, except we've been hunting that elusive eighteenth hole!'

There was a lot of baritone laughter and chat at this comment.

'Dad?' said Mikey, dashing up to Frank's side.

'Later, Mikey my love. Your father needs to don his glove. PALOMA,' he shouted, moving through the hall towards the barbecue area, 'WHERE IS MY ROASTING GLOVE? I need to CHAR ME SOME DEAD FLESH, BY GAD!'

There was a noise of laughing approval among the Spanish contingent. Mr Parker was just so funny and English. They never knew what he was going to do next!

Sally watched as her husband strode off and bit her bottom lip uncertainly. Amerjit rolled his eyes at her with a knowing twinkle, gave her an affectionate hug and followed Frank through the gigantic white-carpeted front room towards the hallowed barbecuing area. Dr James Livesy was up next, like waiting to kiss the bride in a wedding queue. His lids were half-closed as he held Sally by the wrists and pecked her languorously on each cheek.

'Your skin looks fabulous,' he whispered with a wink.

'Yours looks like a lizard,' Sally muttered as she let herself be kissed.

Sounds of Paloma and the staff fussing and laughing around Frank could be heard coming from the terrace. Frank's stride was long and strong – he covered distances quickly.

'Hello, Tim,' said Sally, looking down at her feet.

'Hi there, Sal,' he said, hanging back and putting his hand on Sally's waist before kissing her on both cheeks. He always lingered with these kisses, hanging on just a bit too long. Sally always felt uncomfortable during these embraces, and moved away from him with a little cough.

'Right . . . er . . . come on through, Tim. You must be starving after all that riding around on a golf buggy.'

3

The braying noise of seventy-five barbecue-goers, three mojito cocktails to the wind, blasted out over the back lawns at Cedar Vale. By the time it reached the swimming pool, the noise had simmered to a drone, before hovering briefly around the mini Versailles formal garden and then out, skimming over Frank's security laurel hedges, to be released into the Surrey countryside.

Meat consumption was never high on the Parkers' Must Try to Conserve the Planet list. Flesh of all shapes, sizes and hues was displayed across Frank's horseshoe of barbecues; he never worked fewer than three. Behind this butcher's bazaar stood Mein Host, face flushed with hot gas and meat fat, glowing with delight at playing to such a large gallery. His gauntlet reached as far as his elbow and he wielded not one but two barbecuing implements. An oversized pair of tongs in one hand, and a fork large enough to dig a flowerbed in the other. He felt like an Arthurian knight, jousting with the sizzling flesh before him. Stabbing the satsuma-infused guinea-fowl breasts as if they were Charlemagne's army, and doing a roistering jig with the tongs around the various hand-stuffed sausages and sirloin steaks.

And there in one corner of Frank's colossal barbecue was his own little Xanadu. His cheap-as-shit burgers, two pounds for six, probably filled with all manner of testicle,

33

eyeball and hoof, but a taste of his Hayes & Harlington past. When nobody was looking, Frank liked to fill a filthy soft white roll with two of these foot-and-mouth disasters and gulp them down as if they were manna from heaven. Only Paloma knew his dirty little burger secret. She would wink secretively at him when the coast was clear, and Frank would clag up his palate as fast as his jaws could chomp.

Sally was more of a bird when it came to food. Peck, peck, peck like a hedge sparrow. And tonight she couldn't get even a beakful down. She'd loaded her plate with a couple of marinated larks and some intricate salads, but the only greenery that interested her was the lime in her mojito glass. She had a lump in her throat; she was more likely to conquer Snowdon in a pair of six-inch high heels than Paloma's groaning buffet.

Frank licked his lips and surveyed his vast kingdom. He looked fondly over to his prized possession of John Deere sit-on lawnmowers. They'd been waxed and buffed, and were amassed behind the rose arbour he'd had built for Sally's fortieth birthday. He looked over his livestock, seven dogs in a pack, eyes fixed on the sizzling meat. Kurt, Brigitta, Liesl and four others. He could never remember them all, but they were named after the Von Trapp family. Sally loved *The Sound of Music*. He'd taken her to Austria for their first wedding anniversary. They'd gone with two rucksacks and fifty pounds' worth of schillings. They'd lived on bread and cheese and the sun never stopped shining all weekend. They drank cheap wine and laughed and laughed. He had a sudden pang for those backpacks and Sally with a scarf on her head like Maria. But then Frank looked around at his Camelot and thought that life really didn't get much better than this.

He gave his little apron-paunch a satisfied pat – a gift from one of his clients, the apron featured Michelangelo's

34

David, giving the illusion that Frank himself was the nude statue. He felt like David. Big and important but a good deal better hung.

'Oi, Ken! King of the barbie! Stick one of your poncey guinea-fowl doo-dahs on here, mate!'

And a Spode porcelain plate with gold-leaf trim was shoved under Frank's nose by one of his more abrasive hedge-fund clients. Bruce Fowler had made his money selling arms in the Arabian Peninsula. An estuary man, watery of eye and sandblasted-red of cheek. Frank obliged with a jovial laugh – Bruce was a good lad and a loyal client. It was time to pass the barbecue weaponry over to a member of staff now, and mingle with his guests.

He passed briefly by a group of Sally's friends with their shiny white jeans and even shinier white foreheads. Local women mostly, whose kids all attended St Bede's. Francesca Daly-Jones was holding court, showing off an expensive gold necklace that had a bunch of keys hanging off it.

'So this was a Monday Present.'

'Monday present?' asked Karen, a stocky lady with legs filling high boots.

'It's pure husband guilt shopping,' said Francesca to the group. 'Tim'll show up after work with booze breath and a little something in a Lalique bag. "Happy Wednesday, darling", he'll say, or whatever day it is,' and with a slight roll of her eyes, Francesca yanked the chain hard so that her friends could admire its plethora of gold keys, each set with a different jewel. High-pitched squawks filled the circle like crows over a carcass.

'It's scrummy!' yelped one with a burnished clementine tan.

'I feel like a jailer with this bunch of bloody keys,' Francesca continued, 'maybe I should lock Tim up and throw them away. Ha!' She tossed her luxuriant hair and pouted her coral lips together. Her friends flicked gold-ringed fingers, hoicked expensive blingy sunglasses up on to their hair-straightened heads and shifted their weights from one caramel-coloured high heel to the other.

Sally had been lingering behind the circle of women, mesmerised by the dynamics at play. She breathed deeply through her nose and approached.

'Hiya, hon!' said Francesca, giving Sally an awkwardly placed pair of kisses, neither of which landed on her cheeks.

'How the hell do you manage to look so good, Sally Parker?' said Karen, giving Sally the classic female flick-over. The eyes flick up and down, almost imperceptibly, and take in hips, boobs, face, chin, legs and stomach. The flickover is a classic manoeuvre and is usually only carried out by girlfriends who aren't as supportive as they appear. Sally had had this from girls and women all her life. It wasn't her fault that she was slim and pretty. It was just her genes.

'Well, look at her plate compared to yours, Karen!' said Francesca loudly, prodding an unwanted finger into Karen's large sirloin. 'Sally's not going to put any weight on eating a tiny bird skeleton, is she?'

Sally blushed and drank further into her mojito. She was aware that her group of friends were starting to fuzz pleasurably at the edges.

'Classic Frank,' said Sally, 'there's enough to feed an army on that barbecue. Samantha, have you tried the guinea fowl? It's Paloma's – what do they call it on those cooking shows? – signature dish!'

'How *adorable* to have a live-in housekeeper with a signature dish!' said Francesca, whose cheekbones looked like they might crack, she was smiling so hard at Sally.

'So does she have a signature pleat when she does your ironing, hon?' she added, still grinning like a gargoyle.

There was supportive tittering from the group. Sally flushed harder, looking intently into her mojito. She shouldn't really be drinking this with the Valium, but was loving the buzz which now muffled her earholes, eyeballs and entire head.

'No, Francesca, but she does a very good signature cunnilingus every now and then.'

Everyone looked at Sally. There was silence in the circle of friends and Francesca disengaged her smile from her cheekbones slowly, leaving just a pair of dead shark eyes behind.

'Jus' joking!' slurred Sally as she slid out of the group with a low backwards manoeuvre. She'd spotted Amerjit's wife. Her heart was beating just a little bit faster. She giggled to herself; it was fun to see her friends lost for words. She was beginning to enjoy this barbecue. She felt as if she could say whatever came into her head. It was freeing.

Frank looked over and smiled at his wife, who looked very happy. And so she should, he thought, she had everything she desired. She was wearing those cropped white jeans that he adored and a lovely fresh white and pink candy-striped shirt. Nobody could pull off a crisp shirt like his wife. And that's exactly what he wanted to do – pull off his wife's crisp shirt.

Frank looked at her gym-toned body with pride, and then yawned. He felt a tad tired. It was probably all that hard golfing. Sally appeared to be talking to herself. He couldn't make out what she was saying but he just loved the way her mouth formed those lovely words of hers.

*

Laura Piggott had a mobile phone in each hand, her tongue slightly protruding from her mouth in concentration as she flicked her eyes from one phone to the other.

'Laura!' said Sally a little too loudly, clapping her on the back. 'You look like you need some meat inside you! Come to the barbecue, me old china!'

Sally really was enjoying the barbecue now. She felt perfectly safe in her own fudged head. It was delightful. Laura Piggott looked up briefly and then scanned both of her mobile phones again.

'I'd love to, Sally, but it looks as if I'm going to be called back into work. It's economichaos out there. This is worse than '87.'

Laura Piggott was a woman of Amazonian proportions and a jawline to give Dan Dare a run for his money. There was a whiff of helmet about her haircut and she liked a pinstripe. She was the Chief Economics Correspondent for Sky News as well as having her own weekly show, *Piggott's Projections*, where she would baste, grill and eat alive anybody who dared challenge her bastion of fiscal knowledge, worn like a breastplate across her impressively muscly chest.

Sally was desperately trying to remember what had happened in '87, to make some pithy link with the current economic situation, but all that came out of her mouth was,

'Aaaaaargh! MEL AND KIM!!'

Laura looked up briefly from her pair of mobile phones. 'What?'

'FUN, LOVE AND MONEY!!!' Sally was singing loudly into Laura's face, and was delighted to find herself doing some long-forgotten dance manoeuvres right there in front of her. 'F . . . L . . . M!!'

Nearby guests looked round and smiled briefly at Sally,

who raised her empty mojito glass to all and sundry with an impressive

'FUN, LOVE AND MONEY!!'

Laura gave Sally the look of someone who has not only smelled dog shit, but has been forced to eat it in the form of a soufflé. The moment was broken by Amerjit, tiptoeing up to hand his wife a mojito.

'Here you are, babe.'

He looked carefully at Sally.

'Hey! Nice moves there, Sal! Takes me right back to Hayes '87!'

'You know I can't drink when I'm on call, Amerjit,' Laura interrupted.

'I'll have it!' laughed Sally, grabbing the mojito out of Laura's hand and clamping her lips around it.

'On call?' Amerjit's eyebrows danced up to attention.

'Yes, Amerjit, on call. I don't know if you've noticed from your particular corner of financial services, but the country is very likely about to plunge into an economic crisis as bad, if not worse, than Black Wednesday. And you're trying to foist some dodgy eighties cocktail on me?' Her right-hand phone buzzed. 'Great. The Dow Jones is in freefall. Call me an Uber, please, Amerjit.'

Her husband rummaged around in his trouser pocket.

'Sure . . . er . . .'

'Quickly, Amerjit.'

'Er . . .' and he fumbled around with his phone. 'Hang on, my Wi-Fi's been playing up today. Hang on a minute . . .'

'Your WI-FI's been playing up? What about your WIFEY, Ammers? Has she been playing up too?' said Sally raucously before falling backwards into another guest, she was laughing so hard.

'Fucksake, Amerjit,' snapped Laura.

'Hang on, babe, here we go . . . now . . . what do you want, an Uber X? OK, there seems to be a driver nineteen minutes away—'

'NINETEEN MINUTES AWAY? Oh, of course! That's what you get when you're in the arse end of suburbia. I am the Chief Economics Correspondent for Sky News and you expect me to wait NINETEEN MINUTES to get into a vehicle?'

'I'm the Chief Economics Correspondent for Sky,' mimicked Sally in a rather pathetic baby-voice, directly at Laura.

Amerjit looked confused.

'Are you OK, Sally?' he asked.

'Of course she's not OK,' said Laura tersely, 'she's a suburban wife with nothing to do all day, and now she's pissed out of her head on cocktails paid for by her husband.'

'Laura . . .' Amerjit placed a hand on his wife's arm.

Sally's smile faded and she steadied herself, with one eye slightly squinting to get her balance. She looked at Laura through the larger of her two eyes and pointed at her, causing the mojito to slosh dangerously out of its glass.

'I'll have you know, Miss I'm ChiefCospondent of the Sky Economicsnews, that I'm not only pissedoutmyhead but I'm also on psciption drugs, so pu' thatinyourpipeand-smokeit!'

Amerjit looked stumped for words. Laura shook her head briskly.

'Get your keys, Amerjit. Let's go.'

'Sure, babe. I'll drive you to Sky,' and he attempted a winning grin. 'I'll drive you to the sky and back!'

'Please tame that quiff, Amerjit. You look ridiculous.'

Amerjit spat into his hand and started to flatten down his hair. Laura was already on the march towards the house.

'Sal, are you OK? Can I get you anything?' Amerjit asked her while keeping an eye on his wife's fast-receding back. Sally just put both her thumbs up and lost the remaining mojito in the process.

'Thanks for a lovely party, Sal,' Amerjit said on the move, 'and say bye to Franko, yeah? Tell him I'll bell him in the morning!'

And with that Amerjit and Laura were gone.

Sally sighed and spotted Frank, who was deep in conversation with Charlotte, one of his accountants, and Simon Khan, his Head of Risk Assessment.

'. . . .and it's got a warm top note of berry, that vintage,' explained Charlotte. 'I keep mine in a cooler in Cardiff. Two hundred bottles. Much better investing in wine than property, Frank, I'm telling you. Give me the grape over the brick any day. I'm going to retire on that bloody wine, just you wait and see!'

'I bet you will, Charlotte. You'll be pissed as a fart, sitting on your money like an old hen—'

Sally almost fell into Frank, who had to catch her to prevent a collision with Simon.

'Sal, you all right there? You look like you might need a glass of water, babe!'

'Laura,' and she looked from Frank to Charlotte to Simon and back to Frank again, 'is a massive bellend. Massive. She's buggeredoff to do her SkyChiefConomics-Cospondentthing. Sthingabout 1987.'

Frank stroked his wife's left cheek lightly. He couldn't help himself.

'Well, we've been talking about wine here, babe. And it looks as if you've maybe had a bit too much of it!'

Frank laughed and Charlotte and Simon joined in politely. 'Charlotte, I want to invest in two hundred and fifty bottles of your 1926 wine for my gorgeous pissed wife!'

Sally disengaged herself from Frank's sleeve and stared at him. Although she didn't manage to stare him in the eye, it was more of a stare into his mouth.

'WINE! WINE! YOU? You only drink BacardinCoke. WINE? You pretentiousoldtwat. WINE!!!!'

Sally started laughing and the more she laughed, the more it tumbled out of her. It was nice to laugh out of buzzing lips. Mojito and Valium. What a double act. Why had she never realised this? This was the way forward. She ignored her husband's crestfallen face.

'Come on, Sal, that's enough now.'

'Ithankyou.' Sally bowed deeply in front of her husband and his colleagues before swaying off to find Stephen; she'd spotted him over by the food.

He was standing, talking to nobody, with a plate piled high with various thighs and drumsticks. She went over to him.

'Stevn, Stevn, my liddle Stevn,' she slurred, trying to hug him, 'although not so little any more . . . hmmm . . . Stevn eatsomesalads . . . c'mon lesseatsalads . . .'

'You're drunk, Mum,' said Stephen, oozing grease out of his mouth as he spoke, 'and I hate eating salad.'

He proceeded to chomp through another guinea-fowl drumstick, and then moved straight on to a sirloin steak, the corners of his mouth overflowing with brown marinade.

'Sally, hon, are you all right?' Francesca Daly-Jones had sprung up behind her. When Sally turned, Francesca swiftly formed her mouth into a concerned position. She lowered her voice. 'The girls and I were a bit worried. That cunnilingus comment? So unlike you. You've been stressed recently, haven't you, hon? Is this party too much for you? It's just that with our big Charity Ball coming up, I'm worried that if you can't cope with this, then how are you going to feel with the whole of Surrey here, expecting the biggest night of the social calendar?'

Sally had never noticed it before but Francesca's nostrils had a habit of flaring whenever she said the word 'hon', which she did very frequently.

''Cesca,' said Sally, starting to laugh again, 'yournostrils are normous. NORMOUS!!'

Francesca gave Sally a tight-lipped smile and felt one of her nostrils self-consciously with her fingertip.

'Sal, love, are you all right?' Frank was by her side. 'Do you want Paloma to get you anything?'

'I WANT PALOMA TOFUCKOFF!' shouted Sally.

'Sal, come on . . .' Frank now tried to hug her into submission. And then Mikey bobbed up out of nowhere.

'Dad. I've got to talk to you about something. I had a chat with a contact of mine—'

'Not now, Mikey, I'm trying to control Mum.'

'FUCKOFFPALOMA!!' Sally's yell was muffled by Frank's chest.

'Shall I get Dr Livesy?' suggested Francesca with a deeply worried look on her face.

Mikey's face fell. The time was never 'now' with her Dad. 'Now' was important; 'now' was everything to Mikey. She paced from one foot to the other, looking like she might want to cry. And then she darted off.

'Where's Ammers?' said Frank, looking round anxiously. 'Where's the old tosspot? I need help here!'

Dr Livesy broke up the group, clapping Frank on the back. 'Come on you old bastard. Isn't it time you gave your big speech-aaaaage? Some of us have homes to go to, you know!'

And Frank laughed a big laugh but his eyes looked worriedly at his wife.

Sally gave Livesy a big punch on the chest.

'HA! MY DEALER!!!' she shouted raucously into his face.

Francesca put a comforting arm around Sally, whispering loudly, 'Hon, shall we go get you a glass of water?' and manoeuvring her away from the menfolk. Several of the girlfriends clustered round to check out the state of their hostess. Frank rubbed his eyes and suppressed a slight yawn. If Sally was anything short of perfect it made him anxious.

He rubbed his eyes again and puffed out his chest. Time to address the throng. He moved to his favourite speechifying spot on a large stone. He was not a tall man. This was a lovely place for him to hold court. Stone and flowers. Soft and hard. Just the way he wanted to come across to his audience. Another little yawn escaped his lips. Why did he feel so tired?

Frank was never tired.

'Tiredness is for pussies!' was one of his favourite phrases. Frank was king of the forty-eight-hour marathon with no sleep – gym, Skype meeting, office, flight to Zurich, charm the nadgers off some clients, cut a deal, hammer some fondue, flight back from Zurich, schmoozing, charity event, conference call with Tokyo, more schmooze, build a night-time deal, seal another deal, back into work, shave in the car, smash down some beers with the lads in Finsbury Square then back to the gym. Frank was unstoppable. Indestructible. Insatiable.

He tinkled his glass lightly with a spoon. And in his peripheral vision he saw his niece Emily emerge on to the patio. Oh God, she was carrying her flute. He was all for his niece giving the odd concert, it was enriching and enlivening, but she had a habit of doing so uninvited. And it peeved him that none of his other kids could play a note. They'd all tried, for God's sake, at vast expense. A troupe of music teachers had been enlisted to bring various instruments into the house to enrich and enliven his other three children. Stephen puffed away on the clarinet but never even made it to Grade One. Cleo wanted to play the sax because she'd read somewhere that Billie Eilish used to play the sax. And Mikey. Mikey didn't want to learn violin, but a violin teacher was enlisted. Mikey took one look at her, got her into conversation about jam-making and then proceeded to form a loose business plan based on damson jam-selling in the Chobham area. The teacher was dispatched by Mikey at the end of the session never to be seen again.

Frank cleared his throat. He noticed that Emily was giving him a reassuring thumbs up. It was rather off-putting. And what about Cleo? Shouldn't she be here to hear her dad's wise words? Stephen was lurking by the dessert table looking the other way; Sally was being contained by her friends, thank goodness. Though he hoped to God she wasn't going to heckle. From where Frank was standing, it looked as if Francesca was restraining Sally in some kind of Heimlich Manoeuvre. Was that a good thing or a bad thing? And Mikey – where was his little girl? Nowhere to be seen. The ducker and weaver. And where was Ammers? His best friend had buggered off from his own party and wasn't around to get the crowd going when Frank made a gag. Twat.

Frank looked out at the crowd of expectant faces – women groomed like a stable of finely polished ponies, some with puffier lips than others, some with very large and darkened eyebrows. Statement chains, real gold twisted around tanned necks, some sagging, receding hairlines on the men crafted carefully to look as if they were meant to be that way. They waited for his pearls to flow.

Another tinkling of spoon against glass, a clear of his throat, a light tweak of the bollocks and he was ready for action.

'They say an Englishman's home is his castle, and I can tell you, if the heating costs are anything to go by, Cedar Vale is most definitely a castle!'

There was a murmur of appreciative laughter. Then Dr Livesy's voice piped up. 'Who's up for a beveraaaage in the Castle?'

The Castle was the local, frequented by the commuting set.

Frank looked sharply at Livesy and forced a laugh out in his direction.

'Anyway. As I was saying before I was so rudely interrupted by my good doctor and neighbour here. Some of you may know him. He's the one with the perma-tan who's got you all addicted to antidepressants.'

There was a wave of appreciative laughter now. Frank the stand-up had the crowd right in his palm. He was very gratified to see James Livesy looking annoyed, but a little anxious to spot Sally trying to escape Francesca Daly-Jones's clutches.

'Now, unaccustomed as I am to standing up and making a complete tit of myself,' a crest of warm laughter enveloped Frank, 'I'd just like to take this opportunity to say that I am so proud to know you all. Some of you are clients. To you I say, keep the money coming in, I'll make you more of it. And the invoice is in the post. Some of you are my accountants. To you I say, if you can cook a roast as well as you can cook the books, I'm round at yours next Sunday dinnertime. And lastly and most importantly. Because these are the most important people in my life –' a little pause for effect – 'my golfing buddies!'

There was a big laugh. Frank was loving this. He was truly in his element.

'No! Not really. You're all wankers . . . especially my best mate and so-called business partner Amerjit who's buggered off, which makes him the biggest wanker of all.'

A huge roar from the golfing buddies at this.

'No, and I mean this most sincerely, folks. The most important people in my life? My family. Team Parker! Where are you?'

There was a silence. Emily, in the front row, put up one hand. There was no sign of any other Parker.

'Hello Em. And, well, the rest are around somewhere. And if you see them, please tell them that I said this. They are the reason I get up in the morning and get driven to work in an effing great big car and then spend hours losing hair, marbles, sperm count, God knows what else, to make their lives better. Sally, wherever you are, you are my rock. My linchpin. My Blarney Stone. Yes, like ye olde Blarney Stone of the Emerald Isle, I do like to kiss you every time I see you . . .'

Massive laughter at this. Where was Sally to hear this solid gold material? Frank was on a roll but registered a look of worry when he noticed that Sally was no longer with her girlfriends.

'Without you and the kids, Sal, I am nothing. And Paloma, where are you, my darling?'

Paloma stopped feeding the dogs the remains of the sirloin steaks and looked up, pleased as punch to be singled out in Frank's speech.

Sally, meanwhile, had wriggled away from her friends and parked herself behind the enormous ornamental statue of Pan next to the swimming pool. As Frank played to the gallery, she had suddenly realised she had a lot of mojito to shed, and pulled down her crisp white jeans to take an enormous pee, horse-like in volume. She had managed to get herself into a standing position with her trousers up halfway over her thighs, when she heard Frank falter briefly before the next bit of his speech boomed over towards the swimming pool.

'Without you, Paloma, nothing would happen in this house. I mean that. Nothing. We wouldn't eat, we wouldn't have anything to wear in the morning, we'd be an utter shambles. You are our clock. You are our compass . . .'

Sally's world stopped. Suddenly she could hear nothing. See nothing. She was aware of who she was and where she was but everything she had known ceased to be. She saw herself from high above as a tiny little speck in an oversized field. An enormous tractor pulling a threshing machine was heading straight for her, its thrashing blades about to mince her up. That was all she deserved, really; it would be a relief to be minced up and fed to the crows . . .

'My friends, you all need a Paloma in your lives,' Frank was starting to wrap up his speech, 'it's basically like having a missis, but because you're paying them, they don't nag you. It's a win-win, I'm telling you! And so I say to all of you – my extended family – as head of HNB hedge-fund management . . .'

Somebody gave a little whoop of appreciation.

'I know! Who'd have thought I could lead anything, eh?' quipped Frank. 'I can tell you we've had a large two years with me at the helm, so you know what? Let's make the next two EVEN LARGER!'

And with this Frank raised his glass high and everyone did the same.

'To HNB!' Frank bellowed.

'To HNB!' they echoed back.

'And now,' Frank smiled, 'you know that this has become something of a Cedar Vale tradition. Gentlemen, please . . . TAKE TO YOUR LAWNMOWERS!!'

There was much scuffling, putting down of glasses, laughter, and general drunken movement towards the John Deere lawnmowers which were ready in their serried ranks, awaiting some of Surrey's richest and finest-clad buttocks. The golfing buddies were the first to reach their steeds, and were soon sparking up the lawnmowers with shouts of 'Oi oi!!!' and 'Where's The Stig when you need him?' and 'This engine's got more poke than your Jag!' and other such merry male joshing.

Frank was in heaven. He loved the John Deere lawn-mower race. Yes, he'd lost a couple along the years due to some rogue driving, and poor old Roger Mitchell-White still had the large scar across his cheek from where he'd taken a tumble. But there he was, Jolly Roger as he was now called because of his piratical scarred face, mojito in one hand, the other revving up his John Deere with the best of them.

Frank felt like a Roman emperor sitting in the Colosseum watching his gladiators fight it out. But where was his Agrippina? He'd thought he'd seen Sally hiding – crouching? – behind Pan during his speech, but now there was no sign of her. Well, she was missing out on the best bit of the party.

'ON YOUR MARKS, GET SET . . . GO!!' roared Frank, and the lawnmowers were off with all the smoke, smell and clamour of a sloth-paced Grand Prix. Frank was in his element, hopping from one foot to the other in sheer excitement. All his friends, neighbours and clients were part of the Frank Parker Circus, and he was its ringmaster. The lawn would be right royally scuffed, but his team of gardeners would airbrush it in the morning. He only wished his family were here to stand shoulder to shoulder with him and relish all of this. Where were they all?

Frank's eye was caught by a smaller figure on a lawn-mower at the back of the peloton who didn't look as big and male as the others. It was a slight person in white and pink who had no control of the lawnmower whatsoever. In fact, they were driving the John Deere away from the pack and perilously close to the pool house, an Alpine chalet that Frank had commissioned after seeing one just like it on a skiing holiday. It wasn't looking good for the little pink and white person at all. Their lawnmower veered and crashed through a piece of statuary and on to the patio surrounding the pool, crushing several sun loungers before plummeting headlong into the water.

Frank shouted to his staff and several of them sprinted towards the pool. News filtered through the lawnmower race that somebody was down. Lawnmowers stopped. People started running. Frank arrived at the scene just in time to see his wife hauled from his £180,000 pool, trousers down by her ankles, soaked and bedraggled and coughing up, by the look of it, a large mixture of swimming-pool water and mojito.

4

The light barely made it through the heavy white damask curtains, which many thousands of Asian silkworms had worked their little tushes off to provide. With pelmets trimmed lustrously in pomegranate and gold, they lined a whole wall of Sally and Frank Parker's hangar of a bedroom.

Sally kept her eyes squeezed tightly shut, even so, cringing away from the dim light in her supersize bed. She had seen it on holiday, made an offhand comment about quite liking it, and the next thing she knew, Frank was having that exact bed shipped over from Dubai to Cedar Vale.

Paloma sniffed, leaning towards her with a slightly funereal bunch of lilies and twigs arranged in cellophane and raffia.

'Miss Parker. These flowers are from Miss Daly-Jones. You want me to read?'

Sally tried to croak out a no, but Paloma had already started, in a loud monotone:

'Get better soon hon. Francesca and Tim PS maybe get some refresher driving lessons? Smiley face kiss kiss kiss.'

Paloma pursed her lips. 'I made you liver and ginger smoothie. With salt. Good for your condition. You are dehydrated, Miss Parker.'

And she plonked a tall glass of grim-looking, viscous beige liquid at Sally's side.

Gradually the random fragments of yesterday evening's barbecue began to order and present themselves to Sally, in her wrung-out dishcloth of a brain. Oh God. She had the vaguest memory of straddling the John Deere and rather enjoying its thrum between her thighs. Did she remember Tim Daly-Jones licking his lips and baring his teeth at her in a lascivious way as he was sparking up his lawnmower, or was that her new best friend Monsignor Valium de Mojito playing tricks with her? She was never, ever, EVER going to drink another mojito as long as she lived. And she was never, ever, EVER going to swallow another Valium. She could have died! Did the kids see it? And where was Frank?

Oh GOD. She'd said something to Francesca about cunnilingus and nostrils, she was sure of it. GOD, OH DEAR SWEET GOD. And had she really sung a Mel & Kim hit, with accompanying dance manoeuvres, to Laura Piggott, Sky News's Chief Economics Correspondent?

'The children?' Sally murmured.

'Colette organise everything, Miss Parker.'

'The dogs?'

'Janice Dawes organise everything, Miss Parker.'

'Frank?'

'Mister Frank organise himself, Miss Parker.'

So just another regular day in the Parker household then. Everything organised by somebody else. Sally couldn't even take charge of her own dogs. Janice Dawes, the local dog groomer, was frequently relied upon to walk and board the pack. Sally was just a bit part in Cedar Vale life, banging fruitlessly on the double-glazed windows from the outside while all of life went on inside, nobody hearing her pitiful cries.

She lay back into hotel quantities of pillows, and wondered how she was going to navigate her way into this weekend without a) falling over or b) being forced to discuss the John Deere and other episodes from the previous evening with her husband.

She ran her parched tongue around the inside of her crusty mouth, and had a word with herself.

'Come on Sally Parker. You can do this! You've got three A levels, for God's sake!'

Decent grades in English, Latin and French that had taken her absolutely nowhere. She'd married Frank straight after taking her exams, to the utter disgust of her mother, who refused to attend the wedding. It had been a small affair at a Catholic Church in Effingham, a drizzly day in July with twenty people in attendance. Neither Frank nor Sally had been part of the in-crowd at their respective schools. They shared in common a complete ease with being alone. They didn't quite fit. Sally was too pretty to be taken to the bosom of the girl gang. They were too jealous of her. And Frank had his own fish to fry. Plus he was often made to feel alienated in the group because of events happening within his family. Frank and Sally were like 'two square pegs in search of two square holes', as Sally always put it. 'But we just found one big rectangle to fit into together, didn't we?' At the age of eighteen, they'd joined their square pegs together and that was that. They were a two-person team from then on. With Amerjit as a cherished gooseberry, their beloved third leg.

She hoped he wouldn't be too upset with her after the barbecue. Laura Piggott she had never much liked, but Amerjit she cared for deeply.

Sally sighed. It was all too much. She closed her eyes and tried to drift back to sleep.

*

Frank passed Paloma coming out of the bedroom, a disapproving frown wedged on her face, and gave her a wink. He'd managed to drag himself up early with the first phone call from an anxious client. A couple of hours of the classic soothing Parker patter later, and everything was hunky-dory again. Frank thought he'd earned a cheeky nap. He also needed a bit of a recharge before he talked to Sally about what the hell she'd been playing at last night.

He marched through the door, ready to throw himself down for a rest, but halted mid-stride at Sally's small, pale, sleeping face engulfed by their massive bed. She looked about sixteen, as if the last thirty years had just dropped away, and he was back in his dad's truck, that summer they first met.

Frank's dad, Jack Parker, was pure Hayes born and bred. He came from Irish stock and worked in the local Tarmac plant, the main employer for any male under sixty in the vicinity. Jack was a grafter and worked at the plant all week, then ran his own business on the side at weekends, tarmacking people's driveways and front paths. He knew Tarmac like the back of his hand, and the backs of his hands were imbued with the stuff.

Frank had grown up with that hot bitumen aroma in his nostrils. Even now, when he smelled it, it took him right back to the Hayes of the seventies and eighties, Frank riding up front in the truck, proud of his dad's muscly tattooed forearms with their soft down of blond hairs manning the wheel. He was all man, Frank's dad, and Frank loved that about him. He loved the smell of him and the way that he smoked cigarettes and handled a pint glass.

Frank had some of the best times of his childhood in that truck, the two of them driving off to some job, Frank by his dad's side all the way and proud to take home some proper cash at the end of a hard day's work.

Sometimes Frank's younger brother Kyle would join them too, but he was getting into Gary Numan and chasing girls, so wasn't nearly as reliable as Frank. If there was a sniff of cash to be made, Frank was right there. What with the money he was making on Uncle Phil's fruit stall and the Tarmac cash, Frank was squirreling away a tidy sum.

'For a rainy day, eh?' his dad would say with a wink.

'No, Dad. For my business. I'm going to be rich as Creasers!'

And Jack Parker would chuckle at Frank's mispronunciation of the word.

'It's Croesus, son, and beware. Not much good came of him, you know.'

All of Jack Parker's spare time was taken up with reading. He knew his classics, had a penchant for the poetry of Yeats and a rather surprising passion for the writing of Jane Austen. Frank had always been a bit mystified by this and quizzed his father about it.

'It's simple. You always know where you are with Miss Austen, son,' Jack would say. 'Whenever you're in doubt, ask yourself "What would Lizzy Bennet do? What would Emma think? How would Fanny react?" And my favourite of all, Frank, Anne Elliot. What advice would she give to you?'

'Who's Anne Elliot?' asked Frank.

Jack Parker's voice became almost reverent now.

'Anne Elliot is the lead character in *Persuasion*, Frank, the finest of all Miss Austen's works.' Frank loved the way his dad never referred to her as 'Jane' but always opted for the more formal 'Miss Austen'. Jack was warming to his theme now.

'Anne Elliot is nearly twenty-seven when we first meet her in *Persuasion*. She's unmarried and thinks that her life's over. In those days she was on the shelf. Past the sell-by date. And then she meets the dashing Captain Wentworth, who she'd rejected once before, and realises she made a terrible mistake.'

'So that's it then, is it, Dad?' asked Frank.

'No, son. It's not. What Miss Austen is saying is that it's never too late. You can change. You can try again. You can have that second chance at life.'

Jack's eyes glazed over and his voice was dreamy now. Frank felt as if his dad had departed from the Tarmac truck and had floated off into a world of crinolines and bonnets.

'Dad! Dad!' said Frank somewhat urgently. He didn't want to lose his dad to the Bennets and the Bingleys, thank you very much.

'Sorry, son,' said Jack softly, 'I was just thinking. How lovely to be able to have a new chapter like Anne Elliot. To change; to remain true to yourself but also to move on. If you know what I mean.'

Frank didn't really know what his dad meant, but it didn't matter. He just loved spending time with him in the Tarmac truck and hearing his soft and rasping Hayes voice.

It was mainly people's driveways that the Parkers worked on. Jack Parker started to get a name in Surrey for being a safe pair of Tarmac hands. He did a couple of jobs in the Effingham area and then word spread to Bookham and Fetcham and he was soon having to turn down work. Everyone wanted a tarmacked drive in the Surrey of the eighties. It was a badge of honour to have a smooth drive-way that you could park your one, two, sometimes even three cars on. A lot of driveways were built on hills, and the name of Jack Parker soon became synonymous with the perfect tarmacked hill.

'Tarmac covers over a multitude of sins, son,' Frank liked to say, 'cracks, fractures and secrets.'

'Secrets?' Frank would ask, enthralled.

'Everyone needs some Tarmac in their lives, Frank, don't you think? Wouldn't you like to be able to Tarmac over some of your secrets? I know I would.'

Frank didn't like to think of his father having secrets. He liked having his dad real and present and smelling of Tarmac.

A job came through one day for a posh house near Haslemere, out of Jack Parker's usual patch. Randwyck Manor it was called, and Jack and Frank set out there early one Saturday morning in the truck. On the way, Jack found reason to land on his favourite default topic.

'Well, well, you and I going to the poshest part of Surrey, son. Imagine how the Bennets felt when they were invited over to Netherfield, or indeed how Lizzy felt when she arrived at Pemberley, for God's sake.'

The sixteen-year-old Frank knew enough about *Pride and Prejudice* from his dad to hazard a guess.

'Awestruck?'

'Yes, son, but also sure of herself. And that's how I feel going to this Randwyck Manor. I feel sure of myself. And so should you. The Parkers are the best at Tarmac in Surrey. We are secure in that. That's all we have to think about.'

Nevertheless, Frank noticed that his dad smoked way more roll-ups than usual on the journey there.

Jack needn't have felt nervous at all. Randwyck Manor, which stood about two miles from Haslemere in some of the most breathtaking countryside that Surrey has to offer, was a crumbling dump. An unloved Gothic neo-monstrosity with a dark aspect to it, strange ghostly turrets all around its roof and gloomy, shuttered windows. Jack and Frank bumped along the long and potholed driveway up to its grand entrance, which was about as grand as the back entrance of Leatherhead Leisure Centre, Jack couldn't help remarking with a chuckle.

The lady of the manor was a Lucinda Tennant, who appeared out of the darkened doorway like a spectre in faded silk shirt and tweed trousers. She had beautiful bone structure and a ballet-dancer posture, but she had the coldest blue eyes that Frank had ever seen. They'd turn you into an arctic roll, those eyes. They were eyes which life had endlessly disappointed, so they had given up their sparkle.

She looked the Parkers up and down as if they were dirt brought in by her dog, a nasty little cavalier spaniel that wouldn't stop yapping. She didn't invite them into the house but waved in the general direction of the driveway and announced that she wanted the whole thing tarmacked over. Jack Parker had enough aesthetic sensitivity to know that a quarter of a mile of tarmacking was not going to look the prettiest. He said so, but Lucinda waved it away with another supercilious hand gesture. It was what both she and her husband, an invalid who never left the house, wanted.

Jack suggested that maybe it might be nice to mix it up with some gravel or stonework, something to complement the era of the house?

Lucinda raised a haughty eyebrow.

'You're quite the Capability Brown, aren't you? Don't lecture me about architecture and design. You tarmac for a living, Mr Parker.'

Jack had a red spot on each cheek, which his son had never seen before. It made Frank feel all churned up inside, so he looked Lucinda Tennant squarely in the face and blurted, 'Pemberley or Netherfield wouldn't have Tarmac on their drives.'

Jack shot him a warning look, but Frank maintained eye contact with this old bag. Lucinda Tennant settled her cold blue marbles on Frank, and then threw back her head and laughed.

'The tarmacker knows about Netherfield and Pemberley. Whatever next?'

'This driveway's about five hundred metres long, Mrs Tennant. You know that's at least four weekends' work?' Jack advised her.

Lucinda sniffed.

'Then you'd better get started, hadn't you?'

And with that, she turned on her heel and was engulfed by the black hole of Randwyck Manor.

Jack and Frank looked at each other and, when it was safe to do so, burst out laughing.

'Hammer House of Horror,' chuckled Jack.

'Hoity toity old bag,' said Frank.

They set out their tools and Jack started the process of heating up the Tarmac while Frank did a proper recce of the area. After twenty minutes or so, he was aware of a prickly sensation on his neck. It wasn't unpleasant. It just felt as if someone was watching him. He looked up and his eye was caught by a small figure in one of the upper windows. A blond curly-haired girl was looking down at him and it gave him a strange flutter in his chest. She disappeared from view and he got back to work. But he had the same prickly feeling intermittently over the course of the morning, like she was watching his every move.

She was indeed watching his every move, from the confines of her chilly bedroom which even the posters of ABC and Simple Minds did little to modernise. Around lunchtime, she emerged out of the front door and into the light.

Frank had the sensation of seeing a moth emerging from the darkness of a cupboard. She was the most beautiful girl he'd ever laid eyes on, with straw-coloured curls set around a gentle, inquiring face, and, unlike her mother's, eyes as soft and blue as a spring morning. Her beauty wasn't one that knew itself. It wasn't a 'look at me' sort of flicking hair, wiggling hips kind of self-centred beauty. She gave off something much more powerful even though she was slight. Frank had an overwhelming sense of nature in all of its freshness when Sally stepped on to that driveway. She had whispering of trees and a reassuring crunchiness of a forest floor about her. Everything was aligned with her, but not altogether perfect, which prevented her from being bland. She had a slight beakiness about her nose – Frank was reminded of a small bird – and she was sure of foot, like a goat. Frank was sure that if she ever allowed him to sniff her hair, it would smell just like hay. Sally was the sort of person that breathed oxygen out as well as in.

When she arrived on the drive and stood, in shorts, plimsolls and T-shirt, side by side with Jack and Frank, offering her hand for them to shake and looking at them with dancing eyes, she brought an energy with her. It wasn't overwhelming or exhausting. She just made you feel that the day had a bit more colour in it. She was assured without being smug. She was quiet but full of humour. Frank knew pretty much immediately that he would marry her.

He told his dad this on the way home, who looked at him and said, 'Don't rush into it, remember Lydia and Mr Wickham.'

But Frank was kick bollock scramble in love and counted the hours and minutes until he could be back at Randwyck Manor again.

*

Sally was not struck with that particular bolt of lightning; like a deer she had to sniff the air and see which way the wind was leaning before she could start to gambol. But it was a pretty extreme set of weather conditions that began to envelop her heart over the next week. Hail and a heat-wave maybe. A thick fog followed by the most intense bright sunshine. She definitely felt a stirring of the elements and found herself longing to see the energetic, engaging son of the tarmacker again. Frank was his name. She liked it. It sounded open and honest, and, well, frank.

On their second Saturday she made sure she was in her trendiest pedal pushers with her coolest T-shirt, and a bit of make-up to accentuate her blue eyes, but nothing too obvious. Lucinda noticed her eyeliner at breakfast that morning as the two of them sat silently at the cracked Formica table.

'Your eyes look very . . . distinct this morning.'

'I've put some eyeliner on, Mummy.'

'I can't think why. There's nobody to impress, is there?'

There was a silence. Lucinda looked up from her boiled egg and scrutinised her daughter.

'Not the Tarmac boy, I hope?'

Sally's silence said everything. She excused herself as quickly as she could and hid upstairs, holding her breath, until she heard Jack's truck rumbling up the driveway. She waited a few minutes before she dared go to the window. Her heart was in her mouth; she thought it would pop out and jump around her bedroom. What if Frank hadn't come? What if her mother saw? What if? What if?

She sidled up to the window and peeked out just a fraction. Her heart leapt as she saw the reassuring form of Frank, which she realised she'd longed for all week. She smiled as she watched him move the tools out of the truck, taking his jumper off to start the day. His hair was ruffled and curly, his movements sure and athletic, and she pretty much skipped on both feet when he smiled directly up at her window.

Under the benevolent eye of Jack, and the unseen glower of Lucinda, Frank and Sally's friendship quickly blossomed into young love, and four weekends of tarmacking stretched into six. Jack realised well enough that the lovebirds needed more time to cement (and tarmac) their relationship. He was being paid for the whole job rather than by the day, but didn't mind taking extra time over it; he was so happy to see his son experiencing true Miss Austen-style depth of feeling. He let them go off on their own for walks in the Surrey hills, assuring Frank that he was fine to work on his own. Jack even brought Kyle along for two of the Saturdays. He managed to get his feet stuck in some Tarmac and fell asleep in the truck, but Jack laughed it off; Frank's happiness was infectious.

And so the driveway at Randwyck Manor was finished. Jack was pleased with the job but thought that the overall effect was horrible. A shiny black runway, like a five-hundred-metre slug, leading up to a loveless Victorian shell of a house.

Lucinda Tennant looked down her nose at the finished driveway and gave Jack his cash as if she were doing him a favour.

'Thank you, Mrs Tennant, I hope you're pleased with the results?' ventured Jack before they got in the truck to leave.

'The drive will do perfectly well,' she said, 'but that will not,' she added, glancing at Sally and Frank who were sharing a joke a few metres away.

'Let me make this crystal clear, Mr Parker,' she continued, 'whatever this dalliance is, it will cease from this day forward.'

Jack shook his head, and blew out some breath from his lungs.

'That's like trying to stop the planets from turning, Mrs Tennant.'

'This has nothing to do with astronomy, Mr Parker. This is an earthly matter and it is simple. It is not in my family's interests for my daughter to consort with your son. She has seen him working with the sun on his back and with the heady smell of Tarmac in her nostrils, but that is all, a passing fancy. She will not see him again. I'm sure you'll agree with me that it is not wise for –' she searched for the words – 'your sort either, to be running around after something that will never be attainable. I hope we understand each other, Mr Parker,' and with that she closed the subject with those disconcerting blue eyes of hers.

Jack Parker looked over at Frank and Sally, who were teasing each other, trying to step on each other's feet. He turned to meet Lucinda Tennant's stare and shook his head gently.

'Pure Lady Catherine de Bourgh,' he said slowly, 'and just like her, Lucinda Tennant, you are totally lacking in any real class.'

Lucinda's mouth opened to say something but no sound emerged. Jack smiled and called Frank over to the truck. They made their easy way down the smoothest drive in Haslemere, with Frank looking behind him at Sally's receding figure.

Love, as we are told by writers, painters and songsmiths, can conquer all. And over the course of the next two years it appeared to do just that. Despite everything Lucinda said to try to crush, sully and belittle the relationship, Frank and Sally saw each other twice a week, unfailingly. Frank had already planned out their marriage and life together by the time he was seventeen. Sally laughed and said they should wait. Lucinda brewed and stewed and the atmosphere in Randwyck Manor became unbearable for Sally. Her ancient father continued to crumble in a room with a hoist, commode and array of carers, as the lines around Lucinda's mouth went deeper and ever downward.

Sally was a valiant sort, and kept herself going with her studies and her love for Frank Parker. It was simple really. Until the inevitable day came. She'd been preparing for this most of her life.

She was now seventeen and about to do her exams. One Sunday morning her mother called her back into the so-called breakfast room, the sort of room that the late Romanian dictator General Ceauşescu and his wife would eat in, with lots of appliances from the 1950s.

It was clear that Lucinda was not going to mince her words.

'Sit down.'

Sally did as she was told.

'This stupidity has got to stop. You will soon be out in the world, young lady, where you will find a very different place from the one to which you have become accustomed here at Randwyck.'

Yes, Sally was thinking with every fibre of her brain, and I cannot WAIT!

'Girls like you are destined to have a good marriage to a man with prospects. From somewhere solid like Shropshire. Not Tarmac boy from whichever ghastly hole he emerged from,' and on the word 'hole', Lucinda's nostrils widened into ghastly holes as large as a rocking horse's.

'His name is Frank and he comes from Hayes,' said Sally evenly. 'It's not a ghastly hole actually, although it is under the Heathrow flight path,' and she smiled sweetly. She had learned during her seventeen years that nothing riled her mother more than speaking to her in an even tone with a sweet smile to finish.

'I'm going to lay my cards on the table,' continued Lucinda. 'If you marry Tarmac boy, I will disinherit you. You will come to nothing. And all of this –' she swept an arm around the chilly room with its detritus and broken old pieces of hideous crockery – 'that Randwyck has to offer you will be taken away.'

There was a long pause. Sally held her lips together for fear of laughing. With the rules of primogeniture the way they were, she knew the most she and her sister Nancy could ever hope to inherit would be some broken egg cups and a tablecloth. All of the property would go to the first-born son, in this case, her younger brother Miles. Lucinda extended her neck like the Empress of the Nile, and Sally cleared her throat carefully.

'I'm not interested in your cards, Mummy,' she said quietly, 'and I don't really want your table either. Thank you for having me and for keeping a roof over my head for seventeen years. But . . .' and Sally paused here. She'd known for a long time that she was going to have to make this speech to her mother's face, and she wanted to be sure to get it right.

'To survive in this world,' Sally continued, 'and make a good life, I need to be everything that you are not. Where you are cold, I need to be full of love. Where you are ungiving, I need to be gentle.' As the speech came out Sally felt slightly mortified as she realised how like the Prayer of St Francis of Assisi it was, but she was on a roll now. 'Where you are ungenerous, I need to be as kind as I can possibly be.' Sally smiled briefly at her mother. 'That's all really. It's not rocket science.'

Her mother looked as if she'd been petrified, her swan's neck still at full extension. There was a mighty silence in the room. It had weight; you could have packed it up in blocks and put it in the attic. Lucinda Tennant got up and left the room. And that was it. Their relationship was set in aspic from that moment onwards.

Sally's mum popped into her mind now, as she wobbled into her enormous bathroom with its his and hers separate basins, its his and hers separate showers, and its his urinal – bought by Frank for a dare from a nightclub in Dublin – and hers sit-down loo. And then there were the bidets with the gold taps. The sight of those his and hers bidets always made Sally think of her mother. Lucinda Tennant despised bidets with all of her being, she called them 'non-U' along with hostess trolleys (Frank bought Sally a golden one as a joke for their tenth wedding anniversary), non-purebred dogs and referring to lunch as 'dinner' and supper as 'tea', which Frank had been brought up to do, and boy, he enjoyed saying both as much as possible in his mother-in-law's presence.

Sally's visits to her ailing father became rare; her mother made it as difficult as possible for her to see him. Lucinda refused to visit the married couple until fifteen years into their marriage, coincidentally the year that Frank had made it on to the *Sunday Times Rich List*. She would visit maybe three times a year, her nose held aloft as she perched with her Finishing School legs crossed over one another in one of Frank's oversized white leather armchairs. She would look about her with a mixture of intense scorn but also a deep longing. She couldn't bear the fact that Sally had staff and she didn't. She hated everything about Cedar Vale and the way it was done out so lavishly and showily, but she wanted it. She wanted it all.

After her husband died, a few years after Sally's wedding, Lucinda had been left rattling around Randwyck Manor all alone. Miles, her only son, wanted to put as many miles between himself and her as possible. He was busy spending whatever money he could earn as DJ and rave organiser, on coke and pills. Nancy, the eldest Tennant child, had pretty much run away from home at the age of fifteen, to be found selling vegetables in a market in Rome. She lived in squats, learned to paint and then partnered up with Italian activists and performance artists for a few years, before disappearing off to Thailand with a guitarist. She had always been a wild one, Nancy. Lucinda had taken down every single photo of her in the house (there were only three to be fair) and she did exactly the same with Sally's the day she married Frank Parker. There were plenty of photos of Miles around Randwyck, even a terrible oil painting of him as a boy in velvet plus-fours and waistcoat. He had mean eyes even at the age of seven.

The only reminder of Sally and Frank was Randwyck's tarmacked drive, which was standing the test of time well thanks to its superior craftsmanship. Randwyck Manor was almost totally dilapidated, and Lucinda Tennant wandered around its dank interior for years on her own, in a fur coat, come summer or winter.

The year after she deigned to speak to Sally again, Frank paid to have some rooms renovated so that she could live with some central heating, though she barely acknowledged the gesture. And then, one day, the prodigal Miles came home. Penniless and mannerless, he installed himself under the eye of his doting mother, who was determined she would give him everything he desired, to ensure that he never left her alone again.

Miles lived in a room off the drawing room, where he got up to God knows what. Now that she had him home, all that Lucinda Tennant longed for was to be Lady of Randwyck once more, to get the fire roaring again in the hall so that she could patronise the local nabobs over a Christmas sherry. The only reason she visited her daughter and her scrofulous Tarmac boy of a husband, was to mention how *kind* it would be, and how they *owed* it to her, to share some of their ill-gotten gains and help her to get Randwyck Manor back on its glorious feet again.

Sally sniffed as she looked into her (part of the his and hers) mirror. She still had Valium eyes. She needed to throw that stuff away. She had to get a grip of herself. Big time.

The 1812 Overture rang out. Who was at the door? She couldn't remember making a plan for anyone to visit. Paloma would know, she guarded the family diary like Cerberus.

Sally put on a floaty cream silk dressing gown, and wandered barefoot out on to the landing, then started to descend the grand staircase. As soon as she saw the familiar battered leather suitcase at the door, she felt herself flush with embarrassment. Frank's Welsh granny, Bronwen Llewellyn, Great Britain's most frugal nonagenarian and the beadiest woman on the planet, had arrived.

5

'It's over, Amerjit.'

Laura Piggott was too preoccupied to make eye contact with her husband. She was hunched over both her mobile phones at once, head to toe in fur, with a fur muff and a fur ring round her head like the Royals wear skiing at Klosters. She was perched on a bed made entirely of ice. She cut quite a figure in all that fur, and if her jaw hadn't been so lantern and her eyes a tad less granite, there might have been an air of Dr Zhivago about her.

'Fucksake, why is the Wi-Fi so patchy? This is SWEDEN, the Sweden where the GDP Growth Rate is projected to trend around one point two per cent in 2019!'

Amerjit Singh was also clad head to toe in fur, but the figure he cut this morning was not so much Dr Zhivago as an anxious bear. The hat that Amerjit sported was one in the traditional Russian style, with flaps that come down over the ears and then tie up underneath the chin. The flaps were untethered this morning, and one of them punted gently above his left ear, giving him a confused look.

Amerjit had always been tentative around his wife, ever since he'd spotted her at an Economists of the Future evening in Canary Wharf, soon after he'd finished his Master's at Princeton. He was actively on the lookout for a life-partner. All his school and uni friends were married; like a set of dominoes they'd all got hitched in quick succession. Amerjit was in danger of getting left behind and his parents were going spare.

'Your cousins are all married. Your sister is married. Why are you not married, Amerjit?' they'd say whenever he went back to Hayes. 'When are you going to give me some grandchildren, Amerjit?' his mother Pinki had pleaded. 'Your sister's given me grandchildren. What about you?'

He felt the family pressure building beneath him, so when he saw this foxy woman in the serious green suit which both accentuated her taut physique and gave her a perky Robin Hoodish air, he was determined to get in there with the merry men that were buzzing around her. Laura Piggott was definitely one to watch in the City – the *Financial Times* had named her Economic Temperature Changer of the Year, and she wasn't shy in showing off her confidence and acumen.

On first meeting, she immediately threw down the gauntlet with Amerjit about the impact of artificial intelligence on business growth. He was up to speed, and she liked the fact that this smart guy in the gorgeous suit was practically the only man in the room who hadn't been to public school.

He was really smart, but on his own terms, and definitely not because he'd been born with a silver spoon in his mouth. She embarked on a mission to test Amerjit out, and keep him on his Armani-clad toes. Laura loved testing men to gauge if they were man enough to take her on; and Amerjit in turn found this really sexy. The roster of women he'd been out with after university were more keen to chat about their law conversion courses or the endless country weddings they'd attended. Laura was exciting and aloof, and he was determined to warm her right up with some good old Singh heat.

In the early days of their courting, they'd had lots of

sparring, most of it over economics and finance, followed by lots of very wild and athletic sex the like of which Amerjit had never encountered before. It was a heady combination, the money chat and then the shagging, and it kept them both entertained for years right up to their wedding, a smart affair held close to the Bank of England. Amerjit then spent the early years of his marriage trying to do less of the sparring and more of the snuggling, and Laura gradually came to despise him for it. He didn't want to fight her, he just wanted to love her, thaw her, but Laura Piggott was not a woman for slippers, movie nights and onesies. As her career soared, her pedestal got higher and higher, and soon Amerjit was going to need an industrial cherry-picker to reach her.

'I've got two minutes till my taxi arrives, Amerjit, so I'll make this quick. I can't go on with this marriage. As I think I've been hinting at you for the last six months, but you seem to have become selectively deaf on the subject— Fucksake, Laura Piggott?'

She answered one of her phones brusquely. 'Hi, Guy. Yes, I'll be on the two p.m. flight out of Stockholm.'

She stood up and listened intently. 'On air at six o'clock? That's cutting it fine, Guy, but I'll definitely be up and running for the nine. And through the night of course, and for as long as this economic shitshow carries on. You might as well get me a zed bed in the studio because I won't be leaving it for the foreseeable!'

She laughed loudly and paced the ice floor as she listened to her news editor on the other end of the line.

'Yes, this . . . Swedish trip . . . has been an unfortunate blip. I'm sorry I had to leave London so suddenly. What's the temperature like in the markets?'

Her eyes took on a look of real concern now, like a mother hearing bad news about her child's health.

'Holy mother of God. Right. Anyone talking about quantitative easing this morning or is it just get in a boat, head for Dunkirk and start bailing?'

Amerjit hadn't blinked in about a minute. His eyes were frozen in bewilderment as if somebody had pressed the pause button. His wife carried on chatting animatedly; Amerjit could see her mouth moving but all he could hear were underwater noises.

She finished the call to Guy and looked briefly at Amerjit.

'Well, the cats are not only among the pigeons, Amerjit, they seem to have eaten, digested, and shat them right out.'

She busied herself with packing a few last items into her Louis Vuitton grip bag.

'Laura?' Amerjit's voice sounded as if somebody had been at his vocal cords with a cheese grater. Laura looked up and sighed.

'What now, Amerjit?'

'I wanted this to be a special weekend. I don't want our marriage to be over. I love you, Laura.'

She folded her arms.

'This weekend has come at a bad time for me, Amerjit. The country's in economic meltdown. And as far as our marriage is concerned, in pure economic terms, you've invested in me, Amerjit, but it hasn't yielded. It's what we call a ringer. You should know that. You work in finance. I don't want to be your ringer, Amerjit. Oh, I almost forgot . . . my ring.'

And she pulled her wedding ring off and left it on the sidetable made of ice. Amerjit was really trying hard to blink, but his eyelids felt wooden and numb in the frozen air. As he spoke, his words made little clouds of white condensation.

'You mentioned an "unfortunate blip" on the phone, Laura. Is that all I am? Your "unfortunate blip"?'

Laura snapped the lock on her grip bag, stood tall (a good inch higher than her husband) and stared down at him.

'Sometimes we need a blip in our lives to focus us, Amerjit. So we can have an emotional declutter and move on.'

'But I don't want to move on. I'm happy with where we are, Laura.'

The hotel phone bleeped on the ice sidetable.

'Ah,' she said, 'that's my taxi. Goodbye Amerjit,' and she picked up her bag and moved towards the door. She turned to him as she was leaving. 'This is not a good time, economic or otherwise, to be a ringer, Amerjit.'

Amerjit moved towards her. He wanted to grasp her furs and drag her back into the room like Daddy Bear. He wanted to talk to her, laugh with her, cry with her. He wanted to hear her say that she was prepared to try again, smooth over the blip, and move forward together. He wanted their two furs to merge and roll as one on the ice bed. He wanted baby bears.

But as he moved towards her, his foot hit a wet patch on the ice floor, and as the word 'Laura' came out of his mouth at an unfortunately strangulated pitch, he stretched his length on the slippery area, hitting the deck like a felled grizzly as the door shut firmly at her heel.

Amerjit had really hurt his elbow, and also his left cheek, but that was not the cause of the tears that began to flow from his finally animate eyeballs. And they were tears that felt even hotter than normal, his frozen face causing them to burn like unstemmable geysers. He tried to brush them away but the fur gloves were too large for a delicate job like that – it was like a football goalie trying to apply liquid eyeliner. And then the snot came. Gallons and gallons of snot on to the frozen floor. Amerjit became quite obsessed with its string of jellylike substance and started to move his gloves around in it while he let out a long howl.

Laura couldn't leave him; it couldn't be over. They had an extensive collection of Murano glassware together, a pair of matching his and hers £4,000 bikes. He'd been planning a surprise cycle trip to Transylvania for them both, deep in Dracula country and staying at top-of-the-range hotels. Who would accompany him on that trip now? Certainly not Frank: he'd rather go to Disneyland.

And now his thoughts turned to Frank. Amerjit felt uneasy about how he'd run out on his buddy before his big speech at the barbecue. Their barbecue. They were a double-act now, the two of them against all the other hedge-fund management companies. And the markets were going to shit. This made him cry even louder. He felt as if he were crying out seventeen years of tears and snot here all over the ice floor. Seventeen years of tears since the fateful night he'd met his unscalable, undefrostable wife.

From the open front door of Cedar Vale, Bronwen looked up at Sally with a look of the purest bead, and saw through her wan smile immediately.

'You'd forgotten I was coming, hadn't you?'

Sally had indeed but now, through the mesh of her hangover that seemed to have enlarged her tongue to the size of a leg of lamb, she did remember something about Bronwen stopping off at Cedar Vale for a night or two on the way to visit a cousin.

'You look green around the gills, Sal. Is that grandson of mine being a good boy?'

Sally moved in to kiss her, which felt like putting your lips into a little bird's nest, partly soft and feathery but also dry and twiggy.

'I've brought Welsh cakes,' said Bronwen. 'Looks like you should put a few of them away, Sally. Now where am I staying? Hidden away at the back, is it?'

Bronwen didn't do stairs without a stairlift, so Frank and Sally had had an annexe dayroom and bedroom built behind the utility rooms for her regular visits.

'You parking me behind the tumble dryers with the Polish laundry lady again, is it?' chirped Bronwen.

She grunted loudly and bent towards her suitcase, a move which always guaranteed somebody else to swoop in and do it for her. On cue:

'Let me do it, Bronwen, you shouldn't be lifting that,' said Sally, who immediately regretted her swift bob down.

'Well, my sciatica's been playing up something dreadful.'

Sally noticed that Paloma didn't step in and offer to carry the suitcase but stood watching with her arms crossed. Sally could sense the housekeeper's glee as she picked up the suitcase and struggled not to vomit all over it.

'No, don't worry, I'm fine, Paloma. Could you please go and make Mrs Llewellyn a nice pot of tea?' Sally said curtly. She was in no mood to walk on eggshells around her housekeeper today.

'So, you were up till all hours getting legless and driving the lawnmower into the pool, I hear?' said Bronwen loudly, as they moved through the kitchen-diner towards the utility complex.

Sally was speechless.

'She shouted at Paloma to eff off as well!' This was Cleo, bounding down to give her great-granny a hug. They loved each other, these two, and would sit and pore over *Heat* together for hours.

'Well, that's no bad thing,' said Bronwen dryly. 'I hope to God the bloody lawnmower's out of action now, is it? One less of those silly boy-toys the better, I say. They're all just penis substitutes, anyway. His grandfather, who had the one penis and managed perfectly well with it, thank you very much, would be turning in his grave to think that his grandson had squandered hundreds of thousands of pounds on a set of penises. I mean, how many penises does one man need?'

Cleo bellowed with laughter and put her arm around her great-granny.

They were all halfway across the kitchen by this point, somewhere around the vast red cappuccino machine with six nozzles, which Frank had persuaded a bar owner in Milan to sell him.

Bronwen ploughed on.

'Enough's as good as a feast, I always say, and Wyn, God rest his soul, was a firm believer in this. That, and don't count your chickens. And we had chickens too. Never counted them. Didn't want to tempt fate, see? Imagine that. Actually counting your real live chickens and then something terrible happening? The irony! I mean you've got to look at the reality of the situation. How many of those flipping lawnmowers does Frank have stuck in that silly garage with its doors that open by themselves?'

'At least twenty, G-G,' said Cleo.

'What a prat! And only the one chest freezer in there. I mean that doesn't make sense, does it, Sal? How can you equate one chest freezer with over twenty lawnmowers? And they all have names, don't they?'

Fortunately they'd arrived at the annexe door by now, and Sally could deposit Bronwen into her lodgings, dump the suitcase and leave Cleo to look after her.

'Granny Bronwen,' murmured Sally, 'I'm just going to go and see how that tea's coming on . . .'

Bronwen rolled the beady eye towards her once more.

'Yes, Sal, but from which teapot? Eh? Doubtless you've got one hundred and four of those. Frank paid for all of them, no doubt? Have you got names for them too?'

While Sally smarted at these comments, Cleo roared with laughter, which made Bronwen chuckle and wheeze, 'Maybe they should meet the lawnmowers, eh Cleo? They'd get on famously, I'll bet!'

Cleo actually ruffled her great-grandmother's hair at this comment, like a footballer.

Sally laughed politely.

'Well, I'll tell the others that you're here. I'll just pop back and see what they're all up to!'

She could have answered her own question right there – she knew exactly what they'd be up to. Stephen would be gaming, Emily would be studying and Mikey wouldn't be there at all.

'I'll be right back!'

'That's right, Sally, you just leave me here in the land that time forgot. Luckily I've got Cleo so I won't starve. I'll just be quiet and do what a ninety year old is supposed to do. I'll go and wee in that armchair over there, shall I, Cleo? Or fall over and bash my head on that glass nest of occasional tables.'

Sally rolled her eyes as she shut the door on gales more laughter from Bronwen and Cleo. She'd never laughed with her grandmother-in-law like that, and made a note to herself to try and be more upbeat and funny. She had a brief flashback to the barbecue, and put her hand out on the wall to steady herself.

Out of the two of them, Frank's grandmother was the woman least likely to fall over at this moment. Bronwen

Llewellyn was the woman who, out of sheer grit, never sat down to put on either sock or shoe in the morning. She would stand there on one leg, like a flamingo, and insert one foot after the other into first wool, then leather.

Sally's head was really starting to throb now. She must do something useful today. She must show Frank's grandmother that she was proactive and in charge. What could she do in this state? She'd get dressed. Good. A plan.

She padded back through to the kitchen; she needed some drugs, something to take the edge off. Codeine, maybe? Or a double shot of Day Nurse?

She could hear Frank's voice on the phone, uncharacteristically loud for a Saturday; it definitely wasn't his Weekend Voice, it was his Office Voice. He took in the sight of Sally in her silk dressing gown, smiled briefly and then rubbed his eyes. He looked knackered.

'Well, let's make sure we send some flowers to Simon. What a wally cycling home from here to Islington! How long is he likely to be out of action, then?'

Sally started to pour out some Day Nurse into a glass, discreetly so that Frank couldn't see what she was doing. She topped it with a mint leaf to make it look like it was a smoothie. A neon-yellow smoothie. Maybe she'd have time to listen to her podcast this morning? That would give her a good idea of how to set about her day.

She sat at the breakfast bar and focused her attention on Frank. She presumed that whoever was on the end of the line was talking about Simon Khan, one of Frank's colleagues at HNB.

'Jesus. That must have been a hell of a collision. And tell me, Kerry, where the hell's Amerjit? Do we know? I've been trying his mobile all morning.' Frank slumped down in one of the country kitchen chairs. 'Well, he was here last night, little toerag. He didn't say anything about a Swedish mini-break. Bloody tit, he's only just had a two-week jolly in the Maldives, hasn't he? Well listen, we need all hands on deck with Simon out of the picture. You'd better track Amerjit down and tell him to haul his spotty arse back to London. OK? And I'll leave him another message too. I'll call you later, all right? And can you get all the files that we need out and ready? I'll call in the operators with their pocket calculators. Cheers, Kerry.'

He shook his head and rubbed his stubble thoughtfully.

'What's up?' asked Sally.

'I could ask the same of you, babe! Nice work last night. Poor John Major's never going to see the light of day again.'

'John Major?'

'My sexiest lawnmower that you drove into the pool last night, Sal! Or had you forgotten?'

There was an edge to Frank's voice that Sally wasn't used to. And Bronwen was dead right, he did have names for his lawnmowers. Were they all named after Tories?

'RIP John Major. I'm sorry, Frank, I was feeling anxious so I probably overdid it on the mojitos . . .'

'You were heckling me and telling Paloma to eff off—'

'Ssh, Frank, she might hear!' whispered Sally.

'Then I do my big speech and there isn't a single member of the family watching except for Emily.'

Sally put her glass sharply down on the breakfast bar.

'What do you mean, "except for Emily"? Emily is a member of our family, Frank. Emily is your niece.'

'I know that, Sal, you remind me of that at least a hundred times a week. Of course she's my niece.'

'She's more than just a niece, Frank.'

'How can she be more than a niece, Sal? I'm her uncle! She's my niece!'

'She's lived with us like a sister to her cousins, for fifteen years.'

'And don't I know that, Sal,' said Frank, warming to his theme. 'I did exactly as you asked me, I took her in when your loop-de-loop sister ran off with whatsisname and for fifteen years I have paid for her food, her clothing, her education—'

'Is this a bad time?' Emily had appeared silently at the kitchen door without them noticing.

Sally looked at her husband with pure venom, which is easier with a hangover as the poison is pretty close to the surface. She turned to her niece.

'Frank and I were just talking—'

'I know,' and Emily turned glacially to her uncle, 'I heard.'

And with that she was gone. If Sally had had the energy she would have run after Emily, smothered her with hugs and told her everything was fine, they were just having a stupid argument. But she was weakened. And scared. She found it difficult to talk to Emily about Nancy at the best of times. And with a raging hangover . . . well . . . it would have to wait. Sally made a mental note to seek out her niece and have a good heart-to-heart in private.

'Well done, Frank. Great work,' said Sally sarcastically.

'I didn't hear her creeping about, did I? The point is, I gave that cocking speech and there was less than twenty per cent of the family there to support me.'

'And who was that supportive percentage, Frank? Emily!'

Frank sighed.

'Emily, perfect as always. While my own kids were off AWOL and my wife was behind a statue with her trousers round her ankles.'

Sally was genuinely shocked.

'You never saw me behind the statue?'

'Of course I saw you behind the cocking statue, Sal! Everyone could see you behind the statue!'

'Oh GOD, NO!' Sally held her head in both hands. The shame of it. She would never live this down. She felt the prick of tears at her eyelids.

Frank softened as he always did with Sally.

'I'm sorry, babe. That was harsh. There's just a lot going on at the moment. The markets are in freefall, the radio's full of it today, we're heading into some very choppy waters and bloody Simon Khan, our hilariously titled "Head of Risk Assessment" did not assess any kind of risk in cycling home through central London last night, pissed as a fart with no lights. Muppet. He's in intensive care as we speak. Stupid bastard.'

Frank was pacing now. Pacing and yawning at the same time.

'His poor family, Frank,' said Sally quietly.

'I know, his poor family. And poor us. The last thing you want to do is lose your effing Head of Risk Assessment when your whole business might be at risk. JESUS, why am I so tired? I'm going up to have a kip.'

Never in her thirty-year marriage had Sally heard Frank say these words. It was, what, midday, and Frank was going back to bed? Bizarre. Sally shivered. A cold breeze blew right through her for a moment.

6

It was early Monday morning in the Parker household after a Sunday where not much had happened apart from Sally escaping to the Park Club gym and spa for a full six hours. She'd kept telling herself that she'd stay for just one more workout, but one became two and then there was the spa, and she wanted to listen to her podcast. And there were lots of lovely magazines to read. But the truth of the matter was that Sally just couldn't face being pinned out like a lab rat under the intense gaze of Granny Bronwen.

She knew how it would pan out. After an hour in her company Bronwen would start to delve into the whys and wherefores, and Sally just didn't have the strength to go below veneer-talk. She'd also wanted to escape from Frank, who spent most of the weekend either barking into a variety of mobile phones or kipping. It was most odd. She needed time and space to herself.

It was a beautiful September morning with the promise of an Indian summer's day ahead. And Granny Bronwen was due to leave, thank goodness.

Emily was usually up first on a school day, ticking things off a checklist written neatly on to a Post-it note the night before.

Today's note read, 'Flute lesson. Netball kit. Maths project. Geography homework. Physics homework. Mum's birthday.'

Emily put a line of neat blue biro through all of them apart from the last. She let the pen hover over 'Mum's birthday', and then scrubbed out the words until they could no longer be seen or read. She wanted those words not even to exist. She scrubbed so hard that she actually made a hole through the paper. Job done. She was ready for her day.

Frank Parker was like Margaret Thatcher in his sleeping habits. Not his lawnmower Margaret Thatcher, for yes, he did have one named after her. Like the real Thatcher, Frank had only ever managed to bag four to five hours' kip a night since he was thirty years old; maybe six if he was ill or drunk. But on this Monday morning he was still flat out, sprawled like a starfish in the Dubai bed at eight a.m. He'd spent a lot of Sunday afternoon in it too while Sally was in the gym. Unheard of.

He'd slept through his five thirty alarm. By five thirty-five he should have been into his cross-trainer and kettle-bell programme, in the depths of his musky basement gym. Paloma always had his pecan-milk Bircher muesli with chia seeds ready for him at six a.m. when his driver picked him up on the dot every morning. Trevor Smith had been his faithful chauffeur these last ten years. He, more than anyone, had been party to the high-octane roller-coasterings of Frank Parker's working life.

Sally had taken the executive decision not to wake Frank up, and went out at eight a.m. to give Trevor the latest update.

'I'm so sorry about this, Trevor. Frank's not well. He's really not been himself since Friday,' she explained. 'I think we'll let him sleep it off, shall we?'

Trevor nodded, slipped his jacket off and took out the *Daily Mail*. 'FREEFALL BRITAIN!' blazed the headline.

'You seen this, Mrs Parker?' asked Trevor. 'Looks like the economy's gone Pete Tong.'

Sally scanned the headlines vaguely.

'I know. Terrible.'

'Don't you think Mr Parker should be up and about trying to sort this mess out?' said Trevor. 'I hope my two grand's safe, and all! I gave that to Mr Parker and told him, "You look after that dosh, like it was your own flesh and blood!"'

Sally looked thoughtful. She had no idea that Trevor had given Frank some of his own money to invest. She bit her lip and found it hard to meet his eye.

'I think I'll just leave him for another half an hour. The mess can wait! You relax, Trevor, I'll get you a cup of tea.'

And she went into the house wondering what Trevor might do with the money that Frank had invested for him. Might he want to buy a new car? A conservatory? She hoped to God that Trevor's money was safe.

Bronwen had been up and about since seven and was in the kitchen. She pounced on Sally as soon as her foot fell on to the imported Syrian flagstone floor. Sally almost jumped out of her skin.

'Oh! You scared me, Bronwen. Can I get you a nice cup of tea? I'm making one for Trevor—'

'I did already,' said Paloma, sweeping past with tray, pot on a doily, and some homemade fruit-and-date bars laid out on a plate.

'Great. Thanks.' Sally's jaw clenched.

'She's always pipping you to the post, isn't she, Sally?' Bronwen's sharp eyes scrutinised Sally as Paloma left them alone. 'When's the last time you made breakfast for Frank and the children?'

Bronwen's voice was much quieter now, almost chapel-hushed. 'She's a bit of a Queen Bee, that woman. Running the hive here, isn't she? She'll have you down with the drones if you don't watch out, Sally, see? Mark my words, you'll be slumming it down in the dunny while she's up in the penthouse suite, dripping in honey!'

Bronwen got very close to Sally and her voice dropped to a whisper, 'Take back the reins, Sally Parker, take them back.'

Sally badly wanted to run out of the kitchen and far, far away from this windbag who'd been whingeing her way through their weekend, making 'helpful' comments about the children (most of them gallingly correct), the house, her annexe, the dogs, the décor, the food. Apart from the brief respite during her essential little escape to the gym, Sally had to deal with Bronwen solo because of Sleeping Beauty up there in the bedroom, getting his forty flipping thousand winks.

She was saved by the appearance of Emily, trotting into the kitchen for her breakfast.

'Morning, love,' said Sally. 'What can I get for you?' she added pointedly, looking at Bronwen, to show her that yes, she could provide as good a breakfast as Paloma's.

'Hang on,' Emily looked around, confused, 'where's Paloma?'

Sally felt her balloon burst; she noticed that Bronwen was smiling smugly.

'She's outside talking to Trevor,' she said earnestly. 'I'll get your breakfast, Em. What would you like? I can make you anything . . . er . . . French toast? Eggs sunny-side up? Porridge? Smashed avocado with some seeds on toast?'

Emily looked genuinely surprised.

'Wow. Are you sure, Sally?'

'Yes! I do know how to make breakfast, you know!'

'Er . . . OK. I'd love some French toast then, please.'

'Sure!' said Sally with a confident smile.

And turned to face the cupboard with a grimace. Sally had no idea how to make French toast. Did it involve bread? What made it French? Was it something to do with a hollandaise sauce or was that something to do with Benedictine monks?

Bronwen was keeping a very sharp eye on proceedings and Sally knew that it was going to be impossible for her to go undercover and delve into a recipe book. She would have to style this out big time.

Humming a very jolly tune, she got a saucepan, some bread, eggs, flour and butter, and also some sugar – she was sure that French toast had a sweet element to it. She began cracking eggs confidently into the saucepan and then hit a bit of an impasse. Should she go for a separate roux sauce in another pan, or should she dip the bread into the eggs and sort of take it from there?

Emily waited silently at the breakfast bar, staring into space.

'Penny for your thoughts, love?' asked Bronwen softly.

Emily laughed.

'I'd need more than a penny, Bronwen,' she said. 'I've got at least twenty quid's worth of thoughts whirling through my head at the moment.'

Sally was breaking up the bread with a fork, which was harder than she'd anticipated, and examining the mixture. It didn't look quite right to her. She tipped in a bit of flour and then started to mix it round with the eggs and bread. It started to get very stodgy in the pan, but she carried on humming.

'I'm sure I've got twenty pound in my purse, Em. Come on, try me.'

'Today is the ninth of September,' Emily said, now transfixed by her aunt Sally trying to stir bread, eggs and flour round the pan, 'and it's a special day for this family.'

'September the ninth . . .' repeated Sally, 'it does sound familiar. September the ninth . . .'

She tipped in some sugar and thought it looked terrible in there, so added half a pint of milk for good measure. There was now a pale slop swilling around an island of stodge. This was not the French toast she remembered.

'September the ninth is familiar because it's your sister's birthday, Sally. Today is my mother's birthday and no, I'm not going to try and phone her because last year when I phoned her, she didn't pick up, and the year before that her number was out of order.' Emily was standing up at the breakfast bar now, her eyes shining bright and hard. 'You might well deduce from this that my mother, your sister, doesn't want me to make contact with her. Not that anyone cares whether I do or not, because nobody in this fricking family remembers that today, September ninth, is Nancy, my mother's, fricking birthday!'

There was a stunned silence, broken by Bronwen.

'Let's not have so much of the effing and jeffing, Em.'

'On the contrary,' said Sally, rushing round the breakfast bar and enveloping her niece into an enormous floury hug, 'you can eff and jeff all you like from here to kingdom come. I am so, SO sorry, Em. Of course it's Nancy's birthday. September the ninth. How could I forget?'

Emily extricated herself from her aunt's embrace and stared at her.

'Because we've all forgotten her. She has made herself forgettable. She last came here two years ago. On June the fourth. She doesn't care. And now nor do we. And if that's how the French make their toast then I'm amazed there hasn't been another revolution.'

And with that she left for school.

*

87

Cleo, like her father, had slept through her alarm, and was now heading for a half-hour late entry into registration. Not that the thought of this gave her any juice to fly out of bed in a panic, grab her rucksack and hurtle downstairs and through the front door.

No. She put her clock on to Snooze, adjusted her eye mask and thought she'd just give herself an extra seven minutes of sweet shuteye. It was only the start of double psychology she was missing. She knew all about psychology anyway – she'd watched every series of *Made in Chelsea* forensically, hadn't she? There was all the psychology you needed, on a plate.

Further down the landing and under the myriad fake Tudor beams which were quite a feature of Cedar Vale, Stephen was struggling over his laces. He could do them up all right once he was down there, it was just the getting down there that was the problem.

He looked lovingly towards his games console area. Thank God for it. It was the one console-ation in his life, he told himself, sniggering at his little pun. He'd soon be back with his virtual friends, ruling virtual cities and flying around the place in jet-propelled pods. He loved life online. Everything was so much easier. Much better than the real thing, really. Nobody nagged him about his weight online. As far as they were concerned, he looked like Timothée Chalamet.

He could hear Colette clattering down from her flat, shouting randomly:

'Anyone want a lift to school?'

'Yes please!' shouted Stephen back at her.

Even though St Bede's was eight hundred metres from their front door, it was always comforting to sneak into school from the Jeep.

Mikey rejected Colette's lift and skittered out of the house, breakfastless, and on to her beloved BMX bike, mobile phone already up against her ear.

'Dom? Dom? Can you hear me? It's Mikey!' She crooked her head over so that she could speak freely. 'I know, Dom, I've seen on my phone. It's madness, isn't it? The Dow Jones is bonkers, there's a lot to talk about. Yep. I'll see you in the pavilion . . .' and she was off on her bike and away down the drive.

Back in the kitchen, Sally and Bronwen had been left with the two awkwardnesses. The first, Nancy's birthday, which hung like a bad smell in the air, and the second bad smell, a pan chockful of inedible mess.

Sally was saved by a cacophony of beeps coming from Frank's three mobile phones, sitting on the breakfast bar. He had one phone for his hedge-fund clients, one for friends and family, and one for his HNB colleagues. The phones were jumping out of their skins, and each time they buzzed they edged forward a little; how much pleasure it would give Sally to see those three phones commit suicide, buzzing and inching inexorably onwards to throw themselves to their deaths off the side of that marble slab.

Sally picked up two of the phones and read out some of the messages distractedly.

'Bruce Fowler – "Frank where the hell are you? Pick up your phone". Genevieve Corbett – "FRANK YOU NEED TO TALK TO US IMMEDIATELY. CALL ME IN GENEVA". Goodness, old Genevieve from Geneva's got her knickers in a twist, everything in capitals. Sean Harris – "Frank call us ASAP this is getting urgent" . . . and that's just the one phone.'

'It appears that the shit is well and truly hitting the fan,' said Bronwen matter-of-factly.

'Yes Bronwen. Yes indeed,' and Sally breathed in, heading towards the vintage copper-coloured turbo kettle that she'd picked up for £549 at a promotional gadget fair last year.

'Well,' said Bronwen, folding her arms, 'don't you think you'd better wake up the aforementioned fan? Before he gets absolutely covered in shit, as opposed to being gently spattered by it?'

'I was . . . er . . . just about to do that, thank you, Bronwen.' Sally's voice was higher than usual. 'I know you're ninety but I'm sure you can still make a cup of tea, can't you?'

And she turned on her heel.

Sally found Frank so deep and lost in the land of Nod that, at this rate, she was going to have to send in the Gurkhas to try and retrieve him. She tweaked his feet, sticking out from the end of the duvet. She tried shaking him, prodding, nudging him, said his name increasingly loudly into each earhole. Nothing. He was definitely alive, snoring contentedly like a large badger.

She went into the bathroom and filled a silver-plated tooth mug with water. She started with a gentle spray, misting his chest area like a priest blessing his congregation. It didn't even register. She got a bit bolder and flicked some water right into his face. He stopped snoring for a full two seconds, but then started up again with the badger rhythm. She'd never in her life seen Frank like this. What the hell was going on? What was wrong with him? He didn't have a temperature. He looked a bit pale, but not scarily so. She'd have to call Dr Livesy if this continued.

Sally went back into the bathroom and searched for a bigger vessel. The bin. It was a beautiful pedal-bin completely carved out of walnut wood, fabulously expensive and only five of them in existence. Sally had picked up two at a craft fair in Dorking. It was empty, of course. Paloma's cleaning team never allowed a bin in the house to get tainted with any rubbish. She filled it with water and lugged it into the bedroom.

'I'm sorry, Frank. This is going to be really wet.'

And with one big swooping action, she flung the water into a flying arc, dousing Frank from head to chest. If he didn't wake up from that then she'd have to call an ambulance.

It did the trick. Frank jackknifed up into a sitting position, properly drenched. He suddenly seemed young and vulnerable, like a little boy who'd been pulled out of a paddling pool. He blinked out of sleep-puffed eyes.

'Jeez, Sal . . . the bed's soaking . . .'

'It's nine fifteen, Frank. You slept through your alarm.'

'Wha . . . ?'

'Trevor's waiting to take you to work. There's quite a bit of action on your phones.'

Frank hauled himself out of the wet bed and tried to make sense of it all. His favourite Armani pyjamas with the Taj Mahal motif were absolutely wet through. His wife was standing over him with the walnut pedal-bin, and the clock indeed said nine fifteen. It was Monday. The Tokyo markets would be finished for the day by now. And what about New York? What was the time difference in New York? He couldn't actually remember. They were behind. Were they behind? So what did that signify?

He answered his own question with a magnificent, lion-sized yawn. What he really wanted to do was to get into some nice dry jim-jams, perhaps the Versace ones with the cherubs and guns pattern, and tuck himself back under a glorious fifteen-tog duvet in one of the guest suites. Nobody would find him there; they were all the way down at the other end of the house. He could just bury himself away for a day, maybe two? A mini-break. Amerjit was constantly on mini-breaks, for Pete's sake, so why shouldn't he have one?

'Any news from Amerjit?' snapped Frank.

Sally hadn't heard anything of Amerjit since he'd scrambled away in Laura Piggott's wake on Friday night. Right now, she was more concerned with her husband.

'I'll get your suit out, shall I?' she said, with an anxious look. The only time she'd ever had to dress Frank was when he'd been properly ill about six years ago. And even with full-blown red-eyed flu he'd still dragged himself into Finsbury Square.

'I'm sure you'll feel fine once you get there, Frank. Maybe running HNB is too much for you? Or you overdid it at the barbecue?'

There was a pause and she flushed, realising the pot and kettle nature of that comment. And normally Frank would have been right on this with some whip-smart retort, but he simply sat on the edge of the bed in his wet pyjamas, staring out of the window on to the back garden. Sally wanted to reach out and touch his face.

'Nothing from Amerjit, I'm afraid,' she said quietly.

This sad figure sitting on the edge of the bed could be Frank in thirty years' time in an old people's home. Thirty years' time, fine, but not now! Was he showing early signs of dementia? Frank Parker wasn't built for dementia, illness, death or anything less than one hundred and twenty per cent, supersized turbo action. This was the man who played squash before breakfast with a client while cutting a deal on a phone at the same time. Yes, he'd been known to hold a racquet in one hand and a mobile in the other. That was not an ill, demented man. Frank Parker was invincible. He was Superman.

'Frank?'

No response.

'Frank?'

'Hmm?'

'Shall we get dressed, Frank?' she said loudly, suddenly sounding like a care worker. Sally held out his suit for him and he looked blankly at her. He had deep black bags under his eyes, which started to redden and water as he clenched his mouth tightly to try and prevent a massive yawn from escaping.

'Well! I'm going to leave you to it,' said Sally, placing the suit beside him and heading for the door sharpish. She was finding it hard to be in the same room as him, like this. Even Bronwen would be preferable company to this strange, hollow version of her husband.

She got halfway down the stairs and stopped. The familiar feelings started to rise up. A fluttering in the chest, a dizziness in the head, a pounding in the heart. She needed a pill, but was too chicken to go back into that bedroom and get one. She couldn't bear to see Frank sitting there on the bed like that; and it'd be worse to see him from behind, he'd look even more vulnerable.

She was saved by the 1812 Overture. For once, its brassy jangle was a welcome and comforting distraction.

One of Paloma's nieces went to open the front door. She was called Angela and was from Seville. Sally couldn't recall how long she'd been at Cedar Vale. She was only supposed to come for a month but had been here for at least three. And how much was she being paid? Was it cash? Sally simply couldn't remember. She made a note to herself to try and find out.

Angela opened the front door and Sally felt a sudden rush of faintness to her head. For there, standing on the doorstep was her younger brother Miles.

Miles Tennant made even the simple act of standing look as if it were too effortful for him. He wasn't actually standing. He was poured against the side of the doorframe. All of his right arm and shoulder made contact with it, while his waist and legs slouched underneath like an after-thought. A good two-thirds remained of his original hair, thick and tawny, mapped out on his head in an archipelago. His cornflower-blue eyes could still muster a twinkle when he wanted something out of you, but at rest they looked like a tired animal's that's been too long in the zoo. They can no longer engage with visitors who come up to the enclosure. They've seen too much – in Miles's case, way too much of the eighties rave scene, mainly in fields in the county of Oxfordshire.

The classic Miles uniform was dark blue Paul Smith jeans, expensive trainers, a 'funky' (his term) shirt and a jersey tied in the Italian style over his shoulders, knotted lightly at the front. A pair of sunglasses was never far away, usually sitting up on his head. A musk of Trumper cologne and a light chewing noise followed in his wake, as his jaws constantly had to work against a piece of gum to mitigate his many years of amphetamine consumption.

Sally felt exhausted just looking at him. She had nothing to say to him really; she didn't want to hear the latest news of their mother, and anyway she knew that the only reason he was here was to check that the Bank of Frank was still going to invest into his awful rave-based Randwyck Renovation plan. It would, Sally suspected, be less than a minute before he mentioned money. She couldn't help smiling to herself. What a prize prannet he looked, loung-ing there in his noncey outfit with his silly sunglasses on his head.

He twirled a set of chunky car keys lazily around in his hand and looked his sister up and down.

'Hey, big sis,' he drawled, 'digging the yummy mummy look.'

Sally looked down at her gym kit and trainers. She wasn't sure if she liked being referred to as a 'yummy mummy' by her brother. She didn't want to look him in the eye and settled on his Jack Wills lemon-striped 'funky' shirt.

'Well, are you going to invite me into your palazzo, Sags?' he said, easing past her. 'I guess you've been listening to the radio this morning?' he continued, sloping through hall to kitchen, as if it were a safari lodge in Botswana and he were about to pick up a large gun. 'It's legit, off the chain, stone-cold chaos out there.'

Miles liked to pepper his speech with what he thought of as 'youth speak'.

'Frank must be LARGING it in the City today!' and with this he did a little move of the arms, as if he might be at a rave.

'Frank's here. He's getting dressed upstairs,' Sally replied.

A pause.

'What?' Miles laughed with a single short blast. 'That is JOKES! Parker's got a NERVE. What's he playing at?'

'He's not been playing at anything really, Miles. He's been sleeping. A lot.'

Miles threw back his head and blast-laughed once again.

'What a LIGHTWEIGHT! He'd better wakey, wakey, risey and shiney because there's been some pretty fucking cataclysmic action in the money markets!'

Sally smiled to herself. Less than a minute before 'money markets' was uttered. Her brother was so predictable.

'Let's cut to the chase, Miles. Have you come here to play happy families, dispense brotherly and avuncular love? Or have you come to talk money?' Sally folded her arms and looked at him.

Bronwen had nipped out of her annexe as soon as the 1812 Overture had started up. She couldn't resist any action and here she was, rolling in as if on silent casters, only measuring up as far as Miles's armpit.

'Well, hello there, Mrs Llewellyn,' said Miles, trying to do a Welsh accent that was veering dangerously towards Pakistani, but thankful however for her timely intervention. 'Wales must be feeling the loss of its favourite gorgeous granny! You look delicious as usual.'

And Bronwen actually blushed. Damn Miles, Sally thought. He could charm the birds out of the trees. But the birds had to look sharp because he'd soon wring their necks and bake them in a pie. Or make them into some raver's feathery headband or something equally sinister.

'You are the G, Mrs L,' Miles continued, giving Bronwen a sidling smile. 'You're the G for GANGSTA. I've got some business plans cooking with my sis, but I heard you were in the hood and I couldn't resist dropping by!'

Sally rolled her eyes. 'So you have come to talk about money, Miles. Well I'm afraid Frank is a bit out of action at the moment—'

Miles's gaze shifted past Sally and he grinned.

'Out of action? Who's out of action?'

Sally and Bronwen turned in unison and looked to the top of the staircase to see Frank begin his descent. He was definitely wan around the jowls, but Sally was relieved to see that the old Parker swagger was back as he pimp-rolled down the stairs. At least, from a distance he looked swag. The closer he got to them the craggier his eyes seemed, and she noticed quite a heavy five o'clock shadow around cheeks and neck.

'Come to fleece me, have you, Miles?' said Frank with a half-hearted boom.

'Come on, bro!' said Miles, joshing.

'Let the fleecing commence, Miles! Get those clippers out!'

'I need to dip you first, Franko,' laughed Miles.

'This sheep has been DOUBLE-DIPPED, Miles, that's the recession for you!'

'Ha!' retorted Miles. 'Well, you'd better lie down and show me your woolly gonads, bro, because these clippers are buzzing!'

Frank laughed and then clapped Miles heavily on the back, which winded him a tad. Both men laughed and Sally laughed a little too, out of relief mainly. It was good to see Frank back on form and putting her brother in his place.

Outside, in Miles's Audi, his mother had been completely forgotten. Lucinda was trying to get out of the passenger seat but was having difficulties with the seatbelt. Trevor was parked out there too and would normally have assisted, but he was having a sly twenty winks himself with his seat tipped back.

'Miles! Miles! Come here and help me!'

Lucinda's voice was croakier these days. Her eighty-three years were beginning to take their toll on her high-status posture too.

'Miles!' she continued to rasp, but to no response.

Frank was collecting his things together for a hard day's graft at the office. Well, Paloma was, handing him smoothie, phones, keys and his favourite mid morning snack, a good old-fashioned Wagon Wheel.

And Miles was following his brother-in-law round like a pet Labrador.

'Come on, Parker, you know you're going to make money out of my plan,' droned Miles. 'It's going to be Surrey's premier Trance Palace for the rich and addled. They're going to be FLOCKING to get off their faces in our beautiful hedonist Church of the Risen Raver. Get your cheque book out, you tight tosser, it's payday.'

Frank kissed Sally distractedly and shoved his tie into his pocket.

'We'll name the chill-out room after you, Frank!' Miles insisted. 'No, sod that, we'll name the Resuscitation Area after you. Ha ha! The Frank Parker Resuscitation Suite, that's got a ring to it, hasn't it, Sags?'

Sally didn't like Miles calling her by her childhood name. Frank laughed and put his arm protectively around his wife. And squeezed her too tight. Whenever he was in the presence of his brother-in-law, Frank felt the need to flex his muscles.

'Well listen, Miles, you colossal dick, jump in my car and we can talk about it on the way to London.'

'And watch the fires as we go. It's pretty hairy out there, Frank.'

'Miles, I like hairy. I've lived off hairy for many years and there's no reason why I shouldn't do so for the foreseeable. Granny B, we're taking you up to the bright lights of London, aren't we?'

'Yes, you are,' Bronwen sniffed, 'to see the respectable side of my family. Cousin Blod and her dull-as-ditchwater husband Alan. And by the way, you can stop with that lewd language, thank you very much.'

'Come on, Gran, you love it when we talk dirty,' chuckled Frank.

He went to his grandmother and attempted to swoop her into a hug and off her feet. He got as far as the hug, and then had to stop. He was too weary.

'Here, let me do it,' and Miles picked her up like a bag of shopping, even giving her a little swing round for good measure.

'Hey!' she squealed, 'careful of my sciatica! I'm nearly ninety-one, you know!'

Miles set her down with a flourish and Bronwen positively beamed from top to toe. Frank gave them both a regretful look. Bronwen hadn't been this animated all weekend. It was probably the best thing to have happened to her in the eighteen years since her husband had died.

Sally felt like the party pooper. 'Bronwen, your bags are in the boot, Trevor will drive you on to Camberwell once he's taken Frank into the office, is that OK?'

'Not really. I have no desire to hear Cousin Blodwen wittering on all day about how delicious her dried fruit ring is,' she said, poking Miles in the chest. 'I'd rather spend the day with young Miles here!'

'He's not that young,' said Sally, 'he's forty-three.'

'I've always wanted a toy boy, me!' said Bronwen. 'Miles, will you be my toy boy?'

'We can low-key discuss it in the car, G. Come on, you Welsh raver, let's get you into Trevor's love machine,' and Miles ushered her to the front door.

As they went through the doorway, they almost knocked Lucinda sideways as she came through from outside.

Sally had no idea she was to be paid this visit by her mother. She felt something bilious rise into her throat. She was furious with Miles, who was clearly intent on dumping her here.

'Shit,' said Miles to his mother, 'I almost forgot to give you these, Mothership.'

He handed her the keys to the Audi and lowered his

sunglasses. 'You won't get very far without them, you fruit bat!'

Lucinda gave her son a stern look.

'Miles, you left me stranded in that car—'

'Morning, Mother-in-Law,' said Frank mock-jovially as he took a call from a mobile phone. Lucinda tried to smile at Frank, but her mouth turned downwards into a death mask. Miles ushered Bronwen away too quickly for her to interact with his mother.

'Will you be home for dinner, darling?' Lucinda called after her son somewhat feebly. But Miles was halfway to Trevor's Daimler and didn't reply.

Sally watched all of this wryly. Her brother not only had his mum like putty in his hand, but he was allowed to rub his bottom all over the putty and then throw it away if he wanted.

Lucinda hobbled through the hall, giving her daughter the once-over as she passed.

'Sally,' was all she said, with her signature sniff.

'Would you like a cup of tea, Mummy?' Sally asked politely.

'Do you have any decent porcelain?' was her mother's reply.

Sally rolled her eyes.

7

'Do you want the radio on, Mr P?' asked Trevor.

'Is it going to depress me?' said Frank.

Trevor laughed.

'Well, what would you rather hear about – the economic situation or some feminist on *Woman's Hour* who weaves her own tank-tops?'

'Economic situation, Trev,' said Frank, rubbing his eyes. He was still feeling ragged. The first thing he'd do at the office was get Kerry to book an appointment with Dr Livesy for this very afternoon.

Bronwen was up front enjoying her role as Trevor's copilot, leaving Frank and Miles to spread their thighs out on the back seat. It was almost a competition back there as to who could sit more crotch-central. Frank thought he had the edge on Miles until Miles hoicked up his Paul Smiths and suddenly had two more inches of splay to give.

Frank's phones were on overdrive.

'Aren't you going to answer any of those calls, Parker?' said Miles.

'I don't like to speak too much on the phone in the car, do I, Trev?' Frank said in a jolly way. 'I shall have all that to look forward to when I step into my office. Look at this, they're getting their knickers in a right twist. I don't even need to look at the markets, I can tell by the amount of exclamation marks in these texts! Yadder, yadder, yeah,

yeah, we'll see what our risk assessment is, then bish bash bosh, everyone calms down again.'

Frank pulled his tie from his pocket and hung it raffishly around his shirt collar.

'Miles, listen to me. We're swimming in a big sea with many an up and a down. You can't ATTACK the tide, you have to surf it . . .' and then mid-sentence he yawned as widely as a cat, displaying all of his fillings.

Miles looked thoughtful and then moved on to brass tacks. He didn't mince his words.

'So we're still good for the three million loan?'

'I promised it to you, didn't I?' said Frank. 'Have you ever known me renege on a promise?'

'And three mill still OK? I mean, what with all this going on . . . ?'

'Miles, I could lose three mill down the back of the sofa. Of course it's OK, you twat.'

Miles smiled a lizard smile.

'I'll sort the build, obvs, and all the frippery and shit. Then we open up business with a bit of hoopla to seven hundred Surrey trippers, off their gourds on chems, you get forty per cent as we discussed, and we will be, my blood, sitting sweet on a project which will hopefully see us well into our very disgraceful old age. I wouldn't be surprised if we were low-key rolling out several more of these babies in the next, I dunno, five years? The trance scene's going mental, and I mean MENTAL, again. In fricking Bosnia, of all places! Never went there, although I got pretty bloody close on my gap year. What d'you think, Frank? Frank?'

Miles turned to his brother-in-law who was leaning back into the headrest, snoring ever so gently.

*

Sally poured her mother a Lapsang Souchong out of her very finest teapot with a delicate willow pattern on it. Lucinda checked underneath her saucer to see the pedigree of the porcelain.

'Not a patch on Royal Doulton,' was her comment.

'Sugar?' said Sally tightly.

'Goodness, no.'

'Biscuit, Mummy?'

Lucinda gave her a sly eye.

'What about those ghastly cheap chocolate things with marshmallows?'

'Of course you can have one of Frank's Wagon Wheels if you want one, Mummy,' said Sally, reaching for Frank's private biscuit tin. Lucinda devoured one lustily while muttering 'ghastly things' and 'dreadful biscuits' with Wagon Wheel spitting out of her thin lips.

Sally watched her mother while sipping her tea, and thought of her sister Nancy. Would Lucinda remember that today was Nancy's birthday? She sighed. She had neither the will nor the energy to open up the Nancy subject.

'How's Randwyck?' asked Sally as an icebreaker.

'Cold,' said Lucinda.

'Have you got the heating on?' inquired her daughter.

'When I can afford it,' said her mother. 'I suppose I won't freeze to death as long as you and your hedge-fund boy give me the money you promised me.'

Sally breathed in calmly.

'You know that my husband's name is Frank. And he's a forty-eight-year-old man, not a boy. He has promised out of the goodness of his heart to pay for some more refurbishment at Randwyck and is discussing it with Miles as we speak, I imagine.'

Both women sipped their cups of tea, Lucinda rather noisily, to fill the awkward silence.

'Well, well,' said Lucinda quietly, 'the son of the tar-macker made something of himself. A miracle really, considering what became of his parents.' Lucinda fixed her steely eyes on to her daughter.

'And how is Frank's . . . how should I put it . . . father?'

Sally felt the blood rising into her head and swirling around her fists. If her mother went any further down this track, Sally was going to lay her out flat with one single punch.

'Frank's parents are fine, Mummy. They live abroad, as you know.'

Her fists were clenched, ready to plant at any point.

'I suppose they had to leave the country after all that scandal, didn't they?' She looked at her daughter sideways, egging a reaction out of her.

Sally thought of her podcast upstairs. Clean and calm, it had said this morning. Clean and calm thoughts. Sally tried to think of a newly washed pair of socks, lying in her lavender-infused drawer.

'It was their choice. More tea?' and she lifted the pot with a little sniff, almost like her mother.

'When did you get so high and mighty?' said Lucinda with pep. 'Was it when you first employed your charlady?'

Paloma had just come into the room and nodded briefly to Lucinda.

'Did it give you a little sniff of power, knowing you had somebody at your beck and call?'

'Please don't talk to me like this,' Sally said, looking at the floor.

Lucinda was glancing around the room with venom building up behind her eyes.

'I don't know how you live with the smell, Sally,' she said at last.

'Of what?' said Sally, her heart starting to bump.

'The smell of your money.'

The same way that you live with the smell of your bullshit, thought Sally, but she didn't have the guts to say it out loud. Her heart was fluttering now, making her long again for one of Dr Livesy's nice little pills.

'It's an unpleasant smell, new money.' Lucinda was warming to her theme. 'You see, old money smells of leather, vermouth, wood smoke and cigars. New money smells of –' and she sniffed Sally's kitchen like a bloodhound – 'desperation.'

Sally leaned back in her chair and looked at her mother. How many more times could she put up with being talked to like this? How many more strips of Valium would she have to pop as a buffer against this bitter old woman? Sally made a mental note to put it on her to-do list: grow a pair. Grow a mighty big pair.

She cleared her throat as if preparing to speak loudly. But she bailed at the last minute and said under her breath,

'Well, you'd better get used to the smell, because this new money's going to pay for the refurb of your house.'

'Speak up, Sally, you're mumbling,' snapped Lucinda.

'More tea, Mummy?' Sally asked her mother through gritted teeth.

Trevor's Daimler arrived at Finsbury Square, an hour and a half later, where Trevor had to shake Frank to wake him up. Frank got out and went round to the passenger seat to say goodbye to his grandmother.

'Bye, Granny, you take care and come and see us again soon,' and he leaned in to her, dishevelled with sleep. 'And I'll visit you in Llanfairfuckwit or whatever it's called.'

'Frank, less of the language,' but Bronwen smiled. She was high on testosterone from the car journey with these likely lads. 'You always say that you'll come and see me in Wales, which is part of your heritage, Frank Parker, and you never do, do you?'

'I will, Granny, I promise.'

'And you never renege on your promises, do you, Frank?'

'No, he bloody doesn't!' said Miles quickly.

Bronwen reached into her little carpet bag and took out a white envelope.

'This is for you, Frank,' she said.

'What's this, a book voucher?'

'Make sure you read that, please,' she chided.

'Look at the state of your bag, Gran. At least let Trev pick you up a Mulberry, or a Burberry, or whatever, while you're in town?'

Bronwen tutted in response.

'Mulberry, Burberry, loganberry, gooseberry. What a lot of old nonsense. I like my bag, Frank, I won it back in seventy-four in the Penmaenmawr Christmas Bingo. More than two sheets to the wind I was, and your grand-father had to practically fireman's lift me all the way home to Llanfairfechan. Now you take care of yourself, young man. You look peaky.'

'I'm sound as a pound,' said Frank.

'Hmm,' sniffed Bronwen, 'I'm not sure that phrase holds much water at the moment.'

Frank laughed.

'I'd better go, Gran.'

'Well, before you do, have you been in touch with your father?'

Frank looked as if he'd been scalded.

'Why would I do that?' All warmth and humour had gone from his voice.

'Because he's still your dad, Frank.'

'Er . . . I really don't think he is, Gran.'

'Life is short, Frank, and you might regret it.'

'You go and buy yourself a nice expensive bag on me and forget all about it, Gran. Best way. Take care of her, Trevor.'

Frank shut the passenger door firmly and waved the Daimler away. Miles gave him the peace sign through the back window. What a douche; it was almost impossible to believe that Miles and Sally had swum in the same gene pool.

He sighed and moved his hands through his unruly hair. No time to think about what lay in the past – he had enough to deal with in the present. Was it him or did everyone in Finsbury Square appear to be talking urgently into a mobile? On that thought, Frank looked ruefully at his three phones. He was going to have to do a lot of Frank Parker fast-talk today, he could feel it in his bones. And his bones felt tired. Dog tired. And with that he dragged them into the Finsbury Square monolith that housed HNB to start his working day.

Emily was sitting in her GCSE French class, looking out of the window. It was most unlike her. She was usually the person with eyes and brain focused solely on the teacher, ready to lift her hand as fast as a ferret out of a pipe, ready to answer (usually correctly) any questions. They were analysing a passage from Albert Camus' iconic novel *The Outsider*.

Emily was finding it hard emotionally to get beyond the first sentence.

'Mum died today. Or maybe it was yesterday.'

These chilly words kept worming their way around her head, first in French, then in English. Round and round like existential washing in the drum. The idea that the protagonist couldn't even remember if his mum had died today or yesterday blew her mind in all its bleakness. And it made perfect sense to her. If her own mother were to die today, on her birthday, would anyone remember if it were today that she'd died or yesterday? If nobody, not even her closest family, had the decency to even remember Nancy's birthday, then who was ever going to remember the day of her death?

Emily was aware of a darkness starting to envelop her, a pit of something swirling and unknown, a vortex created by both Albert Camus and the realisation of her own strange family situation. The Parkers were her family, of course, but they weren't her family. She was motherless in a family with a mother. She was a little rowing boat tied to the cruise ship that was the Parker Family, being pulled along in its wake. She had no control of her destiny; this was huge.

She felt a sudden urge for a tattoo on each wrist, one saying 'Albert' and the other 'Camus'. She had some birthday money left over. She would go to Dragonfly, Leatherhead's premier tattoo and piercing parlour, this very Saturday and get a consultation. She had her fake ID. Hell, maybe she'd go the whole hog and have 'Nietzsche' inked all over her chest. Would that involve sitting in her bra for hours though . . . ?

'Emily?'

Miss Jahn's voice scythed through the morass of dark fog that had settled over her.

'You've been looking out of that window for the last ten minutes. Is there something out there more interesting than Albert Camus? If there is, I'm sure the class would love to share it.'

Emily looked at Miss Jahn, resplendent in her Boden Catalogue outfit, a sweatshirt with strawberry motif and palazzo pants with tulip print. How very optimistic, thought Emily dourly. Spring will come again for Miss

Jahn, the birds will sing, the sky will be blue and all will be well. And Miss Jahn's mother won't die, either today or yesterday.

'I'm looking outside, Miss Jahn,' said Emily after several long beats, enough time to get the whole French class looking at her, 'and like the protagonist of Camus' novel, I am the outsider looking in. But in this case, I'm the insider looking out.'

Emily said all of this in a voice that was not natural for her; it was sombre, slow and monotonous.

Miss Jahn smiled briefly and then addressed the class,

'Righto. Well, it's good that somebody's feeling the existential angst that the novel illustrates. Can you all turn to page fourteen now please?'

The only question Cleo had relating to her existence at this moment was whether her shellac nails were too much, colour-wise, with her Hollister crop top. The teacher was droning on about this Australian guy called Freud, and Cleo couldn't help wondering what on earth all the fuss was about.

A class discussion started about Freud's use of dream analysis, and students were opening up about their own dreams and what they might signify in psychological terms, using their knowledge of his theories.

Cleo perked up. She loved this kind of thing. They sometimes did celebrity dream stuff in *Grazia*.

'Anything to contribute, Cleo?' asked Mr Dunn the teacher.

Cleo gave her thousand-megawatt smile once she realised that everyone was looking at her, and ran her tongue around her mouth just to check that she didn't have anything stuck in her straightened teeth.

She sighed and put her head on to her hands.

'Dreams . . .' she murmured dreamily.

'Yes, Cleo, that's what we're discussing, in Freudian psychoanalytical terms,' said Mr Dunn dryly.

'Dreams are so weird, aren't they?' added Cleo. 'I mean sometimes you have them and sometimes you don't, do you know what I mean?'

Mr Dunn took off his glasses and rubbed his eyes.

Cleo expanded on her thesis.

'I dream of a boy,' she announced, and somebody in the class tittered, 'a gorgeous boy who appears out of nowhere. On my doorstep. And that's it. I'm his. For ever. Did anyone see on *Love Island* where they talked about their dreams, and one of them said that they'd actually dreamed about the other? And then it turned out there was a massive coincidence, and that person had actually been dreaming about the person that had been dreaming about them? It was so amazing! I think Freud could learn so much from *Love Island*. Surely they get it in Australia?'

Stephen was having an equally productive physics lesson, taught by the aptly named Miss Starr. While she waffled on about the solar system, Stephen was enraptured by her pair of heavenly bodies, currently doing gentle battle with a floral gilet.

Stephen was fine at school. He was middle ranking in most of his classes, which was fine. He wasn't teased too much for being overweight, apart from being called Fatboy Slim or Big Steve occasionally, which was kind of fine. Being son and heir to the most relentlessly active man that has ever set foot on the planet, had taken its toll on Stephen. He would simply never be fast nor strong enough for his dad.

One fateful day when Stephen, a naturally tentative boy, was four, Frank hauled him up on to the trampoline and forced him to jump with him.

'Come on, son! Higher! Higher, Ste! Come on! Jump!'

The forceful pounding that Frank inflicted on his side of the trampoline made Stephen ping up into the air uncontrollably, like a stone being ejected out of a slingshot. Higher and higher, the little boy was flung until he was crying, a stream of snot flying out of each nostril.

'Come on, Ste! Stop grizzling! Commit to the jump!' And on Frank went, shooting his son ever higher into the air.

Stephen's legs started to flap uncontrollably until one of Frank's alpha leaps sent his son flying right off the trampoline. He squealed in an arc across the sky, before ending up in a winded thud on the lawn.

Stephen broke a leg and a wrist, and from that day onwards never trusted his dad with playtime again. It forced him naturally into the arms of his mother and nanny, the latter whom delighted in feeding him snack after snack to cheer him along. Anything Stephen did or felt, good or bad, was met and rewarded with a snack from Colette's unending supply. And Frank watched in despair as his only son retreated into the soft undemanding confines of the biscuit tin.

Stephen would continue to be fine if people, and that included his family, just left him to his own devices. And he had many devices. A PS3 and also 4. iPad, MacBook, sixty-two-inch flatscreen TV, two iPhone 11s, Game Boy DS (very retro) and two sets of VR goggles plus his own popcorn, ice-cream, chocolate-fountain, slushy, sushi and Turkish-delight devices. His parents, ironically, had bought him these mouthwatering contraptions while also being desperate for him to lose weight. They'd put him on Atkins, 5:2, the Carol Vorderman detox, the Canadian Military, and even enrolled him at Junior Weight Watchers, which was enough to send him running to the custard creams. No diet plan had had any effect whatsoever. In fact, he'd gained another half stone over the summer. Stephen had been mortified one evening to overhear his parents discussing it.

'Do you think he can actually see his todger, Sal?' Frank asked his wife anxiously in their bathroom.

'How should I know, Frank? It isn't really the sort of thing a mother asks her fifteen-year-old son. Why don't you ask him?'

Stephen existed fine in the comfort zone of his own flesh. And it was comfortable. OK, it was not comfortable in the height of summer, and it wasn't particularly comfortable in a plane or on any other form of public transport. But he didn't take any forms of public transport apart from planes, because his able assistant in snack crime, Colette, drove him everywhere in the navy Jeep, which always had several caches of sweets or chocs in the glove box.

Stephen sighed and tuned back into Miss Starr's astral projections. The thought of that glove box would keep him going through the rest of the school day.

Sally had finally seen off Lucinda, and was focusing on deep breaths in blissful silence when Colette announced her return with tyres squealing and a strong smell of Silverstone.

Colette was the worst parker in the world. Frank made jokes about this regularly. 'Call yourself part of the Parker family with parking like that?' he would crow. 'You're not a Parker, you're an imposter!' and the nanny would laugh dutifully.

Colette would actually speed up as she came down

the drive towards Cedar Vale; it was a miracle that any of the peacocks were still alive the way she manhandled that Jeep. Every time she blazed into Cedar Vale, she created an afterburn arc of gravel around the fountain; one of Sally's favourite cars, a little Mini convertible, had been pretty much written off by one of Colette's jazzier handbrake turns, and Surrey's tentative hedgehog population had surely been seen off for good by Melbourne's answer to Jeremy Clarkson.

Sally had wanted to bring up the subject of Colette's parking with her for about five years now. And this lunch-time, with the house to herself again, Sally felt like she was ready to have another try.

'Right, Colette, I really need to talk to you about the parking situation.' Sally rehearsed the words firmly to herself in the kitchen, bringing her fists down strongly on to the morgue-like marble. 'This . . . er . . . laddish way of driving the Jeep has got to stop. I know Frank finds it amusing, but I don't. OK? There are going to be some new rules around here, Colette.'

She was cut short by the nanny bouncing into the kitchen, her considerable thighs filling some puce leggings and a neon-green fanny-pack strapped around her waist. She was wearing an unfeasibly tight T-shirt emblazoned with the legend 'WHAT HAPPENS IN PRAGUE STAYS IN PRAGUE', although the 'PRAGUE' was hard to follow as it negotiated the ley lines of her ample chest. Her fleshy lips were wrapped around an eco-cup full of almond flat white decaf, her go-to. She had a habit of slurping the remains from the eco-cup, which made Sally want to rugby tackle her to the floor. As Colette slurped she narrowed her already close-set Björn Borg eyes, which made her eyes pretty much disappear altogether. She waved her big ginger bush of hair around.

Colette's hair could be found everywhere in the house. In the washing machine, down the backs of radiators, in every sink or shower, clumps down the loo, on the hall carpets, and enough around the driver's seat in the Jeep to knit into a merkin. The other week Sally had dipped her spoon into her chia-seed and pecan Bircher muesli and put it in her mouth to find the longest and thickest ginger hair working its way around her teeth. She'd almost thrown up while trying to disentangle it from the bolus of mashed-up oats.

Colette drained the flat white noisily, belched and slapped her eco-cup down on the Carrara marble. Right. This was Sally's big moment. She put her feet into a gentle boxercise position, feet aligned with hips and shoulders, knees soft, calves and core engaged. She was ready for this. She cleared her throat lightly to herself and then launched in strongly.

'Right. Colette—'

'I've been thinking, Sally?' Colette steamrollered right over her. It was the conversational equivalent of a burn-off at the lights. Sally was left for dust, her mouth hanging open like a trout's. 'And actually I've been talking to Frank about this? But that Jeep is getting really raggedy and I think it's probably time for an upgrade? It's three years old already and I worry for the kids and their safety? There's a fabbo new model on the market with amazing hold on the road and airbags to die for?'

Just like you, thought Sally sourly as Colette scratched her left breast somewhat graphically.

'And while we're on the subject of upgrades,' Colette continued loudly, 'I've been speaking to the agency and it seems like my wages need a bit of an upsize too? It's been a whole year since we looked at our arrangement? So, I know it's asking a lot, but a pay rise of let's say two thousand a year plus a Jeep upgrade is going to be a bit of a deal-breaker for me?'

And with that she scratched her scalp so vigorously that Sally saw maybe thirty hairs loosen and fly out, then float over towards the eight-slice Harrods toaster.

'Right . . . er . . . and you've spoken to Frank, you say?' Sally rasped. Her confidence was now utterly shattered.

'Yeah? He was cool with it?' and Colette narrowed her eyes again. 'But of course if you don't want to go down the whole upgrade route . . .'

Colette watched Sally carefully. She knew she had her over a barrel. It would take a lot of work to find another nanny. There'd be the phone calls, the exhaustive inter-viewing of candidates, the chasing up of endless references, setting up a new taxation system. Plus agency fees and chatting it all through with Frank, and Colette knew how exhausting it was to try and get his attention even for a minute. There was no way on God's earth that Sally would have the tenacity, desire and grit to see all that through. Plus the actual sacking of Colette. Sally just didn't have it in her. Sally was jelly in Colette's hands and both women knew it.

'So, you've . . . er . . . talked to Frank about all this, you say?'

'That's right, Sally? Frank's across all of this?' said Colette, sweet as pie.

Colette knew exactly how this was going to play out now. Sally would agree to her demands, make some sort of excuse and go off urgently to utilise her Platinum Family Plus Nanny Membership at the Park Club.

Colette watched Sally as a spider does when it spots an insect crawling into its web. Not long now before her quarry was trapped.

Sally breathed in and smiled brightly.

'Well, I guess that's all fine then, Colette. Yes. Sounds sensible. I'll talk to Frank tonight. Thank you.'

And Colette nodded. No word of thanks needed. No acknowledgement. The insect was already mangling itself up into a little ball as the web's sticky ginger strings strangled it.

Colette stood her ground by the marble breakfast bar.

'Actually, Colette,' said Sally on cue, 'do you know what? I'm late for something at the Park Club. I'd better dash otherwise I'll miss it. See you later. You're good for school pick-up this afternoon?'

Colette smiled.

'No problem, Mrs P.'

8

Frank Parker usually loved the feel of his wood-panelled office. Brett Grover had vacated it and now it was his very own. Frank Parker, Business Manager of HNB, one of the City's hedge-fund management companies to watch. Not bad for a fruit seller from Hayes. When he ran his hands around its comforting walls, he was reminded of a hunting lodge with a view over the Serengeti.

For that is exactly what the City of London was for Frank, a vast expanse of hunting ground. If you were a big-bollocked Lion King like him, you spent your days on the sun-baked rocks, surveying the impala and other grass-dwelling hors d'oeuvres down there on the lower terraces. There was much evidence of the hunt all around his office. Pairs of antlers hung, thrown in casually amongst the photos of Frank on golf courses around the world and the pieces of heavy-jowled Victorian portraiture that Kerry, his faithful PA, had found in online auctions.

There was an ostentatious display of family photos, too. Wedding photos of him and Sally, both looking like kids, and his suit so cheap. School photos of all four children. Stephen, hiding behind a fringe in every picture, with a non-committal smile. Cleo, smiling as if butter wouldn't melt, but with a mischievous look in her eye. And Mikey, always looking directly into camera, just like he did, from every photo frame. Mikey was his evergreen; she'd come wheeling and dealing out of the womb and hadn't changed an iota to this day. Frank reckoned she'd still be the same when she was working for him in this place. He must start grooming her up for the job, and tell her she was going to be his successor. He wasn't sure if he'd ever communicated that to his youngest daughter. And finally, Emily. There were probably more photos of his niece than any of the others, due to her dizzying myriad achievements.

There she was holding that bally flute, then clasping the coveted St Bede's Debating Prize, and there she was, second from the left, in the Lacrosse A team. Another showed her winning the County Chess Cup and, in the glitziest of all the photo frames, there was Emily curt-seying to the Duchess of Cornwall. She had been chosen to present her with a bouquet at the opening of the new Leatherhead Meadow Hospice for Children. To be fair, Frank had stowed a hefty amount of cash into that hospice, so the choice of Emily as flower girl may not have come as the biggest surprise, but still.

Frank had asked Sally if it wouldn't be nicer to have Emily and Cleo greet the Duchess together. But Sally insisted. She said she wanted to create important memories for Emily, ones that would show her that she was loved as equally as her cousins. Frank often asked himself whether this was strictly true. Was it possible for them to love Emily as much as their own children? *Should* they love her as much?

That had been a red-letter day for Emily and a real honour for the Parker family too. Frank had even winked at the Duchess as she was holding the scissors, ready to cut the oversized ribbon that hung across the hospice entrance.

Tim and Francesca Daly-Jones were invited by the Parkers to come and shake the Duchess's hand. And the look of pure rictus-smile venom on Francesca's face as the Duchess of Cornwall turned and said something privately to Sally was pure Hollywood.

Frank shook his head. He just wasn't getting the comforting sense of power from his surroundings today, even though he'd shut himself away in his wood-panelled sanctuary. He picked up the photo of Emily and the Duchess and sighed. There was something arms-length about his relationship with his niece. In a way they were cut from the same cloth, they were both grafters, both confident, but she was far better educated, fluent in two languages and could quote Shakespeare with ease, had a prodigious general knowledge and, for the first time ever this summer, she'd managed to whip Frank on the tennis court. At the end of the match Frank was a mess of sweat and latent anger as Emily skipped around the court laughing at him. Why was it always Emily? Why couldn't the others excel at something that got them into the local papers? Why hadn't they filled a trophy cupboard? Why were they so mediocre at school? True, Mikey had energy and spunk. But why wasn't it directed to the netball court, or the chemistry lab? Frank was convinced the only thing that was ever going to get Mikey into the local press was a crime.

Frank eased himself carefully down on the Persian rug laid out in front of his old-fashioned bank manager's desk. There was only one photo on that desk, a badly taken, faded picture of Sally in shorts standing outside the Wimpy in Hayes. From 1989 that Wimpy was the scene of many an illicit rendezvous, stolen teenage kiss and, finally, Frank's proposal of marriage. How they loved that Wimpy!

Frank loved that photo, too. Sally was standing almost on tiptoes – she used to do that when she was excited about something. Her face was brimful of life, hope and promise. 'It's all ahead of us!' her face seemed to say. Frank sighed.

He hadn't seen his wife stand on tiptoes with excitement for years.

Frank had a sudden wish to transport Sally back to that Hayes Wimpy of 1989. She'd order the spicy bean burger of course, and Frank would have a cheeseburger and chips. If Amerjit was with them, which he was bound to be, he'd go for his standard chicken burger.

'Who's paying?' Amerjit would say mischievously.

'Empty your pockets, Ammers,' Frank would demand.

And Amerjit would put a pack of Polos, pencil, 20p and a hopeful condom on to the table. Frank would then empty his pockets; forty quid in cash, three tokens for the pool table and one of Sally's hairbands. There was no contest; Frank was the great provider even at the age of sixteen.

They'd discussed everything in those red moulded plastic Wimpy seats: life, death, the merits of Gary Numan versus Yazoo, and everything in between. They'd made out a lot too at the moulded plastic table, which made Amerjit squirm and throw paper napkins at Frank's head. When it was just the two of them, Frank sometimes managed to get his hand under Sally's shirt in Hayes Wimpy. Life was so easy then.

In his overpriced office here in the City of London, Frank had an overwhelming yearning to be back in that Wimpy, next door to Dye Another Day Hair Salon.

Frank let his eyelids rest gently over his eyeballs; he was just on the point of relinquishing his nervous system to slumber when the door burst open and every single available member of HNB pounded into his sanctuary.

'Frank, this is very serious.' Kerry started proceedings immediately. Her face was flushed and her top lip glistened with sweat. 'Our computers have been flashing red at us for two days. We need a risk assessment specialist to understand the minutiae of it.'

'I already told you,' Frank said slowly, rubbing his eyes and attempting to get up off the rug, 'Simon Khan had a bike accident—'

'Well then, someone else needs to step in.' This was Eduardo the Oxbridge graduate who'd been with them three months; keen as mustard, but still too green to join the Golfing Pride. 'And there's no sign of Amerjit.'

'Where in the name of arse is Singh?' said Frank, now fully upright but a tad wobbly of leg.

'We last heard from him in Sweden.'

'Sweden?' barked Frank. 'What the hell's he in Sweden for? A fricking ABBA reunion?'

There was an uncomfortable silence. Then Roger, Amerjit's PA, coughed and spoke up.

'I don't want to speak out of turn, but—'

'Do!' Frank interrupted him. 'Do speak very out of turn indeed, my friend, and just tell us WHY THE HELL AMERJIT SINGH IS IN SWEDEN?'

Roger was blushing now.

'He phoned me two days ago. From an ice hotel.'

'An ICE HOTEL? What in the name of my arse is THAT?' roared Frank.

'It's a hotel. Made of ice,' said Roger quietly.

'Oh, for fuck's sake, don't tell me, he's on some spiritual detox or some aura-rebuilding spa retreat, is he?'

Frank was warming to his theme now and wagged his finger in the general direction of his colleagues.

'And if that wanker's on another of his JUICING holidays, I swear to God I'll rip the pips out of him and pulp him in my Nutri-Bullet faster than a display team of flying fucking prunes!'

Frank gritted his teeth and shook his head slowly to himself.

'Amerjit and his juicing. That man is taking the pith.'

Frank looked up expectantly. He'd left space for a laugh. None came. Eduardo coughed lightly.

'As I was saying,' Roger continued smoothly. 'I took a call from Amerjit in Sweden two days ago and he informed me that he was there with his wife on an emergency mission, to . . . to . . . repair their marriage.'

Frank rubbed both of his hands vigorously up and down his forehead as if he wanted to relieve it of twenty-five layers of skin. He had to sit down. He was utterly bone-rattlingly exhausted. He slumped into his large leather chair and spun himself round to take in the faces looking at him in a semicircle of worry.

'We've been missing all of our key players, Frank. You, Amerjit and Simon; all at the same time. HNB has been left very vulnerable.'

This was the calm and sensible voice of the cleverest person in the room, Adewuya, a Harvard grad and HNB's deputy head of research. 'We've been firefighting for the last couple of days but we've run out of hoses. It's unprecedented out there, Frank. Are you actually up to speed with what's happening? This isn't a glitch, it's not something we can all guffaw about in two years' time when we sip our cocktails down at the Lamb and Flag and say, "Ooh, remember that shit storm we surfed?" This is worse than '87. It's worse than '08. Billions were wiped off the markets in a matter of hours, Frank, and we've been left wide open.'

There was silence in the room. Frank wanted to stand up, like whatsisface at Agincourt and do the big speech. Or he wanted to pull some gags out of the bag. Something. A metaphor. An analogy. Anything. But more than all of this, what Frank really wanted to do was to feel his gentle, dark eyelids slip over his eyeballs again where they fitted so well and snugly, like little blackout blinds. That was what he craved now more than any glorious speechifying.

Six pairs of eyes looked intently at Frank, six pairs of eyes which all had their own silent stories to tell. A shopping-list of stories:

'We're relying on you, Frank Parker.'

'I've booked an eye-wateringly expensive holiday in St Lucia for my entire family, Frank Parker.'

'I've just had a forty-thousand pound loft extension done, Frank Parker.'

'My kids are really happy at their private school, I don't want to pull them out at this crucial stage of their education, Frank Parker.'

'I'm planning a tummy tuck and facelift in Armenia next month, Frank Parker.' (This was Roger.)

And finally, the rather accusing eyes of Sabrina the intern:

'I've actually got used to buying my lunch at Waitrose. I can't go back to eating Subway, Frank Parker.'

With a superhuman effort, Frank stood up and planted both hands on to the mahogany desk in front of him. He was momentarily distracted by a figure in the room that he didn't recognise; a tired man with the saggiest hangdog eyes he'd ever seen, a man like an empty space with a jacket too big for him, like an eleven year old's blazer on the first day of secondary school. This was not the figure of a business manager, a player, somebody who called the shots. What the hell was he doing in Frank's office? Frank was on the verge of asking Sabrina to politely show him the door when he realised that the loser in the room was him. Frank was looking at a reflection of himself in a gilt mirror in the corner of the room.

He rubbed his eyes again and delved deep into his lungs to try and summon up some volume and authority.

'Well, Simon Khan's a silly bastard for coming off his bike. What kind of a douche rides a bike in London anyway? I've not been myself of late and on that note, Kerry, please make me an appointment with Dr Livesy for as soon as possible.' Kerry beetled off to do his bidding immediately. 'Roger, you need to bring Amerjit to ground. Today. Book him a flight back from Randy Scandi-land. Today. I want him in this office. Today. I'll handle all this,' Frank gestured to the three mobile phones on his desk, 'and I promise you, Adewuya, we will indeed be nursing large Sex on the Beaches down at the Lamb sooner than you care to think possible. And maybe we won't be guffawing. But we will smile fondly as we think back to this –' Frank paused and surveyed his audience – 'purple patch.'

Five pairs of eyes watched him silently.

'And then we'll all go to Go Ape and get shit-faced on a . . . what is it? Team-bonding exercise. Roger, I want to see you ripped to the tits in a pair of overalls and begging for your life up a very large tree. Adewuya, I'd like to see you the wrong side of five pints coming down a zip wire. And now ladies and gents . . .'

Frank paused for effect here. His employees knew what he was about to say: this was a Frank Parker catchphrase.

'Stand by your beds! It's time to make money!'

Frank watched his troops file out, none of them able to look him in the eye, some of them shaking their heads. He allowed himself a brief, wincing glance in the mirror.

'You are out of your depth, Frank Parker. And get yourself a shave, you tosspot.'

And with that he gave an enormous, chief-of-the-pride yawn, a yawn that seemed to go on for minutes and then mutate into various different sub-yawns. It was a glorious yawn, but it was actually physically demanding, yawning that deeply. Frank needed a rest after that yawn, so he flumped down in his chair and picked up the three mobile phones. He was aware that his hands were aching; maybe he was coming down with something? It hurt to hold the phones in his hands. He breathed in resolutely, looked as if he were about to start tapping out a message. Then stopped.

He looked over to his door to check that it was closed. He'd just have a sharpener. A little ten-minute kip to refocus the synapses. He had this; he'd been here before, hadn't he? This was all going to blow over. He was the boss now, wasn't he? He could set the terms. He put the phones back down on the desk, put his head back, and let himself climb gently up the wooden stairs to Bedfordshire.

Sally was hiding in one of the large green glass cubicles at the Park Club, luxuriating under the outsized droplets of rainfall shower. There was not only Aesop shampoo on tap, but conditioner, body wash, body scrub and an endless supply of muslin cloths and deep white fluffy towels; and lovely lighting too. In every mirror of the Park Club you looked your best. And the temperature was always perfect. Warm but not stifling. The Park Club was like a womb, and Sally spent a good two hours a day in there. It had huge sprawling grounds where you could while away the hours with a copy of *Hello*. She needed the rest, frankly. It was exhausting having to hide from so many staff at home all the time. The Park Club was the perfect place to disappear and unwind.

Sally had just done a really demanding Body Balance class and was frothing up the shampoo on her head with aching arms when she heard the familiar voice of Francesca Daly-Jones in a nearby cubicle.

'. . . well, I mean she was SO out of control on that lawnmower, it was tragic. Did you see it?'

'I KNOW,' said another female voice that Sally couldn't quite pin down, 'it was like watching . . . I dunno . . . Lindsay Lohan or something, wasn't it?'

'Not cool,' said Francesca. 'God knows what she's going be like at this Charity Ball. Let's hope she doesn't pull down her pants and wee on another statue!'

There was laughter at this comment.

'What are we going to do?' Francesca went on. 'Have a round-the-clock suicide watch or something? I mean, I know we all discussed it on our last group dog-walk, but she's definitely getting worse. She's becoming a liability. I can feel it.'

'She still looks gorgeous, though, Francesca.'

A pause.

'Weeeell. Depends what you think of as "gorgeous",' Francesca spoke loudly and brightly now as she turned on her shower, 'and it doesn't last. People on meds and booze lose it pretty quickly. Look at poor Amy Winehouse. Soon it'll be less the sweet little Sally and more of blotchy-nosed puffy Sally who pisses on her shoes Sally. She'd better watch out.'

'We're due at Cedar Vale tonight for a Charity Ball meeting, aren't we?'

'Oh God!' laughed Francesca.

'Let's try and keep her away from the booze cupboard.'

'And the bathroom cupboard!'

Sally heard both shower cubicles open, then shut, the two women tinkling merrily with laughter before leaving. All was silent again apart from the noise of Sally's water splashing down on her. She sat down on the floor of her shower cubicle and let the warm water hose her. She had to do this for a while, to be sure that Francesca Daly-Jones and her friend were gone from the changing rooms when she finally peeped round the door like a scared little prune.

Frank sat opposite Dr Livesy in his surgery. It had the air and smell of a goodly sized drawing room in a Victorian country house. The only sign of anything medical was a skeleton in the corner (with glasses on, of course) and a very old and expensive stethoscope that Livesy liked to leave nonchalantly on his expansive desk, the sort of desk at which Isambard Kingdom Brunel might have doodled up some new bridge. The only sound came from a walnut grandfather clock, in the corner of the room, magically slowing down London Time with each and every languorous tick. The Sloane Square traffic was mercifully muted by pricey and tastefully rendered double glazing which covered every floor-to-ceiling sash window.

James Livesy was about to play tennis near the Chelsea Physic Garden by Albert Bridge. His tennis whites looked as bleached and crisp as the sails of a privately chartered yacht in the Med. His long physique was lean but pampered. The crow's-feet around his eyes sat bright white in his Mustique-tanned skin, and his public school knees hadn't quite lost their knobble. He liked to smooth his receding hair with careful long-fingered hands, and he wore a pair of righteously expensive Harrods trainers on his long, bony feet. He sat, rubbing his smooth cleft chin, while observing his patient in the chair opposite.

'Bit wild and woolly aren't you, Parker? Didn't get time for the holy trinity this morning – shit, shower and shave?'

Frank looked wanly back at James Livesy. He couldn't summon up a laugh. He couldn't summon up any reaction at all. He just wanted to curl up like a dormouse.

Livesy narrowed his eyes. He'd known Frank a long time. They'd met through a mutual friend in the City, and sounded each other out on the golf course before Livesy became a fully paid-up member of Team Parker as the family physician. Frank Parker was one of Livesy's healthier clients – he was a machine of a man; his heart, lungs and digestion functions were textbook. If you were to remove all of his major organs today and show them off at the Royal College of Surgeons, there would be audible gasps. Medics would marvel at the structure and strength of his arteries, how pink, moist and firm his flesh was, how robust all his vital signs were.

Frank had given up smoking in his early twenties, played proper man sports like squash and golf, and had the great joy that a burgeoning wage packet allows of eating the best foods and drinking the best bean shoot, nutmeg, prune and grass-clipping smoothies that money can buy. Apart from the occasional question mark over his cholesterol levels, and a very rare bout of constipation, Frank Parker was sound as a pound.

Slumped here in front of James Livesy with the autumnal Chelsea light fading on him, Frank looked more cadaver than live human being. Like somebody had taken a spoon and hollowed out his insides, the way children do to pumpkins at Hallowe'en.

James Livesy was reminded of the teddy, Worcester Bear, that he'd taken to prep school with him. He squeezed and loved Worcester Bear during so many tearful nights that the bear had lost most of his insides.

'You look like you've lost your stuffing, Parker. In fact, are you getting enough stuffing? Is that what this is about, you old bastard?'

Livesy was pleased with that. He picked up a brass letter opener with his right hand and began working at the underside of his left thumbnail. It was almost arousing to prod that hidden bit of flesh behind the nail. Gently poised, the sharp tip of the knife worked away at a tiny bit of detritus that Livesy gouged and then fished out. How very satisfying that felt. He was hoping he didn't have a semi on. It would show in these tennis shorts. He began work on the next nail.

'So, Doc, what's the matter with me?' asked Frank, suppressing a yawn and leaning back in his chair. 'Why do I feel so tired all the time? Is this the Big C? Or something else terminal? Am I about to cark it?' Frank shifted about in his seat. 'If that's the case I need to know ASAP so that I can get everything cushty for Sal and the kids.'

Dr Livesy was working on nail three now. This was the most absorbing and satisfying thing he'd done all week. He was so glad he'd discovered a use for that damn brass letter opener, which a Saudi prince whom he'd treated for crabs had gifted to him.

He continued gouging and said,

'You've had the bloods done. We'll know the results this afternoon. And I'm going to send you off for an MRI scan-aaaage now. OK? You sure you didn't just overdo it at the barbecue?'

'No more than usual.'

The nub of the letter knife was just jabbing at a particularly sensitive piece of skin on his little finger. Bliss.

'And Sally OK?' said Livesy quietly. 'She gave Lewis Hamilton a run for his money on that lawnmower, didn't she? Bloody hell. Still –' the letter knife arrived at the sweet spot under the nail and Livesy couldn't help a little moan of pleasure escaping from his lips – 'it was a bonus to get a bit of the Sally Parker wet T-shirt contest!'

Livesy gave Frank a wicked grin; he just loved to provoke husbands. Frank didn't like it when men alluded to his wife in any way that was predatory or lascivious. And on any other day Frank would have been up on his feet immediately, ready to take Livesy down, both physically and verbally. Not today though. It was as much as he could do to stay upright in his chair and remain conscious.

The grin dropped slowly away from Livesy's face. He looked empty with disappointment, like when Matron used to take Worcester Bear away to be laundered. And that happened a lot; the combination of pubescent boys and teddies at boarding school requires an awful lot of laundering.

'Has it all got to you, Parker? Left to run the joint and finding it a bit too much, are we?' Livesy glanced down at his Rolex. He was going to be late for his tennis partner. 'Now come on, bugger off out of my office. Go and get your body Chernobyl-ed and I'll call you when we've amassed all the results, blood-aaage and everything.'

Frank stood up, yawned, and nearly fell over as Livesy thumped him on the back.

'Bear up, you old sod, go home and get some zeds.'

Frank rubbed his eyes and said through a yawn, 'I wish I could. It's mayhem out there.' He gestured vaguely to Sloane Square. 'I think we've just about kept a lid on it at HNB, but it's getting pretty minty.'

'I'm sure the world of finance will keep on turning without you, Parker. Go home and get some shuteye-aaage.'

And that is exactly what Frank Parker did.

9

The black cab came to a halt in Finsbury Square, which is in one of the nicer quarters of the City of London. There is a quaint Dickensian feel to it, almost as if some kind-hearted clerks, dressed in Victorian garb, might suddenly leap into the square and perform a full dance routine with their quills. Amerjit Singh leaned forward from the back seat, took clumps of money out of his wallet, some three hundred pounds in total, and shoved every last note through the little window for the shocked cab driver to scoop at. The driver didn't take it upon himself to correct Amerjit's counting skills, and, open-mouthed, was pocketing the cash as fast as his chubby hands could manage.

Amerjit took off his charcoal grey Armani coat, laid it carefully on the back seat of the cab, and emerged on to the pavement. Leaving the cab door open behind him, he proceeded to walk at a moderate pace down Finsbury Square, taking off his jacket as he did so. When it was fully off he hung it on a nearby railing, and then set to work on his tie, which he placed on a convenient bush.

'Oi, mate!' the cab driver shouted after him. 'Your coat! And your bag! Mate!'

Amerjit was oblivious. A half-smile played on his lips as he carried on walking and unbuttoning his Savile Row duck-egg blue shirt. City workers were starting to look at him. Two well-heeled girls carrying soya flat whites nudged each other as he passed them by. He was bending right down now, still trying to keep walking but unlacing each pointy Paul Smith shoe as he went, and then casting each one aside into the gutter.

'Mate! Oi! MATE!' The cab driver's voice was getting more distant now.

The sight of a shoeless man walking through Finsbury Square at four o'clock on a Monday afternoon was starting to create a stir. And the commotion intensified as Amerjit undid his Gucci belt and let his Dolce & Gabbana trousers slide gracefully down his legs, as he kept on walking. He now resembled something out of a Brian Rix farce, 'Ooh Madam My Trousers Have Done a Runner at the End of the Pier' or some such, as he waddled along the pavement with his Gabbanas bunched around his ankles. With a couple of swift foot flicks, he was free of them, however, and Amerjit left the pavement to walk on the road in nothing but a pair of Hermès socks and silky boxers from Stockholm airport.

He took off his vintage 1964 Omega watch carefully and handed it to a passer-by who looked at the watch, and then at Amerjit, mouth agape. Cars were hooting at him now. He was adding to the rush-hour build-up. London didn't have time for the foolish idiosyncrasies of an emotionally exhausted hedge-fund manager in his underwear.

City workers were watching and laughing now, and a couple of tourists got their mobile phones out. Amerjit rounded the corner of the square, cast his Gianfranco Ferré glasses aside into a drain, popped his thumbs into the waistband of the Swedish boxers, and took his pace down to a nice gentle stroll. Baristas emerged from coffee shops to get a better look, and a security guard outside an investment bank started talking earnestly into a walkie-talkie. If it had been London Fashion Week, this might have been part of an impromptu catwalk – ad hoc, sight specific. This was no fashionista event; this catwalk model very much had the look of somebody who was about to do a streak.

To the sound of now insistent honking, Amerjit shimmied the boxers down over his buttocks. He got a loud wolf whistle from a guy up a big ladder. With one swift hand movement at the front, the silken material swished down to mid calf and then, in a wisp and a jump, eighty-five pounds' worth of knickers were gone, left to float around the gutter of Finsbury Square.

A moment of sheer Britishness filled the air unexpectedly. Would some plucky bobby emerge and rush over to cover Amerjit's helmet with his own helmet? Maybe a game lady with an umbrella could do something useful? Or a nice man could unfurl his *Times* and usher Amerjit kindly away to his club? The sound of a wailing police car answered these questions. Carnival time was over. The British fete was on the turn. People started to run away from the weirdo streaker. Some were screaming. Whatever the streaker was planning to do with his nudity, they didn't want to get caught in the crosswind.

All was quiet and ordered at Cedar Vale. Mikey, in an unexpected twist, was actually at home watching her favourite Disney movie, *Mulan*. She liked to imagine that she, like Mulan, could head off an invading army on horseback and show her dad a thing or two in the process. Up in her penthouse room, Emily had her head down in the Camus. Cleo was lying on Emily's floor reading the latest edition of *OK!* magazine, twirling her hair around her fingers as she did so.

Stephen was gaming by himself, smashing down a city and then building it up again, all with the power of two opposable thumbs. He was happy as Larry; happier than

Larry, actually, because Larry had probably never tried Oreo sandwiches. This particular delectation was Colette's new fad, the cookie sandwich. She'd tried one down at the Redback on a drunken Friday night: two pieces of white bread slathered in butter, and then filled with your favourite biscuit, be it custard cream, bourbon, garibaldi, whatever. She described it as the Oz version of the Scots' deep-fried Mars Bar; something so calorific as to be almost illegal. Dirty, craven and utterly delicious.

Apart from the sound of Stephen's jaws munching his cookie sandwich, the house was silent.

There was not even a dog bark or snuffle to break the magnificent quiet that seeped into the bricks of Cedar Vale. The Parkers' canine community were boarding over at Janice Dawes's boarding and grooming emporium, Paws Fur Thought, for a few days. It was to give Sally a break – she found it exhausting having so many pets, and it gave the dogs a chance to have their claws and coats clipped and some hydrotherapy too.

Colette was upstairs in her flat, Skyping her mum back home in Melbourne. She was telling her the great news about the pay rise and car upgrade, while brushing out her hair over the cream shag pile carpet. Paloma was ensconced in her domain downstairs, putting the finishing touches to the enormous dinner she'd prepared for the household. A rich red pepper soup followed by a pork and quince casserole, with a fruit salad to finish. She was feeling very warm and satisfied. She and her niece Angela had spent £548 on a groceries shop in Waitrose today (she had her own housekeeper's credit card, courtesy of Frank) and she'd managed to cream off at least a hundred quid's worth of stuff for herself. She'd squirrelled away profiteroles, luxurious marmalade, a huge celebration cake, some gorgeous rose oil bath soak, some Chinese ready-meals, two birthday cards and three of her favourite celebrity magazines. All of it stored safely in her pretty garden flat behind the garages.

Life was good for Paloma. She was queen of her castle and could consume what she wanted, when she wanted, all at a pin code's tap away. She was so content she sang a little Spanish pop song to herself. She sipped her red pepper soup. The seasoning was perfect. And the pork smelled succulent in the oven. Mr Parker's favourite.

Sally did not announce herself with the 1812 Overture at the grand front door, but instead used a hidden side entrance through the laundry area to gain access. It was perfect. Nobody knew if she was coming or going and, if she was lucky, she could creep upstairs without anyone even noticing she was there.

She'd have made a good burglar in a previous life, she thought to herself, as she crept across the rich violet and peacock green mosque carpet, which covered the main dining-room floor. She'd spotted it on a trip to Oman while she and Frank were sightseeing in Muscat, and she didn't know how in the name of Allah Frank had pulled it off, but he'd done a deal with the imams with much smiling and drinking of sugary tea, and the carpet followed the Parkers home several weeks after their return. Frank's sweet-talking and bartering must have been off the scale.

Since her shower at the gym, Sally had had a lot on her mind. Francesca Daly-Jones and the troupe of local friends were due this evening to discuss the Charity Ball, taking place at Cedar Vale the following week. Thankfully she was not chairing the ball committee meeting, but as hostess for the evening she must appear in charge. No dips into the bathroom cupboard tonight; a clear head and a bright and breezy approach were required.

She would show the good women of Leatherhead and Chobham that she had her house in order. As mother, employer, wife, neighbour, hostess and chatelaine she would be unimpeachable this evening. This was the turning over of a new leaf and as Sally crept up the stairs to avoid her children, she felt a new zing in her step.

She was also going to take a long hard look at her friendship with Francesca Daly-Jones. Sally had put up with a certain amount of jealousy from girls since puberty. She'd always been slim, small and pretty and that was that. Girls didn't like it. It made them feel darkly jealous and even violent towards her. Francesca was attractive in a fresh-skinned, plenteous hair type of way, but she smiled in a downward direction that was unfortunate, and she had an arse that was visible from space. It was extraordinary. Each buttock could have featured on an Ordnance Survey map. When Frank and Sally saw it for the first time on holiday, unhoused from its tight jeans and the long shirts used cunningly to conceal it, they were spellbound. They whispered about it in their room at night; and it was the main reason that Francesca would never properly be able to love Sally. While Sally's arse was well proportioned and pert, her own was bigger than the elephant's in the room.

Sally couldn't help the fact that her friend had a colossal butt. It wasn't her fault. She was going to make changes. She was going to reassess and if necessary, trim back her relationship circle. She had counted Francesca as a friend. The Daly-Joneses had three children of similar ages to the Parkers and had done holidays and many a Sunday lunch together. Izzie Daly-Jones had been a friend of Cleo's until age thirteen when Izzie discovered netball and Cleo *TOWIE*. Milo Daly-Jones wasn't remotely interested in being Stephen's friend since he'd signed up as a teen model with Boden Catalogue, and Mikey thought that the eleven-year-old Poppy Daly-Jones was the prissiest, girliest, most idiotic girl she'd ever had the misfortune to have to share a ninth birthday at Franco Manca with. But Frank, Tim, Sally and Francesca were a foursome often seen out and about in the high-end eateries of Byfleet, Esher and Weybridge. That would have to change. Sally was going to move away from the Surrey school and charity mums set, maybe start a course or two.

She sat in a throne-like chair in a nook, tucked her little feet under her bottom, and thought of all the books she would soon read in this seat. History of art books. That was it! She was going to do a history of art course. If she stuck with it, she could even do a degree someday. And she'd have lots of history of art-loving new friends. Sally hugged herself. The house was quiet and gorgeous, and she realised that she loved her life during stolen moments like this.

Her reverie was shattered by the 1812 Overture.

She left the sanctuary of the chair, crouched down and peeked through the banisters to see who'd arrived. Paloma opened the door to a gaggle of people. She recognised Kerry, Frank's loyal PA, at the front of what looked like most of the HNB crew, plus some new City faces, men and women in smart work attire. Frank's team of accountants was there, three of them, and there were two smoked-out people carriers parked out on the driveway.

Sally's heart started to pump a little harder. Why were they all here? This was unprecedented. What was going on?

'Where's Frank?' Kerry asked Paloma.

Paloma shrugged her shoulders in a non-committal way.

'Is Mrs Parker here?'

The same shrug from Paloma.

'Is there somewhere we can set up? We need an operations area, would in here be OK?' said Kerry, motioning towards the dining room. Kerry, ever the calm and practical solver of a thousand Frank Parker problems, looked exhausted.

Paloma ushered them all in and they trouped over the mosque carpet; they set up a bank of computers on the dining table and, with worker-bee deftness, charged phones and tablets in silence. There was an air of urgency but also a tinge of melancholy.

Where the hell was Frank?

The 1812 Overture sounded once more, the dying ring of the previous one still hanging in the air. Sally was starting to feel light-headed; her fingers had the beginnings of pins and needles buzzing near the tips. She needed a beta-blocker. This felt like the onset of a panic attack. But how would she get to her bathroom cupboard without being seen? If she crept down the corridor and across the top of the grand staircase, she'd be completely visible. The children could appear from any of four different places. She was surrounded. Where was her phone? She needed to speak to Frank's driver; Trevor would know where he was.

Angela opened the front door this time. It was a group of men Sally didn't recognise. Workmen by the look of them, with big boots and toolboxes.

'Mrs Parker? I am Piotr. We are here to plan the construction in the garden. For the party?'

Upstairs and still looking through the banisters, Sally actually gasped. How could she have forgotten? Of COURSE they were coming this evening. She and the charity committee were creating a whole *Great Gatsby* theme for next Friday's ball. There was going to be a big working casino with room for a Big Band, built outside under a huge gazebo, complete with real glass chandeliers and 1920s furniture. They'd even invented a signature cocktail called Wall Street Crash, to be served at the Prohibition Bar. It was going to be the highlight of the Surrey social calendar. It would take three days to construct and dress; Sally had found a theatre designer to come with props and hundreds of metres of voile and velvet to make it look gorgeous. It would cost eight grand, paid for in cash.

'Don't let them in, Angela, don't let them in, please, please, please,' Sally whispered with every fibre of her being.

But Angela stood back politely and let six Poles stalk across the chessboard hallway.

Paloma sounded the dinner gong and various doors started to open upstairs. Stephen was usually the first down, his stomach the most reliable of alarm clocks. Sally watched her children tumble downstairs for supper; they were all intrigued by the commotion – who were all these people and what on earth was this war cabinet in the dining room?

Mikey was in there straight away asking questions. Sally could tell she was excited even from behind as she hopped from one foot to the other. Emily followed close behind Mikey and started engaging with the HNB staff. Sally was in awe of her confidence. She talked, nodded and bit her right fingernail, which she always did when she was concentrating. Sally hoped she felt better than she'd done this morning. She made a mental note to talk to Emily more about Nancy.

Cleo went in next and started openly flirting with the best-looking guy she could find, twirling her hair round her fingers and generally getting in the way. Sally made a mental note to talk to Cleo about her flirting. Stephen shambled in, gave a general cheery wave to everybody and then sloped off to the kitchen in search of supper. Dear old Stephen, he didn't have any interest in Frank's world. He didn't seem to have much interest in anything. Sally made a mental note to generate some enthusiasm into her son. And then the bloody 1812 Overture struck up again.

This was getting ridiculous. Sally gripped the banister for dear life.

It was Emily who opened the door to Francesca Daly-Jones and five other ball committee members, who all tripped in with their car keys, bags and flicky hair. The ladies could see that the dining room was abuzz with strangers, and this got them gossiping immediately. Sally could see Francesca's animated face, lit up with the delicious intrigue of it all.

Francesca immediately started talking to the Charity Ball committee in a lowered voice, almost behind her hand. Her arse was well camouflaged in a brown and orange tunic over some brand-new Victoria Beckham jeans and high boots. Sally felt her palms pricking with sweat. She could see that Paloma was looking for her. She'd be upstairs any minute and then what would Sally do? She had to get out of here.

Kerry emerged from the dining room with her ear glued to a phone. She spoke loudly in the general direction of the HNB staff,

'We really need to find Frank. I've got Amerjit Singh's mother on the phone. Amerjit has been sectioned under the Mental Health Act and is currently in Homerton Psychiatric Unit in North London.'

This news was like a piece of meat being thrown into an enclosure of hyenas. Francesca and her friends fell on it and moved into Sally's kitchen to feast fulsomely, perched on Terence Conran breakfast bar stools. Francesca was already on her mobile, doubtless providing Tim with a live commentary of events as they unfolded.

Paloma mounted the staircase. Shit. Sally was up on her bare feet in a trice and running towards the guest room suites. She had an escape route in mind. She padded across the larger of the rooms, opened the window and stepped out on to a balcony. Her many Park Club classes had made her very agile, and, cat-like, she was soon over the railings and on to the expansive roof of one of Frank's garages. She hoicked herself over the edge of it and curled her feet around a drainpipe, which she shinned down with ease.

She tiptoed round to the largest garage that housed Frank's precious collection of thirty-two John Deere lawnmowers. She tapped the code into their own Alcatraz-style locking-system (Frank always used Sally's birthday to remember a sequence of digits) and opened the doors gingerly.

Each lawnmower, like a hulking silent pet, had its own snuggly rug covering it. And on each of the rugs was embroidered the name of the lawnmower. TED HEATH and DAVID MELLOR to name but two.

Sally spotted one lawnmower in the far corner that was riding rugless.

'Frank,' she whispered loudly, making her way towards the naked lawnmower, 'Frank! Are you in here?'

She became aware of a gentle rasping sound, almost like a cat's low purr. She noticed a rug-covered bulk with the name MICHAEL HESELTINE embossed on it. There was her husband rolled up in its womblike warmth, like a snoring sausage roll. Apart from an advanced five o'clock shadow over most of his face, he looked like a little boy.

Sally knelt down beside him and was touched by how innocent he looked. In some ways she loved this version of Frank; uncomplicated, undemanding and, most blissful of all, not talking.

'Frank!' She spoke at almost normal volume now, very close to his ear. 'Frank, wake up! All of HNB are here, Frank. Excuse my language, you know I don't eff and jeff very often, but I think it's fair to say that we're fucked.'

No response from under Michael Heseltine.

'FRANK!' Sally shouted. There was no time to scale her volume up gently. 'FRAAAAANK!!!!' she bellowed down his earhole. There was the added clamour of a mobile going off loudly, rendering sleep impossible.

Frank gave a bleary smile to his wife and whispered a 'You look lovely, Sal . . .' before fumbling around in his pocket for the insistent phone. He looked defeated by the name 'James Livesy Private' flashing up at him. He just didn't have the wherewithal.

'Here,' Sally grabbed the phone, 'I'll speak to him.'

'Hello, Sal-aaage,' said the silky voice at the end of the line. Sally could make out the hum of an expensive restaurant in the background, 'has that T-shirt dried off yet?' Sally wanted to throw the phone away; the sound of his voice made her feel sullied. 'I thought that Frank might like to know that his results have all come back.'

'Results?' Sally was genuinely surprised. Frank hadn't told her he was having tests done.

'Yes . . . er . . . just a sec, Salaaaaaaage—' James was interrupted at this point and Sally could hear him talking to somebody else. ' . . . I'll have the 1976 Châteauneuf please, my darling . . . round and fruity, a bit like you, although I don't know if I'm allowed to say that in this hashtag day and age . . .' Sally could imagine the poor sommelier biting their lip, having to serve this creep.

James Livesy's voice came back to her again. 'Sorry, Sal . . . now, Frank's results. Look, we're all good on the biggies. Nothing scary. And scans are all good. But judging by the bloods and taking into account his general state, I have made my diagnosis . . . sorry my darling, no focaccia, got to keep this supermodel waistline . . .' Sally sighed. '. . . I'd say what we're looking at is narcolepsy, Sal.'

'Narcolepsy?'

'Yah, it's not unknown in the City. Stress-aaage and all that. Nobody's invincible. Even the rock star fund managers like Frank.'

'You've got narcolepsy, Frank,' said Sally loudly to her husband. And on hearing the news, he fell asleep again.

10

The good county of Surrey is full of vales. If you look on a detailed map you will be treated to many of them, even beyond the environs of Tolworth and Hook. Names such as 'Godalming Vale', 'Willow Vale' and 'Vale of Gomshall' delight the eye and ear. Even Cedar Vale is there on the map. It has enough acreage to merit a marking, and that gives it heft. It is not a Three Little Piggies confection to be huffed, puffed and blown down. Cedar Vale is a location, not just a house. You can argue in a car over directions to it. Other people can see it. It's on the map. And Sally Parker found herself clinging to it, the solidity of it, the soundness of it. Whatever was going on outside its environs, she knew that inside Cedar Vale she was safe.

As the days passed, Sally Parker kept a muffler around her brain and nervous system. The odd Valium. Not all the time, just the odd one maybe once or twice a day, as she watched her husband's livelihood crumple around them, mirrored by the general crumpling of the country's economy too. Sally had once been enthralled at the sight, on TV, of a pair of water-cooling towers being blown up in slow motion. Or was it blown down? The general movement of the explosion was downwards, like a woman in a huge Scarlett O'Hara ballgown curtseying, while the whole edifice of the dress collapsed and billowed around the tiny

144

figure within it. It was one of the most compelling things she'd ever watched. It was graceful, beautiful almost, so still with the sound muted, and utterly unstoppable.

Watching HNB Capital Management's demise was a bit like those water-cooling towers all over again. Big of girth, solid, penile, the company was brought to its knees quickly and almost gracefully, one minute it was there in Finsbury Square, all English Castle brick and yeoman's timber, the next it was like a paper lantern being sent off into the night before blowing away into ash. And Sally watched, like a fish gaping from a goldfish bowl. Frank tried to watch too, in the moments when he was awake.

But the show went on. The hairdresser and make-up artist still came on the afternoon of the Charity Ball. And the theatre people trotted in to do their titivating, to plaster over the cracks. Sally knew that if she could just keep moving one foot in front of the other, maintain the smile, clink the glasses and nod in the right directions, she could style this ball out. With Frank, the styling was a bit harder to achieve now. Two bags the size of bin liners were now a fixture under his eyes, and his overall look was now more Cornish fisherman than City slicker.

As guests arrived and they moved through the Charity Ball together, Sally acting as scaffolding to Frank's crumbling edifice, smiling eyes scanned them and, as soon as the Parkers passed by, looked greedily to each other for gossip or just heavenward in shock. HNB clients boycotted the ball, unsurprisingly, which left the great and good of Surrey – charity people, mums, the school community, reliable Rotary and Golf Club luminaries – and made the event feel parochial and gossipy.

Sally, looking stunning in a Swarovski crystal-encrusted all-in-one minx of a jumpsuit with a little 1920s flapper hairdo set with crystals to match, floated through the night, pulling Frank in her tow. People clapped him on the back but got no response; they tried endlessly to charge his glass but found it unchargeable because it was always full. The vintage champagne bubbles flattened then died in Frank's flute. He had neither stomach nor energy to drink it. Eyebrows were raised, if that were physically possible on the collective of shiny Botoxed foreheads.

There were four others looking on from a bird's-eye view. The Parker children had, of late, found themselves away from their screens and in the company of each other much more than usual.

They were currently based in Cleo's room, which looked out over the back garden. Mikey was sitting on a sofa-sized beanbag, playing with some particularly virulent UV purple slime, letting it slide to and fro between her fingers.

'So, guys, the economy is very much like this slime—'

'Mikey, you're legit weighing me down with all your slime chat,' complained Cleo. 'It's SOOOOOO boring. Can't we talk about something interesting, like the amount of WORK that woman down there in the boob tube has had? Oh my GOD those are, like, the dodgiest fillers I have EVER SEEN!'

'Slime's way more interesting than fillers, Cleo.'

'Mikey! Bey! Your insults are like a DAGGER in my heart!' laughed Cleo as she fell back extravagantly on to the cream sheepskin-covered sofa.

'To be fair, Cleo,' Emily reasoned, 'a lot of what you say can be pretty BS and meaningless.'

There was a pause. Cleo put on a face like a hurt kitten.

'Sorry, Cleo,' said Emily, 'I'm feeling pretty existential and Camus-like at the moment.'

She was met with a blank stare from all of her cousins.

'He was a French writer? Albert Camus? Oh. Never mind.'

Cleo pushed out her bottom lip.

'Well, I may say some empty stuff sometimes but at least I don't sound . . . pretend . . . pretending . . .'

'Pretentious?' asked Emily.

'Nailed it,' said Cleo, smiling, 'like that dude who was on series two of *Geordie Shore*. G-G Bronwen and I thought he was SO pretentious. We used to ring each other after every episode! He was always talking about, like, poetry and stuff.'

Stephen, who so far had remained silent, looked bemused at this coven of girls. He admired them – they were powerful when they got going.

'Hey guys,' he said gently, putting down a rather delicious plateful of speakeasy burgers from the party, which Colette had deposited outside the door for them, 'I think we maybe need to have a word with Mum and Dad about what's going on. I mean, Dad's clearly not right. Have you ever seen him with a beard before?'

'Uncle Frank is having a mental and physical meltdown, Stephen,' this was the cool voice of Emily, 'he is firing emotional and intellectual blanks at the moment.'

'Hang on, Em, that's a bit mean.' Mikey was always ready to defend her dad. 'He's just super tired. He's been working so hard. And what with the economic collapse . . .'

Emily gave her a withering look.

'There's tired, nodding-off-in-front-of-the-TV tired, Mikey, and then there's Frank, our paterfamilias, falling-asleep-in-the-dog-basket tired. That's right, Team Parker. I found Frank ASLEEP IN THE DOG BASKET. What sentient homo sapiens actually does that?'

'Emily,' said Cleo seriously, 'our dad is not a homo sapiens. He's only ever been out with women.'

Emily put her head in her hands.

'Yeah, just watch it, Emily!' said Mikey vehemently.

'Didn't you ever listen in your biology classes—'

'Guys! Guys!' Stephen held up his hands to placate them. 'Let's not fight. We need to come to some sort of agreement. Are we going to try and talk to them? Find out what's actually going on?'

'Oh, I know what's going on!' piped up Mikey, bursting out of her skin to be next to speak. 'No amount of quantitative easing has been able to save the markets from their downward spiral—'

'SHUT UP MIKEY!!!' Cleo and Emily were for once in stereo agreement. Cleo added a flying leather cushion to be extra sure of shutting her younger sister up.

'OK, Mikey,' said Stephen gently, 'I know you're up to speed with the financial world, and that's cool, but what we need now is some clear thinking—'

Stephen was interrupted by a frenzy of ginger hair coming around the door.

'Y'alright, munchkins?'

It annoyed all four of them that Colette persisted in calling them by this vile childhood nickname. There was a bit of silent eye-meet among the cousins.

'Are you going to tuck us up into our little fairy hammocks and sing us lullabies, nanny dearest?' This was Emily speaking in a little gnome voice.

There was a silence. The girls' loathing for Colette had been out in the open for a few months now, but their attempts to persuade Frank to sack her had failed. Stephen still felt a degree of attachment to her, but that was snack and school-lift related.

Colette eyed them coldly.

'Are you all on the rag, girls?'

'I haven't started my periods yet,' said Mikey.

Emily looked at Colette with a direct gaze.

'Can't you try and sugar-coat that comment with

something, Colette? Just a veneer of something sweet? Oh no, you haven't got anything sugary left because you've fed it all to Stephen.'

Colette stood in the doorway and worked her tongue around the inside of her mouth.

'Bed before midnight. If I hear another word out of you, I'll make sure your Wi-Fi's turned off.'

And that was her goodnight to them.

'WOW, EMILY!' shouted Cleo as she fell back again on some cushions. 'You are so amazing. How do you come up with that sugar thing and make it sound, like so clever and so mean?'

'It's called an analogy, Cleo.'

'I think I had one of those once. I had to go to the doctor,' said Cleo absent-mindedly, reaching for a mini burger.

'Seriously though,' this was Mikey, 'it's so embarrassing that we've got a NANNY. When are Mum and Dad going to get rid of her?'

'She's not so bad really,' said Stephen, looking at the floor.

'Well, they'll probably have to start letting key staff members go in the next few days,' said Emily, snapping her laptop shut, 'if my projections are correct.'

She smiled at her cousins.

The Parker dogs were blissfully unaware of all this. While the children watched the *Great Gatsby*-themed Charity Ball fizz and pop into the night, the pooches were slumbering happily at Paws Fur Thought, Surrey's most chichi grooming salon. And that is some claim, because Surrey is positively heaving with glamorous dog emporia: K9, outside Kingston and a pun on the Kingston postcode, Four Legs Good of Epsom, complete with its own doggy detox room, and Pooch Paradise in the village of Fetcham with a doggy music group called 'The Hound of Music' every Wednesday.

Sally's dogs were as well-groomed as the children they were named after: Liesl (Sally's favourite), a bichon frise; Friedrich, a collie; Louisa, a cockapoo; Kurt, a chocolate lab; Brigitta, an ex-racer greyhound; Marta, an ageing bulldog; and finally Gretl, an enormous St Bernard. The Von Yapps, as Frank sometimes called them, had their own car to ferry them around in, and Janice Dawes, owner of Paws Fur Thought, had the keys.

Janice was a forty-something woman of trustworthy build and a generous line in Puffa jerkins, the go-to clothing for any dog walker worth their kibble. Janice had one in every shade from the green and brown palette. From olive to dun, and all with the insignia 'Paws Fur Thought' emblazoned proudly on the right breast. She had thick hair, not unlike the coat of a Patterdale terrier, and what she couldn't achieve with a barking voice and enrichment dog treat was not worth knowing. She moved as if she were permanently in the ring at Crufts. With speed, agility, precision and purpose. Her trousers were mainly of manmade fibre, and her shoes were always the thick-soled slip-on variety. She had an open, ruddy face peppered with bright eyes and bushy eyebrows. Dogs were Janice's life and she made a very decent living off them; she'd spotted a vast niche in super-high-end dog grooming in this nook of Surrey.

The other love of her life was Mrs Teasle. A perfect evening for Janice was to sit in her back office poring over the accounts and fondling Mrs Teasle on her lap. It was hard for her to actually reach the computer keyboard with a large Alsatian in the way, but Janice had long arms and made it work.

Janice's business acumen was strong and she grafted hard. She was keen to expand her empire into the Ashtead area with a second grooming parlour, called simply 'Simon Groom' after her favourite TV presenter from the eighties. She was even hoping that Simon himself might come and cut the ribbon. She was on the up and life was comfy, although something hankered in the heart of Janice Dawes. She yearned for change, for a bit of adventure. She had always envisioned herself and Mrs Teasle exploring the world together, like Bonnie and Clyde, but minus the murders. One day, Janice often used to say to Mrs Teasle, they would leave all this behind and hit the open road.

Housing all seven of the Parker dogs was a stretch for Janice, but she loved it. She adored those dogs. She had a very soft spot for Sally too. There was something about her, her petite frame, her childlike trust, her kindness, the way her breasts curved gently underneath her cashmere cardi. Janice would do anything for Sally. Or for her dogs of course.

The little darlings were snuggled in various baskets in Janice's flat above her shop in Leatherhead High Street, like doggy pigs in the proverbial shit. Janice always gave Sally's dogs an extra special going-over, and Janice liked to think of Sally as she scrubbed their bellies and trimmed their claws. Janice would shortly be winging a £1,200 invoice over to Sally, plus she could look forward to a handsome cash tip; Sally was always very generous. In fact, she'd spotted a spritzy greengage-coloured jerkin in a catalogue recently – the cash tip would cover the cost of that. Janice popped an enrichment treat in her mouth – she couldn't resist it.

It was the morning after the grand Charity Ball at Cedar Vale. Sally had kept it together. She'd simply had to, with

Frank being so off form. No statues had been peed on, no lawnmowers in the swimming pool. She'd just got through it while hanging on to her husband's woefully limp tuxedo. Where had he gone? Where was the essence of the man? Distracted, she made her way slowly down the staircase to breakfast. She didn't really know if the evening had been a success, she couldn't tell. She'd seen people smiling, dancing, eating and making all of the usual faces they do when they're at a party. The time passed from eight p.m. to three a.m. It happened.

She sat in the bay window, nestled into the comfort of the pistachio-coloured Selfridges sofa, with Paloma's eyes upon her. There was an uncomfortable silence, an airlessness, in the kitchen. Sally cleared her throat lightly.

'Thank you for all of your . . . er . . . help . . . with the ball, Paloma. It all seemed to go very . . . smoothly.'

A pause. Paloma said nothing.

'I think we must have raised lots of good money. For charity –' still no response from the housekeeper – 'which is wonderful, isn't it?'

Paloma started to break eggs into a bowl and whisk them with a fork. Sally chewed her lip thoughtfully. 'Is anything . . . er . . . the matter, Paloma?'

Paloma put down the fork and looked at her employer, deadpan.

'Are you fucked?' Paloma demanded suddenly and hoarsely.

'I'm sorry?'

'If you are fucked, Miss Parker, I must know.'

Sally had to bite her lip properly now to stop the sudden urge to laugh.

'By "fucked", Paloma, what exactly do you mean?'

'Fucked. Money tits up. Nada left in bank.'

'Well, Paloma, I will certainly give the matter some

thought and . . . er . . . as far as I know . . . well, really the person you should talk to is Frank, because he knows how—'

Sally was interrupted by Colette and Emily entering the kitchen,

'Hi Em, darling,' said Sally with her arms open. Emily gave her a cursory non-committal dip rather than full hug.

'I'm off to lacrosse practice.'

'I'll drop her there but if you can pick her up, Sally?' Colette was brittle this morning. 'It's my day off, so . . .'

'Great. Lovely, I'll come a bit early, Em, I'd love to see how the team are doing.'

'We're top of the league,' said Emily, deadpan. 'Don't worry about picking me up, I'll get a lift. Bye.'

Sally definitely needed to sit down and talk with Emily. Ever since the debacle over Nancy's birthday Emily had not been the same girl. Sally made a mental note to tackle the Emily and her mother issue. She flashed a bright smile at Colette as she was leaving, but got nothing in return. She tried to give Paloma a winning smile but the housekeeper was in no mood for niceties this morning.

'I need to know if you're fu—' she said loudly, but was interrupted by Sally's mobile. It was Kerry phoning from HNB. She'd only ever phoned Sally once before, when she needed to check Frank's blood group as he went in for an emergency appendix removal.

'Sally, it's Kerry.'

'Hi Kerry!' answered Sally, as if they'd just bumped into each other at a cocktail party.

'We're fucked,' Kerry announced.

Silence.

'Right,' said Sally slowly, her heart starting to churn in its old familiar way. 'It's funny you should say that actually, Kerry, I've got Paloma with me here in the kitchen asking me that exact question. "Are you fucked?" she asked me, and it's good to hear it confirmed by you, Kerry, to be honest. It's good to hear the truth. I'll pass that on to Paloma straight away.'

She turned to talk to the housekeeper. 'We're fucked, Paloma!' She said this with a broad smile, and turned back to the phone. 'And I'll let Frank know, shall I? When he wakes up, which will probably be in about . . . ooh . . . five hours' time, there's usually a twenty-minute window before he falls asleep again, so I'll let him know then. OK? Actually, I'll make flash cards. Big ones. With big black marker pen lettering on two separate large cards. One will say "WE'RE" on it and the other will say "FUCKED". Great to hear from you, Kerry! We'll speak soon. Sorry I can't chat, life gets a bit busy when you're . . . you know . . . fucked.'

And with that she hung up, and leaned against the breakfast bar with both arms straightened out in front of her and her head dangling in the middle like a punctured balloon.

Paloma was staring at her, open-mouthed.

Sally breathed in, reinflated the balloon at the end of her neck, and straightened up to face her housekeeper. She shrugged her shoulders with a smile.

'Well, what a coincidence!'

Paloma adjusted the waistband of her black trousers, smoothed her crisp white shirt. She coughed lightly, popped the whisked eggs into the fridge, took a cloth, squeezed it, wiped over the breakfast bar, and left the room without further word.

Sally let her face muscles relax, put her hand up to her forehead and scratched off a single Swarovski crystal in her fingernail. She examined it and was just about to sink deep into the armchair when the 1812 Overture struck up.

'Oh no.'

She had a feeling Paloma wasn't going to be doing any front-door opening this morning. She went into the hall, tightening the cord of her dressing gown. This was the last thing she needed right now, somebody at the door. If it was that chirpy postman making some comment about the doorbell again she might have to floor him. She frowned and reached for the big brass door handle.

What met her on the doorstep made her frown deepen and the words 'Oh God, no,' escape from her lips unthinkingly.

A familiar figure, hat perched on the back of his head rakishly, a roll-up fag wedged tightly into one corner of his mouth, a filthy pair of long shorts which only a teenager on E can get away with, an item of clothing looking suspiciously like a poncho, some kind of tie-dye kerchief, bare arms covered with cheaply rendered Celtic tattoos, various bits of leather laces wrapped around wrists and one tied round the neck, and the *pièce de résistance* as Sally looked downwards – the feet, two hairy slabs encrusted in ancient sandals, that bore the look of one who has lived on or perilously near to a festival site for the last ten years with no access to running water. And half-hidden behind this person was an enormous rucksack. And even more worrying than the rucksack, a wizened old guitar propped up beside it. This was not a visitor who was going to pop in, have a cup of tea, and then be on his merry way. That rucksack said, 'I'm here to stay, kiddo. I've got a myriad stinking bits of washing in here. I'm going to pollute your drum many, many times before I leave. I'm in for the long haul.'

Sally tried to breathe slowly, letting her tummy muscles expand, as Simone the Park Club yoga instructor encouraged them all to do twice a week. In her head, Sally tried to hear the voice of her podcast, visualise a calm place that

155

she loved, far, far away from here, and breathe, expand the tummy muscles, calm place, and breathe. She shut her eyes for a nanosecond to try and block out the figure on the doorstep before her.

'All right, Sal?' his voice cajoled.

She opened her eyes to see Frank's younger brother Kyle still twinkling at her with those same goddamn Parker blue eyes. The look that made you feel giddy, annoyed, tickled, excited, tired and slightly fed up all at the same time.

'Well. This is a surprise, Kyle,' said Sally and crossed her arms.

'Namaste,' said Kyle as he put his palms together in prayer and then bowed to her.

Sally glanced at his rucksack.

'Are you planning on . . . er . . . staying, Kyle?'

Kyle licked his forefinger and held it up to the air.

'Till the wind changes,' he said, mysteriously.

Sally shook her head.

'What, are you Mary Poppins now?'

Kyle smiled at her indulgently.

'Is it not delightful that I'm here to pay my big brother and my gorgeous sister-in-law a little visit?'

And Kyle removed his trilby to reveal an unwashed mane of grey-black crinkles, balding conspicuously at the back. He darted in for a kiss on the lips, which Sally only just averted by turning her head quickly.

'So, what's cookin', Sal?' said Kyle in a lazy, wannabe David Essex tone.

Sally turned her back on him and he followed her through the front door and into the hall. She stopped beside the life-size bishop piece on Frank's chessboard. Sally spoke loudly and clearly for all at Cedar Vale to hear.

'We're fucked. Kyle. That's what's happening.'

11

For the first time in days, Frank made it down to the dinner table. In maroon tracksuit trousers and grey hoodie, he looked like a PE teacher who'd been through a harrowing and prolonged Ofsted inspection. His haunted eyes had grown several more crow's-feet in the last two weeks, and his complexion was greyer than the hoodie. His beard was starting to fill out and his hair, normally kept strictly above the collar line, was now starting to straggle over the nape.

He sat in his usual place at the head of the table, with Sally to his right and Kyle to his left. Normally he'd be half-sitting, half-standing, holding court, carving the roast like he was playing squash and booming with bonhomie. Tonight he cut a smaller, deflated figure in his chair. It was rare to have all Parkers round the dinner table at once, especially on a weekday; Frank was never usually home before eight p.m.

'So. This is nice,' said Sally brightly. 'Delicious, Paloma.'

Paloma and Angela were dishing out a huge chicken and chorizo casserole with saffron rice. Paloma flared her nostrils.

'Mmm. That smoky aroma takes me right back to Bogota, my friends,' said Kyle, doing a full body stretch with arms and legs out like starfish. Sally was distressed to see a tuft of pubes poking out on an expanse of white belly.

Frank yawned and Sally caught a whiff of his stale breath. He put his elbows on the table and rubbed his eyes with the heels of his hands, as if he were trying to dislodge them. This was like having dinner with a pair of tramps that you'd taken in for a hot meal, thought Sally to herself in a rare moment of callousness.

'Why were you in Colombia, Kyle?' asked Emily.

'Isn't it where all the party drugs come from?' said Cleo.

'Now there's a story,' said Kyle, pleased to have an audience. 'It all started in the mid nineties, when I was asking myself a lot of the big W questions. The Why? When? What? Who? type questions. The biggies.'

Frank was now slumped against the back of his chair, a bad sign these days. Sally glanced at him, hoping he wasn't going to fall asleep. She was sitting on the edge of her seat, her teeth set into a little smile which hadn't travelled to her eyes.

'I know those type of W questions,' Mikey piped up, 'but I usually have the answer. If I'm asked "Why?" I say, "Why not?". "When?", I say, "Now would be fine". "What?", I say, "I dunno, but I'll Google it" and "Who?", I say, "Who's paying?"'

Everyone round the table laughed at this outburst. Mikey beamed with delight. It wasn't often that she got a Royal Flush of praise.

'Wise words, Mikey,' said Kyle. 'They remind me of a shaman I chanced upon in the Andes. A wild and woolly human he was, with a penchant for bedding young virgins—'

'Right, tuck in everyone, who wants salad?' said Sally, quickly taking the conversational tiller.

'What was that about young virgins, Uncle Kyle?' said Stephen through a mouthful of chicken.

'Wow,' said Cleo, 'virgins! I didn't think virgins, like, existed any more these days.'

'Well, I've got some big W questions for you, Frank,' said Emily, putting down her fork. 'WHAT is going on with you? WHY are you sleeping all day in a tracksuit and WHO is going to tell us the truth?'

'And I'm not going to lie,' added Cleo as backup, 'like WILL you lose the nonce beard, please, Dad?'

There was a silence. Paloma stopped clattering with the Le Creusets at the end of the table and looked silently at Frank. Sally looked from her glass of wine to Frank. Kyle gave his brother side eyes. Everyone looked at Frank.

'Hey, bro,' said Kyle earnestly, 'this might be time to take hold of the talking stick. A method we used campfire-side in the forests outside Medellin. Annibal the storyteller showed us the talking stick, and if you wanted to talk, man, you had to wait till you were passed the stick. Woe betide you if you uttered a word and couldn't feel the wood in your hand. Frank, imagine this fork is the storyteller's stick,' he held a fork towards Frank, 'now when you hold it, bro, you take ownership of your story . . .'

Frank put the fork down petulantly by his plate.

'Fork off, Kyle.'

'Frank, please,' Sally chided.

There were some muffled giggles from the children's end of the table. They hadn't all been sat for a meal together for ages; this banter was golden.

Frank coughed and looked carefully at his plate. His voice was quieter than usual.

'I will tell you the truth, and I'm sure Sally will back me up.' Frank turned to his wife for support, but she was staring fixedly into her dinner plate.

'OK. In my line of work,' he continued, undaunted, 'you go with the wind. That's another big W for you.

Now, your kite is your client base, your assets, your reputation. Sometimes the wind's favourable, it goes in the direction that you want it to, and it lifts your kite higher. Now my kite's been known to fly high, way, way up high, higher than everyone else's kites. Sometimes the wind drops and that forces your kite to drop too. And sometimes the wind changes direction and you have to know how to steer your kite back. That's what's happening at the moment. Your kite can be blown out of your hand and the wind can be so powerful it can even knock you off your feet.'

'I feel you, bro,' said Kyle, half-closing his eyes and leaning back into his chair. 'I've been blown many times—'

Cleo snorted a mouthful of water over her plate of food.

Kyle's eyes were almost closed. He patted his hands on his stomach as he warmed to his theme.

'It's an ill and also cruel wind that blows nobody any good, and I have been at the receiving end of that ill wind, my friends. I remember when I was crossing Chile with a, let's call him a llama-whisperer—'

'Kyle,' Sally interjected, 'Frank's still holding the talking stick.'

'Sorry, man, my bad,' said Kyle. 'The stick is yours.'

Kyle gave him a mini-namaste with palms together. Mikey copied him and did the same to her siblings, which made them snigger.

'Now,' Frank yawned deeply, 'where was I?'

'You were talking about wind and . . . er . . . your kite, Frank,' said Sally, still looking down into her plate.

'That's right. My beautiful, expensive, silken kite that I've been so used to flying. The kite that's made me the talk of the town,' and at this he looked round the table at his family slowly, one by one, totally serious. Mikey looked as if she might be sucked across the table and into Frank's gaze, she was concentrating so hard.

Frank brandished the talking fork in front of him.

'The rock star of the City, I've been called. Ha! My kite and I were flying so flipping high that I was the tiniest blob in the faraway and nobody could even dream of catching my coat-tails. I was invincible. I was so high I was breathing a different air up there. I was flying high, tiny, tiny, but also immense. I was God-like. Everybody wanted a piece of me. Everything I touched turned to gold.'

'Very much like the Midas myth,' said Emily, wiping her mouth neatly with a linen napkin.

'Yes, Emily,' said Frank seriously, 'I was that Midas.'

'And we know what happened to Midas, don't we, Frank?' said Emily sharply. 'His avarice and stupidity got the better of him. He turned all objects around him in his palace to gold.'

'What, even the stuff that was already gold?' asked Cleo, wide-eyed.

Frank closed his eyes briefly. This was draining.

'I think it's a bit difficult to turn something to gold that's already inherently gold,' said Emily kindly.

'Could be, like double gold? A bit like double denim?' suggested Cleo.

'You're a moron, Cleo,' said Mikey.

'And you're dyslexic, Mikey, so welcome to the moron club,' shot back Cleo.

'Girls. Girls,' said Sally faintly.

'Dyslexia actually makes me super good at other things, anyway,' said Mikey.

'What, like hanging around with that pervert Dom in the school pavilion every lunch time?'

'He's my business partner,' said Mikey defiantly.

'Yeah right, Mikey. And I'm Millie Bobby Brown.'

'Cousins!' Emily sought to bring the table to order. 'Let me finish my tale of Midas!'

'You are a moron though, Cleo,' said Mikey, under her breath.

'Dyslexic douche-bag,' whispered Cleo loudly.

Emily looked round the table and continued her story.

'So, King Midas, fool that he was, started to turn animate things into gold. He turned a rose to gold and it gave him no perfume. But worse was to come. At the zenith of his avaricious, idiotic behaviour, he went to hug his daughter—'

'Yes, all right, Emily, we all know how the story ends,' Frank interjected loudly.

Emily held her cutlery like weapons, lowering her voice dramatically as she neared the conclusion of her tale. She was eyeballing Frank now.

'Midas held his girl fatefully in his arms, his precious flesh and blood, and she too turned to gold. He had accrued more—'

'Just to say,' Kyle whispered across the table to her, 'digging the story, Em, but you're playing pretty fast and loose there. Are you actually holding the talking stick?'

Frank cut across him.

'I think you're confusing avarice with talent, Emily. And I certainly never behaved with, what did you say, stupidity, or was it idiocy?'

Sally laid a gentle hand on Frank's.

'Frank, it's all right. Em was just telling us a great story, and you told it really well, sweetheart, you really brought the Midas myth to life.'

'Well I did win the Year Nine Public Speaking Prize.'

'Thanks for reminding us, clever clogs,' said Frank crisply.

'She was brilliant in that,' said Stephen loyally.

Frank was not prepared to let this go.

'Midas is an obvious myth to use for one of the City's most successful hedge-fund managers, Emily, but it's only part of the story. It's way too simplistic. As a hedge-fund manager you're not just waving your magic wand to create money, you know. It's a dance with the markets. It's subtle. It takes years of expertise and—'

'I'm not going to lie, Dad, sounds a bit bullshitty to me, no offence.' This was Cleo, laughing. 'I mean, sorry . . . wind, kites and dancing? It sounds like one of those crusty festivals that play rubbish folk music for old people. Eeurgh!'

'Believe me, Cleo,' said her father, 'when you've analysed and played the markets for as long as I have—'

Paloma and Angela chose that moment to sweep out of the dining room as one, heads held high. Mikey sat up in her chair, eager as a beaver to join the conversation.

'Dad. Dad. Dad!'

Frank shut his eyes.

'Yes, Mikey,' he said wearily.

'Please may I have the talking stick?'

The fork was passed to her.

'Thank you. I really liked what you said with the talking stick, Dad. I wouldn't of understood it half so well without the kite and the wind stuff.'

Frank sighed, his eyes still shut. 'Wouldn't HAVE understood it, not OF understood it, Mikey. Jeez, is this what we get for one of the most expensive educations in Surrey?'

Mikey continued, 'But I need to ask you one thing, Dad. Would you say that since Brett Grover left you in charge of HNB you've been a bit out of your depth?'

There was an embarrassed silence. Frank looked at his youngest daughter, tried to formulate some words with his mouth, but none came.

Mikey continued,

'You probably feel like I did when I had to do the lifesaver's badge at school. I had to put a brick down my pyjamas and swim around the pool. It was horrible, I felt like I was sinking. Is that how you're feeling, Dad?'

Everyone looked at Frank in silence. Again his jaws moved around some silent language which was eluding him at present.

Mikey ploughed on.

'With your fund, yeah, the big fund of other people's money that you manage now because Brett Grover isn't there to pull the trigger, which to be honest must feel kind of shit-scary—'

'Language, Mikey,' said Sally who was now in a monogamous relationship with her dinner plate.

Frank shut his eyes.

Mikey carried on regardless.

'Isn't it true that your investments recently have been, kind of like, wobbly? In the last year and a half you've put a lot of your . . . well . . . THEIR money into things like tech companies? Which are OK, but if the companies are, how do I explain this, too futurey then they don't perform well?'

Frank half-opened his eyes, like a lizard. Mikey was on a roll.

'Now, I don't know much about tech companies, but I hear things on the grapevine, Dad, and I've heard if you invest a lot of money in these tech companies then your kite can really flap about and just crash to the ground.'

The whole of the Parker clan was now staring at Mikey.

'Plus,' she continued, 'because of just, like, general feelings of wobbliness in the world with recession and stuff, that's made the money markets iffy, and without Brett Grover—'

'STOP GOING ON ABOUT BRETT GROVER!' snapped Frank, hitting the table so hard with his fist that the cutlery jumped.

Mikey's cheeks went very red and she put the talking fork down.

'Frank, please,' said Sally, eyes down into the dinner plate again.

'I'm not going to lie, how the hell do you come up with this bullshit?' said Cleo.

'Cleo. Language,' said Sally.

'I'm interested in this grapevine, Mikey,' Emily was chipping in now. 'What is this grapevine? Who's on it?'

'It's Dom,' said Mikey.

'Again. The perv who works for the PE department,' said Cleo, aghast. 'He's SO OLD, he must be at least fifty and he has proper disgusting greasy hair.' She pulled a face.

'Shut UP, Cleo,' said Mikey.

'Dom is your financial grapevine?' said Emily, starting to giggle.

'Yes,' said Mikey, 'Dom used to work in finance. He reads everything about it. We have really interesting chats in the pavilion.'

'What, while he pervs over you in your PE kit?' said Cleo. 'Aren't you a bit worried that it might be a bit, like, hashtaggy, Mum and Dad? A bit like that guy, what's his name, Harry Wine and Dine?'

'Harvey Weinstein,' Emily corrected her.

'Oops! Sorry!' giggled Cleo.

Sally looked concerned. 'Mikey, how much time are you spending with this Dom?'

'Enough time for him to show her his long bushy grapevine!' said Cleo, and Stephen and Emily laughed.

Mikey stood up at the dinner table.

'You just don't know anything about anything. We talk about the economy. You're all stupid idiots.'

And she ran out of the dining room.

Sally got up to go after her.

'I'll go, Mum,' Stephen said. 'I'm due on *Crackdown* in about two minutes anyway.'

'*Crackdown*?' asked Kyle, suddenly interested.

'It's a game,' said Stephen, heaving himself out of his chair. 'It's amazing.'

'Reminds me of an unusual situation I had during a military coup in Paraguay. We were hiding out with a bunch of tribesmen dudes. Out of nowhere we hear boots trampling over the forest floor, then loud voices and guns going ack-ack-ack —'

Cleo interrupted her uncle's story by standing up.

'I'm not going to lie, I'd love to stay here and chat shit but I've got some homework to do and the repeats of *TOWIE* are on.' She sauntered out of the room, picking at her nails.

Emily stood up.

'I'm sorry if my Midas story bored you, Uncle Frank,' she said. 'It's strange, when you don't have a mum or dad around whose job it is to believe that everything that comes out of your mouth is pure genius, you can feel a bit unsupported, you know? By the way, everyone, my mother Nancy, who I know is shit and probably never wants to see me again, has a birthday. It was on September ninth. Just in case you might want to remember it next year.'

And she ran past Stephen and out of the dining room.

'Emily!' called Sally, standing up.

Stephen paused in the doorway.

'I know how Emily feels sometimes. And I've actually got a mum and a dad,' he said, and disappeared.

There was a brief silence before Kyle spoke again.

'That was touch and go in Paraguay. I thought we were done for. Militia men with guns. Heavy duty, man. One of my nine lives was definitely hanging by a thread that day . . .'

Sally sat down heavily, wishing that at least seven of Kyle's nine lives had been extinguished that day.

'Frank, we need to talk. About Emily, about Stephen, about Cleo and about Mikey.'

'What, you mean our kids?' said Frank with a hint of sarcasm.

'Don't give me that tone, Frank. We're sinking. They're sinking. They need us, but we're like those stupid life rings that have been cut adrift from their post, and we're no help to them either. We should be attached to those posts, Frank. And instead we're just bobbing around on the sea with them and we're all going to start sinking, Frank, I can feel it—'

Frank tried to suppress a yawn but the effort of it made his entire mouth tremble and his eyes water copiously.

'Was that a yawn, Frank?' said Sally, standing up defensively.

Frank looked sheepish.

'Well, thank you very much, Frank,' said Sally with a wobbly voice. 'I'm trying to talk to you about our imploding family and you just yawn in my face,' and she turned on her heel and headed out.

There was silence in the room, which now only contained the two Parker brothers. Frank drummed his fingers on the table.

'Do you want to leave the room too, Kyle?' he asked bitterly. 'It seems to be all the rage, leaving the room. Be my guest.'

Kyle got up from the table.

'You know what, bro, I'd love to stay but I've got one hell of a turtle's head on the brew. I think my belly's only used to Central American food,' and he headed for the door. 'By the way, bro,' he said, turning back into the room, 'who's this Brett Grover dude?'

Frank gripped all of his hair in exasperation and leaned right back in his chair.

Kyle disappeared, leaving Frank to his despair. He looked around him at the dinner-table detritus. No sign of Paloma nor Angela to clear it up. Frank stood and piled up a couple of plates lazily, one on top of the other, the cutlery still on them. He put them down again. He was too weary for this. Mikey was right. He felt the weight of many, many bricks weighing his body down, and he was sinking in a pair of wet pyjamas. He shuffled off to bed.

In the west wing of The Chantry, nestled deep in the Surrey countryside towards Esher, Amerjit Singh was settling in for his nightly group therapy session. He and four companions were taking advantage of deep armchairs in which their whole bodies could buffer themselves.

Amerjit had begun to look forward to his time spent in their comforting confines, with a cup of something hot and milky inside him. He was loving not having to wear a suit. He'd been told that the last one he'd worn had ended up strewn halfway around Finsbury Square, but Amerjit had only patchy memories of that. He'd been in soft cotton jeggings and a fleece-lined hoodie for a while now, and it was blissful. No constricting collars, tie or rubbing waistbands.

Roland, a softly spoken Scot in round glasses, was running the session. It was nice to sit and talk amongst a group of people and hear only affirmation back. After so many years of marriage to Laura, Amerjit was not used to having someone actually agree with him. Or if not agree, then at least try to find the positive.

They were having Share Time, a chance for each person to vocalise their thoughts and feelings on the day's events before bedtime. Amerjit was trying to maintain his cool because one of the group was a well-known TV comedian and game-show host, Tommy Zubin. On screen, Tommy was an unstoppable force in sharp suits with an endless repartee of even sharper one-liners. He always wore zany brothel creepers; they were the Zubin signature, and he had them in a dazzling array of different colours. Amerjit was dying to ask Tommy how many pairs of shoes he really owned. He'd read an article about them once in *GQ* magazine. Frank would be amazed if he could see Amerjit now, sitting so close to Tommy Zubin and hearing his innermost thoughts every day. It was strange, Tommy's thoughts were not the whizz bang wallop kind of thoughts that he was so famous for. He seemed very, very tired and quiet, smaller and wrinklier than he was on the telly.

Amerjit couldn't help smiling at him expectantly, waiting for him to come out with a killer one-liner. He was trying desperately not to be too goofy in front of Tommy; it would make the celebrity feel singled out and judged, and that was against Chantry rules. Everyone was a blank canvas, an open, clean book; everyone was on their own unique journey. Tommy would occasionally catch Amerjit's eye and then Amerjit couldn't help but grin back at him. Tommy would then lower his eyes with a slight shake of the head. Amerjit spotted this; he was going to have to be careful.

'So,' said Roland gently, 'are we ready to hear from you, Amerjit? In your own time, if you'd like to tell us what you'd like to share.'

Amerjit repositioned himself in the chair so that his knees were tucked right underneath his chin.

'Well,' began Amerjit, 'I've just been realising today how comfortable I feel in clothes that don't have a structure.'

There was a supportive murmur from the group.

'OK,' said Roland, smiling, 'that's a good positive thought.'

'I mean, who knew that tracksuits were so comfortable?' said Amerjit. 'I studied at Princeton in America after I did my degree at Cambridge, and I got into a little sport while I was there. Yeah, we wore tracksuits, but they were, I don't know how to explain this, aggressive tracksuits. They had piping and stiff pockets and competitive things emblazoned on the breast. The ones we wear here are just so soft. And I'm loving that.'

'That's great, Amerjit,' said Roland encouragingly, 'I'm really glad to hear that. Anything else you want to say this evening?'

Amerjit didn't know what came over him, a sense of euphoria maybe at being here among such supportive folk, but he blurted out,

'Tommy, how many pairs of brothel creepers do you actually own? Like, I've read it's sixty pairs, is that right?'

There was a stunned silence in the room. Tommy cursed under his breath and started to get out of his chair. Roland had to take charge.

'Whoa, Amerjit. You know we don't bring the past into this space. This is clean space, it's about the here and the now.'

'I'm sorry, Tommy,' said Amerjit, mortified, 'it's just that I read it in GQ—'

Tommy stood up.

'Amerjit. Please. Tommy. Sit down.'

The comedian sat down reluctantly and looked at Amerjit like he wanted to deck him.

'I'm so sorry,' said Amerjit, his voice thickening with tears. Roland subtly moved the large box of tissues towards him. 'I wish that Laura and I had found more time to wear tracksuits, well, maybe not a tracksuit for Laura, although I could definitely see her in some kind of sailing gear. She'd suit that, a captain's cap would go well with her strong neck –' Amerjit's lower lip was starting to wobble – 'in fact, it's one of the things I first noticed about her; that plus her incredible grasp of the Asian markets. It's a powerful combination for a Sikh boy who'd never set foot out of Hayes. I miss her chat. I mean I can see her if I want to. She's all over the media.'

Amerjit paused and took a tissue absent-mindedly from the box.

'I miss the tough stuff. The icicles, her intractable nature, her aggression at times. I know it sounds weird and like I've got some kind of a victim complex or something. I've messed up so badly. She's so angry with me. Everybody is. Laura and Frank. I ran away from the sinking ship. I just ran. Like a rat. He's never going to speak to me again. What colleague just runs when the waters get choppy? I've lost my wife, my best friend, my job, all in one fell swoop. Gone. Everything. Dust to dust. Ashes to ashes. Funk— Jesus. Even Bowie's gone. Bowie's bloody gone. I loved Bowie, I bloody loved Bow . . .'

And Amerjit could not finish the word as the sobs took over his upper body. His hoodie shook with loud, wet sobs. Roland watched him, nodding, saying nothing. This was all part of the Chantry process.

*

'Frank. We really need to talk.'

Sally was sitting on their top-of-the-range memory-foam mattress from Harvey Nichols. She watched as Frank shuffled around towards his side of the bed, as the Lalique carriage clock sounded half past eight. Why were his shoulders so rounded? He never used to slouch like that. He was shuffling like an old man going into a betting shop. Sally felt resentment rising in her throat.

'We need to sort things out, Frank. We're going to have to make some serious changes.'

Frank peeled back the duvet in its sumptuous William Morris Victorian bird-print cover.

Sally continued:

'The company's gone bust, OK. I don't want to go into the whys and wherefores but maybe Mikey's right. You've been out of your depth running it, and . . . well . . . I've never really delved into our accounts because there's always been somebody else to do that for me. I don't know what we've got in terms of savings, but I have a feeling that our money is quite, well, fluid around here. In that it seems to slosh in and then slosh out again . . .' She was starting to get lost in the fiscal minutiae. 'Lots of overheads and everything? Our life? All this?' She gestured vaguely around the bedroom. 'Well, I'm going to have to get my head around all of it pretty sharpish, aren't I? With you being so tired all of the time.'

'I'm not tired. It's an illness.' Frank slid under the duvet with a light groan and sank back into the pristine puffed-up pillows. 'I'm not bunking off, Sal, I've got narcolepsy.'

'Yes, well, whatever it is, it sounds made up to me!' Sally blurted loudly, blushing at her own uncharacteristic fit of pique. She noticed Frank's defeated face. 'I'm sorry, Frank, that was uncalled for. Look, you just need to get over this . . . illness . . . and then we can start up again. But in the meantime, we need to cut back our expenses. We need to access some money while you're out of action. We need to sell Cedar Vale, move somewhere smaller, then live off what we make from the sale. We have to cut our cloth, Frank. It's the only way we're going to get out of this nightmare.'

Frank looked down at the duvet as if he were suddenly deeply interested in William Morris's depiction of a nightingale's beak. He said nothing.

'Frank? Are you listening?'

Frank didn't say a word.

'Frank?' repeated his wife more urgently.

'I've got this, Sal. We've been here before,' he said quietly.

'We haven't been here before, Frank. You wear a tracksuit on a daily basis. You've got a beard to rival the Archbishop of Canterbury's –' she paused for a moment – 'oh no, it's not the beardy guy any more is it? He's pretty clean-shaven now. But you know what I mean.'

'You don't have any faith in me, do you?' Frank looked at his wife sadly. He was mumbling now. 'Go on, say it. Tell me that I'm no Brett Grover. Tell me to my face!'

Sally had a faraway look in her eye.

'You know what, I've got to take the reins, haven't I?'

'Yes, and keep my balls in a jar by the front door while you're at it,' said Frank, petulantly.

Sally got up from the bed.

'You're being ridiculous, Frank.'

'Sit down, Sal, there's something I need to tell you.'

Reluctantly she sat back down. She was thinking how unattractive his beard was. There was a bit of rice caught in it and it was making her feel slightly sick.

'Your financial plan sounds highly plausible, Sally. Cutting our cloth and all that. Cedar Vale would have been the perfect asset . . .' Frank's voice trailed off into nothing.

There was a pause.

'What do you mean, "would have been", Frank? I don't like the sound of that "would have been" one bit.'

Frank looked up at his wife.

'Well. There's a slight glitch in all of this.'

Frank stopped. Sally stared at him, holding her breath.

'Glitch, Frank?' she asked tentatively.

Frank coughed lightly.

'Cedar Vale doesn't belong to us, I'm afraid.'

'What?' Sally's voice was suddenly an octave higher.

'The house isn't ours, Sal.'

At that moment there was movement near the bathroom door and Paloma came into the bedroom holding a plunger in one hand and a gruesome ball of what looked like sodden pubic hair in the other.

'I plunge the bidet.' She nodded at Frank and sniffed at Sally.

Frank and Sally just stared at the housekeeper dumbly. Paloma held her head erect. 'I heard everything in the bathroom. Everything.'

12

Paloma and her niece departed early the next morning. Sally had a Valium veneer of serenity. Sometime very soon she would have to kick the habit. But not today.

The three older children had just left for school, reluctantly, late and on foot – for some reason, Colette had not appeared brandishing the Jeep keys today. Mikey would no doubt career off on her BMX at any moment.

Valiantly, Sally helped Paloma and Angela with their bags to the door. She was ever the gracious chatelaine, but in reality she was mortified to her hair roots, which were showing dark now. That was another thing she'd have to get done. But not today.

She remembered being on this very spot, nervously awaiting Paloma's arrival at Cedar Vale all those years ago. Sally and Frank had watched as a small, brisk figure walked up the drive with an old-fashioned leather suitcase in one hand and cool box in the other, the sort you pack a picnic into. It was like Maria arriving at the Von Trapp mansion but minus the merry guitar-waving. Paloma had brought a beetle-browed disapproval with her, which was to be her default setting from that day forward.

Paloma's cousin Feliz pulled up in a Transit van and loaded up her possessions, which now amounted to fourteen large boxes, six oversized checked laundry bags, an array of carrier bags and the same little cool box and leather suitcase that she'd arrived with all those years ago. Sally couldn't help but notice a few of her own items poking out here and there: a hairdryer, some rather expensive dinner plates with gold lily motif, a Harrods towelling dressing gown and some silk flowers. Sally said nothing. These were the spoils, the booty left behind after the sack of Cedar Vale; take all the loot you can grab. Sally realised that she was going to have to get used to this.

'Paloma, I don't know what to say,' Sally stammered at the front door. 'I'm so sorry it's ended like this. You've been . . . er . . . so indispensable. Like a piece of furniture. That sounds wrong. A living piece of furniture that we have . . . er . . . admired and occasionally sat on.' Paloma folded her arms silently and let Sally squirm into her own conversational cul-de-sac. 'I mean that you're like a piece of furniture we've become accustomed to having in our house. You are so . . . solid . . . no. I don't mean solid, although you are very strong and your centre of gravity is low which has made you so reliable and . . . er . . . you're so good at lifting heavy things.'

Paloma stared at Sally and pursed her mouth drawstring tight, watching her, like a worm, writhe on the end of her big fishing rod. Sally plunged further into the mire of her own making.

'Basically, what I'm trying to say, Paloma, is that you're a good egg. That's a real compliment in English. I don't know if you have the same expression in Spanish? But, like an egg, you have given us solid, solid . . . there's that word again . . . like an egg, a good egg, you've given us protein and . . . also . . . carbs, salads and delicious, delicious canapés. Thank you for all of those many and varied canapés, Paloma . . .'

Sally was beginning to run out of steam. She was finding it comforting to repeat the word 'canapés'. It was a nice word to turn over and again in her mouth. She managed one more 'canapés', to herself, before Paloma uncrossed her arms, recalibrated her leg stance, and then gave Sally the full laser beams. Sally was taken back to being twelve again, waiting outside the headmistress's office. She felt a strange watery feeling in her front bottom, and the sensation that her face was burning up like a furnace.

Paloma worked her tongue slowly over her teeth, looked her former employer up and down, took in the flattened, rumpled hair with dark roots, the stressed face, the mismatched skirt and sweatshirt, and was that a ladder in Sally's tights? That was a first. Sally was normally groomed like a show-pony. She moved closer to Sally so that she was now about a foot away from her face. Paloma's eyes narrowed and even though smaller than Sally, she somehow managed to look down on her as she spoke.

'You. Are. Very. Lazy. Bitch.'

Paloma capped her sentence with a chin flick upwards, showing off her flaring, slightly hairy nostrils. She then turned on her heel and through the front doors.

Sally felt as if she'd been punched in the bosoms. She caught a glimpse of herself in the bespoke Graham and Green mirror, with its silly cherubs clinging to the frame. Three grand, that mirror had cost.

This last couple of weeks had taken its toll somewhat. Gone was the coiffed hairdo and her eyelashes needed tinting; so did her eyebrows. She looked undefined, foggy of face. There were new wrinkles around her jowls and an almost permanent tic in her right eye. She moved closer to the mirror to see if the tic was visible; she was living with her very own dormant alarm system to remind her that at any point, her entire body could explode into a clarion call of primal panic. Sally looked at herself.

'Who do you think you are, Sally Parker?' she said and then laughed bitterly, remembering she'd asked that of herself even before everything collapsed. But she did not look away. She clenched one fist and then the other, and lifted them so that she could see them reflected in the mirror.

'Deluded, yes. Frightened, maybe. But are you lazy, Sally Parker?' she addressed herself directly in the eye. She let her fists drop slowly. She hated to admit it, but the answer was a very definite yes. With her harsh words, Paloma had managed to peel back Sally's skin and sprinkle the tiniest bit of salt on to her raw exposed flesh. It reminded her of her mother, she was a salt-sprinkler too, as was Francesca Daly-Jones with her seemingly innocuous comments, always delivered with a smile.

Sally looked around her. So much money had gone into the construction of this Cedar Vale dream. When she'd first stepped through the door, Sally fell head over heels in love with the space and quiet of it. If she'd had her way, Sally would have kept it minimal, but life with Frank's gargantuan disposable income meant that every breath of space was filled. A set of Venetian blown-glass chandeliers bought at Carnevale, 'wow factor' pieces Francesca had called them; endless paintings on the wall which meant nothing to Sally; lots of silverware, tureens, platters and oversized roasting dishes. Frank loved them but they reminded Sally of school trophy cabinets. And glass cupboards full of rarefied knick-knacks. Twee porcelain ladies on a swing or carrying trugs of flowers; hideous Chinese vases large enough to squat in; *objets d'art* randomly picked from antique shops; and the most eye-wateringly expensive curtains that money can buy. Pelmets, tassels, swathes and heavy hems, Cedar Vale was drowning in overpriced haberdashery.

Sally paced like a tiger trainer around the hall.

'Trappings and spoils,' she said to herself out loud as she circumnavigated the vast chessboard floor. She laughed. 'I am trapped. I am spoiled. And maybe I have become lazy,' she continued aloud, 'but I and I alone will be the judge of that.'

Sally stood up straight. It was time to take ownership. She marched through the front doors, down the steps and right up to the Transit van. 'I will never be called lazy by anyone else,' she said defiantly.

She felt suddenly awake and clear of brain as she stalked up to the Transit's passenger window.

'I AM THE AUTHOR OF MY OWN LAZINESS,' she shouted as she stuck her head inside to find Paloma, alarmingly close, lighting up a fag. Sally knew that she was no longer the rightful owner of Cedar Vale, though she had no idea who it belonged to, and it meant that she and Paloma were now on neutral territory. The gloves were off, and Sally wanted to feel something real in her fist.

'So you think I'm lazy, Paloma? Because I've had a few thoughts about you too.'

Sally was hearing a loud voice that she didn't quite recognise. It was less honeyed around the edges; it didn't come from her throat. It came from lower down. Sally Parker was using her chest voice for the first time in three decades. Her GCSE drama teacher would be so proud.

'You have always made me feel uncomfortable in this house, Paloma, because you are sour, jealous and uncompromising.'

Paloma said something in Spanish to her cousin, who started to turn the key in the ignition.

'Not only that, Paloma, but you are manipulative.'

The Transit van sparked up and started to crunch slowly over the gravel. Sally walked alongside the passenger window as she continued,

'And you are also divisive. You're like Mrs Danvers from the book *Rebecca*. She was a cow and also wore a lot of black. Just like you.'

The vehicle was starting to accelerate, forcing Sally to jog briskly alongside. She was yelling now.

'And for your information your pastry is SHIT even though everyone always goes on about how fricking crumbly it is.' Sally was slightly out of breath now but forged on valiantly. 'And if I'm a bitch, Paloma –' the Transit van was drawing away too fast now for Sally to keep up. She was left in the middle of the drive bellowing her concluding words – 'THEN YOU ARE AN ARSE-HOLE! A BIG OLD SHITTY ARSEHOLE WITH DINGLEBERRIES HANGING OUT OF IT!'

Sally started to flick the V-sign manically from both hands in the direction of the van. Then she reduced it, pleasingly, to just the one middle finger. She accompanied this with hoarse random words that came to her, like 'DOUCHE!' and 'DICK-SPLASH!' She'd told Cleo off in the past for using that sort of language, but here it was being put to good use. Sally was on something of an adrenal high; she was so absorbed that she failed to see the vehicle driving up the other way. A sleek navy Range Rover filled with four smart yummy mummies stopped, just as Sally shouted:

'YOU VINDICTIVE SHIT-PASTRY BASTARDY OLD SHITBAG!' as loudly as her pipes could muster.

Francesca Daly-Jones looked out of the Range Rover, dimples on display.

'Everything OK, hon?'

Three perfectly made up faces appeared at various other orifices of the car.

Red faced and croaking, Sally managed a quiet, 'Trappings and spoils, Francesca, trappings and spoils.'

'Sorry, hon, what was that? We've got Simply Red on in here, the girls and I were having a bit of a boogie!'

Francesca leaned over to turn the music down and Sally flexed her fingers and looked at her hands. She had scared herself, but mixed in with the fear was also a great sense of release. She formed her right hand into a fist again and beat it into her left hand.

'Oh hon. You look . . . tired. Do you want a lift up to the house?' asked Francesca.

'No. I'll walk,' Sally said gruffly, 'thanks.'

Francesca gave her a conspiratorial look and then lowered her voice.

'I expect you want to cool down after that outburst! Who was the lucky recipient of that little tirade, hon? It didn't look like Ocado. Was it a delivery person?' she inquired breezily, clearly digging for gossip.

'No. It was Paloma,' said Sally, turning round and starting to walk back to Cedar Vale.

'Shut up!!' Francesca almost shouted with excitement. She turned to the women in the car and started talking at them in a stage whisper. Sally could make out the words 'Paloma' and 'bastardy old shitbag'. She had given the gossip gannets much flesh to peck over.

Sally smiled to herself as she walked away from the Range Rover. A male peacock screeched nearby. Did the peacocks still belong to them? Or was it just the house that wasn't theirs? She'd have to have a serious chat with Frank. She inhaled deeply. As long as she put one foot in front of the other. And then the other foot in front of the other. And so on. It was doable. She kept on walking. It was odd. She felt abnormally light and strangely in control of her footfall. The sun was out, she could feel it in her hair. She enjoyed each step as it scrunched into the gravel. Her calves felt lithe. She could do this.

On purpose she walked right in the middle of the drive so that Francesca's Range Rover couldn't overtake her. Sally would dictate the speed at which they arrived at the front door. She slowed down a little. The Range Rover had to slow down behind her. Sally felt powerful. Her throat was sore after the shouting debacle, but it was a nice kind of scratchy sore, a bit like Bonnie Tyler must feel after a gig.

On arrival at the front entrance, the women emerged, still chattering, from the car and the hair flicking started.

'. . . and GOD it was so stressful, Joshie forgot his violin,' moaned Karen.

'Oh, nightmare,' answered Samantha. 'Maisie always does that. Did you have to go back to school and drop it off?'

'Yeah,' said Karen, pouting, 'nightmare tailback all along the Chobham Road. I missed my spinning class.'

'Shit. That's just awful,' said Becks, joining the gaggle.

'Girls!' Francesca marshalled them like a Head Prefect. 'Have you got the list of all the things that we need to go through this morning?'

'Yes,' said Becks, 'I'm chairing this event, aren't I?'

'Yes, you are,' said Francesca, smiling and twirling her little Mulberry purse around her wrist, 'but we have a slight change to this morning's agenda, girls. Because at the very top now, is "What the fucking hell happened between Sally and her housekeeper on the drive this morning?" Sal, we'll need you to spill!'

The girlfriends laughed and looked at Sally. She looked through their expectant faces, at some far-off place, as if she were planning a journey.

'Sally?' nudged Francesca.

'I'm so sorry,' Sally said after a five-second pause, 'I've no idea why you're here.'

Bronwen Llewellyn was helped back into her neat skirt and shirt in the sparse examination room on the first floor of Bangor Hospital. Bronwen looked as small as a wren, with not a bite of fat on her.

'Can I help you with your pop socks there, Bronwen?' asked the kindly nurse.

'No thank you. The day I can't put on my own pop socks is the day you'll take me down the Llanfairfechan High Street in a wooden box.'

There was an awkward moment. The nurse smiled ruefully.

'Well, let's hope that won't be happening for a little while yet, Bronwen.'

'It'll happen when it happens,' sniffed Bronwen. 'Now where's my handbag?'

The nurse passed Bronwen her carpet bag, smiling.

'Don't I even get a cup of tea and a biscuit, or does the National Health Service no longer stretch to that?'

'I'll get you a cuppa, Bronwen,' said the nurse, and caught Bronwen's look, 'and I'll find you a biscuit!'

'And plenty of milk and four sugars. Not sweetener. If anything's going to kill me, that muck will.'

The 'girls', as Francesca called them, were all sitting down in various comfy armchairs in Sally's kitchen. Sally had given them the briefest outline of Paloma's departure, but nothing more. She was determined not to extend Feeding Time in the big cats' enclosure. She made cups of tea for everybody in the Fortnum's pot, and put farm shop biscuits on to a Harvey Nichols pistachio-coloured cake stand.

'These biccies are so scrummy, aren't they?' said Francesca, nibbling away at one. 'Wow, are they from Gaysford's Farm Shop, Sal?'

'Yes,' said Sally, pouring the tea.

'I bought some biscuits in there the other day. Cacao nib and ginger pod. Delicious. But,' and she paused lightly here, 'they are expensive, you know, Sal.'

Sally continued to pour the tea silently. Francesca kept looking at her.

'I think I paid eight pounds for the packet.'

There was silence in the room. The girls looked at each other. Sally put the pot down gently on the table.

'And?' she inquired.

'Well. All I'm saying is that, in these uncertain times, would one do better to downgrade one's biscuit box and just go for a good old cheap and cheerful Jammie Dodger or a garibaldi from Tesco?'

Francesca smiled sweetly and popped a bit more biscuit into her mouth.

Sally smiled right back at her.

'If one is so genuinely concerned about the status of one's biscuit box, then one really should think about getting oneself a life, doesn't one think? Would one like any more tea?'

Francesca's smile withered on her face. You could have heard a pin drop. Sally thought how peaceful it was in her kitchen now that Paloma was gone. Except it wasn't her kitchen any more.

'Right,' said Becks, sensing an atmosphere, 'it's time to call this meeting to order. Get us! We've all left the kids at breakfast club and we're just wasting time nattering!'

Francesca was scowling at Sally. Becks smiled at both women broadly.

'Okey-dokey! So, ladies, we're here to plan our fabby Charity Clothes Auction again. Hashtag Girl Power! And we're going to raise even more cash than we did last time. So, two years ago we managed to raise, hang on, look at me all official with my notes! A whopping thirty-two grand!'

There were excited whoops among the girls. Except for Francesca who was now looking at Sally icily.

Becks was enjoying her role; it reminded her of when she used to work in an insurance office.

'Okey-dokey. The most important thing for us to do today is to pledge our items of clothing. We can't have a Clothes Auction with no clothes, can we, girls?'

Becks was stopped in her tracks by the appearance of a dishevelled and barefoot man at the kitchen door, wearing boxers and an old Depeche Mode T-shirt.

'Well, hello, Captain Birdseye,' said Francesca, sitting upright, 'you missed quite a farewell to your beloved housekeeper this morning!'

'Morning Francesca. Ladies,' said Frank with a gravelly morning-after voice.

Sally felt keenly the lack of his footwear. And trousers. It made her prickle with anxiety. And she wished he'd just shave off that bloody fisherman's beard.

'What's this? A mothers' meeting?' Frank picked up a satsuma and started to throw it in the air. Then dropped it and had to pick it up with a grunt. 'And you tell that dick-head husband of yours, Francesca, that I want a rematch on the golf course. Tomorrow!'

'Tim'll be at work tomorrow, Frank,' said Francesca pointedly. 'It's Wednesday.'

There was a pause.

'Of course. I meant on Saturday.'

Francesca smirked. She was enjoying herself.

Frank shuffled to the fridge and opened it.

'Where's breakfast, love? Has Paloma prepared something?'

'She's gone, Frank,' said Sally quickly, 'on . . . er . . . holiday.'

'Really?' said Francesca with very wide eyes.

'Where's the bread, Sal?' asked Frank.

'We're out of bread,' replied Sally, giving him a loaded look.

'Eek, no more bread,' said Francesca. 'Now all I want from your lovely wife here, Frank, is her most expensive designer clothes please! It's that time of year!'

'Be my guest, 'Cesca,' said Frank.

'Frank—' Sally tried to intervene.

'Sal, that's OK with you, isn't it?' said Francesca. 'You donated LOADS of clothes to the auction last time.'

All eyes were now on Sally and Frank, looking like worn-out hostages only recently released from several years of captivity in their own kitchen. Except it wasn't their own kitchen. Sally straightened her shoulders back.

'Of course, it's more than OK, Francesca, go on up. I'll join you in a minute,' she said confidently.

Francesca shot her a venomous little look, before smiling widely all around.

'Come on, girls! To Sally's wardrobe –' and off they all clattered – 'which is the size of frigging Chessington World of Adventures!' Francesca added, out of sight.

Frank and Sally were left on their own, a state which both seemed to be avoiding assiduously at the moment. Sally crossed her arms.

'So, are you going to explain, Frank?'

Frank slumped down at the breakfast bar with a Gaysford's biscuit which, by Francesca's reckoning, would be worth about £800.

'Explain what?' said Frank, dead-eyed.

'The house. You said last night that it wasn't ours.'

Frank sighed.

'Sal, babe, when we saw this house for the first time all those years ago, you fell in love with it. I made the guy an offer and he refused. Said he didn't want to sell. So I've been renting it off him for the last seventeen years.'

Sally's eyes were starting to brim.

'What?'

'A lot of people abroad do it this way, Sal. They rent. It's only the Brits that are obsessed with "our home is our castle" and all that bullshit. It actually shows more financial acumen to rent—'

Sally marched several paces and flashed him angry eyes.

'Oh, don't tell me about financial acumen, Frank –' there was the old chest voice coming out again – 'I just want to know, do we have a roof over our heads or not?'

Frank put his hands through his hair.

'Well, why can't we just carry on renting?'

There was a pause.

'We can't afford to rent this house with our current cash-flow issues.'

They were interrupted by the twang of a guitar as Kyle came into the kitchen in the shortest dressing gown ever seen on a human. It barely skimmed his buttocks, and Sally was worried that he wasn't wearing anything underneath it. He flumped himself down into an armchair in the middle of the bay window. Yes, Sally's fear was confirmed. She got a vivid eyeful of her brother-in-law's middle-aged meat and two veg.

'My muse has woken me up early today. And she won't be serving me breakfast in bed. She's telling me to catch the wave. So, it's kind of a troubadour riff I've had playing around my head the last couple of days, you know?'

And Kyle started to strum a simple chord on the guitar – G major – which, if his pain-filled face was anything to go by, was the most difficult of all chords. He grimaced his way into another chord and then accompanied this improvisation with a rather strangled voice.

'The road has been long. The road has been muddy. The road takes me home. Back to my buddy.'

'Er . . . Kyle?' Sally was loath to interrupt the muse but felt she had no option with the view of Kyle's genitals filling her eyeline.

'Wait, Sal, the muse pushes me ever onwards . . .'

Kyle shut his eyes and stopped twanging. He looked soulfully out of the window, a bittersweet, strained expression coming over him. And he returned to his guitar.

'The road has been long. The road has been winding. But when I see you, your persona – no that's not right – your charisma . . . is blinding.'

Frank put his head in his hands. Sally went over to the sink. She felt as if she might throw up. And then the gaggle of girlfriends came trotting back into the room.

Becks, Karen and Samantha were thrilled to see a half-naked man with a guitar lounging in the armchair.

'Well, hello there! Sally!' said Becks fruitily. 'Where have you been hiding this one?'

Kyle winked at the women and treated them to a cheeky naval salute, thankfully with his legs now together.

'In the words of Iggy Pop, I'm just a passenger, ladies. Just stopping till the crops are brought in, then I'll be hitting that ol' yellow brick road once again.'

And with this he bent over his guitar and strummed something that wasn't quite a chord. Kyle's legs looked dangerously as if they were about to start opening again; luckily Francesca stepped in centre stage to mask him. Her arms were piled high with Sally's most expensive clothes. Sally was taken aback by the sheer volume of gear Francesca had taken, but gritted her teeth, and said loudly,

'Didn't you want to take more, Francesca? I've got a ton more stuff.'

'You are so GENEROUS, Mrs Parker,' Francesca said with a shake of her mane. 'Just look at all the clothes she's given us. I mean, what the hell? We've got Stella McCartney, Beckham, Juicy Couture, Tu. Who's Tu?'

'It's Sainsbury's,' said Sally.

Francesca dropped it as if she'd just handled cat poo.

'Eeurgh. You can keep that, Sal! Oh my GOD, I'm going to cry. A Valentino, a bit of Miu Miu, there's some Gucci and just look at this. Sally, do you mind if we take this?'

Francesca gave Sally little girl imploring eyes. She was holding up the most beautiful and fragile piece of clothing that Sally owned, a vintage Chanel kimono. Sally had only ever worn it once, to an HNB dinner in Mayfair. All eyes were on her.

'Come on, Sal,' Frank interrupted. 'I'll buy you another one!'

Sally nodded.

'Yes?' said Francesca. 'Is that a yes?'

Sally continued to nod.

Francesca jumped up and down clutching the clothes, squealing like a toddler, the kimono scrunched in her grasping hands.

'Oh! I almost forgot. I found this on your bedside table.'

Francesca handed Sally an envelope. Sally recognised Colette's writing immediately and knew that the nanny's resignation letter would be inside.

Francesca's eyes travelled enquiringly from the letter in Sally's hand, up to her face. All eyes were now on Sally expectantly.

'I know exactly what this is,' said Sally brazenly. 'It's from Colette. She always writes a really sweet note when she's going off –' there was a pause as she collected herself – 'on holiday. Colette's gone off on holiday.'

13

Mikey knew that if she wanted to catch Dom, the best time was before school. She parked her BMX outside the sports pavilion and went round the back to Dom's little hideout. He liked to sit in a broken wheelie chair, feet up on a big crate full of cricket pads, and have a draw or two on his vape. Dom was nearly sixty and was continually trying to retire from St Bede's, where he'd worked since the age of forty-five. Prior to that he'd been a trader in the City where he'd burned out his immune system. Looking after the school grounds for the last fifteen years suited him perfectly.

'All right, Parker?' he said when he saw Mikey's face round the door.

'All right, Dom. What news?'

'All good,' said Dom, reaching down under the chair and pulling out an old Charles and Di biscuit tin. He smiled so that his whole face wrinkled up like a chamois leather.

'We've done good, Parker!' he said, eyes glinting.

'How much?' asked Mikey.

'Here we are. Three grand each. Nice one, Parker, that was all your doing.'

Mikey's face flushed with pride. She'd never made this much cash before. She pulled herself up to her full height, and looked serious.

'The wind was blowing in the right direction, Dom,

I knew it. Our kite was high –' she looked down at her hands full of notes – 'and look what blew in!'

'You could buy three hundred thousand penny sweets with that, Parker,' said Dom, laughing.

Mikey's eyes shone as she took in this piece of information. She looked tempted for a moment, but a look of earnestness came over her.

'No way. We're going to reinvest, Dom,' she said, looking at her phone. 'I'd better bounce. I've got Citizenship Class first thing. Good to do business with you, Dom,' and Mikey was gone.

Cleo, Stephen and Emily were walking in a huddle down the lane that ran along the back of Cedar Vale towards St Bede's.

'I'm not going to lie, my bag is THE HEAVIEST on a Wednesday,' said Cleo, stumbling along with chunky-heeled patent boots on.

'How come?' asked Stephen, puffing a bit behind her.

'I've got, like, four kettle bells in here for my PE essay.'

'Why do you have to carry kettle bells to write a PE project?' asked Emily

'Because, derr, I'm going to draw diagrams of them and I want to know what they look like!' Cleo explained to her cousin.

'But why do you have to carry four?' said Emily.

'Em, wise up, coz! They're all different sizes.'

'Yes, but kettle bells all look the same, so you only need one to draw from and then you just draw the next one bigger.'

'Em, for somebody clever you can be very, very obscure.'

'Obtuse,' Emily corrected her.

'Well,' panted Stephen, struggling to keep up with the

girls, 'I went to ask Colette to give us a lift, but I couldn't find her anywhere.'

'Of course you couldn't,' said Emily, 'she's buggered off. So have Paloma and Angela.'

'All right, Inspector Agatha Christie. How do you even know all of this?' asked Cleo.

'I have a very absorbent brain, Cleo,' answered Emily. 'BTW, Agatha Christie was a writer, not a police inspector.'

'She's right,' confirmed Stephen.

'All right, geeks! God, it's like living with a pair of Harvey Weinsteins.'

'What?' said Stephen, genuinely shocked.

'I think Cleo means Albert Einsteins,' said Emily with an eye-roll. 'OK, losers, I'm going to be late for my Latin class. *Valete*, guys. Which means "laters" in Latin.'

She started to jog off, then called as she turned back to them,

'I suppose you could say *"valeters"* actually, that's funny!' and she ran on ahead with her rucksack bumping up and down.

Cleo and Stephen laboured along the lane.

'You're so sweaty, Stephen. Look at your face, even your eyeballs are legit sweating.'

'Well, I don't often get the chance to walk this far, Cleo,' Stephen explained.

'What, the, like, quarter of a mile to school?'

'Yeah, I'm knackered.'

Stephen stopped, completely out of breath.

'Maybe if you just cut down on the Oreo deep-fried sandwiches?' suggested Cleo.

'Maybe if you just cut down on being an interfering dick-weed?' replied Stephen curtly.

Cleo stopped and folded her arms grumpily. Stephen stopped too, glad of the chance to catch his breath.

'You've got no clue about what's going on, have you?' said Stephen.

Cleo thought for a moment.

'We need to stop drinking bubble tea to save the planet?'

'I don't mean like that. I mean us. Our family, Cleo.' Stephen started to walk.

Cleo followed him with a perturbed face.

'What d'you mean?'

'It's going to be one hell of a humdinger of a fan,' said Stephen to his sister, who returned him an empty expression. 'The fan, Cleo, the one that our collective shit is about to hit. Prepare for scattered showers. This is going to get messy.'

Cleo paused to collect her thoughts.

'Can't Mum and Dad just, like, buy a new fan if the other's so shitty?'

There was a large lorry parked up outside the Finsbury Square building, where HNB Capital Management occupied the whole second floor. Burly men in blue boiler suits were carrying out heavy furniture, brass lamps, a skip-load of Victorian art, a ton of computers, and a Downing College Eights rowing oar – Amerjit's, from his Cambridge years. Kerry, loyal to the last and still wearing a crisp grey jacket and pencil skirt, was overseeing the evacuation. She managed to save Amerjit's rowing oar from being tossed into the back of the lorry – she knew how much that oar meant to Amerjit. She didn't notice the Daimler draw up on the other side of the road.

'Here we are, Mr Parker,' said Trevor. 'Shall I drop you off here?'

'I don't know,' said the slumped figure quietly on the back seat. 'I might just stay here for a minute, Trevor.'

Trevor parked up gently and put his hazards on. He sighed.

'Can I ask you a question, Mr Parker?'

'Shoot,' said Frank.

'You remember the two thousand pounds I gave you to invest for me in your fund?'

If truth be told, Frank had totally forgotten about this. Paltry sums of money like that were given to Kerry to deal with, filed away with less important things, like picking up the dry cleaning and remembering to go to school parents' evenings.

There was an awkward pause.

'I do have a vague memory of that, Trev . . . er . . .'

'It's nothing really, it's just that my missis has been cut back to two days a week and the kids are heading for college, so I was wondering, what with the way things are at the moment . . .'

There was a pause. Frank coughed to fill the silence.

'Winds and kites, Trevor. Winds and kites. I'll ask Kerry to look into it for you.'

'I don't want to overload you, Mr Parker, and I'd better chip off anyway. The parkies round here are a nightmare.'

'Yes of course,' said Frank. 'See you later, Trevor?'

There was another pause.

'I've had to take another job, Mr Parker.'

'Another job?' said Frank carefully. 'What, a full-time job?'

'Yes, Mr Parker, what with everything being a bit uncertain . . .'

There was a pause. 'Good for you,' said Frank, finally. 'We've had some good times in this car, haven't we, Trevor?'

'Yes, Mr Parker, we have.'

'Remember when you drove all that way to Frankfurt

to pick me up when the ash cloud hit and none of the planes were flying?'

Trevor chuckled. 'Those bratwurst baguettes on the autobahn were unforgettable.'

There was another silence. Trevor looked at his watch discreetly.

'I mustn't keep you,' said Frank. 'All the best, Trev. I'll phone you when this cash-flow issue resolves itself, and when that dickhead Singh emerges from whatever K hole he's in and Khan finally gets over his numb-nuts bike accident.'

Trevor couldn't look at Frank. 'Yeah, you do that, sir.'

Frank got out of the car and swayed as if he was about to topple over.

'You OK, Mr Parker?' said Trevor, opening his window. 'How are you getting home?'

'Oh, don't you worry about me, Trevor,' said Frank with a jaunty salute. 'I'm Frank Parker, I'm the rock star of the City! Getting home is like Dorothy clicking her red glittery heels together.'

Sally was totally alone at Cedar Vale. Unheard of. Even Kyle was out at some free Psychic meeting in Leatherhead Town Hall. She padded round the kitchen in her socks and tipped some delicious caramel-smelling coffee (Gaysford's Farm Shop, £14.99 a packet) into the cafetiere. The kitchen was looking rather different since Paloma's departure. There was a huge pile of washing-up not only in the sink but surrounding it, and the floor and surfaces were not their usual glistening selves. Sally decided that as soon as her coffee was finished, she would set to. It would be a fun challenge. Lazy, my arse.

As the kettle boiled, she wandered through into the vast

laundry room that Kasia, the laundry lady, had recently vacated with a cursory goodbye.

In the corner of the room stood the industrial washing machine, like a Dalek. It was a top-of-the-range German model, and so hi-tech you needed some kind of qualification from NASA to get it going. Emily did lacrosse, netball and swimming regularly, each with its own affiliated kit, and it was all laid out here in front of Sally on the floor in a big mucky heap, together with Mikey's mud-infested weekend clothes, and a mountain of teenage attire reeking either of Cleo's latest Calvin Klein perfume or Stephen's sweat.

Kasia always managed, like Rumpelstiltskin, to turn this mess of dirty clothes into miraculous piles of cornflower-fresh laundry in her beautifully categorised linen cupboard. It was magic, now Sally thought of it. Sally told herself that she was looking forward to being that magician. It would be *her* motherly hand crisping up everyone's collars and sorting everything into piles. Lazy? Watch this space.

She went back into the kitchen, poured boiling water on to the coffee grains, and gave herself the luxury of sitting and watching the brown liquid swirl, until the granules settled at the bottom. She breathed in the fortifying aroma. As she tucked herself into a Peter Jones armchair in the bay window, cradling hot coffee and looking out over the splash of early autumnal colours, Sally allowed herself a moment of peace.

She breathed deeply. This atmosphere of calm felt exactly like a story she'd read about Poland in 1939 – the end of a hot summer, leaves just on the turn, the calm before the storm. Sally listened. She couldn't hear any heavy artillery in the distance. No sound of soldiers' marching feet. All she could hear was a pair of blackbirds twittering near the ornamental fountain. And there was a dripping sound. She told herself it was nothing, but stood up to try and pinpoint the source. She was suddenly struck by a feeling of wondering if this might be her last moment of peace for a long time.

'Bankrupt, Mikey?'

'Yes, Mrs Kowalska. We're bankrupt.'

'OK,' said her form teacher, slowly taking in this information, 'that's a big word, Michaela. Do you know what it means?'

All eyes were now on Mikey; the entire class was craning round in their chairs.

Mikey explained:

'It means that your source of income, which means the money you earn, cannot match your outgoings. That's the money that you spend. It basically means you're fu—'

'THANK YOU, Mikey,' Mrs Kowalska interrupted Mikey just in time as the class exploded into shrieks of laughter. 'Class! CLASS!' said Mrs Kowalska, raising her voice and clapping her hands to try and control the twenty eleven year olds who were suddenly behaving as if they were on day release. 'Michaela PARKER! We do NOT use that kind of language in this classroom! I would like you to stand outside in the corridor until the bell goes. Do you understand?'

'Yes, Mrs Kowalska,' grinned Mikey, pleased to get the whole room's undivided attention.

'Hey, Mikey,' said one of the pupils nearest to the door as she walked past, 'is it really true then, that your dad's gone bankrupt?'

'Yup,' Mikey responded casually, 'we're fucked.'

Frank stood behind a tree in the middle of Finsbury Square and watched Kerry, still upholding impeccable standards of calm, marshalling the removal guys. Frank knew that he should cross the road and give her some moral support; as her boss, that was the least he should do. But he was overwhelmed with the desperate need to lie down.

A light drizzle came down, freshening up his grizzly face for a moment. There was an alleyway behind him which he slipped into. He laid out his coat and slumped on it with his back up against a wheelie bin. He loosened his tie right off, undid the top button on his trousers and fished for his phone. He pulled out an unfamiliar envelope as he did so. He couldn't remember for the life of him what it was. It was very crumpled and his name was written in spidery writing on the front. Bronwen. That was it. He didn't have the energy to open it right away; he had more important things to do.

He dialled Dr Livesy's private number, and, as had happened every day for the last couple of days, the ringtone was a longish, single beep rather than the usual two; a sure-fire sign that Dr Livesy was living it up somewhere in Europe. Tuscany for the grappa tasting? Cannes for some late sunshine? Maybe further afield, in a spa in the Atlas Mountains having his corns shaved off by Berber tribesmen?

'Bollocks,' muttered Frank.

Then he dialled Amerjit's number, which of course went straight to voicemail.

'Ammers, you tosser. I'm sitting here watching our livelihood being loaded up into a lorry. When you're finally out of your straitjacket and Nurse Ratched's given you your medication, can you kindly call me? We're fucked, Amerjit, we need to make plans. Oh. And are you all right, mate? I hope you're all right.'

Frank hung up and closed his eyelids, which felt blissful over hot and aching eyeballs. He let everything drift for a few moments, the traffic, the clicking of city workers' heels marching by, the insistent 'vehicle . . . reversing . . . vehicle . . . reversing . . .' from a nearby lorry. And then he heard a light metallic chink as something hit the floor beside him.

He opened his eyes slowly to see a fifty pence piece that somebody had thrown down for him; for the sad bearded man with the terrible eyebags, slumped in an alley wearing a suit too big for him. Poor guy. The City was awash with this type of flotsam and jetsam.

Frank picked up the coin and turned it over in his fingers. A single, hot tear appeared in the corner of his eye before it squeezed out and rolled slowly down his cheek.

The drizzle turned to rain. It was starting to splash gently on his Church's £550 loafers.

'Fifty pence, love,' said the dinner lady as Stephen held out a chocolate bar towards her. Somebody punched him in the back and Stephen was pushed forward towards the cash register.

'Oi, Weightwatchers, is it true your dad's bankrupt?' said a loutish boy in a school hoodie emblazoned with 'St Bede's Rugby Trip South Africa'.

Stephen collected himself and his chocolate bar.

'Yeah, maybe,' he said flatly.

'Well, you better go easy on your spending, then!' said the lad, much to the mirth of his two companions who laughed loudly. 'You sure you can afford that chocolate? If you can't, it might help you shed some of this!' with which he punched Stephen hard in the stomach, and the three of them laughed again and left him.

Stephen unpeeled the wrapper off the chocolate bar and stuffed it all into his mouth at once.

*

Sally stood stock-still in the kitchen as the drip of water splashed on and on. To a military beat. Onwards. Insistent. It was marching into her brain. Her heart was picking up pace. She could feel the anxiety starting its familiar journey up her body. On and on it dripped, this water torture. Where was it? Where was Frank? How the hell was she going to stop that dripping noise?

Then she heard the distant rumble of a large-sounding vehicle bearing up the drive towards her. Somebody must have forgotten to shut the electric gates behind them this morning. Probably Kyle. Dickhead. And her heart beat on. And the drip dripped on. Her hand trembled slightly as she put down her cup on to the marble worktop. She had to breathe through this. Whatever it was coming up the drive, she had to carry on breathing and put one foot in front of the other. Survive, Sally, survive. Breathe and walk.

The 1812 Overture sounded just as her mobile phone buzzed. A message from Frank. She had no time to respond, because a bunch of guys in black monkey boots, black army trousers and black sweatshirts were on the front doorstep. They looked like a small private army. Mercenaries. Maybe world war had been declared this morning but she just hadn't heard about it. She put on her best Surrey smile.

'Can I help you, gentlemen?'

'Mrs Parker?' Sally nodded. 'We're from house clearance?' said the man, holding out some paperwork for her to look at.

Sally took stock, and then said smoothly:

'Ah yes. House clearance. We've been expecting you. Would anyone like a cup of tea?'

In Leatherhead Town Hall, Kyle Parker was having a lovely time at the free Psychic meeting. There was a pretty housewife in jeans and tight jumper, around forty years old, who was definitely giving him the eye. Kyle returned it with one eyebrow quizzically raised; in his head he looked like James Bond as he did this. He was looking forward to the tea and biscuit break so that he could engage her in conversation.

A motley group of around thirty sat and listened to Mrs Ranathsinghe, who'd come over from Guildford to enlighten them with her messages from the Spirit World. Dressed almost exclusively in purple, Mrs Ranathsinghe cut an almost imperial figure among the Leatherhead folk, who were readying themselves for another lot of messages from the other side.

Mrs Ranathsinghe sniffed deeply and closed her eyes.

'This one's coming through quite strongly,' she announced. 'I've got a message for a Kylie. Kylie. Have we got a Kylie in amongst us today?'

Kyle looked around him. Nobody was forthcoming, so he spoke up.

'That might be me. Who wants to know? It's not the Inland Revenue, is it?'

There were a couple of little titters from the gathering, including the lady in the tight jumper.

'Are you Kylie?' Mrs Ranathsinghe asked in a dramatically deep voice.

'Not last time I looked!' quipped Kyle. 'I don't *think* I've been out on a world tour recently singing my greatest hits in gold hot pants! But I'm prepared to try anything once! My name's Kyle.'

Tight Jumper gave him a full, toothy smile and Kyle noticed that she had rather gratifying dimples too.

'Kyle. Kyle,' said Mrs Ranathsinghe slowly, 'I'm getting something very strongly through for Kyle.'

'That's my name, Mrs R. Don't wear it out!'

'Is anybody there? Is anybody there?' said Mrs Ranathsinghe enigmatically, extending both arms towards the void. 'Speak to me. Your vessel Kyle awaits you. Speak!'

Kyle began to feel little prickles on the back of his neck. Then he realised it might be his poncho. Whatever, this Mrs Ranathsinghe was very good at creating an atmosphere.

There was a dramatic silence, except for Mrs Ranathsinghe muttering and raising her closed eyes occasionally up to the ceiling. Then she opened them.

'Kyle, I'm hearing from a Jim. Or John. Or Julie.'

'Julia?' asked Kyle.

'Yes, Julia,' confirmed Mrs Ranathsinghe.

Kyle said almost immediately,

'My mum's called Julia.'

'Julia is saying to Kyle, "Don't worry Kyle. Everything will be all right. Let me help you, Kyle. I want to help you."'

Anyone with a bit more experience of the psychic world might have spotted that these messages from beyond were somewhat over-generalised. What really got the goose bumps up at this type of meeting were very specific levels of detail. The 'Uncle David says the 1987 lawnmower is in the topaz-blue shed' or 'Daphne's pearl and sapphire ring will be found under Clacton Pier' kinds of messages. But to Kyle, a novice, this was exhilarating. A message from Julia saying that she wanted to help him, and that everything was all right! Tight Jumper looked over to him with a combination of friendly support and admiration. Kyle gave her the James Bond eyebrow again.

'Have you anything to say, Kylie?' said Mrs Ranathsinghe.

'Kyle. Well, well. I don't know how she found me here. For a dude whose address is simply "Planet Earth", I feel very connected by that. Wow. Thank you. And thank you to my mum!'

Mrs Ranathsinghe nodded indulgently.

'I'm pleased for you, Kyle. It's always comforting when a spirit friend can pass over with positive news.'

Mrs Ranathsinghe closed her eyes again, about to move on to another message, when Kyle piped up again,

'But my mum's still alive. She runs a bar in Tenerife, in Los Cristianos. Does that work, I mean, does it have to be a dead person sending through messages?'

Frank had made it as far as the entrance to Liverpool Street station on his shambling feet, but the weariness was biting into his bones now. Why wasn't Sally answering his calls? He was desperate for her to come into London and pick him up. He was ill, for God's sake. He needed his bed. He checked his pockets. He had a tenner. He searched around for a credit card in his pockets but found nothing. He simply wasn't used to leaving the house with any means of payment on him; Trevor was his transport and his ATM, Trevor took him everywhere. Trevor would have picked him up from Jupiter if Frank had asked him.

Would ten pounds get him to Victoria Station in a cab to get the train back to Leatherhead? But then how would he pay for his train ticket if he spaffed it all on a cab? Maybe he should just get a cab back to Cedar Vale and then hope that somebody could pick up the tab? He always kept a few grand stashed at the bottom of an Italian vase on the hall sideboard. All good. This cash-flow problem was going to be fine, as soon as he and Ammers got themselves back on their stupid middle-aged feet. They'd go to a nice spa together, the two of them, do a healthy juicing program for three days to get their nutrients up, then they'd talk tactics. HNB Capital Management would be up and running again in no time, and they'd be able to laugh at all this as the jacuzzi bubbles tickled their balls.

Frank entered the main concourse of Liverpool Street and looked at the clock. Just before two p.m. Frank was amazed. He hadn't been inside a London station for ages; when had it all got so busy? There were literally people everywhere; it was utterly enthralling and exhausting. He rubbed his eyes and looked for an Underground sign. He needed a little sit-down on a bench first. Just to fill up the sleep coffers to be sure of having enough energy to get home. He sank down beside the ticket machine, looked up at the orange neon boards with names like Manningtree and Norwich, and felt himself glazing over. He'd just have a quick ten winks and then he'd be on his way.

'Would anyone like another cuppa and a biscuit?' said Sally with a lump in her throat. It had been lodged there all day.

'Don't mind if I do. Phew. You've got a lot of gear, here, Mrs Parker,' said the chief house-clearance guy.

'You don't have to take away everything, do you?' Sally asked.

'We'll take the luxury goods, the expensive-looking stuff, and then it's up to you to talk to the landlord about everything else.'

'So does our landlord get to keep all this nice stuff?' asked Sally.

'Nah, this goes to the Revenue.'

'Aah,' said Sally, pretending to understand, 'so, you'll leave us our bed, then, will you?' she said, trying to raise a smile.

'It's handcrafted, so it's classed as a luxury item, I'm afraid.'

Sally dropped both arms by her sides, limply.

'What will we sleep on?'

The man in black shrugged.

Sally's thoughts were interrupted by the 1812 Overture, followed by her children. At which precise moment a removal man passed by with an Xbox.

'No!' wailed Stephen. 'No! No, you can't! I'm on Level Eight – I've built an entire world! Those machines are my life!'

'Say goodbye to your life, Ste,' said Cleo, laughing, before she spotted her own laptop, hair straighteners and exercise bike trooping down the stairs.

'No! No! I'm not going to lie, I can't live without my straighteners!'

'Muuuum,' Sally could hear Mikey somewhere beyond the kitchen. 'I think the washing machine's leaking. There's a massive pool of water in here. Quick! Come!'

'Er . . . just a moment, Mikey. Oh Stephen, love, I'm sorry about your Xbox—' Sally was cut short by Emily, who thrust a slip of paper under her aunt's nose.

'You probably don't want another bill right now, Sally, but this is the invoice for the Vienna music trip?'

'Oh. Great, Em. That's . . . er . . . wonderful, love.'

'Also, I've been thinking, Sally. I really need to talk to you. I think I need to leave this family. To go and find my mother. I'm questioning my existence every minute of the day. It might just be the Camus, but I think it's more than that. I need my mum, Sally, I mean you're great and everything but . . .'

Sally felt like she was about to faint.

'Maybe this isn't quite the right time, Em. Let's find a moment to sit down and—'

The 1812 Overture blared again and in trouped Janice Dawes with the seven Von Yapps, all barking loudly at the sight of these strange men in black turning the house upside down. Liesl was so distressed she started to poo. This was becoming a living cack-ophony.

'Oh heck,' said Janice Dawes, 'I'll clear that up.' She clocked Sally's unusually scruffy appearance and watched as her delicate little face crumpled. For Janice it was an intimate moment of stillness between them.

'Sally, are you OK? Can I do anything for you?'

Sally gave her a look of pure helplessness. Only to be interrupted once again by the 1812. This time it was Kyle, bounding in like yet another big family pet.

'What's going on here?' he said, approaching one of the removal guys. 'Hey man, don't touch my guitar. And my bong. That was gifted to me by an elder in the Chilean borderlands, and it's supposed to have special powers.'

One of the removal men took the two large Italian vases off the Serbian sideboard and was making off with them, like an abduction.

Everywhere Sally looked there were people speaking loudly, demanding things of her, teenagers complaining, Emily looking at her with an expression of exasperation, water leaking, dogs barking or pooing, burly men taking away her prized possessions. The only island of comfort in this madness was the reassuring figure of Janice Dawes who stood in the middle of it all, unflappable in a pea-green body warmer.

'You can do something for me, actually, Janice,' said Sally. 'Can you hold the fort until Frank gets home? There's food in the fridge. Kyle can help. I need to go. I really need to just . . . go.'

Sally grabbed her Burberry handbag, still on its heavy brass hook (Graham & Green, £26.95) by the front door. And she was gone.

14

Amerjit was really getting used to the idea, relishing it even, that it was very important to resolve his own issues before he could even entertain the thought of helping others. He reclined fulsomely in a heap of the plumpest pillows you could find this side of The Ritz. He was starting to sleep really well in The Chantry. The mattress was memory foam and the duvet just the right tog. Room temperature was also perfectly judged; the view from the window serene and unintrusive. Lush, rolling lawns with surrounding woodland in the foreground, and gentle Surrey fields in the distance. The room was uncluttered with possessions, apart from a book, *Just the Way I Am,* borrowed from the honesty shelf downstairs. Next on Amerjit's reading list was a new publication that had got the chattering classes aflutter – *Women Are Also from Mars* – which looked very interesting.

He was relishing the simplicity of his new life. No phone, no stressful accoutrements such as an overfilled sponge bag; just a simple bar of soap, toothpaste and white toothbrush were provided. Best of all, he had no artery-furring job to go to every waking hour of the day. All he had to think about were his therapy sessions, getting lots of kip, and eating regular, nutritious meals. It cost £4,900 a week to be here, all inclusive. Amerjit did some quick mental calculations and worked out that he could probably stay here for the next eleven years. It was tempting.

There was a very light tapping sound; even the door knocking was Zen here. A nurse with a gentle Scandinavian face popped her head round. She was uncluttered too; no distracting jewellery or eye make-up; everything about her was calm and calibrated.

'Morning, Mr Singh, nothing to worry about. Just to say that your mum and dad have promised to settle up for your stay at The Chantry, and they'll also be here to collect you when your treatment finishes. What supportive parents!'

And she closed the door with a smile.

'Nothing to worry about,' Amerjit repeated these words back to himself. He could feel an imaginary shirt collar tightening around his neck. Nothing to worry about? Why were they going to pay his Chantry bill? Why were they coming to collect him? How much did they know? He sat up erect in the bed and did some breathing exercises Roland had shown them on Day One. He was determined to make the most of the next four days, the next ninety-six hours were his everything. Ninety-six hours? He felt his heart begin to pound . . . and release the shoulders . . . let the belly grow . . . and breathe . . .

Sally also woke up in an uncluttered room with only the skittering of mice under the floorboards for company, banished to the eaves of Randwyck Manor, where in bygone days servants would have been housed. It felt to her as if the temperature were below freezing, surely impossible in an unseasonably mild late September?

She checked her phone but it must have died sometime last night and she'd forgotten her charger. She'd slept fitfully under a sheet that was browning at the edges and a moth-eaten paisley eiderdown. Her mother had insisted that she borrow a night-dress and gave her the ugliest in her collection, a green thing with cap sleeves and a stain around the hem. Sally was glad to get out of it.

She hopped from foot to foot in the icy room, turning yesterday's pants inside out; she hadn't planned to stay the night. All she wanted was to ask her brother a favour and then go. She'd phoned him and, of course, Miles was out on the town somewhere in Guildford and wouldn't be back at Randwyck till midnight.

Sally had waited in a pub car park round the corner from Randwyck Manor until she knew it was her mother's bedtime. Lucinda retired to bed early these days, around eight thirty. Sally timed it to perfection; she only wanted to spend ten minutes in Lucinda's company, maximum.

After an awkward encounter, during which her mother managed to mention Frank and Sally's loan for the Randwyck refurb twice, Sally was left huddled by the blow heater in the kitchen, awaiting the return of the ever-prodigal son. Miles never came home.

This morning, as Sally made her way down to breakfast, she could hear a far-off radio crackling. There was the sound of a crow squawking out on balding grass that had once been a croquet lawn. Sally looked up at the sombre stained-glass window, filling the hall with a lugubrious pond-coloured light. Randwyck Manor was hideous and uninhabitable; despite this, Sally knew that her mother wanted to reinvent herself as 'the lady of the Manor'. It mattered not that the place was crumbling around her ears and stinking of mouse wee, every one of its foundations and timbers corroding with damp or dry-rot, Lucinda still had the satisfaction of looking at the map and seeing it written there: 'Randwyck Manor'. It was a place of historical significance; some minor baron had parked a mistress there back in the nineteenth century, and these things mattered.

Sally went through to the back kitchen and felt the 1970s lino sticky under her feet. Everything was as it had been when she'd first met Frank here all those years ago. Except dirtier. There was an overpowering odour coming from the pantry, partly savoury, rotting and meaty, but then mixed with something very sweet, like Turkish delight or cheap bubble bath. Sally had to pull her sweat-shirt subtly over her nose.

Lucinda was there, top to toe in tweed jacket and trousers, with a rabbit fur coat on top. Radio 4 was on at full volume, so Sally crept in unseen. Her mother still had good bone structure but was starting to stoop around the shoulders; a dowager's hump, they call it. Lucinda insisted on wearing a string of pearls and lipstick every day, to be on standby if the bishop or any local dignitary dropped by. In reality, the only people that came to Randwyck Manor were the postman, the Jehovah's lot (only the once after Lucinda told them to 'eff orf back to Mumbo-Jumbo land'), and the vicar to say his annual 'Happy Christmas'. Oh, and a twice-weekly visit from Miles's drug dealer, a girl called Rizla who lived in Ashtead.

Her mother wore a vivid orange lipstick, and only ever hit a seventy-five per cent success rate with the colouring in. The bottom lip looked a lot fuller than the top, giving Lucinda the air of a ventriloquist's dummy. She'd also drawn in some thin eyebrows in what looked like mauve pencil. The whole effect was alarming, and that was only the side view. Her mother was ferrying a boiled egg from pan to sink, like the slowest egg and spoon race ever run.

Sally had an almost pathological desire to scream with laughter. She held it in by clenching her pelvic floor muscles, which in turn made her release a loud piggy snort. Her mother turned round and gave Sally the benefit of the make-up full frontal. She looked her daughter up and down out of those cold Wedgwood-blue eyes.

'Why are *you* here?' was her morning greeting.

'Er . . . morning,' said Sally, trying to sound upbeat. 'Do you want me to help you with that egg?'

'I'm perfectly capable of boiling an egg. You look dog-tired.'

She loved to say this to Sally. She knew it never failed to deflate her sails.

'Do I? It's probably something to do with our situation at home. Frank's not very well and—'

'My distant cousin Clarissa was a Mostyn-Owen, did you know that?' said Lucinda. 'She threw it all away by marrying that rich scoundrel who was related to whatsis-name who was caught up with that slut Christine Keeler.'

Lucinda placed her egg into the chipped egg cup and sat down painstakingly. She stared at her daughter.

'Tell me,' she asked again. 'Why are you here?'

Sally didn't know what to say. She scanned the shambolic kitchen for some form of distraction.

'I'll put the kettle on.'

Lucinda began to peel the shell of her boiled egg with gnarly arthritic fingers.

'Where's your husband?' she demanded.

'He's not well, Mother. He's been diagnosed with narcolepsy.'

Lucinda looked up from her egg sharply.

'Sounds like he needs a good kick up the backside. Narcolepsy indeed. Why does everything have to be given a label these days? In the old days he'd have been told to shut up and join the army.'

It hurt to admit it, but there was a part of Sally that was actually tending to agree with her mother. Not the army part, but the kicking up the backside part. She was sure that what Frank was suffering from was psychological, some sort of stress block, and it was frustrating beyond belief to watch him, day in and day out, just falling asleep all the time.

They were interrupted by the arrival, eight hours late, of Miles. 'Well, well, here comes the cavalry!' he said to Sally with a night-on-the-tiles croak in his voice. 'Have you come to check out your investment, Sags? Where's your layabout husband? Licking his wounds in some City skin-bar, no doubt.'

Lucinda looked at her son and her eyes softened with unadulterated devotion.

'Would you like a boiled egg, darling? Sally can very easily do you one. You need some breakfast, a big growing boy like you with your hollow legs.'

'I'm all right, Ma,' said Miles, kissing his mother on the top of her head. 'Don't want to unleash last night's vodka back into the system – might wait a tad before I introduce any solids into the mix. Make us a coffee, will you, Sags?'

Here they were, in their forties with their mother over eighty, and it was as if they were children again, slipping into the same roles that they'd always been destined to play. The only thing missing was their elder sister, Nancy.

Sally sighed and put some no-frills instant coffee into a chipped Doulton cup, rinsing a greasy teaspoon on the way. She battled with the door of the 1970s fridge to be greeted by one stick of floppy celery, a half-drunk bottle of Tesco's own vodka and a bowl containing some solidified sausage fat. Coffee in hand, Miles straightened up his posture and assumed a languid lairdly air.

'Come on, sis,' he said, 'don't you want to see where all your husband's ill-gotten gains are going to be invested?'

Back at Cedar Vale and Frank was finding it physically hard to get up from his camping mattress, which now occupied the floor of the marital suite. With the carved Lebanese cedar bookshelves carted away, piles of stuff filled the room, including, to Frank's horror, Sally's bloody bichon frise nestled on a pile of jumpers. He could hear the wailing of a loud 'Fraaaaaaaaaaaank!' on repeat, from downstairs, so after enduring about thirty seconds of it he thought he'd better get up. He reflected that last night was the first time in about twenty years that he and Sally had spent a night apart. He had a sudden pang for her. Her phone was still going straight to answerphone every time he tried it. He needed to see her, sit down with her, reassure her with a big hug, tuck her hair behind her ear and have a laugh about this bizarre mess they were in.

'Well, take your time, Frank! There are some builders at the door,' said Emily, looking at him deadpan, 'the guys from the Charity Ball.'

Frank gave her a curt look and loped towards the door.

'Morning, guys,' said Frank through his beard, 'excuse my relaxed attire. You have the look that says we owe you some dosh, am I right?'

'Half up-front, half on completion. Four thousand, six hundred pounds and thirty-four British pence,' said Piotr.

'Great. Absolutely great. Er . . . just a sec. I can get that for you right now from my special bank,' and Frank turned to the place where the large Italian vases had always sat, on the Serbian sideboard. Which wasn't there any more.

There was a short silence.

'Ah,' said Frank. 'Kids, have you seen what's happened to those large vases?'

All four were shambling around the hall looking directionless.

'I'm not going to lie to you, Dad, I've totally lost my laptop right now,' whined Cleo.

'I've lost my entire social life. Dad, I need my devices back. Are you serious that we have to walk to school AGAIN?' moaned Stephen.

'I think the vases were taken with everything else, Dad,' said Mikey, 'but I can help you out—'

Frank turned to the builders.

'Right. I've got a few cash-flow issues at the moment. How about I cut you a deal? Would you like to take five grand's worth of goods from the house? Everyone else is,' he added, with a gesture of largesse around the hallway.

Piotr looked interested.

'I prefer cash. But OK, we can talk.'

'I'll give you a John Deere lawnmower, probably worth about six grand new, pristine condition, how about that?'

'There are only a few lawnmowers left, Dad,' said Mikey, tugging at her dad's sleeve, 'and the removal guys are coming back for more.'

'And this is my accountant,' Frank continued. 'She's very persistent. The lawnmowers are in the largest of the garages, Piotr. Be my guest, fleece me of my most prized possession!'

Piotr went off in search of booty, leaving Frank with his arms hanging limply at his sides.

Mikey looked up at her dad. Her big squirrel eyes were full of worry.

'And that,' Frank said to her, 'is how you conduct business. Swiftly, no nonsense. Give them no room to question.'

Mikey tried to give her dad an encouraging smile.

'Frank, all of my sports kits are filthy and I'll stink,' announced Emily, 'and that pool of water by the washing machine's getting bigger every day.'

'You'll just have to wear a dirty kit today, Emily. Spray the armpits with something, nobody'll notice.'

'Are you actually serious?'

'Yes, Emily. I've got more important things to worry about right now than your personal hygiene.'

At which point Kyle came out of the kitchen, dressed in nothing but Y-fronts and apron, holding a very smoky frying pan.

'Anyone for more Colombian fritters?' he asked jovially. 'I can easily defrost more prawns.'

'I'm not going to lie, Uncle Kyle, I've only just eaten them but I think I'm about to evacuate my vowels,' said Cleo, clutching her stomach.

'Or your bowels, maybe, Cleo?' asked Emily wryly.

'Probably both,' said Cleo seriously.

'Frank, this is getting ridiculous,' said Emily, planting herself directly in front of her uncle. 'I had to do my homework lying on the floor last night because I had neither desk nor chair to work with. I slept on a wafer-thin mattress, there's no Wi-Fi and I haven't eaten a single vegetable for two days.'

'Kyle's Colombian fritters had a tin of sweetcorn in them,' Mikey corrected her.

Emily continued, 'And to add insult to injury, I now have to wear a sports kit that honks. We can't go on like this, Frank, this is akin to child abuse.'

Frank stared at his niece. Emily stared back at him. Uncle and niece, both stubborn as mules, with jaws set at each other. Stephen, Cleo and Mikey looked on, disconcerted as to how this would turn out. Frank broke the deadlock by throwing back his head and laughing. He laughed and laughed and tottered around on the empty marble chessboard floor. He wiped his eyes he was laughing so much. The rest of the family looked at each other and then started to laugh uncertainly; Frank's laughter was catching. Even Emily couldn't resist a chuckle.

'You!' managed Frank, through gales of wheezing. He pointed at his niece. 'You are the absolute enth degree, you are. You geek, always getting the right fricking la-di-da answer when my own children are stumbling about in the dark of their own dumbness. You! You're too clever for us by half, Emily, this must be a living HELL for you. This philistine family, with our unsophisticated ways and lack of washing machine. I'm sorry if this is all beneath you, Emily, I really am, I'm sorry if we don't have conversations at the dinner table about Plutarch and the films of . . . that Italian bloke—'

'Bruno Tonioli?' suggested Cleo.

'Oh Christ, CLEO!' shouted Frank, covering both eyes with his hands and staggering away from his family.

'What?' said Cleo, looking around at everybody. 'He's Italian, isn't he?'

Frank stood a few feet away and howled into the emptiness of the hall. Kyle, still holding the frying pan, stood motionless. Nobody said a word as they let Frank's howl subside. Nobody was laughing now. Emily looked perturbed.

Stephen was the first to speak.

'You can't speak to Emily like that, Dad, it's too much.'

'I agree,' said Mikey, close to tears.

'And that thing you said about the dumb of our darkness.'

'The dark of your dumbness, Cleo,' said Frank in a whisper.

'Whatever,' said Cleo, 'that thing you said is literally hashtag thingy. You could actually get arrested for that.'

'D'you know what, Cleo?' said Frank with eyes glittering dangerously at her. 'I'd love to get arrested at this point in time. I'd rather be locked up in a prison than stuck here with this nightmare. Somebody for God's sake get me out of here!'

'You and me both,' said Emily quietly. 'I wish you'd never taken me in; I'll always be an outsider.'

Stephen, Cleo and Mikey rushed to their cousin and hugged her silently as tears started to trickle down Emily's face.

Frank put his hands in his pockets. He didn't know where to look. He was so tired all he wanted to do was curl to the floor and shut them all out with sleep.

'See what you've done now, Dad?' said Stephen accusingly.

'Yes, Dad. You've ruined her mascara,' said Cleo angrily, 'and Emily always applies mascara faultlessly. It's one of her best skills.'

'I think you'd better say sorry, Dad,' said Mikey, barely audible.

All of the children turned to Frank. He blinked. He could feel his authority slipping from underneath him like quicksand. He didn't utter a single word, but stood, blinking, his hands in his pockets.

Kyle tried to reach for metaphorical oil to sluice on to troubled waters.

'Hey, dudes, that's some kind of nuke-strength chat right there. And you're plucking out some pretty vicious arrows from your quivers. Why don't we all sit around a bong together, sing us some Andean riffs, and just chillax for a while, yeah?'

'I'm eleven, Uncle Kyle,' said Mikey. 'I don't think it's legal for me to smoke a bong.'

'I'm fifteen, Kyle,' added Stephen, 'and I think I'm right in saying that bongs went out in the 1980s?'

'They actually didn't,' said Cleo, 'you still get them on Big Ben. Ten bongs when it's ten o'clock, nine bongs when it's nine o'clock, seven bongs when it's—'

Stephen turned gently to his cousin. 'Come on, Em, let's go.'

And he ushered her away, with Cleo and Mikey following, not one of them able to look Frank in the eye.

Mikey turned back to Frank and gave him a mournful look.

'Do you know when Mum's coming home?' she asked.

'No. I don't,' he replied.

'OK,' said Mikey, turning to follow the others with lowered head.

Frank sat down clumsily on his human-sized chessboard and leaned up against the one lone pawn which the house clearance men hadn't taken.

Kyle crouched down beside him.

'Is it stalemate, Frank?' he said, proud of his analogy. 'Or has the old queen still got some moves?'

'Oh fuck off, Kyle. Go and spout your bullshit to somebody who gives a fuck.'

'I'm only trying to reach out to you, bro.'

'Yeah? Well I'd rather you reached out, Kyle, and got me my multi-million-pound business back.'

Frank's mobile phone chirruped and he picked up angrily. 'Frank Parker speaking, and I need a kerjillion pounds, have you got it?' Frank was stopped in his tracks. 'It's the bank,' he mouthed to Kyle. He then listened intently for several minutes, during which time Kyle picked at the remains of the Colombian fritters in a desultory manner.

Frank hung up.

'Well?' Kyle asked brightly. 'Can our capitalist bastard friends lend you a helping hand?'

Frank laughed bitterly.

'They've turned off the taps. Foreclosed. Everything. No more cash. Nothing. Shit.'

Miles led Sally through two chilly reception rooms where stuffed birds in glass cases and armchairs spewing out their insides were on display. Sally had a musky dampness in her nostrils – she looked in vain for a corner of comfort in this grim house. A pile of old medical equipment was stacked up in a corner and she recognised her poor old dad's rusting hoist. The grand fireplace housed no logs, just a cheap electric bar heater. The jumble of commodes, walking frames and elephant's foot full of umbrella corpses made it feel like a room of the dead.

'Welcome to my humble abode, Sags,' said Miles as he pushed open a creaking door leading off the main drawing room. Sally walked into what looked like a student hovel. DJ decks sat on a tatty Victorian dresser, normal lightbulbs had been changed for red ones, giving the room an eerie bordello glow, and the smell of Miles's unmade hamster-cage bed could not be masked by the plethora of joss sticks placed around it. Sally's stomach lurched a little as she spotted an extra-large box of condoms placed casually by the bed on top of an outdated copy of the *Yellow Pages*.

'So,' said Miles, 'my cunning plan is basically to turn this whole wing of the Manor into Surrey's first Trance Palace.'

'And does Surrey want a Trance Palace?' asked his sister.

'It *needs* a Trance Palace,' said Miles confidently. 'You've got your white stiletto brigade falling out of Barbarella's every Saturday night, and the only decent festival round here is Dorking Calling, which is yawnsville indie and doesn't even have camping. Randwyck could low-key be an omni-weather, first-class, premier rave site. People will legit come here from miles away.'

And with that he slithered to his decks and flicked several switches until the room was filled with techno. Miles did his signature dance move; it was his only dance move, and it involved him making a small box with both of his hands. He'd been wowing the raves of Britain with this dance move since 1989.

'And how does Mother feel about Randwyck being turned into a Trance Palace, Miles?' shouted Sally over the techno.

'Haven't squared it with the mothership yet, but she'll be cool. I'll give her some ear defenders,' he yelled, 'or she can join in. Be good to see her Jaeger headscarf bobbing along to the latest mash-up! Ha ha! The Jaeger-Bomb, that's what we'll call her, brilliant!'

Sally did not respond to this Class A quip.

'And what about Frank? Has he been in touch about the finances, Miles?'

'We had a man-to-man, Sags, yes. He thinks the business plan has legs.'

'Just a shame *he* doesn't,' said Sally, shouting more loudly.

'What?' said Miles, turning the techno down.

Sally breathed in and looked her brother squarely in the eye.

'Frank possesses neither legs nor anything else of use to him at the moment, Miles. He's lost everything. We're flat broke.'

Miles turned the music off altogether.

A crow squawked on the back lawn.

'Shit,' said Miles blankly.

'We're about to be kicked out of Cedar Vale, Miles. Which is why I'm here. To ask you a favour. Would you mind if we could come and . . . just camp here or something? Till we get back on our feet?'

Miles reached for his stash. He started to skin up a joint.

'Shit, Sags. This is terrible . . .'

'I know, Miles,' said Sally, relieved to be able to open her heart out to her brother. 'I feel like we're about to jump off a precipice, there's no safety net, and we're about to—'

Miles cut her off as he sat down with a jolt.

'This has absolutely fucked me up, Sally. How else am I going to get the money for the Trance Palace now? Fucksake, Frank promised me . . .'

At this moment their mother, still wearing her moth-eaten fur coat, tottered into the room. She looked at both of them. Miles gave his mother 'little boy lost' eyes.

'Miles, you look upset, darling. What have you said to him, Sally?'

'Frank's lost all his money,' Miles chipped in. 'No Randwyck refurb, Madre.'

Lucinda narrowed her eyes at her daughter, and proceeded to give her the once over, icily.

'When you married that boy, I always knew you'd come to nothing, Sally.'

Sally looked at her feet. She'd been here so many times before.

'Bit harsh, Ma?' said Miles, lighting up his second joint of the day.

Sally needed to leave the room; the smell of Miles's weed was starting to make her feel sick. She drew back her shoulder muscles and clenched her fists slightly. She took a deep breath and looked up from the floor to meet her mother's stare.

'You say I've come to nothing. That may be so, but at least I get to wake up every morning with the knowledge that I am not you.'

A shadow seemed to pass over Lucinda's face. Sally had not finished.

'At least I have many years ahead of me in which I can try to be something, Mother, rather than dying a slow damp death in a crumbling shithole with an emotionally retarded balding man-child of a son.'

The joint in Miles's mouth stuck to his bottom lip as he looked at his sister, open-mouthed.

'It's good that you've got each other,' Sally said, looking from mother to brother, 'because you lost Nancy ages ago, and now you have lost me. Again. Goodbye, Mother. Good luck with your Trance Palace, Miles.'

Lucinda turned to her son. 'Trance Palace, Miles?'

Sally turned on her heel and left the chilly room, and Randwyck Manor, for the last time.

Frank had stayed on the chessboard for most of the morning. Kyle was kind enough to place a cushion under his brother's head when he began complaining of aching joints and disturbed vision.

'Hey, bro, d'you want the quacks to check you out? Shall I drive you to the krankenhaus?'

'Call me an ambulance, Kyle. Can you stay here and hold the fort? Feed the kids, manage the house? Whatever I've got is getting worse. I need some proper medical care. Where's Sally, for God's sake? I've been leaving messages for her since yesterday evening,' he said with real despair in his voice.

Kyle patted his brother's arm consolingly.

'Franko, sometimes the ladies need their space. She'll come home when her waters tell her to.'

'Talking of which, there's a fricking flood back there, Kyle. You'll have to get hold of an emergency plumber.'

Kyle nodded sagely.

'I've seen worse floods on the plains of Ecuador, bud. I've got this.'

Sally was in need of windscreen wipers for her eyes, as she cried all the way round the M25. She swerved the Leatherhead junction completely and headed towards Gatwick airport. Her mind was made up. For all her bold words to her mother, she had come to nothing and she didn't want to pass on a fat lot of nothing to her children. It was best for them if she made a clean break. Got out of their lives. Her sister had done it. Why shouldn't she? Her face was a sodden mess but her mind was strangely crisp and clear. She'd left her pack of Valium back at Cedar Vale yesterday evening, so was running a pretty clear system. Maybe that's why she couldn't stop crying. Reality was starting to present itself in a very uncompromising way.

She turned into the airport and parked the Range Rover valiantly but badly in the Long-Stay Car Park. She was intending to be away for at least a few weeks, maybe for ever. She thought of her sister Nancy. She had so many questions to ask her. Nancy had escaped Randwyck Manor at the tender age of fifteen. And got all the way to Rome! That was pretty impressive, now Sally thought of it.

She marched into the North Terminal and scanned the departure boards. She'd put her passport in her handbag for safekeeping when the house clearance guys had shown up. Amsterdam? Too close. Delhi? She'd probably need a visa for that. Moscow? She didn't have the right cold-weather gear. Palermo. Quite close to Rome. Sally had never been to Sicily. She had a smattering of Italian. Bingo. She'd go and make a new life in Sicily. She looked in her purse. She had about forty quid in cash. She checked her face in her compact mirror. Tiny eyes and big swollen lids greeted her, but there was a look of something new. Was it defiance? She punched her numbers into the cashpoint machine and waited a few seconds while the card was checked. And then a few more seconds. Strange, it didn't usually take this long. Then a message flashed up.

'This service cannot be provided at present. Please contact your bank.'

Sally tried every ATM in the terminal and was given the same treatment. She didn't think she had enough moisture in her body to produce any more tears, but sat down in the café area and grizzled like a toddler.

Mikey came home to Cedar Vale to find Uncle Kyle in charge, if 'in charge' means sprawled on the floor in a tie-dye sarong, watching re-runs of *All Creatures Great and Small*. The house-clearance men had kindly left a small TV set behind.

'What's for tea, Uncle Kyle?'

'Colombian fritters.'

'We had those already.'

'My resources are restricted, Mikey. Has anybody been shopping –' Kyle was distracted by James Herriot inserting his entire forearm into the rear end of a cow – 'Wow, James!' he said, addressing the screen, 'there's a fine line between man and the animal kingdom that should not be fudged, buddy,' and he bit the top off his fifth beer bottle.

'I'm going out, Uncle Kyle. I've got work to do,' said his niece. 'By the way, where's Dad?'

'Gone to hospital, kiddo.' Kyle was now transfixed by Herriot sluicing the cow barn down with a bucket of soapy water.

'Mum?'

Kyle shrugged his shoulders.

It was after four p.m. and people in transit were starting to thin out at Gatwick airport. Some trundled off in hopeful sunhats towards their departure gates, businesspeople clicked across the floor wheeling their neat little cases; many travellers already had neck cushions glued to their shoulders, like Elizabethan ruffs.

A cleaner in a black uniform and pushing a trolley was picking things up off the floor with a hooking device. She moved towards a row of chairs near the duty-free section and stopped as she noticed a blonde woman sobbing audibly. The cleaner fished out a paper hanky and offered it to her.

Sally stopped crying, saw the hanky and the kind face of the cleaner, and sobbed some more.

'Th . . . th . . . th . . . ank you s . . . s . . . s . . . so much,' she managed after a while.

'It's OK. Take your time.' The cleaner sat down beside her. 'You're sad because your flight is cancelled? I see this all the time here. Go to Customer Services, they can help you.'

Sally sniffed.

'I wish I was crying over a cancelled flight. I'm crying because . . . my mother has emotionally abused me all of my life, my sister ran away before I even really got to know her, my husband told me the house I live in is rented, we'll have to leave it, my children think I'm a rubbish mother, my niece thinks I'm a rubbish AUNT and that's impossible. It's easy being an aunt. How can

226

anyone be a bad aunt? We've lost all our money and everything has gone to shit.'

She sniffed and spotted the name on the cleanliness supervisor's badge. 'Zeena, I'm sorry for burdening you.'

Zeena looked at her thoughtfully.

'You know, life is not so bad. I come from Iraq. I'm a Marsh Arab and Saddam wanted to exterminate all of us. I have no men left in my family. Husband, father, uncles, cousins, all murdered. I have one son and one daughter; we came to the UK eighteen years ago, and life was difficult, but now it's OK. My children work hard. My son, Mahmud, will be an MP one day. You'll see.'

Sally had never felt so small in all of her life.

Zeena continued:

'You have a husband, you have a family, you're OK. You'll see. Stop crying. Go to them. Life is good.'

And Zeena stood up and took her trolley once more.

'Being an auntie is easy though. Nobody on this Earth is bad at being an auntie. Impossible. I have nothing to say to you about that.'

Sally smiled and looked down at the hanky in her hand, screwed it up small and then breathed in sharply.

'It was good to talk to you, Zeena. I'm going to do as you said and go home now. Thank you.'

15

After four hours, Frank finally arrived at Epsom General Hospital. In the ambulance he explained in lengthy detail to the two paramedics what was wrong with him. They were pleasant, professional but nonplussed, looking at each other with slightly sceptical eyes as he took them through his long list of symptoms.

He stood in front of the reception desk at A & E, waiting his turn to register for the triage nurses. When he got to the front of the queue he proceeded to tell Clyde, the receptionist, in intricate detail as before, the nature of his illness.

'It's actually about the physical need to get into bed, Clyde. Not just the desire. It's like an addiction, a curse, a—'

'Much as I find the journey of your illness fascinating, Mr Parker, there is a queue,' said Clyde, who had a bit of sass about him.

Frank looked behind him at the group of fellow queuers, who had a restive look about them.

'Get a move on, can't you?' complained an old lady in lavender trousers.

'We've got all your details down, Mr Parker,' said Clyde, 'so if you want to just take a seat, one of the nurses will call you forward in a bit.'

Frank looked confused.

'No offence, Clyde, but I need to see a doctor.'

Clyde smiled wryly.

'And I'm desperate to see Gloria Estefan. But good things come to those who wait, don't they?'

'Well, how long do I have to wait to see a doctor here?' asked Frank, exasperation starting to seep into his voice.

Clyde looked around the busy waiting area.

'Difficult to say. Maybe four to five hours?'

'Some of us have been here that long already, thanks to you,' said Lavender Trousers gruffly.

Frank turned to her. 'I'm just trying to get some good service here.'

'Good service?' said a wag further down the queue. 'This is the NHS, mate, not the strawberries and cream tent at bloody Wimbledon!'

The rest of the queue laughed. Frank turned back to Clyde and spoke loudly so that everybody could hear.

'My name is Frank Parker and I paid for most of the new dialysis machine in the Renal Unit here a few years ago.'

He paused for a reaction. None came. He moved closer to the desk and leaned a casual elbow on it. 'There are hundreds, probably thousands of kidneys in Surrey that have me to thank for that machine.'

There were mutterings and laughter from the queue. Frank ploughed on,

'Now, Clyde, if you put a little call through to the doctors with that information, I'm pretty sure they'll stop what they're doing pronto, to come and have a chat with me.'

Clyde stared at Frank and crossed his arms.

'You'll have to sit in the waiting area, sir, like everyone else.'

Frank felt suddenly exhausted. That conversation had all but wiped him out. He shuffled off to the waiting area and heard Lavender Trousers mutter,

'Arsehole,' as he passed by.

He wedged himself between a mother with a yelling baby and a man with sick all over his shirt.

Mikey may only have been eleven, but she was completely ready to sit her driving test. It was almost a daily annoyance to her that she'd have to wait six years to take it. She eased the John Deere lawnmower (a beauty called Cecil Parkinson) into the lane and down towards school. It was a crisp afternoon, and the smell of nearby bonfires invigorated her. She had to work quickly. She reckoned the house-clearance team would be back for a final sweep later that afternoon, so to smuggle a lawnmower out she had to look lively.

It wasn't exactly Formula One, but Mikey still felt pretty cool at the wheel of this beast; she handled the lawnmower nonchalantly, driving one-handed. Her average speed was six miles an hour, so she arrived a full twelve minutes later outside Dom's sports pavilion. It gave her great pleasure when netball practice actually stopped to watch her drive across the playing field.

Dom was visibly impressed with the John Deere.

'How much new?' he asked, inspecting a tyre.

'Six big ones.'

Dom inspected the paintwork.

'What do you reckon you could get for it?' asked Mikey.

'I know somebody who'd pay four grand for this,' he replied, 'so we split it fifty-fifty, two each?'

Mikey shuffled from foot to foot, then looked Dom squarely in the eye.

'Two and a half for me, one and a half for you. I've run more risk than you bringing this deal to the table.'

Dom crossed his arms and thought for a moment. He smiled.

'You drive a hard bargain, Mikey Parker.'

Amerjit Singh was back in his teenage bedroom in a Hayes cul-de-sac. He didn't have a lot of headroom, wedged as he was into the bottom slot of his old bunk bed. The last twenty-four hours were something of a blur to him. His entire family had arrived at The Chantry, like the A-Team, to pick him up before he'd even finished his precious ninety-six hours. Slumped in the back seat of the people carrier, he remembered vaguely his father saying, 'Four thousand nine hundred a week? Amerjit can get that kind of care for nothing at home' to his mum Pinki as they drove him back to Hayes.

Financial information was on the scant side, but he learned from his nephew Veer that his bank had foreclosed on him, freezing all his accounts while HNB was wound up. He had no access to funds and Laura was not answering anybody's calls, leaving her husband, aged forty-eight, now completely reliant on his family.

His mother Pinki had not stopped beaming since his return to the familial nest, and popped into his room every five minutes with delicious homemade snacks: butter chicken, parantha, custard creams and his childhood favourite, gurdh, a fudgy substance with enough sugar in it to give you teeth like Queen Elizabeth the First. He was starting to feel a bit nauseous. The thirteen-year-old Veer was stretched out on the top bunk, his head hanging down over the side, craning to get a better look at his Uncle Amerjit.

Amerjit's sister Priti and her husband Kevin had also turned up. They stood analysing him from the bedroom doorway, with their two younger children in tow. As was his father, who seemed to be permanently shaking his head.

Amerjit also caught sight of an uncle or two who'd been alerted to the return of the prodigal son, and had come round to have a good pry. All eyes were on him; Amerjit felt like a zoo exhibit.

His father was still shaking his head.

'What I don't understand is how a Cambridge and Princeton graduate can come to this,' he said, gesturing to his son. 'The top mathematician of his matriculating year! A graduating cum laude student from Princeton! It just doesn't make sense!'

'He never wanted to read maths at uni, Dad,' countered his sister, also looking at Amerjit. 'You know his passion was always geography.'

'That's right! Blame the bloody parents!' Mr Singh raised his voice. 'We're to blame for giving our children not one but three extensions on this house. THREE! We give them the shirts off our backs to offer them the prosperous future we never had! Go on, have a pop. Just blame bloody us! Geography, my arse!'

Amerjit's grandmother put her pennyworth of tut in, barely visible due to being a good foot smaller than the rest of the Singhs.

'What I don't get –' this was Veer's high voice beaming in from the top bunk – 'is why Uncle Amerjit's bank account has been so totally cleaned out. I mean, can't they leave him something?'

'I blame that bloody Frank Parker,' said Mrs Singh, wiping her hands on her apron. 'I said to Amerjit almost every day at secondary school, you keep away from that slippery-tongued Parker boy. He'll charm the birds out of the trees, that one, but he'll lead you up the wrong garden path. And as for his parents. Well! That was the scandal of the century!'

'Yeah, but Mum,' argued Priti, 'Frank Parker was his best friend. *Is* his best friend.'

'Never mix friendship and business!' This came from an uncle in the corridor. 'Look at the mess Prince Andrew got himself into! Business and friendship. Always a toxic combination!'

'Well, son, you won't have to worry any longer about the Parker problem.' Amerjit's father sat down on a beanbag beside the bunk bed. 'You'll be able to come join us in the business. I'm not going to go on for ever. Who's going to take over? Your sister? She's got her own fish to fry. Your uncles? They'll be dead before I am, the amount of my Glenfiddich they're bloody putting away.'

There were shouts of protest from the corridor at this.

'You can count me out of the family business,' muttered Veer from the top bunk. 'I'm shit at maths. I'm going to be a DJ.'

Amerjit's father ignored these comments.

'Master Blinds is now not only covering Hayes, Hounslow and Heathrow, the blessed triangle of H, but we're branching out, my friends. With myself and my son at the helm, Master Blinds will soon be the toast of Slough, Ruislip and, God willing, Uxbridge. The triangle will have doubled. Into a—'

'Rhombus?' suggested Veer grumpily.

'It's a hexagon, Veer,' sighed Amerjit from the bottom bunk.

'Whatevs,' said Veer.

'You're right, my son, it's a bloody hexagon!' shouted Mr Singh, joyfully.

*

Sally's petrol gauge had been blinking at her ever since she left Gatwick. She was some six miles from Cedar Vale, and was now willing the Range Rover to get her home. She'd completed pretty much a whole rosary of prayers since leaving the airport.

She was driving through one of Surrey's most elite areas. Lanes bisected hills filled with neat little ponies wearing blankets and eating fresh hay from newly built barns. Pubs and snugs twinkled as lights started to go on for the evening. Chimneys smoked in the way that they had done for centuries gone by. Sally passed through village greens that had said a fond beery farewell to cricket pitches for the coming of winter. Surrey folk full of trust left honesty boxes at the end of their driveways for gourds and pumpkins. It was a county brimming with harvest plenty and you could smell affluence in the air.

Sally was praying out loud for a petrol station. She still had twenty pounds, easily enough to get her home, but had found herself on quite remote lanes now and it was gloomy, and starting to rain. And then the Range Rover began to stall.

'Shit. Shit. Shitty shitbags of shit,' remarked Sally as the car gave up its last petrol breath, just as a lay-by hove into view. Sally sat in the silence of the dark car for a full minute, before getting out and locking it. She began walking down the road, never once looking back at the car. She felt something in her pocket and pulled out the scrunched-up paper hanky that Zeena had given her at Gatwick. She looked at it and picked up her pace towards home.

Frank looked up at the clock in the waiting area of Epsom General Hospital A & E, and was surprised to see that it was five twenty. He had now seen the triage nurse who asked him many questions, but still no interface with a doctor. And it seemed odd to Frank, but people who had definitely arrived after him seemed to be being called in to see doctors before him. There was now nobody around him in the waiting area that he recognised. He'd slept on and off in the moulded plastic chair, so felt that he had enough energy to tackle Clyde again.

'Hey there, Clyde,' Frank went in with a jaunty approach.

Clyde was packing his things away into a purple rucksack and now had on a mustard roll-neck sweater. He was not the official-looking Clyde of yore with green tabard and badge.

'I seem to have been waiting here a very long time, Clyde, have I missed my place or something?'

'People who need the doctor more urgently than you get priority. I've finished my shift so you'll have to talk to Slavka. Good luck with the, what was it? Oh yeah, the *tiredness.*'

Clyde stressed the last word like that, which peeved Frank. There was now a new batch of people waiting to be processed by Slavka. He looked around him. He'd had enough of this over-lit cattle pen. Frank had never had to wait this long for anything. Even his babies had been born more quickly than this. He was losing his touch. Right, time to take back control. He looked at the signage near the door and found what he was looking for. He left the A & E waiting area. He needed a doctor, and he was going to find one his own way.

The kitchen at Cedar Vale had seen better days. Gone were the long expanses of glittering marble work surfaces, and in their place was a jumble sale of mess. Cereal packets were littered all over the place along with many plastic milk cartons, and Kyle's Colombian Fritter Factory was still very much open for business, judging by the coating of flour and sticky batter covering the whole kitchen table.

Store cupboards were left open, revealing their chaotic innards. Gone were Paloma's ranks of alphabetised tins and jars, and in their place was carnage. A jar of sundried tomatoes in oil stood on its side with a fork stuck in it, six large pizza boxes had been left, with crusts still in them, on the butcher's block and a loaf of sourdough bread, which looked suspiciously as if somebody had taken a bite directly out of it, was abandoned next to Paloma's condiments cupboard. All cups were out and scattered about with half-dead drinks in them, and a sea of empty beer and wine bottles stood as sad memorials to the places they'd been drunk: by the phone, next to the bread bin, under the table, on the floor. And in the middle of it all was Kyle, slumped with his guitar.

He was halfway through a bottle of rather nice rhubarb gin and had his hand in a big pack of biscuits. They'd come from the farm shop and looked poncey. They were interesting rather than tasty but they were helping to curb his hunger. He could have murdered a steak right now.

His gin reverie was interrupted by nieces and nephew, coming into the kitchen. And dogs barking. Three pairs of feet marched through the door, Stephen at the head. He didn't look happy.

'Uncle Kyle, we've come to talk to you about an urgent matter,' he said. 'We can't eat Colombian fritters any more. We're not going to. We've had enough of them.'

'What is this?' slurred their uncle, pushing his hat to the back of his head. '*Battleship* flipping *Potemkin*? Are you sailors staging some kind of revolution here?'

'I'm not going to lie, I've got absolutely no idea what those words you just said meant, Uncle Kyle,' said Cleo, 'but Emily and I are teenage girls and there are really important parts of our brains that are developing right now, and need food.'

'And my brain needs food too, Cleo,' said Stephen, sotto voce.

'Less so,' said Cleo tersely. 'You've got larger stores.'

Since Frank and Emily's showdown, Cleo had taken a rather protective stance towards her cousin. Emily looked tired. Cleo put her arm around her shoulders.

'Have the dogs been fed, Uncle Kyle?' Stephen asked.

Kyle responded with a shoulder shrug.

'Has anybody seen Mikey?' asked Cleo.

Kyle's shoulders went up again.

'I'll feed the dogs,' said Stephen, moving towards the laundry room, and on opening the door, let out a squeal. 'Oh my God, guys, there's actually a flood in here. Shit! Somebody call a plumber!'

Cleo rolled her eyes.

'And while you're at it call a cook, gardener, housekeeper, cleaner, oh yes, and is there an agency for PARENTS? Can somebody call us some PARENTS, please?'

Kyle stood up, slightly unsteadily. He made a trumpet sound with his cupped hand and then announced,

'Pygmy children! Nieces and nephews! Uncle Kyle is here! Have no fear! I once helped a community in Chile who were having drainage problems in their village. I've got this.'

Kyle moved towards the laundry door with what he thought was purpose, until his left foot met an empty rioja bottle in his path, causing him to stumble into the kitchen island; he ended up half-sprawled over it, clutching at its sides like a novice ice-skater on a municipal rink.

'I've got this,' he reiterated, almost in box-split position at the breakfast bar.

'Uncle Kyle,' said Stephen, picking up the biscuit bag that Kyle had been snacking from, 'you know you've been eating dog biscuits?'

'Oh God,' said Emily, 'anyone got the number for Childline?'

Sally told herself that she was enjoying the march back to Cedar Vale in the persistent rain. It was fortifying, edifying, and she tried to think of herself as a soldier on manoeuvres. This was good for her. Some of the local mums in the area did an overpriced weekly boot camp called Leatherhead Military Fitness; it meant that you were yelled at every Wednesday evening on Ranmore Common by a buff ex-squaddie, whom all the women had the hots for. Sally pretended that this was what she was doing right now, but the fantasy was hard to maintain when her hair was flattened against her scalp, making her look like a distressed otter. She was also wearing flimsy plimsolls, the same sweatshirt she'd been wearing for three days and a Harvey Nicks green and plum velvet coat on top. She didn't look like a soldier, she looked like an alcoholic who'd lost their way to a Virginia Woolf Appreciation Society meeting.

The road was deathly quiet; all that Sally could hear was her own breathing pattern, fast as a shrew, and all she could see were the puffs of mist that each breath exhaled. She heard the approach of a distant purring car and stepped up her pace. She kept her head down; it wouldn't do to be spotted like this. She heard the large car slow down before it crawled along beside her.

'Pervert,' Sally muttered under her breath. She was preparing a volley of swearwords in her head to whoever this kerb crawler was.

'Sal! Hon!' The unmistakable dulcet tones of Francesca

Daly-Jones rang out, with what sounded like Bryan Adams accompanying her on the car stereo.

Sally stopped.

'Hon, you're drenched. Has the car broken down? I saw it in the lay-by back there. Jump in. I'll give you a lift home.'

Sally looked at Francesca through a dripping curtain of hair and saw that the Daly-Jones Chobham Tractor was stuffed to the gunwales with bag upon bag of groceries from Waitrose. Sally spotted some fresh seeded baguettes poking invitingly out of one bag, and felt suddenly famished. She realised that she hadn't eaten properly for nearly twenty-four hours.

'I know. It's ridiculous,' said Francesca, seeing Sally look at the shopping bags. 'I literally went to Waitrose for some pastry for a goat's cheese tart I'm making for dinner. I've ended up spending four hundred pounds in there, I do that every time I go in!' Francesca laughed as she turned down Bryan Adams. 'Don't you find you do that, Sal,' she asked her friend sweetly, 'you just splash all that cash in the supermarket when you don't mean to?'

'It's been lovely to see you, Francesca,' Sally said pointedly, 'but I'd better get on home,' and she started to walk away from the car.

'What?' shouted Francesca incredulously. 'It's four miles from Cedar Vale, Sally! It's starting to piss! What about your car? Where's Frank? What are you doing?' There was panic in Francesca's rising voice.

She glided along beside Sally, who plodded onwards into the rain. 'Oh, I get it!' Francesca was starting to shout now. 'You're giving me the silent treatment, are you? What are you DOING? How long are you going to keep this charade up? We all KNOW what's going on, Sally Parker, you can't keep pretending. Sally! SALLY! LISTEN TO ME! I AM YOUR BEST FRIEND!'

But Sally wasn't listening. She was a soldier on manoeuvres and had to keep marching. Marching onwards. One foot in front of the other.

Frank found himself outside the Renal Unit, unable to gain access. He checked around him and saw a couple of nurses on the approach. He swabbed his hands underneath the hand cleanser outside the doors and, as the nurses came nearer, gave them a slightly muted version of the old electric Parker smile and moved into their slipstream as the doors swished open. Frank had always possessed the uncanny ability to look as comfortable as possible in any location at any given time. It was a vital skill when he was persuading people to give him their money, and it worked for him now. The nurses stopped at their station to chat to their colleagues, but Frank carried on, breezily turning right at the end of the corridor.

He felt his heartbeat race; the old Parker adrenaline was starting to hit his vital organs and he was feeling good again, not a shred of tiredness. Here was the old Frank Parker swaggering towards his next deal.

He saw a sign up ahead and stopped in disbelief. The Daly-Jones Ward, said the sign. Frank felt the energy drain out of him, through his fingertips and soles of his feet. How the hell had that jerk-off Tim Daly-Jones managed to swing this? Where was the Frank Parker Ward, for Pete's sake? He'd paid for that crapping dialysis machine and there wasn't even the smallest whiff of a plaque up. Thousands and thousands that machine had cost him. And how much wonga had Tim Daly-Jones given to get his name up in lights? Frank was going to give him the double barrels when he next saw him on the golf course. Little shithead.

He put his nose into the Daly-Jones Ward and was

gratified to see that it was only an eight-bed bay with a few geriatrics snoozing. Frank spotted quickly that one of the beds closest to the window was empty. He strolled over to it, with a 'Top of the evening' greeting to all as he did so, pulled the curtain so that he could maintain some privacy, unlaced his trainers and got on to the bed fully clothed.

He folded his arms and settled down to have some shuteye. His plan was proceeding perfectly. He'd got himself into the hospital system and would be speaking to a doctor very soon. That old Parker Magic. He still had it in abundance. He smiled and allowed himself to drift off gently. He was enjoying his stay courtesy of the NHS. It had been too many years since he'd been its guest and he was glad to get reacquainted.

He was relishing a dream where he had put Tim Daly-Jones on Uncle Phil's vegetable stall back in Hayes town centre. Except that Tim Daly-Jones had crates and crates of golf balls instead of fruit and veg. Hayes folk came up to the stall for their pound of parsnips, and all that Daly-Jones could offer them were golf balls. He was in the middle of weighing some out for an irate lady who wanted cabbage, and Frank was pleased to see that he looked very out of place there in his Jack Wills rugby shirt and pristine jeans. Surely it wouldn't be too long now before some-body took a swipe at him. Things were just starting to hot up, a bit of jostling had begun, and Daly-Jones was losing his urbane veneer.

'Get off me!' he said as somebody took his arm to shake him. 'You can't do that, get off me, I say!'

'Get off me! Get off me!' Frank shouted, as he was roused uncompromisingly from his slumbers by a male nurse.

'Excuse me. Sir! You need to wake up!' The male nurse gripped Frank's armpit.

Frank sat up in the hospital bed and had absolutely no idea where he was for several moments.

'Golf balls! Five for a pound!' he exclaimed loudly.

'Sir,' said the nurse firmly, 'you are not permitted to be in this ward. I'm going to have to ask you to leave immediately before I call security. Do you understand?'

'Whoa, whoa, hang on just a minute, Mr Nurse, which is an unfortunate combination of words,' Frank retorted, feeling more alert. 'I don't think you know who you're talking to. I'm Frank Parker, AKA Surrey's Kidney Cleanser.'

'I'm asking you to leave right away, sir.'

'And I'm saying that the amount of money I've given this hospital, I should have a permanent suite in it, my friend. Like Elizabeth Taylor and Richard Burton used to have at the Dorchester. The dialysis machine, buddy! Go ask your superior! Go on! They'll find the pictures of me, Frank Parker, at the ribbon-cutting ceremony. Go on!'

'I need to warn you, sir, that I am about to call security.'

'You call security, Nursie, and it will be the worst decision you have ever—'

A loud, drawling voice cut through their argument from the other side of the curtain. It had a languid timbre that gave it an entitled, calm authority when all around it were jabbering and twittering.

'Mrs . . . now, who are we again? Ewa Bielak. Dear Mrs Bielak – now, that's a glamorous name, I bet you know Rula Lenska, don't you?'

And Frank heard the elderly Polish patient actually laugh at this. Whoever this familiar voice belonged to, he was a past master at wheedling his way into the favour of mature Central European ladies.

Frank's male nurse whipped back the curtain to reveal

a tall, tanned doctor in full blue scrubs, holding the Polish lady's hand. She was giving the doctor doe eyes.

'Professor,' said the male nurse to the tall doctor, 'we have a problem here. This man has broken into the ward!'

'Oh *dear*,' said the doctor with mirth in his voice. 'Well, we can't have that, can we, Mrs Bielak!'

He whipped round and his wolfish grin turned to dust.

'Livesy!' shouted Frank into his face.

'Frank!' Dr Livesy shouted back at him. The male nurse looked between the two of them, confused.

'*Professor* Livesy?' continued Frank. 'PROFESSOR Livesy?' and Frank began to laugh.

Livesy looked around him uneasily. Other patients in the bay were beginning to take notice of the fracas in the corner. And several nurses had come from their station to take a closer look.

'PROFESSOR, MY ARSE!' said Frank gleefully. 'If you're a professor then I'm flipping Shirley Bassey, mate!'

'Frank,' said Livesy, mustering all his bedside manner, 'you've been very stressed at work. You need to lower your voice.'

'This man's not a professor,' Frank addressed the whole ward now. 'He's a qualified doctor, sure. The most expensive quack in Sloane Square. I've spent probably a hundred thousand pounds on him. But he's definitely not a professor!'

There was a high spot of red visible on each of Livesy's cheekbones now. His eyes looked at Frank, as cold as the Thames on a February morning.

'Mr Parker, I think you need to lower your voice, you are in a ward full of patients.'

'What the HELL are you doing here, Livesy?' demanded Frank. 'Slumming it a bit, aren't you? I don't think they have a wine list in Epsom General Hospital, or maybe I'm wrong? Maybe the cutbacks haven't quite reached here yet!' Nurses were beginning to whisper to each other as Frank ranted on, 'Oh sorry, I forgot, you're a *professor*. You must be here as a consultant. What are you a consultant in, bullshit? Do tell me, Professor Bullshit!'

Dr Livesy was in no mood for this, and let Mrs Bielak's hand drop limply off the side of her bed. His voice hardened.

'Get out of here, Frank. Now.'

'Why haven't you answered my calls, Livesy? I'm half the man I was, and I need a doctor. Or a professor. Where have you been?'

A thick-set man in navy uniform entered the Daly-Jones Ward and was heading towards the window. The male nurse gestured to Frank, and the uniformed guy nodded.

'Frank, you have narcolepsy. You shouldn't be in the Renal Unit,' said Livesy calmly.

'And you're a FRAUD, Professor Livesy!' shouted Frank. 'YOU shouldn't be in the Renal Unit either!'

Frank was now being dragged physically from the Daly-Jones Ward. He was trying to dig the balls of his feet into the floor, but kept losing his grip. He was too weak for the security guy, who dragged him out like a large sack of catering potatoes.

'Oh dear. Someone's very over tired,' Dr Livesy said with a sheepish laugh to the assembled group, though even Mrs Bielak was giving him a beady look.

'I PAID FOR THE DIALYSIS MACHINE! THIS MAN'S NOT A PROFESSOR!' Frank's voice started to recede as he was pulled out of the ward.

'The man's delusional!' added Livesy, winking at Mrs Bielak.

*

A stiff march through the rain was a bracing and rhythmic way for Sally to recalibrate her thoughts. She'd gone beyond the cold and wet now and had been stripped back to become a pumping organism with the sole mission of getting home.

She had neither house nor car to her name. Her wardrobe had been seriously napalmed by Leatherhead's most fragrant milfs; her hairdo was destroyed along with her reputation as Surrey hostess. And she was seriously doubting if she had much of a marriage any more. But what she did have was her children. Four of them. And this is what kept her going through the rain. Each squelchy plimsoll pace took her closer to them and with straightened back she barked out military-sounding phrases to keep herself motivated.

'Cleo, Emily, Mikey, Ste! Always four! Never three!'

With rhymes such as these she found the journey back to Cedar Vale went by surprisingly quickly.

16

The sickly citrus fumes from the orange smelly tree hanging off the rear-view mirror in Amerjit's car made him want to barf. He'd been sat in his dad's Toyota since five a.m. for the first job of the day, putting up some blinds in an office off the Hayes bypass. He opened the window as he cruised through Hayes's main drag. Nothing much had changed since his teen days. The same ironmonger emporium, the same sweet shop where he and Frank used to pinch black-jacks and fruit salads; a few more chain coffee shops here and there but in essence it was the same little suburb that Amerjit had grafted so hard to escape from all those years ago.

He felt the smallness of it begin to creep into the car. This was starting to feel like a bad dream. He looked at the clock on the dashboard. Just after eight o'clock. In his former life he'd have been sipping an overpriced decaf oat mocha, holed up in some trendy coffee bar in the City chatting to a client about a multi-million-pound invest-ment. He'd be wearing a suit costing several thousand and would have a booking in the bag for himself and his wife for some high-end restaurant that evening.

Laura was never happier than when ingesting eye-wateringly expensive food; a platter of oysters flown down from Loch Fyne washed down with a glass of £850 Cristal was her idea of contentment. Amerjit had booked tables all over the world to try and satisfy Laura's grub lust. His *pièce de résistance*, a year into their marriage, when Laura still found him alluring, was managing to book a table at the world-famous Nöll restaurant in a forest two hours out of Helsinki. The waiting list to get a table at Nöll was six to eight months, but through a contact, Amerjit conjured up a booking and off they flew, first class, to Finland and then straight into a chauffeur-driven car out to the forest. It was hard to get Laura to smile about anything, but she was positively beaming when they arrived at the forest clearing.

Nöll's chef and founder was so high-status and revered that she insisted on meeting her diners before actually agreeing to feed them. Twenty of them waited before she arrived by horse-drawn carriage and stepped down to examine her guests. She was attired in simple grey loose top and trousers, grey trainers and grey-framed glasses through which she looked her diners over in silence. Four of them were rejected immediately and told to go back to Helsinki. They did it in silence, no complaining – this was the Nöll way. Laura was so excited to have been chosen she actually whispered in Amerjit's ear that she was horny and wanted him then and there. Amerjit couldn't wipe the grin off his face.

Nöll was a purpose-built barn set up in a brutally hacked-back clearing in the middle of the forest. It had strip lighting down its centre, and plastic cups for drinking.

'Nöll moulds all of her design on the Stasi,' one diner was heard whispering to another.

Though Amerjit couldn't swear to it, he thought he spotted airline-type food trolleys being delivered round the back, but he told himself that it couldn't be. They must be for some other dinner. Nöll would never ship in pre-prepped meals, not retailing at £895 per head.

The palate cleanser (to remove any traces of impure food) was a simple grey stone to suck on. Everyone did so religiously, several people declaring it to be delicious, quite the most delicious stone they had ever sucked. There was no menu at Nöll. You were simply given what Nöll decided; there was no sending the stone back and asking for sorbet instead; Nöll was all-powerful.

The starter arrived and Amerjit wanted to tell Laura that it looked suspiciously like droppings. But he didn't want to make her cross and lose her horn. Pellets in varying shades of brown were scattered over the wooden plate (or 'trencher' as the waiter, also in loose grey clothes, described it) and Amerjit had trouble getting even one down his gullet.

Laura woofed all of them straight away and was drinking plastic cup after plastic cup of juniper-infused water, which to Amerjit just tasted of water. Now, Amerjit had never tasted any kind of poo before, but he would have testified there and then, on his mother's own life, that at least three of the pellets had originated in the anus of a small forest-floor animal. Some kind of stoat? Or weasel?

The main course was described as 'Steak Beyond Blue'. When this was announced to the gang of gourmands it was greeted with an intake of breath – this was the signature Nöll dish, a bit like having shepherd's pie at The Ivy or the Chicken Royale at Burger King.

What arrived on the trenchers was a slab of raw meat. Simple as that. The 'steak' had never made contact with flame, coal nor gas hob. Not even an ember. It made it very simple for Nöll; there was absolutely no cooking involved in the Beyond Blue whatsoever. Amerjit watched as the other diners oohed and aahed over the raw meat, turning the trencher round, photographing it for envious folk at home. It was suggested that for the optimum palate experience, you rubbed the end of a smoke-infused pine branch all over the steak. Everyone did so religiously and thereafter began the longest and bleakest chewing experience of Amerjit's life. He felt beyond blue both mentally and physically when he'd finished. It took nearly two hours to get through it, and judging by the silence and frequent use of tooth-picks, everyone was finding it as hard-going as him.

Amerjit looked at Laura and was faced with the frankly unappetising sight of a cavewoman in a £2,500 Gucci suit. They were offered essence of silver birch, which tasted like dental mouthwash, to cleanse the palate before dessert. Amerjit now allowed himself to be excited. He'd eaten enough poo and raw meat to last him a lifetime. Come on, Nöll, time to wheel in trollies groaning with pavlova, millionaire's shortbread and hot crumbles!

A small dome of ice was placed in front of everyone on a slate platter. It was flecked with something silvery. The waiter announced that this was a gelato fusion made with water from the Arctic circle, infused with air from a garden in Latvia that produces the best loganberries in the world. The silvery flecks were platinum shavings. Everyone had the gall to applaud. Amerjit had the worst diarrhoea that night he'd ever experienced.

Amerjit sighed and the orange tree twirled slowly above the dashboard. He hated Nöll and her restaurant, but he'd happily dine there and endure the raging trots every night if it meant getting his life and his Laura back.

In a plush reception area of St Bede's School with *House & Garden* magazine laid out on a coffee table next to *The Economist* and *The Week*, Sally and Frank sat side by side on a sofa that was uncomfortably small for the current state of their marriage. In an ideal world, Sally would be sitting about three miles away from Frank right now, but here they were, flank to flank, waiting to be seen by Jim Jordan BA Hons, Headmaster of St Bede's School.

For years, Frank had teased Jim Jordan's receptionist, Cilla, by doing terrible impressions of Cilla Black to make her laugh.

'Surprise! Surprise!' he used to shout in a cod-Liverpudlian accent whenever he bounded into reception. Frank didn't have the energy for that today, and Cilla clearly wasn't in the mood. She was polite, but seemed very engrossed in her computer. Frank was subdued and sat stroking his beard. Sally looked gaunt and the layer of make-up she'd put on that morning did little to mask her fatigue. A brittle silence filled the reception area and Sally picked up a magazine. Jim Jordan appeared at his door, wreathed in smiles.

'Mr and Mrs Parker? Come on in,' he rumbled. 'Sooo-ooooooooooooooo,' he said, showing Frank and Sally to their chairs. Frank tried to adopt the wide-splayed position in his, but it didn't quite work in tracksuit bottoms.

'We have a bit of a cash-flow issue at the moment, Jim,' said Frank, taking control, 'and we need a little bit of wriggle time till things blow over, so it'd be—'

Sally interrupted him. 'I'd say it's more than a cash-flow issue. We've lost all our money and can't afford the school fees. We don't need wriggle time, we need your help.'

Frank looked at Sally, flabbergasted. She'd never interrupted him like this before, particularly in a business environment.

'Er . . . Sally, I'm not sure you're quite as au fait with our finances as I am. Speaking as one of the City's—'

'Speaking *not* as one of the City's top hedge-fund managers –' Sally spoke directly to the headmaster without a sideways glance at her husband – 'I'm very au fait with our finances. You don't need to be an economist to work out that when bailiffs come to repossess your worldly goods on behalf of the Inland Revenue, when your bank forecloses on you, and when you look in your kitchen cupboards and realise that you may or may not be able to feed your family, it makes you very bloody au fait with your finances. We have no finances, Jim. And soon we will have no house. And we can't afford the school fees. So, can you help us?'

Frank watched, slack-jawed, as his wife finished her speech. What the hell was going on? He badly needed some morning shuteye. This was all too much for ten o'clock in the morning.

'OK,' said Jim Jordan, fiddling with a stapler, 'so I've been looking at the situation that we've got here, and I think we can get something positive out of it.'

'Really?' said Sally.

Frank was keen to enter the conversation, which was looking perilously two-handed at the moment. 'Well, Jim, it's also good to know that when I gave all that money for the construction of the school's new swimming pool, we'd be able to call in the loan—'

'It wasn't a loan, Frank,' Sally cut across him, 'it was a donation. Carry on, Mr Jordan.'

Frank didn't recognise this new version of his wife. Was she going to stay? Or was she just a passing phase? Was it the menopause? Surely Sally was too young for that?

'OK,' said Jim after a little cough, 'well, what we basically have here is a scenario where we can offer you a . . . er . . . scholarship situation. Everything paid for, even the trimmings.'

'When you say a "scholarship situation", what are you implying by that?' asked Sally immediately.

Frank couldn't believe the tone and language that Sally

was using here. He looked at his wife's determined little silhouette and felt quite moved; he felt a tear prick in his eye. He also felt pretty aroused. He found himself quite liking the cut of this new Sally's jib.

'Weeeeeeeeell,' said Mr Jordan, 'your fees for all four children are paid up till Christmas. Stephen and Michaela will have no problem catching up with the curriculum if they have to . . . .er . . . adapt . . . and Cleo has proved to be, let's say, maybe more suited to a vocational career?'

He smiled broadly at Sally who returned it with a frosty glance. Jim Jordan continued,

'So, what we basically have here with this scholarship situation is that—'

'You can only give us one scholarship,' said Sally, deadpan.

'Yes,' answered Mr Jordan quickly.

'Even though I paid for that Olympic-sized, self-cleaning, filtered, underlit swimming pool—'

'Shut up, Frank,' said his wife, and turned to Jim. 'And I'm guessing that the scholarship is going to be offered to Emily?'

A nanosecond pause.

'Yes,' affirmed the head teacher.

'We'll have a think about it and we'll be in touch. Thank you.'

And with that, Sally bent down to gather up her things. Frank watched her and followed her out of the room. She didn't look back at him once till they were nearly back at Cedar Vale. He felt like Eurydice following Orpheus through the underworld.

Amerjit pulled the Toyota up behind some stationary traffic. He had another two hours before his next blinds fitting in Hounslow West, so there was nothing to do but drive around aimlessly to fill the time. Amerjit looked out of the Toyota window at Friends Electric, a ramshackle electrical goods shop that had been there since the eighties. He had a sudden flashback to the early nineties, when he and Frank had hired a dodgy sound system and some lights from Friends Electric. Frank bartered and haggled and got the equipment for a song, and Frank and Amerjit threw the best house party Hayes had ever seen. It was for Sally's twentieth birthday, not quite two years into her marriage. Amerjit laughed as he remembered him and Frank, the last to leave the dance floor, hugging each other so as not to fall over they were so drunk, and screaming along with the words to KLF's 'Last Train To Trancentral'. Amerjit felt a pang. He'd been out of The Chantry a few days and still hadn't made contact with Frank. He felt too guilty, couldn't face the aftermath of HNB's demise. And he didn't have a mobile any more.

Amerjit's eye roved over the heaters, hairdryers, car stereos and computers until it rested on the TV section of the shop window. The news was on. Suddenly the screen was filled with radiance. A woman in a scarlet dress was looking straight into camera, and by the look of her serious expression and jaw moving up and down like somebody chewing on raw meat, she meant business.

Her eyes blazed through the camera, out of the TV set, through the window of Friends Electric, across the pavement, through the driver's window of Amerjit's Toyota and straight into his head, circulatory system and finally his heart. His Laura. His beautiful fearless warrior-wife Laura telling the nation about quantitative easing and the FTSE index. How Amerjit longed to play FTSE with her at this moment, under the table of some fancy-shmancy restaurant. He didn't care if she was aggressive towards him, he didn't care if she laughed at him, hell, Amerjit didn't even care if she no longer loved him. He just wanted to be with her, blinded by her knowledge of the economy, lapping up her facts, her thoughts, her everything. He just wanted to lap her up and never let her go.

Amerjit felt his lips wobble and then his nose run. It wasn't long before he was howling like a wounded dog in the Toyota. He needed air; he needed to get out. His clothes felt restrictive. He needed freedom and looseness. He unzipped his Puffa jacket and let it drop to the pavement. He started to unbutton his checked shirt, then moved down to his flies. Amerjit now unlaced his boots so that he could take them off to unshackle himself from his trousers.

Laura was still talking directly at him, her collarbones syncopating with her jaw movements, skimming the neckline of that scarlet dress. In his head Amerjit and Laura were now a million miles away in a far-off kingdom, on a white charger with her riding side-saddle in front of him, still in that scarlet dress. The physical Amerjit, however, was very much on Hayes High Street pulling his pants down in front of the Friends Electric shop window, about to be wrestled to the ground by its owners. What on earth would their customers think of this semi-naked man stripping in front of *Piggott's Projections*?

Sally and Frank arrived back to an empty Cedar Vale, which was a rarity. Kyle was out and the children were all at school. Sally had already made a call about the laundryroom leak and had a stab at the kitchen, but it was still awash with dirty crockery, food packets, homework, piles of unwashed clothes and indeterminate detritus. She put her bag down on the side, took off her jacket, hung it up and snapped on a pair of yellow Marigolds. She sniffed and took in the chaos around her. Frank was properly exhausted; the meeting at St Bede's had rinsed him and he fell into the only armchair left in the kitchen.

'So you're not going to help me with all this?' said Sally, not even bothering to look at him.

Frank shuffled himself forward, to try and get closer to Sally. 'Here, pass me the stuff to dry and I can do it sitting down.'

Sally turned and looked down at him sitting forlornly in the chair. 'I think I'm better off doing it by myself, Frank.'

And she turned on both taps and loud slooshing filled the sink.

Frank sank back into his chair and sighed as Sally started to tackle the tower of crockery, scrubbing each piece gruffly with the washing-up brush. Frank liked watching his wife do this; he hadn't seen her do the washing-up for at least ten years.

'You look very Madam Whiplash in those gloves, Sal!' he quipped.

'Shut up, Frank.'

'That's the second time today you've told me to shut up.'

'Yeah? Well maybe if I'd told you to shut up a long time ago, we wouldn't be in this mess.'

A pause.

'Are you angry with me?' Frank asked her softly.

Sally didn't reply straight away, but pumped suds vigorously. 'Well what do you think, Frank? You've lied to me for seventeen years about this house.'

'I never lied to you about that, Sal,' Frank corrected her, 'you just never asked me about it.' Sally didn't reply. 'You fell in love with this house, Sal,' Frank continued, 'you said this was your forever dream house that you wanted to have your great-grandchildren in. How could I refuse Dave's deal? I did it for you.'

Sally put the brush down briskly on the draining board. She turned to face him.

'Stop twisting things, Frank Parker. You've made a career out of twisting things, ducking things, wheedling things, glossing things.'

'You never complained about the twisting, ducking, wheedling and – what was the other thing?' he said flatly.

'Glossing.'

'You liked all the things that the twisting, ducking, glossing and – what was the other thing?'

'Wheedling.'

'Wheedling, that's it. You loved the life that the – what was the other thing?'

'DUCKING!' shouted Sally.

'The ducking gave you, Sal.'

Sally looked down at her dirty plimsolls.

'I know I did. We all did. More fool me.'

'Well,' said Frank firmly, 'once I've kicked this bloody tiredness thing, I'll be up and bouncing again and able to wheedle, gloss, duck and – what was the other thing?'

'OH, FOR GOD'S SAKE, FRANK. IT'S TWIST, FRANK, IT'S TWIST.'

'I'll be able to twist again,' Frank smiled wistfully, 'like we did last summer!'

Sally put her head in her hands. 'No, Frank. No more stupid gags. We've gone tits-up,' she lifted her face and looked ruefully down at her chest, 'except my tits are down, and likely to go ever downwards. I won't be having a boob job anytime soon, unlike all the other fortysome-things in Leatherhead whose husbands work in finance.'

Sally stood up and plucked a tea towel firmly off its hook.

'Well, at least one of us isn't going to go down the shitter,' she said.

Frank looked confused.

'Emily can stay on at St Bede's with that scholarship, get all those top grades that she was born to get, and then make a great life for herself.'

Frank thought about this.

'But where would she live?'

'Emily's got loads of friends. One of them would love to have her till she's done her A levels. She'll thrive. To be honest I think the best thing we could possibly do for Em, and for my sister, would be to –' Sally turned away and Frank noticed that she was wiping away a tear – 'let her go, Frank.'

'Sal,' Frank's voice was gentle, 'she's been with us since she was a baby. It'd break your heart.'

Sally swung round to face her husband with flashing eyes,

'Don't play the soft, caring daddy all of a sudden, Frank Parker. The kids told me you pretty much asked her to leave.'

Frank rubbed his eyes.

'Em and I have had our ups and downs, but—'

'Face it, Frank. This is a shit situation, and the sooner we start to just OWN it, the better it'll be for all of us.'

Frank looked down at his hands, resting idly in his lap.

'I'm too tired to own anything at the moment, Sal. I'm just too tired.'

Sally sighed. 'I'll sort things out. I've never really planned anything in my life, except for our wedding, and that was a bit of a disaster, wasn't it? But I'll start now, OK? I've been thinking a lot about Nancy. She took control of her life at fifteen. I can sure as hell can do it at forty-eight.'

Frank looked thoughtful.

'I don't think Nancy took control of her life, Sal. She was a mess. Look what she did to Emily.'

'If only I could find her, make things right, get her back with Emily.'

'Well, give Nancy a call then,' he said.

Sally turned to face him. She shook her head and shot her husband a look of undisguised scorn.

'Oh yes, Frank. Everything's so easy in your world isn't it? Just click your fingers and ping! There's your sister who's disappeared off the face of the planet!'

Frank looked confused.

'But Kerry's got her number. Nancy phoned HNB a few months ago, asking for cash. Didn't I tell you?'

Sally looked at her husband in utter shock. She tried to speak but all that came out was a low growl.

'What?' said Frank. 'What have I done now?'

The 1812 Overture rang out. Sally had never been so glad to hear its clang.

A good-looking guy in his fifties was standing in the grand porch, dressed smart-casually in dark jeans, cashmere sweater and long coat thrown carelessly over his outfit. He smelled expensive, Sally noticed. His hair was thick and dark, with some attractive grey woven through the temples. He exuded confidence and calm, and his large dark eyes twinkled when he took in the sight of Sally.

She was painfully aware of how scruffy and ungroomed she looked; she was sure her mascara was smudged, and she'd barely put a brush through her hair these last three days. She was also wearing an outfit that was now a few days' old. The suave gentleman seemed pleased with what he saw, however. He smiled broadly at her and thrust out his hand for her to take. It felt large and solid to hold, like a bear's.

'Dave Aziz. Finally, we meet. You must be Sally.'

'Yes. I am. Sally . . . er . . . Parker.' Sally was furious with herself for sounding gauche and under-confident.

'May I?' Dave Aziz gestured towards the inside of the house.

'Er . . . yes. Of course. Come in, Mr Aziz.'

And they crossed the threshold together. He stood in the hall and looked round him for a quiet moment.

'Looks empty,' he said matter-of-factly.

'We have the Revenue to thank for that, Mr Aziz.'

'Yes, I'd heard. Frank around, is he?'

'Physically, he's here, yes,' answered Sally scornfully. Dave Aziz shook his head and Sally felt suddenly ashamed, like she'd betrayed her husband. She blushed as she continued, 'But he's fine. He's just very, very, very, very, very . . . tired.'

'Classic Square Mile burnout,' said Dave Aziz knowingly. 'I've seen it before. Poor bastard.'

'It's narcolepsy,' said Sally flatly.

There was a slightly awkward silence. Then Sally asked, 'So you're a colleague of my husband?'

'No,' said Dave Aziz, 'I'm your secret landlord, Sally. The one Frank never told you about. I own Cedar Vale. And I'm afraid I've come with some . . . difficult news.'

Sally felt her legs go to jelly. This was happening. This was really happening. She'd known that it was going to happen and now it really was. She was about to be served an eviction notice.

'Go on,' said Sally, trying to sound brave.

'I thought I'd come myself rather than send some random. I've been trying Frank for days, but I think his phone's off-grid. Your rent is paid up to this Wednesday . . .'

'That's two days away,' said Sally with panic starting to rise in her throat.

'Exactly,' said Dave Aziz, 'so you're going to have to be pretty quick about it.' He looked around as he spoke. 'But judging by the small amount of stuff left here, it shouldn't take you too long to move out.'

He saw the features on Sally's face turn inside out all at once.

'I'm so sorry,' Dave said, 'that was insensitive.'

'That's OK, Mr Aziz,' said Sally.

'Call me Dave,' he corrected her gently.

'Dave,' said Sally. 'Right. Dave, is there any way you could extend that a bit, give us more time to vacate?'

'I'm afraid not. I'm moving some relatives in here on Thursday.'

'Wow,' said Sally, genuinely shocked. 'OK. So, there's no period of notice? Nothing that's legally binding?'

Dave Aziz's eye glinted. They looked steely against his dark jeans and soft cashmere.

'That's not how Frank and I did business, Sally. There was nothing legally binding about our handshake.'

Sally shifted her weight from one foot to the other. She wanted to punch Dave Aziz, but she also wanted to ask him to stay and have a cup of tea. She wanted to spit at him, but she also quite wanted to kiss him. Luckily, she didn't have to worry about these conflicting emotions, because a familiar figure in a hairy body warmer came through the front door, carrying a monkey wrench in one hand and huge macaroni cheese in the other.

'Dave,' said Sally, 'this is our dog groom— I mean, my friend. My great friend, Janice Dawes.'

Janice smiled proudly. She was very glad to be referred to as Sally's great friend.

'I've looked up some plumbing tutorials online, Sally. I'm pretty handy with broken washing machines, as it goes.'

'You are the best, Janice!' glowed Sally.

The dog groomer blushed visibly.

'Oh! And I thought you could all use some carbs,' Janice said, holding out the large Pyrex dish of pasta.

Sally wanted to fall down and prostrate herself in front of Janice Dawes, sing songs in her name, and form a new religion immediately, called the Church of the Open Dawes. If Janice had asked her right there in the hallway to divorce Frank and marry her instead, Sally would have done it in a heartbeat. It is safe to say that Sally Parker was feeling a bit untethered at this precise moment.

17

'I don't really get why we're here, Sally,' said Frank, hunched in the back of Kyle's beaten up Austin Allegro, the only vehicle left in the Parker carpool.

Sally was sitting up front with Kyle, and replied to Frank using the rear-view mirror,

'Francesca reminded me recently that she's my best friend. Apparently. So we're going to put that statement to the test.'

Frank didn't like sitting in the back with his wife up front next to his brother.

'Well, why did I have to come then?' he asked grumpily.

Sally turned to her husband to speak to him.

'Because one of us in this marriage is actually trying to get us out of this mess, Frank,' she said accusingly.

'Someone's come off the Valium,' murmured Frank into his fleece.

'I'm sorry?' said Sally sharply.

'Nothing,' muttered Frank like a petulant teen.

'So this is the drive, folks?' said Kyle quickly, sensing the growing heat in the Allegro. They were beside a rustic wooden sign saying 'The Oast House', about three miles from Cedar Vale as the crow flies.

'Yes, Kyle, it's down here,' said Sally curtly, 'although how I can remember that amazes me. What with my Valium-addled Marilyn Monroe itty-bitty fluffball of a brain.'

Frank muttered something inaudible again.

'Friends are the best of times and the worst of times,' said Kyle, sucking his teeth thoughtfully as he eased the Allegro down towards The Oast House. 'My friend Esteban left me for dead in the wilds of outer Medellin when we were hiding out from FARC. That was the worst of times. But then the twat turned up when I was hospitalised, my arse falling out with dysentery; he stayed with me two days and nights resuscitating me with spoonfuls of water and sugar. That was the best of times. But then it turned out he'd been robbing me blind while I was helpless in that hospital bed, the bastard—'

'Was that the worst of times?' interjected Sally dryly.

'Spot on, Sal. But you know what? Esteban did my best-man speech in Bogota three months later. Best of times. But then I didn't hear from him for twelve years. Worst of times . . . you catch my drift? That's friendship, man.'

'Thank you so much for clarifying the best of times, worst of times friendship theory for us, Kyle,' said Sally blankly.

'Hang on,' grumbled Frank, 'best-man speech?'

'Yeah, I tied the knot. Didn't last long. Turned out she preferred being a mercenary in Escobar's army to marriage.'

'Sounds like you dodged a bullet, mate,' said Frank.

'Several hundred rounds of bullets more like,' said Kyle. 'She was packing a semi-automatic even during our honeymoon.'

Frank caught Sally's eye in the rear-view mirror and held it.

'You need to be tooled up in a marriage. It's a battleground sometimes.'

Sally rolled her eyes and cursed both Parker brothers under her breath. The Allegro crunched to a halt in front of a wide, wisteria-clad 1930s house. Willow trees wafted softly in the light rain and garden benches were dotted over the genteel front lawn, which looked ready for a garden party. There was a quaint wheelbarrow and matching trug beside the front porch.

Sally took a deep breath and turned to her husband and brother-in-law.

'Here goes.'

Francesca and Tim came out of the house in matching honey-coloured woollens and pale jeans, with matching honey-coloured dogs at their heels. They were the picture-perfect Surrey host and hostess, with perpetual smiles that said, 'Stiff G and T and a warm cheese straw, anyone?' Francesca looked as if she'd been brushed several hundred times by a groomer; she shone all over.

Sally cut a different figure as she stepped out of the Allegro. She was dressed in Adidas Air trainers from Cleo's wardrobe, faded boyfriend jeans and a fitted blue-checked shirt, with an old biker jacket on top. Her hair was uncoiffed and scrunchy round the edges, and her eyes were uncompromisingly blue. She looked about twenty-five years old. She was not in the best of moods; the Valium was indeed gone and she was feeling everything, raw and sharp.

There were hugs and kisses all round, and Francesca Daly-Jones looked Sally up and down.

'You look . . . different,' she said brightly.

'You look hot, Sal!' quipped Tim, letting his eyes rest for a second too long over her tight checked shirt.

'You look like a student off to a gig, hon!' said Francesca loudly, linking arms and leading her briskly into the house. 'What is it, Curiosity Killed the Cat or something! Now come inside, and let's have a good old gossip, you've been SO elusive, Sally Parker, what WERE you doing walking along the lane the other night? I need to hear EVERYTHING!'

Amerjit was on another bed in another psychiatric ward, but in an altogether different place this time from his beloved Chantry. That halcyon place felt like a hazy dream with its creamy corridors, soft-ticking clocks and sumptuous carpeting.

St Blaise's Hospital, situated on the huge and permanently clogged Uxbridge Road between Ealing and Southall, was a harshly lit brutalist concrete monolith with too many patients and not enough staff. The noise was so intense Amerjit's ears felt as if they were being squatted by a hundred drunken students. He'd been parked on a ward for a couple of nights while the doctors worked out what they could do with a grown man who'd now taken his clothes off twice in a public space. He was clearly high functioning and intelligent. He was miserable but not suicidal; he was confused but not dangerous. It was going to be a case of check him over, prescribe the meds and then ship him out as quickly as possible to make room for somebody way further down the psychiatric U-bend.

Amerjit lay on his bed and watched as an old lady in a onesie was ushered painstakingly down the ward by a nurse.

'DEBATE!' shouted the eighty year old.

'Yes, Mary.'

'DEBATE!' she shouted once again.

'That's right, Mary.'

'DEBATE!'

The nurse carried on steering her with a strong hand under one armpit.

'DEBATE!' blared Mary.

'You want a debate, Mary?' asked the nurse.

For all of her obvious attachment to public speaking, Mary now remained absolutely silent on the subject.

'You want a debate?' repeated the nurse kindly.

Silence.

They continued to shuffle for another minute or two in silence. Amerjit wondered what the future held for somebody like Mary, in her faded panda onesie. The answer came soon enough.

'DEBATE!' she piped up, fervently.

Back at The Oast House, Francesca and Tim were dispensing delicious snacks, straight from Francesca's Aga, off a big Emma Bridgewater platter. Plump pastry parcels filled with spinach and cheese, mini yakitori bites and heaps of mini pizzas. All three guests were lost in the platter, and there was a full minute where the only noise in the room came from chomping jaws. Kyle worked his way through eight mini pizzas and Frank laid waste to the pastry parcels; Sally tried to hold back but faced with the yakitori she was weakened and fell on them like a horse in a nosebag.

Francesca and Tim sat on their powder-blue Heals sofa, with matching floral cushions, and exchanged a meaningful look.

'It's like feeding time at Chessington Zoo in here!' quipped Tim. Francesca tinkled a little laugh.

'You're going to eat us out of house and home!' she said. 'Shall I put some more of those mini pizzas in the Aga? They are scrummy, aren't they?'

'Yes plea—' Kyle started to say through cheekfuls of pizza.

'No,' said Sally, giving him a look, 'we've had plenty. Thank you, Francesca.'

'So. How are things up at Seedy Vale, then?' said Tim who had taken on a rather lordly air, crossing his legs comfortably and easing his bottom further into the sofa. He seemed to be rather relishing this latest turn of events. 'Haven't seen you up at the Golf Club, Frank. Where have you been hiding? Growing a beard by the looks of it! Are you planning on joining ZZ Top?'

Francesca gave her husband a supportive chuckle and squeeze on the thigh, and then asked with a face full of concern:

'Oh Sal, hon. How are you all coping? What's going on? We're so WORRIED about you all.'

Tim took charge of the chat by leaning forward, legs akimbo.

'What you guys probably want to do is just hole up at Seedy –' Tim was clearly pleased with this little nickname, but Sally vowed silently to slap him if he said it again – 'till all this blows over. Nice to have a bit of a staycation, right? Stay at home, put the feet up, keep the head down, and then rise again, Frank Parker! Rise again!'

Frank was delighted that his friend had so much faith in his future, and smiled proudly, until Tim motioned to something in Frank's beard; a large flake of pastry was nestling there, and Frank had to go through the excruciating shame of retrieving it, while Tim and Francesca watched with transfixed disgust.

Frank dug deep to summon up his old booming voice,

'You wait, D-J, I'll be back on that golf course with all clubs blazing. Just watch your spotty arse, my friend, because I will be whipping it from here to Weybridge!' There was a light silence. 'Oh, I know what I wanted to ask you, D-J. I happened to be in Epsom Hospital the other day.'

Francesca rose up in her seat like a meerkat, all ears.

'Hospital?' she inquired quickly.

'Oh! Not for me,' Frank replied swiftly, 'oh no, no, no, no, nothing to do with me at all. I was just . . . er . . . anyway, I spotted the Daly-Jones Ward. You arsehole, Tim! Have you been giving away your dirty millions to help the afflicted masses?'

Tim smiled secretly to himself and sipped lazily at his G & T before responding,

'Nothing to do with me, Parker; some great-uncle of mine was a renowned medic, apparently!'

'Wanker!' shouted Frank at him. 'I wanted to get my spray can out and graffiti a huge dick and balls all over it! The Daly-Jones Ward indeed! Prick!'

Sally looked at her husband with barely disguised shame, and shook her head. There was silence, which Tim filled with a cough. Sally sat up and pulled her shoulders back.

'So, thank you for having us round, Tim and Francesca,' she said carefully. 'We've got a bit of a favour to ask you, actually.'

Francesca widened her eyes with immediate interest.

'Sal, if you want us to throw our keys into a bowl then I'm afraid it's a definite no!' she joked.

'Well, hang on, let's not be too hasty . . .' said Tim. Francesca shot him a look.

'Listen,' continued Sally, 'we won't be taking a staycation at Cedar Vale anytime soon. Headline news – we're being evicted. Cedar Vale never belonged to us. We've been renting it for the past seventeen years.'

Tim and Francesca looked at her with guppy faces.

'Rental!' was all that Francesca could articulate.

'So,' said Sally, 'from tomorrow we're going to be homeless, effectively. And we were wondering if you might be able to put us up for a while?'

Tim and Francesca looked at each other, and the five seconds of silence that followed spoke volumes to Sally. Whatever came out of their mouths after a pause like that was pointless, as far as she was concerned. They had already told her everything she needed to know.

'Now. Let's just have a think about this. Wow.' Francesca spoke first.

'All six of you, you said?' asked Tim.

'Seven,' said Kyle.

'Well. Well. Well.' Francesca was floundering. 'Now, we've got the decorators in doing both guest rooms very soon so that's going to be a bit tricky. Your mum wants to come and stay for two weeks, doesn't she, Tim?'

'Does she?' asked Tim, genuinely surprised.

'Yes, she really does,' said Francesca emphatically, 'and Izzie's got her eighteenth bash next month, that'll be fifty boisterous teenagers invading the house, so that could be difficult. Right. Come on, Team Daly-Jones! Use the grey matter! Let's work this out!'

Francesca made little fists and thumped them on to her thighs to help her think.

'Seven of you?' repeated Tim.

'Plus two dogs?' said Kyle, helpfully. Sally had already explained to the family that they could not keep all seven.

Francesca swallowed hard.

'Plus, CHRISTMAS is in a couple of months but let's not get ahead of ourselves. Wait, I've got it!' Francesca stopped suddenly. Despite herself, Sally looked at her hopefully. 'The barn! You could all go in the barn! There's a big sink and it's really pretty warm, isn't it, darling? Tim and I have done the odd naughty sleepover up in the hayloft and it's great fun. There's a good big table and plenty of room for camp beds and everything.'

Tim and Francesca gave the Parkers their most open smiles. It felt gratifying to have come up with such a wonderful solution to the problem. Sally, Kyle and Frank looked blankly at them.

It was Sally who broke the silence.

'Well, I suppose, like you said, it is Christmas in a couple of months, isn't it? You could have your very own Jesus, Mary and Joseph, plus four children, and two dogs, right on your back doorstep, couldn't you?'

'It'd be great fun!' agreed Francesca warmly.

Sally stood up. The boyfriend jeans looked good on her. Tim was particularly appreciative of the slight gap between low-slung waistband and tight shirt, showing off a taut midriff.

'Kyle. Frank. We're going,' Sally announced curtly.

'Eh?' said Kyle, nearly at the end of his G & T and hoping for a refill. Frank was looking dangerously close to nodding off.

'We can't stay in this hellhole a moment longer,' said Sally.

The Daly-Jones smiles collapsed in unison.

'I'm sorry we can't play Holy Families with you, Tim and Francesca. Maybe another time.'

And she motioned for the men to follow her as she headed for the door. Kyle managed to pinch the last mini pizza on his way out.

Back at Cedar Vale, the Parker children were upstairs, packing.

'This is like a bad dream,' said Emily, folding a jumper neatly into her suitcase.

'Yeah,' agreed Cleo, 'this is what it must feel like to be thrown off *Love Island*.'

'Well, you three are all right,' moped Stephen. 'You didn't get your entire friendship group ripped away from you. I can't believe they took my Xbox, PS3 and 4!'

'Stephen,' Cleo gave him a long-suffering look, 'those droids playing nerdy games with you on a computer are not a friendship group.'

'They're all I've got,' he said sadly.

'Well, why don't you trying making some real friends, then?' asked Mikey jauntily; she was the only one who seemed genuinely excited about the family's forthcoming adventure.

'Oh Mikey,' said Emily, 'why do you have to be, just so, ELEVEN about all of this? This isn't Enid Blyton, you know. It's not *Four Get Evicted and Go Off on a Jolly Camping Spree Together*. We're homeless.'

'Dad will look after us,' Mikey said defiantly.

'A Tamagotchi pet wouldn't survive twenty minutes in his care,' said Emily.

'Oh, DON'T MENTION THAT!' shouted Cleo suddenly. 'You know my beloved Tamagotchi passed away, Em. I've only just got closure from that loss.'

'That was, like, four years ago,' said Stephen.

'So?' said Cleo.

'Anyway,' added Mikey, '*I'm* going to help this family.'

Emily snorted with laughter. 'What, are you going to call Uncle Quentin and he'll come and save us all from the beastly bailiffs and then "Mother" will bake us a ripping plum cake and we'll all have high tea together washed down with lashings of ginger beer?'

'I've got some cash. I can help,' said Mikey.

'Can you give me some?' said Cleo. 'I need waxing strips. My vajayjay is like some kind of forest. The Forest of Dean Gaffney or whatever it's called.'

'It's just the Forest of Dean,' said Stephen.

271

'Whatevs,' said Cleo, standing up in front of her shoddily packed case and four bursting plastic bags. She flicked her hair out fulsomely, to make herself feel like the lead character in a TV show.

'This does feel kind of dramatic, though, doesn't it, guys?' said Cleo with a lurking smile.

'It feels like a crap soap opera,' Emily stood up, 'and I don't think I want to stick around to watch how it unfolds.'

'What do you mean?' asked Stephen.

'I'm sixteen,' she said, looking at all of her cousins one by one. 'I'm officially an adult. When I've got the funds together, I'm going to go and find my mum. I'll be one less person for Sally to feed. Not that she can cook.'

There was silence as her cousins digested this important news.

'You can't just leave us, Em,' said Stephen softly.

'You're our family,' added Mikey.

Emily smiled at them sadly. There was a melancholy silence.

'If you go, can I have your hair straighteners?' asked Cleo.

It was Thursday, and a chilly drizzle settled over Cedar Vale and its surrounding countryside. The westward hills were now clothed in early October fog, and the blackbirds had started to think about hunkering down. The Parker family amassed their cases, mattresses, bedding and remaining belongings around them in the hallway. Janice Dawes was there to help and was lugging essential pots, pans, plates and crockery out of the kitchen. Anything they couldn't take with them Janice agreed to store in her lockup, and they would sell stuff as and when they could. She was also going to take five of the dogs, leaving Liesl, Sally's beloved bichon, and Kurt.

'I don't know how I'm ever going to repay you for all that you've done, Janice,' said Sally during a quiet moment, and she started to pull at a ring on her wedding finger. She held out the beautiful white gold band set with diamonds and amethysts, to Janice. 'Here, I want you to have my engagement ring. It's the least I can give you.'

If Janice had allowed herself to, she would have imagined this scenario being played out on a white sandy beach somewhere in Mauritius, with the pair of them in matching white linen suits, crowns of exotic flowers on their heads and a beautiful sunset lighting up their faces. But Janice Dawes was a dog groomer, businesswoman and realist. She knew that Sally Parker wasn't proposing to her; she pulled her hand away.

'I'm not taking that off you, Sally,' she said, clearing her throat. 'You'll need that to flog for cash.'

Sally smiled ruefully and put the ring back on.

'You are a true friend, Janice. I think you're the first proper one I've ever had.'

And she hugged Janice hard. Janice used every iota of her willpower to ignore Sally's breasts crushed against hers, and the sweet smell of her hair against her cheeks. When they parted she said gruffly:

'I'll move the chairs out, shall I?'

The children sat on the hall floor despondently, three of them on their phones; Sally had no idea how much longer they had on their contracts.

'So, Mum,' said Cleo, looking at her expectantly, 'what's the plan?'

Sally took in her family. Frank had taken himself off to the chessboard and was lying on a roll mat made out of his coat, gently snoring. Kyle was noodling away on his guitar, grimacing as he tried to reach the notes. Mikey was having a serious, animated chat to somebody on her phone, with lots of hand gesturing; Sally had no idea who she was talking to. Emily had a maths book out and was doing her homework. Cleo was taking selfies of herself with sad and dramatic faces. Stephen was playing some game on his phone, involving frantic use of fingers and thumbs. The two dogs just sat neatly, looking expectantly at their mistress.

Sally cleared her throat. She had a sudden longing to be in the steam room, alone, at the Park Club, on half a Valium. What a lovely way to spend an afternoon. She drove the fantasy away with a shake of her head, and addressed the troops.

'In a few minutes Mr Aziz will be here with his relatives to settle them in. We'll then need to leave.'

'Where are we going?' asked Emily, looking up from her equations.

'It's a short-term solution, but we're going to stay in the pool house.'

Everyone looked up.

'What?' said Cleo, forgetting her selfies.

'The pool house?' asked Stephen.

'What, all of us?' asked Emily.

Mikey stalled her phone chat briefly to join in the conversation. 'All of us in the pool house? SO COOL!!' She was hopping from one foot to the other with excitement.

Everyone was watching Sally intently. There was a pause before she spoke again.

'That's if I can get Mr Aziz and his tenants to agree,' she added, 'as we'd be effectively squatting on their property. I haven't actually asked them yet.'

'WHAT?' said Cleo, bursting out laughing. 'Mum, this is JOKES. Hang on, I've got to take a selfie as if I've just heard that news.'

'Has anyone got a better plan?' Sally asked them, looking around.

'Can't we just stay in a hotel?' suggested Cleo.

'For seven of us, sharing two family rooms, the Crown in Bookham would charge us a hundred and twenty a night. That's eight hundred and forty pounds a week. We currently have about five hundred and fifty quid. But we do have stuff that we can sell.'

Mikey piped up, 'I can help, I've managed to—' but was interrupted by the boom of the 1812 Overture.

Sally straightened herself up.

'Time to say goodbye to Cedar Vale, everybody.'

She opened the front door to Mr Aziz, who was standing in the porch, looking freshly laundered in pale pink shirt and black loafers; he was accompanied by a couple in their forties with a teenage boy.

'Hello again, Sally.' He held out that strong hand to her again and looked intently into her eyes.

'Hello . . . Dave,' she stammered.

'This is my cousin Yusuf Jamal, his wife Rashida and their son Amir.'

All were taller than Sally, with great cheekbones and dignified faces. Rashida wore a pretty headscarf. Yusuf was wearing a suit, and Amir had the hugest brown eyes and the thickest eyelashes Sally had ever seen. She shook hands with them one by one. The Jamal family smiled politely at her, but couldn't help having a sneaky look beyond Sally at what was to be their new home.

'This is my family,' said Sally, as her tribe gathered round her, 'this is Kyle, my brother-in-law, my husband Frank's asleep over there somewhere, and these are my children, Mikey, Stephen, Emily and where's Cleo?' Cleo was holding back, still taking selfies.

'I'm her niece,' Emily corrected her.

'Yes. I'm Em's aunt. Cleo, come and say hello.'

Cleo put down her phone with a huff and came forward to introduce herself. She stared blankly at Dave Aziz and shook hands cursorily with Yusuf and Rashida Jamal. Then she got to Amir. Cleo looked at him, he looked at her and they held the handshake as if the world had stopped on its axis around them. They just carried on gazing into each other's eyes. Sally interrupted them.

'Cleo?'

Cleo turned to her mum.

'*Omigod!*' she mouthed at Sally.

Rashida Jamal prodded her son to let go of Cleo's hand. Stephen nudged Emily.

'What?' said Emily gruffly, unaware of what was unfolding in front of her.

'*This was my dream! The boy on the doorstep!*' Cleo mouthed to her cousin.

'WHAT?' said Emily, still not getting it.

Dave Aziz and Sally shared a private look as they caught one another enjoying this touching teenage moment. Sally blushed at the intimacy of it. She felt the hotness of her cheeks, and looked down at her feet uncomfortably. She had to take control; it was time to bite the bullet. She looked up and focused her eyes on Mr Aziz the business-man. Not Mr Aziz the gorgeous man with the sexy jeans and comforting gravelly voice.

'Dave,' she said in a business-like fashion, 'there's something I need to negotiate with you.'

Bronwen Llewellyn was sitting up in her old country-style armchair staring out at the beautiful sea view. There was nothing to see but God's good work; the sky, the sea, the rocks, the birds. She was looking paler than normal, but the bead was still there in the eye. She had her radio beside her, a prayer book, and two Jackie Collins novels. Her friend Myfanwy had dropped in to make her a cup of tea and a sandwich. Bronwen had lost her appetite and found it hard to get anything down.

Her front parlour was spick and span. Shining cups and plates on the dresser, with school photos of various Parker children at different stages, Sally and Frank on their wedding day and the cheekiest picture of Frank at fifteen. He looked brimful of life, his mischievous smile threatening to burst out of the photo frame. Bronwen loved that picture of him.

Her eye fell on the telephone, an old-fashioned avocado green timepiece with enormous dial and handset. She'd been waiting for his phone call for many days now. Maybe he'd mislaid the letter. Maybe he still hadn't read it. Bronwen tutted as she thought of him.

'Silly sod. You'd better be quick or I might have croaked it,' she said out loud to herself and to the empty house.

Four hours later and the pool house was shipshape. With Janice Dawes' valiant help and some old bunk beds she'd managed to dig up, there were now seven beds almost made up and ready for sleeping in. Lucky for the Parkers that the large, Swiss-style chalet was divided into two rooms, essentially one room a big changing room with lots of useful hooks on the wall for swimsuits and towels, and the other a general chill-out room with a handful of wicker chairs. Janice had thoughtfully put a blow heater in each of the rooms.

'This is some crackpot fairy tale,' remarked Kyle as he sat on his camp bed with his guitar, 'we're like those seven dwarves . . . what were their names? Dopey, Speedy, Weedy, Cracky, Heroiny . . .' He wheezed with laughter.

'*Six* dwarves would be a much more comfortable fit for this space, Kyle,' said Sally loadedly. Kyle just smiled at her blankly.

'Or five,' added Emily pointedly as she passed by, putting a pillowcase on her pillow.

Sally glanced at Emily wistfully and then finished tucking in sheets on beds.

Frank had already bagged a lower bunk; the last weeks had taken their toll on him and all he wanted to do was zone out. Janice had put a two-ring electric stove in the large utility cupboard to make a tiny kitchen. She'd also stacked their dried goods neatly on to shelves. There was a small freezer in the bigger room where swimming guests of old would get ice to plop into their Camparis. Those Cedar Vale skinny-dipping party days were well and truly over. The general feel in the pool house today was a budget holiday in Center Parcs, with not enough rooms booked. And without the holiday atmosphere.

Sally looked around and allowed herself a small sigh of relief. The kettle was on, everyone had a bed for the night. There was food in the cupboards, she had five hundred and fifty pounds and, crucially, nobody had died.

'Everyone OK?' she asked generally. She had the odd grunt back but no specifically worded reply, which she took as a positive sign. She hoicked herself on to the top bunk so that she could peer over to spy on Frank. He had a woolly hat on, which, combined with the beard, made him look like some whacked-out old hippy living rough on a beach. She sighed. What was to become of the pair of them? She didn't have time to worry about that, there were a hundred other things to sort out. She hopped down and wandered into the other room to find Cleo draped over a wicker chair, brushing her hair dreamily.

278

'Hi.'

'Hi.'

'What?' said Cleo, letting a small smile curl around her mouth.

'Nothing,' replied Sally, smiling back.

The moment was interrupted by a knock at the pool-house door.

'Come in!' shouted Stephen.

Amir Jamal poked his head around the door.

'My mum's cooking. She wants to know if anybody wants to eat with us.'

'Yes please!' shouted seven voices in unison.

18

Seven people and two dogs living in a shed cum mock Swiss chalet was workable as long as everyone kept to their bed or wicker chair when they were inside. The two blow heaters plus the sheer volume of bodies kept the place pretty warm. Mealtimes had to be rigorously organised and cleared up due to minimal cat-swinging space.

Sally and Stephen found themselves naturally falling into a two-person catering team.

'I'm scared of cooking, Ste,' confided Sally to her son on their fifth day in the pool house. They were portioning out muesli carefully into bowls. 'Paloma was so good at it, and I haven't done it for so long.'

'I reckon I might be all right at it, Mum,' said Stephen. 'I've always loved eating,' he added ruefully.

'I think you're losing weight, Ste,' said Sally, patting her son's tummy. 'This is going to be a good thing for you.'

Stephen pulled away from his mum. Sally saw his crest-fallen face.

'I'm sorry, Ste, that was insensitive.'

'Again and again, the only thing you ever talk to me about is my weight. I've had enough of it. I'm a human being, Mum, not some piece of meat you weigh up at the butchers.'

And he left the tiny kitchen and walked out of the house, slamming the door behind him.

Any sort of exchange in the pool house was a shared experience; it was impossible not to hear everything that was said. Kyle put his nose into the utility cupboard.

'That's a touchy subject with a fella, you know, Sal. If you're a tubster like Ste then it's tough—'

'I'd ask you not to earwig into my conversations, Kyle, and can you please get out of the kitchen?'

Emily's voice came in from the next room.

'Kyle's right though, Sally. It's fat-shaming. It must get pretty depressing for him.'

'Right,' said Sally, standing up in the kitchen/utility cupboard, her face only three inches from Kyle who hadn't yet left the space, 'does anybody else in here have anything to say on the subject of my relationship with my son's weight? Yeah? Just speak up right now.'

Frank's voice chimed in from the bottom bunk,

'I have to agree with the guys, Sally. Ste's got a lot on his plate at the moment. Well, actually he's got less on his plate at the moment due to our reduced circumstances. Probably a good thing for him, now I think of it.'

This was too much for Sally. Frank had done precisely less than nothing for the five days they'd been living in the pool house, except for sleeping and eating.

'Thank you so much for the wise words, Frank. And yes, great of you to point out that we're running out of food. Would it be too much to ask of you, oh great provider, to leave our house and go out and get some? You should be able to manage it, you've had five weeks of sleep!'

Sally was finding it too easy to talk to Frank like this these days. She felt tougher inside, and shorter of fuse.

Frank's small tired face, framed by the woolly hat, appeared from the lower bunk and looked at her mournfully.

He was well aware that Sally's voice was getting gruffer with him by the day. She always used to agree with him

281

with a honeyed tone; now she gave him curt answers, usually completely opposing whatever it was he'd just said. He felt his alpha maleness waning by the minute. He was right down to omega. His existence consisted of waking up and trying to stay awake. What a pointless life, he thought, just trying to stay awake.

Frank opened his eyes wide in the bunk. He'd had enough of this lounging around. Today he was going to be a useful cog in the Parker machine. He was going to become chief hunter-gatherer once more and Sally would talk to him sweetly again.

He heaved himself up and almost put his foot through Kyle's guitar.

'Easy bro, if anyone touches The Lady they'll feel the back of my hand,' said Kyle, swooping down to rescue his beloved instrument. Frank ignored his brother.

'Right, Sally. What's on our shopping list?' Frank tried to barrel out his chest and stand up straight. 'I'm fully prepared to go now and do it. For this family.'

'It's just a trip to Lidl, Frank. You're not saving us from the incoming hordes of Visigoths or anything.'

'What is Lidl?' asked Frank, confused.

Sally slumped into a wicker chair and put her head in her hands. She spoke through them.

'What is Lidl? Frank, it's a value supermarket where a lot of people shop. I was there two days ago. It's just off the Fetcham interchange.'

'OK, Lidl,' Frank was still speaking loudly, 'I shall go to this Lidl now. What do I need to get at Lidl?'

'You don't have to keep repeating the word "Lidl", Frank,' Sally could hear herself nagging. 'We need staples. Badly.'

'Don't I go to an office supplies shop for those? That's what Kerry would have done,' he replied.

Emily laughed out loud from the other room. 'Oh Frank. What a numpty!'

Kyle laughed too, from back in the cupboard.

'Not those kind of staples, Frank,' said Sally, trying not to lose her rag. 'I mean staples that you can eat. Pasta, rice, flour, that kind of thing.'

Frank felt his cheek twitch. It riled him that Emily had laughed at him like that, and his wife's pity was way worse than her wrath.

'Off you go to Lidl, Frank. The money's in the jar by the mug tree.'

Frank cut a shambling figure along the Fetcham Road. He was now a good mile away from Cedar Vale and absolutely exhausted. It was at least another mile to Lidl. What was he thinking? He must have been crazy to endeavour something this momentous. He was just about to sit down on a nearby tree stump when a familiar Range Rover came round the bend, Tim Daly-Jones skippering the ship.

'All right, Parker?' said Tim unsmilingly, looking down from the driver's window. Sally's 'hellhole' comment was still fresh in his mind. 'All you're missing is a couple of carrier bags to complete that tramp look you've got going.'

'Any chance of a lift, D-J?' asked Frank. Tim sniffed and motioned for him to get in. 'Lidl OK with you?'

Tim looked at Frank with pure incredulity.

Back in the pool house, Sally took the opportunity to have some time with Emily, alone. She'd seen the others off to school and Kyle was having a coffee with some housewife he'd met at a psychic meeting, but Emily didn't have any GCSE classes till later that morning.

'It's weird, Sal,' Kyle said as he was leaving, 'it's like I just know that I'm supposed to meet her at Georgina's coffee shop in Ashtead?'

'Is that where you arranged to meet her, Kyle?' said Sally with a small sigh.

'Yes,' he replied, 'but me making that arrangement was predestined.'

And Kyle departed in a cloud of patchouli fug.

'Eeeuurgh! The sights and smells of Uncle Kyle at close quarters!' said Emily, waving her hands to get rid of the odour. 'It's enough to drive anyone to the Housing Office!'

Sally smiled and moved all of Emily's books aside on her camp bed to sit down beside her.

'I'm sorry about the chaos, Em,' said Sally, stroking Emily's shiny brown hair.

'I'm used to it,' said Emily dryly.

'You're so disciplined, Em. You're amazing. Through all the ups and downs of your life, you've just kept on going. It's inspiring.'

Emily didn't look up from her history book.

'Have you got something to tell me, Sally?'

Her aunt laughed.

'And it's always been impossible to pull the wool, or even fur, over your eyes. Remember when I tried to substitute new guinea pig for dead guinea pig?'

'To be fair, the dead one was black and smooth-haired, and you substituted it with a brown rosetted one,' laughed Emily.

'But you were only two!'

The pair of them sat in thought for a moment. Emily spoke first,

'I have a feeling this is something to do with the St Bede's scholarship. One of my teachers mentioned it to me.'

Sally nodded.

'It's a real feather in your cap, Em. A full scholarship till the end of Sixth Form. Congratulations, love! They clearly realise your academic potential. It'd mean that whatever happens to us, you could stay there and have a really stable education.'

Emily nodded thoughtfully.

'And we'd all stay here in the pool house?' she said, trying to put a brave face on it, 'with me trying to revise for exams?'

'Well,' said Sally carefully, 'this is only temporary, Em. I know things haven't been easy for you in the family, so if you wanted, I'm sure we could all come up with a good plan that would make it easier for you and give you the security—'

'I can't help it that I'm his niece,' said Emily. 'I know it pisses him off that I whip his own kids academically.'

'Frank is extremely proud of you, Em.'

'Up to a point. As proud as an uncle can be of a niece. He'd rather it were his own kids coming top in all of their GCSE mocks, let's be honest here. I'm an outsider and a geek, Sally.'

Emily let her head hang down and Sally felt her heart being stretched almost to the point of being ripped out of her chest. 'Listen to me, Em. I have loved you as my own since the day my sister left you with us. You are a gift. Our very special gift from her, and I will never stop loving you. Do you understand?'

Emily hugged her aunt and they sat there for some time, Sally carefully stroking her hair. She never wanted to let Emily out of her sight again, but said in an even tone,

'It's just something for you to think about, Em. OK?'

Emily nodded and nestled into Sally's armpit. She'd always loved doing that, since she was tiny.

*

Unbeknownst to her parents, Cleo had not been at school all week. That fateful Thursday when the Jamals showed up on the doorstep at Cedar Vale marked the beginning of a new era, a new everything for Cleo Parker. For her it was as momentous as the difference between the time BC and AD. Seeing Amir there in front of her, looking into his eyes, that seismic moment of recognition, not just of each other's physical attributes but of each other's very souls, Cleo knew for certain that Amir Jamal was her destiny.

He was a full year older than Cleo, had left school, and up to this point in his life had been at the receiving end of very loving but pressurising parents. Yusuf and Rashida were determined for him to get top grades, succeed and make something of himself in Britain, his country of birth. The moment Amir set eyes on Cleo he realised that what he'd been missing in his life was fun. He loved her easy laugh, relaxed energy and saucer eyes that believed anything he'd tell her. They both had that flushed look of first love. Cleo's skin was dewier, her eyes softer and more sparkly; Amir's movements were more fluid and surefooted. He stood taller, prouder.

Cleo had spent most of her waking hours since Thursday with the Jamal family and was loving every minute. She could tell that laughter had been scant in their little family. And Cleo always brought laughter with her. She often didn't know why, but she did, and it clearly made those around her feel better. Cleo was certainly the only Parker getting her five a day; the kitchen at Cedar Vale was filled with delicious smells from Rashida's oven. Amir's parents were delighted to see the teens together like this.

'It's like Harry and Meghan,' Rashida had said to her husband as they watched the pair of young lovers laying the supper table together one evening. Amir's parents had already started planning when to go and talk to Frank and Sally about their hopes for the teenagers.

Frank and Sally didn't have a clue what was going on. Sally had witnessed the *deus ex machina* moment when Cupid arrived on the Cedar Vale doorstep, but assumed it was just a teen crush. If she had seen the pair of them chatting, laughing, chasing each other round Cedar Vale, poring over Amir's photos of Afghanistan, cooking together and cuddling each other on the sofa, she might have had more inkling.

Cleo was desperate to talk to somebody about all this, and was planning on telling her parents at some point, just not yet. Her ideal confidante would be Great-Granny Bronwen. Now there was somebody who had lived and loved. And she was good at keeping secrets. When Cleo was tiny, she'd broken the lid of Sally's favourite teapot. And Bronwen told Sally that it was actually her who'd done it and never revealed Cleo was the culprit. Cleo had never forgotten that.

She phoned Bronwen at a good distance from the pool house so that nobody could earwig.

'Well, just make sure I get to meet this delicious young man of yours, Cleo,' said Bronwen into the avocado handset which was way too big for her tiny head. 'You'd better come to Llanfairfechan soon or I might not be here!'

'Where are you off to, G-G?' said Cleo with a laugh. 'Are you going on holiday? Amir says he's going to take me somewhere like *Love Island*!'

'Oh, is he now?' said Bronwen. 'And is he aware that it's just a TV show and it's filmed in Skegness?'

Bronwen wheezed into her telephone which made Cleo fall about at her end.

Cleo felt that it was delicious to have a glorious secret. It was her private little fantasy world, which helped her escape the reality of the cramped pool house. She hugged herself at night, in the camp bed beside Emily, imagining what it would be like to spend a whole night with Amir. They were already planning their first sleepover up at Cedar Vale in a couple of days. Cleo was too excited for sleep, and it fed her abundance of wired energy.

For Cleo, the chilly October drabness was cosy and mysterious, the mud underfoot charming and rural, life in the pool house hilarious and quirky. For Cleo Parker, life was better than it had ever been.

Tim Daly-Jones nosed the Range Rover into Gaysford's Farm Shop car park. Frank wasn't quite sure how they'd ended up in here rather than Lidl's but was so relieved to just sit in a car, he didn't really care where he was. He knew this shop's produce all too well, and his mouth watered at the thought of all those fresh staples that he was going to purchase.

Tim got a trolley, so Frank got one too; Parker honour must be upheld, and a poxy basket simply would not do.

'This all right for you, Frank? I mean, I don't want to break your budget or anything,' said Tim, helping himself to a big bag of heritage Shropshire tomatoes retailing at £11.95 a kilo.

'Of course it's all right,' answered Frank, toying with some Jordanian pomegranates at £21.95 a kilo. 'In fact, to be honest, I think Sally's making a bit of a big deal out of all this. I'm sorry it all got so heated at yours the other day. Sal's feeling the stress a bit, but basically it's all dandy.'

'So you're still at Seedy Vale?'

Frank busied himself very quickly with a big loaf of sourdough bread priced at £18.

'Yes, we are at Cedar Vale,' he replied, not making

eye contact with Tim. 'This Lincolnshire Yeoman's sourdough's a bit of a bargain, isn't it?'

Frank beetled off down the aisle. The two men met again at the mahogany checkout inlaid with brass, peopled by staff in boaters and striped waistcoats. They looked like 1950s students about to float upstream in a punt.

At the tills, Frank emptied his trolley of the Lincolnshire sourdough, an enormous handmade coffee and walnut cake from Carlisle, two huge rustic sacks of Umbrian polenta, a large bottle of Viennese cherry liqueur, fifteen Guernsey quinces, five kilos of biodynamically farmed potatoes from the Isle of Man, eight jars of Duchess of Devonshire pickles, a gargantuan terracotta vessel of Dijon mustard and – Frank couldn't resist this because he'd always loved tinned custard as a child – two big vats of Ye Olde Surrey Custarde, made locally, along with a bottle of vintage champagne to woo back the wife.

Frank was first through the checkout, with all his goods going into smart grey tote bags with 'Gaysford's Farm Shop' embroidered on the side.

'That'll be four hundred and forty-eight pounds of the realm please, and ninety pence, good sir,' said Charlie, the rosy-cheeked checkout chappie.

Tim, who was bringing up the rear, said to Frank in a stage whisper:

'I bought some toothpaste in here the other day, mate, it was seventeen cocking quid! It was made from bloody bicarbonate from Shrewsbury or somewhere and salt from Brittany. It's foul. It's like brushing your teeth in sperm. What a rip off, eh?'

And he laughed loudly.

Frank had gone the colour of the grey Gaysford's tote bag. Beads of sweat were forming on his brow. He had taken five hundred pounds from Sally's jar, but was this money to last the whole week, and was it just for food or was it for other things too? Household budgeting had never been his strong suit. He looked down at the five hundred pounds, saw Tim's leering face, and then the expectant eyes of rosy-cheeked Charlie. Frank handed over the money quickly before he changed his mind.

Back at Cedar Vale, Sally was clock-watching. When she noticed that it was eleven a.m., she checked herself in the mirror, applied a whiff of lip gloss and mascara, and decided to take the dogs for their daily walk outside. It felt too weird to stroll around the gardens of what used to be her own house, and she didn't want to disturb the Jamals, so she'd taken to going straight down to the woods at the end of Cedar Vale's southern boundary.

It was a grey but warm October day, and Sally allowed herself to relax and feel slightly optimistic. There was a lot to be grateful for: Cleo was in the best form Sally had ever seen her, she had reconnected with Emily, and Mikey was loving the camping adventure. She made a mental note to sort things out with Stephen; still, three out of four wasn't bad. And, amazingly, Frank was actually awake, out of the house and doing something useful for a change. Plus, Sally told herself, as she told herself religiously every day like a Buddhist mantra, God willing, Kyle would not stay for ever. Soon he'd be off and she would never have to listen to him massacring 'Norwegian Wood' ever again.

There was a reason that she left the house at eleven a.m. on the dot. It just happened that on the morning after her first night in the pool house, she went for a stroll in the woods at eleven a.m. and bumped into Dave Aziz, who also happened to be taking a stroll there at the same time. And so it had chanced to happen on every intervening day since then. Neither mentioned it. Fate or happenstance placed them there together that first morning, and they were simply following Destiny's lead by following the same pattern every day. It wasn't a tryst, it wasn't a rendezvous, they just both happened to be strolling in the woods every day at eleven a.m.; and it had become Sally's favourite time of day. Never before in her life had she loved eleven a.m. so much; it was as important to her as her own heartbeat.

Sally walked through the trees, enjoying the sound that her (or rather Cleo's) Nike Airs made as they scrunched the autumn leaves. Both Kurt and Liesl loved the woods too and went nosying off on their own trail. It struck Sally as crazy that, when she lived at Cedar Vale proper, she'd never really known these beautiful woods. Now they felt like a part of her. Occasionally she would stop to pick up a twig or pluck a berry, allowing herself to look around subtly to see if she could see the familiar figure. She was crouched down bagging up a dog poo, when she heard the nearby cracking of a branch underfoot. She stood up, trying to hide the poo bag, and found Dave Aziz's tall frame much closer to her than she'd expected. In fact, he was inches away from her.

'Boo!' he said playfully into her face.

'I didn't hear you. Stalker!' said Sally, flustered at the smell of his musky scent, and the fact that there was a bag of fresh dog poo in her hand.

'I've been tracking you, Sally Parker!' he said, looking her up and down lingeringly. Sally felt her insides melt, and started to stroll away gently.

'How's life in the pool house?' Dave asked as he followed behind.

'Oh, you know,' said Sally, 'it's pretty palatial in there. I'm thinking of installing a gym, actually. And maybe a basement cinema. If that's OK with the pool-house land-lord?' she said, smiling. 'Thanks for giving us a roof over our heads, Dave. I don't know how we'd have survived, honestly.'

They walked in silence for a couple of paces, Sally still in front.

'And I don't know how I'd survive,' said Dave softly behind her, 'without you, Sally.'

Sally stopped in her tracks. She felt her heart beat faster, but not through panic this time; she didn't want to reach for the Valium to block this feeling, she wanted to feel every iota of its power and beauty. She wanted her heart-beat to go on like this, thumping blood around every inch of her body.

She turned round slowly. She knew exactly what was going to happen next. She stood in front of Dave, locked eyes with him and they looked at each other for what seemed like hours. He traced her cheek softly with his hand, all the way down to her chin. She closed her eyes, carried away by the sheer bliss of it. And then she felt him reach down to kiss her with his soft lips, tasting faintly of something sweet. Sally kissed him back and he pulled her into his cashmere coat. For the first time in a long time, Sally Parker felt safe, warm and cared for.

She was suddenly aware of an unsavoury smell drift-ing up into her nostril area and broke away from Dave's embrace.

'Sorry! Liesl's shits are legendarily stinky!'

Dave looked very slightly put off.

'I'd better go, Dave. I'd better get rid of this . . . and . . . anyway . . . it was lovely to see you . . .' Her voice trailed away.

'I can't go on like this, Sally. I want you. I'm driven to distraction by you.'

Sally looked down at his Russell & Bromley loafers, unable to meet his eye. She admitted, 'I'm pretty distracted too, as it goes.'

'Here's the deal, Sally. I'll let you stay here, in the pool house obviously, for as long as you like, as long as you need, and we can be lovers. We're both married. That's not going to change. But we hunger for each other. I see it in your eyes. What do you say, Sally? How about it? Deal?'

Sally's heartbeat seemed to stop.

'Deal?' she said.

'Yes. Deal,' Dave confirmed.

'So, this is an arrangement, a transaction?' Sally asked, now looking him directly in the eye. 'So what happens? We slink off somewhere, I don't know, a Holiday Inn . . .'

'I'd stump up for a Travelodge,' Dave said seriously.

'We'd shag like rabbits, then I'd skip back to my family and, thank you so much, live in your pool house which I seem to remember my husband actually paid for after he saw one exactly like it in Gstaadt?'

Dave saw that Sally looked angry and was confused. 'What? Is there a problem with the pool house?'

Sally laughed.

'I have many regrets in my life, Dave. But the biggest by a country mile is that I just let you kiss me. I'll never, ever forgive myself for that.'

With which she handed him the dog poo bag and set off at a brisk pace, which soon turned into a run.

'Same time tomorrow?' Dave Aziz shouted after her.

Sally kept running.

James Livesy sat in his Sloane Square surgery, ruminating over his luncheon choices. It was one of the chief pleasures in life to eat alone and watch pretty girls go by. Would he pop down to the river for a little two-course Italian? Or would something funky down the Kings Road be more the thing? A cheeky Moroccan burger with quinoa salad, perchance? His salivary glands were juicing up as he thought of honey-skinned girls with a fancy burger on the side.

And then the phone rang. His blasted secretary. He'd told her never to put any calls through while he was making important lunch decisions.

'I think you'd better take it, Dr Livesy,' her voice was terse, 'it's the General Medical Council on the line.'

'General Medical Council?' Livesy replied gruffly to her. 'What the hell do they—'

And then his face drained of all human colour. The penny dropped right into his guts. He couldn't stomach the idea of lunch right now.

'HOW MUCH?' Sally bellowed directly into her husband's face.

'Sal, come on. There's no need to shout,' Frank tried his best to placate her.

'NO NEED TO SHOUT? YOU NUMPTY, YOU ABSOLUTE ARSEHOLE, FRANK!'

'Language, Sally,' Frank whispered almost inaudibly.

Sally looked as if she were about to cry as she gripped the £51.10 change Frank had given her.

'WHAT ELSE DID YOU BUY WITH THE FIVE HUNDRED POUNDS, FRANK? SOME MAGIC FUCKING BEANS?'

'Language, please, Sally,' said Emily, doing geography homework on a top bunk.

Kyle came through, guitar in hand.

'Folks, come on, I know anger can be a good release but shall we just try and chi—'

'DO NOT TELL ME TO CHILLAX, KYLE. I WILL CROWN YOU WITH THAT FUCKING GUITAR IF YOU TELL ME TO CHILLAX!' bellowed his sister-in-law.

'Language, Mum,' said Stephen just at that moment stepping in through the pool-house door. It had been ages since Sally had seen him, and just the sight of his face made her crumple. Sally ran to him and hugged him with all her might.

'I'm sorry, Ste. I'm so sorry for making those crass comments and for being a crap mum. I love you, darling, I really do.'

'All right, Mum! It's OK. I forgive you. Just watch the language. And chillax, yeah?'

She hugged him even harder.

'Oh, so it's fine if the big man says "chillax", is it?' said Kyle, sotto voce. 'It's all hugs and popsicles when *he* says "chillax"? You hypocrite, Sally.'

Sally wiped angry tears away with her sleeve. Frank sloped into the nearest bottom bunk. Cleo and Mikey came through the door at that moment, and Sally felt an impromptu pool-house meeting coming on.

'Right, here's the deal,' and she shivered inwardly at the memory of the last time she'd heard that word. 'We have one hundred and one pounds ten in cash at the moment. In total. For seven of us to live off. But what we DO have is a very large amount of overpriced polenta, and guys, you'll never guess what! A bottle of cherry liqueur!'

'Mum—' interrupted Mikey.

'Not now, Mikey,' snapped Sally.

'But, Mum, it's—'

'Mikey,' Sally looked sharply at her youngest, 'this is not the time. So listen everybody, we need to get our heads together and come up with some cash-making plans pretty fast. I've got an idea that I'm going to run by Janice. If all of you can come up with something too, then that'd be great.'

Kyle puffed up his chest and looked serious.

'I will tout myself and my lungs, with The Lady in hand, outside the Thorndike Theatre. I was born to busk. Just ask the good people of Bogota Coach Station.'

'Thank you, Kyle. I'll factor in an extra three pounds fifty for that, then.'

Kyle smiled and then realised what Sally had just said.

'Hey!' he said.

'Any other thoughts?' said Sally, now in full chairwoman mode.

'Looking at these ingredients,' said Stephen, 'I reckon I might be able to come up with something pretty good using polenta, pickles and a few things knocking around.'

'Fantastic, Ste.'

'I'm not going to lie, but Amir's mum is the most brilliantest cook,' said Cleo.

'Grammar, Cleo!' croaked Frank from his bunk.

'Her food is like, to die for? It's legit better than KFC popcorn chicken.'

'We can't keep sponging meals off them,' said her mum. 'They've had it tough themselves, coming from Afghanistan and everything.'

Cleo stared at her mum.

'What do you mean? They've lived here for years. Amir was born here. Yusuf drives an Audi, Mum, and works for Kingston University. He's, like, an engineer?'

Sally paused. She was taken aback at how much Cleo seemed to know about these Jamals.

'We're the refugees in this equation,' chipped in Emily from the top bunk.

'Thank you, Emily,' said Sally with a brittle tone to her voice, 'we are hardly that. We can survive perfectly well without relying on others.'

'What about just contacting the council and trying to get into the benefit system?' suggested Stephen.

'We're not at that stage yet, Ste. There are many, many people out there way more deserving of the state than us. Look at us. We've got everything.'

There was a silence.

'I haven't got a desk, chair, or adequate lighting to do my homework.'

'I'll find you a good torch, Em,' said her aunt.

'I haven't got my Xbox,' said Stephen mournfully.

'Just as well,' said Sally quickly, 'you wouldn't have time to create wonderful dishes if you did.'

Mikey spoke up next.

'I haven't got my TV and DVD player but I could probably buy one if I wanted to, because I've got—'

Sally interrupted her.

'It's good for you to be living some stories rather than being fed some Disney version of them, Mikey,'

'I haven't got a job. Or my health. Or any savings,' mumbled Frank from the bunk.

'Or the five hundred and fifty pounds that was our entire budget, Frank,' said Sally somewhat unfeelingly.

'Well, I love it here,' said Cleo, running her hands through her hair and looking winsomely out of the window.

'Are you on drugs?' Emily asked her cousin.

Cleo laughed.

'I kind of love it too,' added Mikey, 'although I wish you'd listen to me. You see, Dom and I—'

'Wooooooouuuh!' shouted Cleo, cutting off her little sister. 'What have you and Dom been up to in the school pavilion?'

'Cleo, that's quite enough,' said her mother. 'I have another piece of news to tell you all.'

Sally mustered up her courage. She was not looking forward to this,

'We're leaving the pool house.'

'What?' said Cleo, standing up. 'I'm not leaving here. No way.'

Frank couldn't join in the conversation because he was grabbing a discreet twenty winks, but there were general rumblings of discontent among the rest of the family now.

'Why, Mum? It's sick in here, and we've only just settled in!' wailed Mikey.

Sally stood up and paced, which was difficult on two foot squared of floor.

'We're basically being allowed to stay here by –' Sally could not bring herself to say his name out loud – 'our erstwhile landlord. For free, like squatters. It's a stopgap; we can't stay here for ever. We've got to keep light on our feet, everybody.' There was something almost SAS about Sally as she spoke and Kyle found himself gently aroused. 'I've got a plan. We'll leave here within forty-eight hours, OK?'

'Well you can all leave,' said Cleo, folding her arms, 'but I'm not going anywhere.'

19

Next morning, Sally and Janice parked up in front of The Oast House in Janice's Paws Fur Thought van, which, satisfyingly, had huge black paw prints painted all over its flanks. Sally noticed that the dashboard clock said nearly eleven o'clock; her chest tightened for a moment as she felt the brief sensation of Dave Aziz's musky cashmere coat around her. She coughed; she and Janice had far more important things to do.

Sally knew that Francesca would be out of the house, at the eleven a.m. Body Conditioning class at the Park Club. Sally had squatted directly behind Francesca's legendary arse cheeks too many times to mention; neither plague, fire nor flood would prevent Francesca from attending that class, so Sally knew that they had at least an hour. If all went well, Sally and Janice would be inside The Oast House for no more than ten minutes max.

The front door was locked, as Sally suspected, but she knew that Francesca could never be bothered to turn on the burglar alarm during the day. And she always hid a spare key underneath the trug. While Janice kept lookout, Sally rummaged around and soon retrieved it. She high-fived Janice with a delighted grin; she hadn't felt this alive in years.

'I feel I should remind you that what you're about to do is illegal, Sally,' said Janice.

'I know,' said Sally, 'isn't it thrilling? You go back up to the top of the drive, and wait for me there, I won't be long.'

Janice nodded, as Sally turned the key in the lock and padded into The Oast House. She slipped off her Nike Airs; she didn't want to leave any incriminating footprints on Francesca's beige carpet. Sally allowed herself a brief moment to breathe in the luxury of the central heating and sheer space and quiet of the hall. As she went up the staircase, she looked at the familiar gallery of family photos, shot in the same studio where the Parkers had done theirs. There they were, all of the Daly-Joneses dressed in white and lined up on the white furry rug, lying down and facing camera with their feet swung up behind them. Yes, even their smiles and poses were carbon copies of the Parker prints. How homogenous all these families were, within the Leatherhead five-square-mile radius. Pathetic, now she thought of it. Sally looked down at her hands, which now had signs of work and care, and she liked them; they looked like the hands of a person, not a cipher. She felt tougher, leaner, more alert. She pulled her beanie hat down a little lower over her ears, and headed straight for Francesca's bedroom.

All was serene in the master bedroom. Sally was struck by the distance between door and bed, a full few metres' expanse of vacuumed shag pile that was so thick underfoot she had to wade through it. Sally had a twinge as she remembered the feel of a crisply laundered cotton sheet, a far cry from the sleeping bag that served as her current cocoon. Francesca had a large double wardrobe which Sally threw open; she had a rummage under the Next jumpsuits and row of Hush catalogue dresses. There was no immediate sign of Sally's designer clothes which Francesca and friends had stolen from Cedar Vale. Sally shut the doors quickly, checked her watch and headed out of the room.

She padded through the beautifully ordered kitchen and couldn't resist a quick look in the fridge. A mellow blue light came on like a spaceship as she opened the door and surveyed the works of art inside: an array of five different juices; a stack of high-end ready-made meals. Sally's tummy rumbled as she read 'Braised Venison in Hunter's Sauce' and 'Kilkenny Stew with Parsley Dumplings'. She had to stop herself from shovelling her hand into a tower of profiteroles; she wished she could just stay in the cool of Francesca's fridge for ever, but the clock was ticking.

She figured correctly that the dogs would be in the laundry room. Sally knew the Labradors, Fortnum and Mason, pretty well, so they didn't react except for a snuffle from Fortnum, while Mason let out an excited bark. She padded over to the utility cupboard; no sign of designer clothes there, and nothing around the washing machine and tumble dryer. Sally suddenly heard an engine noise outside; a vehicle was pulling up outside.

'Shit!' she said loudly.

Sally felt her palms go sweaty. The dogs growled. It was only eleven thirteen; Francesca couldn't be home by now. She'd be lowering those colossal buttocks into some squat thrusts at this stage of the class. Sally decided to just carry on, going through to what Francesca called 'the tack room', even though she didn't have any horses. There, near the back door and shoved into two piles, were Sally's designer outfits. She spotted a pair of beautiful cream Dolce and Gabbana palazzo pants she'd worn to a reception at The Dorchester. Frank had whispered in her ear how gorgeous she looked, and they'd walked into that party holding hands. It felt like somebody else's life. She hoped never to have to wear a pair of palazzo pants again. She liked tight military trousers now. Sally felt her eyes start to fill with tears, and rubbed them fiercely away before they could betray her.

She grabbed as many of her clothes as she could and marched out through the laundry room and back into the hall, just in time to meet Francesca's cleaner, Eva. Eva looked confused.

'Hi! Eva, I'm just taking my clothes back.' Before the cleaner had time to respond, she continued, 'Bye Eva, lovely to see you!'

And Sally walked briskly out of the house, down the drive, and into Janice's getaway van.

Beside a particularly beautiful rowan tree sprouting an abundance of reddish berries, Dave Aziz waited for Sally in vain. It was eleven twenty, but he was still hopeful that she might appear. He felt that yesterday's meeting hadn't gone as well as he'd planned, so had brought her a nice bottle of perfume to make up for it today. The bottle stopper was in the shape of a deer's head; 'Faun' it was called, for that was what Sally reminded him of. She was like a delicate woodland creature, living secretly in his wood, and he wanted to be her protector, her stag. He wouldn't mind a bit of rutting either; he had felt her acquiesce at his touch and knew that she wanted him, he'd known that as soon as they'd first set eyes on each other in the hallway at Cedar Vale.

Maybe he'd got the phrasing wrong yesterday; he needed to work on his pitch. Dave Aziz was a grafter, he hadn't accrued this kind of property portfolio without the odd punch in the guts along the way. He sprayed some Faun and inhaled deeply; his loins loosened. He was prepared to fight. Sally Parker was worth it.

'Buggering shit!' exclaimed Sally as they breezed along in the Paws Fur Thought van. 'The Chanel kimono isn't in this pile! It's worth far more than all this crap put together. We'll probably only get a couple of hundred quid for this stuff if we're lucky.'

'Shall we go back to The Oast House?' said Janice, ever practical, deftly handling the gear stick.

'No. Eva'll get suspicious.' Sally was frowning, starting to formulate a plan. 'You know what, Janice, I think there's a much more satisfactory way of getting my kimono back.'

And she turned to her getaway driver and grinned.

Frank sat staring at the Gaysford's produce gloomily. He wanted to kick the tasteful bags for life from here to Kingston Come and then grind every overpriced grain of polenta into that dick-splash Tim Daly-Jones's face. He had to pull something big out of the bag now; he had to prove to Sally that he was still worth something, that he could still spoil her, that they could build their empire up again.

He felt his eyeballs scratchy with exhaustion but was determined to push on through, helped by an adrenaline buzz that had started to enliven his system. He had a plan and was ready for combat, although he didn't look exactly match-fit in dirty tracksuit trousers, Puffa jacket, bushy beard and the woolly hat that was now a permanent fixture. The hat was starting to smell of warm head cheese now. Frank Parker looked like a man that was starting to fall between the cracks of life. But his heart was still beating, and while there was a heartbeat there was a chance. And 'chance' had always been Frank Parker's middle name. Actually, his middle name was Lesley. All he needed now was a lift into Leatherhead.

He left the pool house in search of his brother Kyle, who could occasionally be found indulging in a spot of alfresco Tai chi. Maybe 'occasionally' is overegging it; he'd done it once. For about forty seconds.

Frank breathed in the fresh October air and looked across the undulating lawn towards Cedar Vale, his erstwhile green and pleasant land. He'd always loved Cedar Vale in October with its melancholy air, his beloved barbecues now safely under their stripy coverings for the coming winter. It was his Cedar Vale. He would expel that Afghan family, nice as they seemed, and throw hundreds of thousands, millions if needed, into Dave Aziz's face, and reinstate his Queen Sally into her rightful palace. He saw himself top to toe in chainmail astride a huge stallion, and so moved was he by this thought that tears welled in his eyes. Now he had a vision of himself, still in chainmail, behind the trinity of barbecues. He was holding court like the Frank Parker of old, impressing a flock of adoring courtiers – tricky to pull off in a crusader's helmet. Everyone present threw their heads back with laughter at Frank's perspicacious wit, and there was Sally, his Guinevere, looking lovingly at him across the spitting burgers, in a big pointy hat and billowing sleeves. This chainmail reverie was getting uncomfortably hot now, he was having trouble seeing out of the helmet. Thankfully it was interrupted by the sound of laughter.

Frank realised he was baking underneath his woolly hat, or maybe he was coming down with a cold. He could just about make out the source of the laughter; two figures not far away were busy snogging among the rhododendron bushes. Frank decided to creep closer and saw his eldest daughter and the Afghan lad engaged in something that the Leatherhead Leisure Centre lifeguards would have something to say about. 'No Running, No Bombing, No Petting' were the rules by which they lived and dived, and here were Cleo and Amir in flagrant floutation of these regulations. They weren't quite in flagrante, but they were flagrantly flouting something and, as Cleo's father, Frank was not sure if he liked this flou-tational flagrancy one fragment.

He drew himself up, determined on scolding his daughter, then stopped. A thought suddenly struck him. If Cleo had this 'in' at Cedar Vale, wouldn't it actually be of use to all of them? The novelty of bunking up together with his family in the pool house was wearing off pretty fast for Frank; if Cleo were the passport to get everyone back into Cedar Vale for an extended visit, then wouldn't that be something worth celebrating? He'd enjoyed his first sample of Mrs Afghan's food. If there was more of that on offer, then he was in.

He carefully backtracked to the pool house, deciding not to disturb the young lovers, who looked like they were moving up on the petting scale. He was shocked to see that it was Cleo who appeared to be in charge of proceedings. How very twenty-first century, he thought to himself. Cleo's hand seemed to be rummaging around in Amir's trouser area while Amir kept his hands demurely away from any danger zones. Frank turned away quickly. It was amazing what you could bring to the petting table on a chilly day if you were in the first throes of love. Frank recalled a day when he and Sally had snogged for seven hours, only stopping for a Ginsters pie, outside on a park bench in February. Extraordinary to think of that now.

Frank heard Kyle tuning up his guitar inside the pool house and remembered that he needed a lift off him. Just then, Janice and Sally appeared, giggling and carrying a big pile of clothes. He went in for a kiss with his wife, but Sally turned her head away brusquely.

'Not now, Frank. Janice and I need to sort these out and try and shift them as soon as,' and with that she went in. Janice followed. Then Frank. He always seemed to be the afterthought at the moment. Always last. Sally was busying herself with clothes-folding.

'Well, if anyone's interested in anything I've got to say,' Frank announced to the room, 'I've just seen the flowering of love's young dream. Cleo and the Afghani lad, in the rhododendrons!' He slumped into a chair.

'Have you got nothing better to do than perv in the bushes, Frank?' asked his wife.

'Well, they were at it there right in front of me. I couldn't help but look,' he said grumpily.

Sally turned sharply and the excessively wide trousers she was holding flapped vigorously in the air.

'At it?' she asked, flatly.

'Like I said. The two of them, snogging each other's faces off, in the bushes.'

'You're telling me this, Frank, as if this is something to be proud of. This is our daughter, Frank. Was she all right?'

'Oh, she's good as gold, very much the hand on the tiller, so to speak. It's him we should be worrying about!' he joked.

'Stop it, Frank.'

Janice felt like a gooseberry in this intimate parental discussion and engrossed herself in origami-levels of clothes-folding.

'You know what, Sal?' blustered Frank. 'I was thinking, good on you, Cleo, you get in there with the Afghans. Cement the relationship and you'll have a nice roof over your head, and then you can invite all of us to stay too. It'd be better than sleeping in this bloody shed.'

Sally held up her hand to stop her husband speaking.

'Firstly,' she said, 'they have a name. I'm ashamed to say that I forget what it is right at this precise moment, but they do. The "Afghans", as you call them, have a name. And secondly, I can't believe you're even thinking of pimping Cleo out like that, just to get a roof over our heads!'

Frank stood up, a little unsteadily.

'You're the one that's been saying we've got to think on our feet, Sal. Well this is ME thinking on my feet. It's business. You scratch my back, I'll scratch yours. It's a deal like any other, Sally.'

'A deal,' she said bitterly. 'I've had enough of that sordid little word.'

There was a silence.

'I'll sort these out into categories for you, Sally,' said Janice quietly.

Frank turned to Janice Dawes, his temper rising.

'Is this it?' he gestured towards Janice. 'Is your friend going to be with us like the permanent third leg from now on?'

'I'm just here to help Sally,' said Janice calmly.

'Well, you sound just like her wife, Janice,' said Frank sharply.

Janice flushed.

'Frank,' said Sally, 'Janice is a lifesaver. She's more of a husband than you are right now.'

Frank moved back a step as if he'd been slapped.

'Wow,' said Frank, 'am I going to have to fight a duel with you, Janice? I'll slap a glove round your chops, shall I, and then meet you with guns at dawn?'

Janice didn't know where to look.

'I'll just put these next door, Sally,' she muttered, and backed away.

There was a pause.

'How *dare* you, Frank?' hissed Sally, when Janice was gone.

'She's always here, busybodying around the place,' hissed Frank back at her.

'At least she's useful!'

Frank adopted a camp impressionist's pose.

'Ooh, can I do this for you, Sally? Ooh, can I do that for you, Sally? Oooh, three bags full, Sally.'

'You're pathetic, Frank.'

'No. Do you know what, Sally? You're pathetic. You've always had Bank of Frank to prop you up, haven't you? Handmaidens to do your dirty work. You think living in this pool house is standing on your own two feet, but it isn't, and Janice is just another of your bloody bridesmaids—'

The conversation ended abruptly with a loud slap. Sally's eyes were ablaze, her cheeks red, and she was shaking. She had never struck another human being before. She'd taken a swipe at her brother Miles once when he'd pinched her as a child, and her mother had locked her in a darkened room for five hours.

There was silence.

Kyle's guitar stopped twanging. The slap had rung around the pool house. Frank slowly lifted his hand to touch his tender cheek. Husband and wife looked at each other as if they were either side of an abyss that neither knew how to cross.

Kyle's face appeared round the door.

'Mofos, if we need to release some aggression, we can set up some kind of manhunt? They do it all the time in Ecuador. Give me ten minutes to hit the woods, then come after me with some weaponry. It can be very cleansing.'

Frank stepped away from his wife and looked at her as if she were a stranger to him.

'I just need a lift to Leatherhead, Kyle,' he said.

'Frank. I'm sorry,' said Sally, stepping towards him.

'You're sorry. And I'm pathetic apparently,' Frank

replied, looking down at his hands. He turned from her and left the pool house, Kyle trailing after him.

Kyle dropped Frank on Leatherhead High Street, near to the arcade where all the posh shops and boutiques were. There was a throng of shoppers spilling off the pavements; teenagers jostling merrily on their way home after school. Frank had never felt so alone, but knew what he had to do. He had to channel some Classic Parker moves. A grand gesture. He had to think big, bold and out of the box.

He stepped into Turtons Jewellers, one of Leatherhead's oldest and most respected family businesses. Frank knew Geoff Turton of old; they'd played golf and had sat on various Rotary Club committees together over the years. There were only a handful of people inside. The jewellery was so pricey that even well-to-do Leatherheadites wouldn't buy those trinkets on impulse. Frank couldn't see Geoff Turton, just a couple of smartly dressed shop assistants in black and white uniforms, and a security guard at the door. All of them eyed Frank as he came in. He didn't fit the average Turtons customer profile one bit; they'd never sold anything to a guy with a beard and woolly hat before.

'Can I help you, sir?' said the younger assistant.

'You most certainly can,' said Frank, a bit too loudly. The other customers turned round. 'I want to know what I should buy for a wife who says I'm pathetic?'

The assistant blushed and looked silently over to her colleague for help. Frank addressed the whole shop now.

'Anyone got any bright ideas? Pathetic, she said, and oh yes, she did also accuse me of being a perv.'

The security guard now had Frank on his radar.

'I don't know, really, sir,' stammered the assistant, 'but the Swarovski stuff is always pretty popular with the ladies,' and she pointed out a tray of crystal necklaces.

'Nah. I'd call that a bit duty free, a bit mid-range, do you know what I mean?' said Frank, leaning right in over the glass counter. 'I know Geoff's got some big bangers behind the scenes. Show me a rock that's going to make my eyes water. The last piece I bought for my wife here was a bracelet in the shape of a leopard. It probably cost more than your house is worth!'

The assistant blushed deeper, and several customers looked away from Frank in distaste.

He was starting to enjoy himself; here was a captive audience. He reached out his arms like a proper orator.

'I expect you're all choosing engagement rings, aren't you? Well, let me tell you this for free. When your marriages are on the rocks, *that's* when you have to start buying the rocks. Rocks to stop the rocks! Ha! Pure Parker!'

The security guard came up to Frank, rested his hand gently on Frank's shoulder and said:

'I'm going to have to ask you to keep your voice down, sir.'

The assistant pulled out a tray of rings and bracelets from underneath the counter.

'Here we are, sir. Is this more what you were thinking of?'

'Just give me numbers,' said Frank grimly.

'OK. Er . . . six thousand, five thousand eight hundred, four thousand four hundred—'

'That's more like it. I'll take that one,' and he pointed to a sapphire and diamond ring.

The assistant looked anxiously at her colleague, who nodded. The tray was unlocked and the ring handed over to Frank, who examined it like a pirate with one eye scrunched up. He was about five paces away from the door. In a deft display of theatre, Frank looked out of the window, pointed, and shouted very loudly,

'Someone's got a knife in Whistles!' so that the security guard momentarily took his eye off him. There were screams in Turtons as Frank bolted for the door. He got about seven metres down the road before he was brought down by the security guard, still clutching the ring.

'I know I've said this before, Sally, but I feel that what you're about to do might well be illegal,' whispered Janice firmly as the two of them crouched outside in the flower-bed, underneath Francesca's living-room windowsill. They were back at The Oast House, although this time under cover of darkness. The drive was full of Chobham Tractors, sports cars and people carriers.

It was Francesca's big night. She was hosting the annual Charity Clothes Auction, this year in aid of a baboon rehoming centre in Zambia, a charity very close to her heart ever since Tim had taken all the family there on safari. They had wept in unison at each and every rehomed baboon they saw, and Francesca promised herself there and then that while she had breath in her body no baboon in Zambia would ever go unrehomed again.

Sally and Frank always wondered why Francesca had such a special affinity with baboons, until they saw some on TV displaying their large and very pink bottoms. They had rolled around laughing on the sofa together till they were howling. Sally banished this cosy memory of her and Frank immediately.

'OK, Janice, it's full in there. They've started the catwalk. As soon as I set eyes on our quarry, I'm in like Flint and you get the van started up. Yes?'

Janice Dawes loved it when Sally went all serious and military on her. Despite the borderline legality of the situation, she'd never felt so happy in her life, in fact.

'Wilco, Captain Sally, I'm literally on it like a car – or should I say van – Bonnet. That's rather lovely actually, Sally. Captains Flint and Bonnet were actual pirates together working in the eighteenth century—'

'Keep it for another time, Janice,' said Sally, her eye suddenly steely. 'Stay alert please.'

Janice flushed.

'Yes, Captain,' she added quietly.

Sally peered again through the window, which was steamed up with the hot breath of Leatherhead's women on the wrong side of two glasses of prosecco. Whooping was now audible, to the accompaniment of The Saturdays, which Francesca had pumped up to full volume on her sound system. And then the moment happened that Sally had been waiting for. To wild cheers, Francesca appeared at the far end of the room, cleared of its sofas to allow the models to walk the runway. Francesca was wearing Sally's kimono. Sally was aghast to see that she had teamed it with a pair of white jeans and suede pixie boots. It was time for Sally to make her entrance and reclaim what was hers. She patted Janice on the back and marched towards the front door.

'Where are Mum and Dad?' asked Mikey, as Stephen ladled out five heavenly scented helpings of polenta with hot stew into his family's bowls. No one knew the answer.

'You're genius at the cooking, Ste, you know that?' said Cleo, genuinely impressed.

'Smells unreal, man,' added Kyle. 'This is top-class scran, dude. Namaste.'

'What is it?' said Emily, sniffing at her bowl.

'It's polenta with a quince and potato tagine and a pickle jus. With some herbs I found in the garden. And some other bits and bobs from our stores.' Four admiring pairs of eyes watched him as he spoke. 'The secret with this is to know your flavours and cook it really slowly so that they don't compete with each other.'

'Wait, how did you know all this?' asked Cleo.

'I've literally had nothing else to do,' said Stephen.

Cleo reached for her mobile to post a picture of the food on her Instagram. She frowned over the phone.

'It's not working,' she said, shaking it.

Stephen and Emily looked at each other and reached silently for their phones. They looked at the phones for a minute, tapped on the screens in vain, looked at each other grimly.

'The day has arrived that I knew and feared would come,' said Stephen seriously.

'Our contracts have run out,' said Emily.

The teens looked at each other as if there had been a death in the family. Mikey pulled her phone out and tapped away on it.

'Mine's fine!' she announced chirpily.

'Mikey, what the actual HELL?' shouted Cleo.

'I may be a dyslexic moron, Cleo, but I can read the words "pay as you go".'

And she gave a smug little smile and sent a text message.

There was a depressed silence from the teens, and then heads bowed down over Stephen's warming and delicious dish.

'What's on the menu tomorrow?' asked Emily morosely.

There was a silence.

'More polenta,' sighed Stephen, as a concerned look drifted across his face, 'and when that runs out, I couldn't tell you.'

*

Sally's unexpected entrance at the Baboon Rehoming Charity Clothes Auction that night was to go down as the stuff of Leatherhead legend. It would be passed down from generation to generation, re-enacted and retold, and for those that were actually present, it was to be the story that they dined out on for evermore, embroidered and enriched until it barely resembled anything like the truth.

The nuggets of the story, laid bare without any hint of embroidery, crochet or quilting, are thus. Francesca was strutting her stuff, halfway down the catwalk, when she was aware of a commotion by the door. A figure in black (Sally had adopted full SAS attire for this event) with scrunched-out hair under a purple beanie hat, wild black eyeliner and just a whiff of red lipstick, had stalked into her living room. The good women of Leatherhead fell quiet, one by one, until all that was audible in the room was The Saturdays. Francesca motioned for the nearest person to shut them down; and then there was total silence. Several people whispered behind hands as Sally stalked up to Francesca slowly; she seemed to be relishing the impression every step that her monkey-booted feet made.

When the women were a metre apart, Sally looked Francesca up and down.

'Ladies,' she announced to the assembled milfs and yummy mummies, 'I have come to take back what's rightfully mine.'

'Oh yes?' said Francesca through gritted teeth. 'You donated it, Sally Parker, it's for charity, remember?'

Sally gave a scornful laugh and turned round to her audience.

'And this,' she said, pointing to Francesca, 'from a woman who cares more about rehoming baboons than she does about rehoming human beings.'

The charity mums began with murmurs but soon the room was filled with loud babble. Francesca, forgetting her composure, looked around wildly. She tried to speak to her audience but no words came out. Sally, magician-like, grasped the kimono from the scruff of the neck, whipped it downwards and backwards so that it peeled away from Francesca's body. There was a collective gasp in the room. It was a literal dressing-down, brilliantly executed.

What happened next was not quite so brilliantly executed. Emboldened, Sally headed for the windows, which were of a faux-Tudor design. She opened one of them, threw the kimono out dramatically, and then hoped to follow it with a similar exit herself. Even though she was slight, it was something of a tussle for Sally and she knocked over several photo frames and a vase in the process. But she had planned for the window exit and was therefore determined to leave by no other means than the window. She managed this in fifty-four seconds; with hindsight Sally knew it would have made sense to use the door.

Frank sat in a holding cell in Epsom Police Station, with nothing but a narrow, hard bed and his own thoughts for company. He was pooped; properly level-five knackered with nothing left in the tank. He lay back on the bed; how had he come to this? For the first time in Frank Parker's life, he felt unsure, that something needed to change. He needed to think. And sleep. He stuffed his hands in his pockets and felt a familiar piece of screwed up paper in the right-hand pocket.

He pulled out Bronwen's small, crumpled letter. It seemed like a century ago that she'd given it to him. Another life; the life of somebody successful with a house, status and a voice. How had he become this incompetent, small, pointless man who needed to sleep all the time?

He sat up on the edge of the bed and started to read.

'*Dear Frank*,' it began, and he smiled forlornly to hear her Welshness.

> *I know what you're like. You'll have forgotten about this letter, too busy making your silly money no doubt, and it'll stay in your pocket till you find it again and it'll probably be too late, you silly sod.*
>
> *I'm dying, Frank, love. It's cancer and it's got your old granny good and proper. Probably due to all the cavorting with the Rolling Stones, getting high and eating all that rich Michelin-star food in the company of Keith Richards. I'm joking. Your grandfather took me to the Crown Hotel only twice and both times we agreed we could have eaten better at home.*
>
> *Anyway, I know things were tough for you growing up and there are still some, what is it you youngsters say, 'unresolved issues' to chat about, so come and visit me. I'm in Wales. It's over the big mountains. Remember?*
>
> *You're a good boy underneath all the bullshit, Frank Parker.*
>
> *Look forward to seeing you, X X X X X X*

Frank stared hard at the letter, and folded it carefully in his hands. He unfolded it, read it again, stayed sitting on the edge of the bed and wept bitter tears.

20

'He's WHERE?' said Sally, hands on hips, in front of Mikey. It was seven o'clock the next morning.

'Epsom Police Station,' repeated Mikey. 'I just picked up his message. On my working phone.'

All of the family gathered round Sally, including Kyle, wearing Y-fronts.

'Kyle, can you get dressed please?' said Sally.

'Want me to don a suit?' Kyle laughed.

'Put on a traffic warden's uniform, a dirndl or a replica of Kate Middleton's wedding dress, Kyle, I don't give a shit, just put on something.'

Kyle bestowed a look of pity upon his sister-in-law.

'Sal, do you think this family crisis might be, I dunno, getting to you? I've got some great stretches we could do.'

'Just put some clothes on, Uncle Kyle,' said Cleo firmly, putting a supportive hand on her mum's arm, 'and if you mention that your phone is working again, Mikey, I'm so going to take you down to Soho—'

'It's Chinatown, Cleo,' said Stephen.

'Der, it's the same thing,' retorted Cleo.

'Oh yeah?' taunted Mikey. 'I'll call the police if you do that. ON MY WORKING PHONE!'

At this, Cleo made a lunge towards her younger sister with her fist up, but Mikey ducked down deftly to avoid it. Stephen moved towards the girls to placate them.

'Girls!' said their mother, taking firm control. 'This is not the time for pathetic fighting. Your father's been arrested.'

Cleo and Mikey looked at their mum and stood quietly at her side.

'Sorry Mum,' said Cleo.

'Sorry Mum,' said Mikey. But then mimed speaking into a phone using her splayed fingers.

'Mikey!' snapped her mum. 'I saw that.'

'Frank's been taken by the feds,' murmured Kyle, wandering off shaking his head, leaving Sally with a tight phalanx of children around her.

'Oh God. Oh God,' she cried, head in hands, 'why's he in the police station?'

'There was an incident in Turtons Jewellers,' said Mikey. 'He says he needs bail. Which is fine, because I've got two grand here in cash,' she added, pulling out a wedge of notes from her school blazer pocket.

There was an amazed silence as everybody stared at Mikey and then at the cash.

'I'm going to need eight hundred of that for the Hong Kong netball tour, sorry, I forgot to tell you, Sally,' said Emily, looking at the cash.

'We've got to do a big food shop today, so I'll need at least a hundred,' added Stephen, looking at the cash.

'My car's low on gas and needs a service,' chipped in Kyle from the other room.

'Would it be too much to ask if I could have my hair and nails done, guys?' said Cleo, looking at the cash. 'I look rank and Amir's taking me out for a special dinner tonight—'

'STOP!' shouted Sally. 'All of you, just SHUT UP!'

Sally's children had never heard her shout like this, and the effect was immediate. You could have heard a pin drop.

'We need to think,' said Sally seriously, 'and plan. Mikey, I'm not going to ask you where that money's come from, though I'm assuming this has something to do with Dom, but you are a hero. And that's the end of it.' Mikey puffed out her chest with pleasure.

'Right. We need to get down to the police station and bail him out,' said Sally, putting on her jacket.

'Or we could just leave him there,' said Emily, darkly.

'Emily, that's enough,' Sally snipped.

She felt suddenly faint and had to sit down.

Kyle wandered back in, wearing a floor-length alpaca kaftan.

'When a man is taken to the edge, Sal, you can say adios to that rule book you've been reading all your life. I remember when I was crossing the Guatemalan border . . .'

Sally was staring fixedly at a point beyond Kyle, way out on the horizon, far beyond them all. Her voice was dreamlike.

'What's happened to my husband? What's happened to us? Why are we living in a glorified Wendy house? Why has my eleven-year-old daughter got a working phone and two thousand pounds in cash?'

'Mum? Mum?' said Cleo, tugging her arm gently.

'Are you OK, Mum?' asked Stephen.

The children were all looking at each other worriedly.

'What are we going to do?' said Sally, smiling slightly dementedly now.

'We should go to school,' said Emily. 'Come on, guys, we're late already.'

Sally snapped out of her reverie.

'Right. Yes. Kyle, I'd like you to go and fetch Frank from the police station.' She was about to hand him the two thousand pounds in cash, then thought the better of it. 'Mikey, please go with him, and you're in charge of the cash. The rest of us can start packing. We move out this evening.'

'But I've got a dinner date,' whined Cleo.

'Where are we going, Mum?' asked Stephen. 'We're getting settled here.'

'To a place where we're not sponging off other people, somewhere that we've actually paid to be.'

'What about school?' asked Emily.

'You go to school, Em. There's not much point in the others going.' Cleo, Stephen and Mikey looked at her askance. 'Sorry! That came out wrong. What I meant was, the others will be more use to me here. Cleo, go and start packing. Ste, can you shop for and plan our next meals, please? Take a hundred quid from Mikey.'

Stephen smiled. There were two lasagnes, a tofu wellington and a butternut squash soup he was desperate to make.

As the family snapped into action, Sally looked around her with something approaching satisfaction, then started rolling up the sleeping bags and working out when she'd need to call in Janice. It felt good to take charge.

'Just one thing, Mum,' said Mikey. 'I could call the police station in advance? I do have a working phone, you know.'

Sally threw a pillow at her youngest child's head.

Amerjit Singh was back in the family nest under doctors' orders to do nothing but sleep, rest and eat. His days in the blind-fitting business had been short-lived, but his dad hoped fervently that Amerjit would join the ranks again soon. Amerjit looked down at his tummy. Gone was the flat washboard that he and Laura had worked so hard on together, in the high-spec basement gym of their Tower Bridge apartment; in its place was a middle-aged roll of dough that had appeared over the last few days courtesy of his mum's irresistible cooking.

He hunched over in the armchair so that he could grab the fat-girth in both hands. Laura would be disgusted if she could see him now. What a waste of a human being he had become. Every year their joint husband-and-wife Christmas card had been sent out to four hundred people. Four hundred friends and acquaintances! And now here he was, back at his parents, with a spare tyre round his middle and anxious bags under his eyes. Come December, those four hundred people would be saying:

'Where's the Christmas card from Amerjit and Laura this year?'

'They normally send such tasteful ones, brought back from their travels!'

'Do you remember the one they picked up from the Azerbaijan silk market?'

'Stunning! But then everything Laura and Amerjit do is stunning!'

'They're such a perfect couple, even their toilet brush is from a design studio in Copenhagen.'

Amerjit thought of the four hundred Christmas-card recipients, like a Greek chorus, bemoaning him and his failed life; their heads hanging as one as they swayed from side to side, groaning the lament of the lost Emperor Singh. Amerjit did feel like he was living out a Greek tragedy; all he needed was for his mother to shag him and his father to eat him. Neither event could be entirely ruled out, he thought ruefully.

Amerjit considered his options. He could either stay here in Hayes and get morbidly obese, or he could escape, find Frank, and start from ground zero again. His thoughts turned to Gary Barlow; there was an example of a man who had had it all, and then had ended up down the

U-bend for a few years eating pies in his pyjamas. But now look at him! Gary had wrestled his own woebegone Greek chorus, cocked a snook at the gods laughing down at him from Olympus, and had reinvented himself into somebody older, wiser, craggier and, let's be honest, much hotter.

Amerjit Singh stood up from his armchair. He glanced at himself in the mirror; the raw materials were not looking their finest at the moment, but if Gary could do it, so could he. This was Day One. This was the Rebirth.

He picked up his rowing oar from Downing College, Cambridge, which Kerry had saved from the removal men when HNB had been dismantled. He held it tight in both hands and sat on a footstool, pretending he was in that college rowing boat again. He sliced through the water, strong and lean, his stomach ridged once more, his life full of purpose and his Christmas-card recipients cheering him on across the river. One, two, three, slice, one, two, three, slice, one, two, thr— the blade of the oar made sharp contact with one of Pinki Singh's favourite wedding vases on a table, and sent it hurtling to the floor where it smashed into smithereens.

Amerjit looked at its sad remains. What would Gary do? Of course! He'd call on his bandmates; there was nothing they couldn't do together. Amerjit needed to get his band back together. He needed Frank.

PC Patel took in the sight of this rinsed-out hippy and the eager-eyed kid clutching two thousand pounds with a certain degree of scepticism.

'I don't know how it works here,' drawled Kyle, 'but in Colombia if somebody's in the pen then you flash the denarii and that usually does the trick,' and he nudged Mikey to show the dosh to the good police officer.

PC Patel looked at the cash, then at Kyle, coldly.

'Isn't it a school day today?' she asked Mikey kindly.

'Inset day,' said Mikey, smooth as custard.

'Convenient,' replied PC Patel.

'Listen,' said Kyle, leaning his elbow on the counter in an attempt to be coquettish, 'my bro Frank's one of the good guys. He's having a wobble at the mo, planets aren't aligned, the ju-ju's agin him, but he's no common-or-garden thief. If Frank *was* a burglar, he'd do it properly, no holds barred. He'd steal something gargantuan, Great Train Robbery-style, you dig?'

'Really?' The PC's eyes widened. 'I hope you won't find yourself saying that in court, Mr Parker. I'd keep that information close to your chest if I were you.'

'No, no,' Mikey stepped in to help, 'what Uncle Kyle's saying is that my dad is just really, really brilliant at what he does. And he gives everything a hundred and ten per cent.'

PC Patel's face softened at the sight of this young girl in front of her. She had the brightest brown eyes, like a guinea pig, and her face was so full of optimism it made your heart melt.

'Have you got any ID, you two?' asked PC Patel.

'Only my face,' said Kyle with what he thought was a winning smile, but his missing molars made it more of a Dickensian leer.

'I've got my cashpoint card,' said Mikey.

'It's normally picture ID that I need, but today I'll make an exception for you, Miss Parker.'

'Thank you so much!' Mikey replied, nearly bursting out of her skin with the knowledge that she, Michaela Parker, was about to save her dad single-handedly from the jaws of prison.

'OK, I can tell you that Mr Parker isn't here,' said the police officer.

Mikey lost a sudden inch in height behind the counter. 'What?' she said, in disbelief.

'The feds haven't moved him on, have they?' said Kyle, gruffing up his voice a notch. 'It's the classic manoeuvre. Jail him, pin something on him, take him hostage, bag him up, move him out to the jungle—'

'This is Epsom, Mr Parker,' PC Patel reminded him, 'and he was released on bail this morning.'

'But I was going to release him!' Mikey's eyes shone with tears. 'Look! I've got the bail money and everything!'

'You keep your money safe, Mikey,' said PC Patel gently. 'Your dad's friend Mr Turton came in and paid.'

'What, Geoff Turton the jeweller, who my dad stole the ring off?' asked Mikey, piecing the jigsaw together.

PC Patel nodded quietly. Kyle whistled through his teeth.

'That is deep. Frank steals from Turton, then Turton, the victim, pays for the man who would do him wrong's release.'

All three of them took the time to contemplate the selfless and extraordinary actions of Geoff Turton.

'And His name shall be called Jesus Turton,' said Kyle reverently.

'Where's Dad now?' asked Mikey matter-of-factly.

'He said something about going to Snowdonia to see his grandmother. Mr Turton gave him fifty pounds to help him on his way, I believe.'

'Ah, Turton! And they shall sing his name from the mountain tops,' pronounced Kyle, loudly, before his niece shoved him towards the door.

Stephen was never happier these days than when his nose was in a recipe book. He had a special ring binder where he would jot down ideas, ingredients, shopping lists, meal planners, general riff about flavours. He'd been poring over his bible for about an hour before Sally found him.

'Ste! You need to start packing. Where's Cleo?'

'She's in the shower room getting ready for her dinner date.'

'It's MIDDAY, CLEO! YOU DON'T NEED SEVEN HOURS TO GET READY!' Sally shouted into the general space. 'Come on, guys, we've got to be quick on our feet. Let's MOVE IT, everyone.' She clapped her hands like a sergeant major. 'I'll be back in half an hour. I just have a last piece of business to attend to.'

And she nodded to Janice, who was always there for her, the Paws Fur Thought van parked up at the ready.

Dave Aziz had a small office in Claygate, from where he ran his property business. It was nothing too flash, just an upstairs room above a solicitor's office. Sally mounted the stairs with trepidation and knocked at the door.

'Come in,' said the familiar velvety voice.

Sally opened the door and there was Dave behind a desk, with a pair of glasses on. She didn't know he wore glasses. It made him look ordinary. The array of framed photos around him added to the effect.

'Nice family photos,' Sally said, pointedly.

Dave coughed; was that a touch of shame in his eye?

'Sally,' he said, on the back foot, which pleased her, 'I—'

'I won't stay long, Dave,' she interrupted, 'I just came to say that we've vacated the pool house. We're moving on,' she smiled.

'Where to?' he asked.

'Nearby. A place where we have a right to be,' Sally said with clarity, and then, looking at him squarely, 'a place which doesn't come with any deal attached.'

Dave looked away from her and ran his fingers through

his luxurious hair, which Sally couldn't help notice was a tad on the greasy side today.

'It's a no-deal exit then?' he said wolfishly. 'OK. If that's the way you want it, Sally.'

Dave Aziz surveyed her over the top of his glasses, which Sally found a bit creepy and school teacherly.

'We'd better settle up then, hadn't we?' he said smoothly.

'Settle up?' Sally shot him a confused look.

'Your outstanding bills at Cedar Vale,' he said, 'gas, electricity, broadband, water.' He held out a sheaf of papers. 'It comes to nine hundred and seventy-eight pounds and thirty-two pence. You can check my maths if you don't trust me.'

Sally snatched the bills from across his desk and looked over them intently, to avoid his laser gaze.

'I don't have it right at the moment.'

Dave looked at her with a quizzical smile. He was enjoying this.

'But we'll deliver it to you in the next twenty-four hours,' she said, meeting his eyes.

'I will always accept other methods of payment, Mrs Parker,' Dave said mischievously, and anger flashed over Sally's face. 'I'm teasing you. You pay me when you can.'

'It'll be within twenty-four hours,' Sally repeated with a deadpan look.

Sally was silent in the Paws Fur Thought van on the way home. Janice kept glancing at her. It wasn't like the new Sally to be so taciturn.

'I'm sorry the van's cramped and smells of dog,' Janice said by way of an icebreaker.

'Don't be ridiculous, Janice. Without you and the van we'd have been sunk,' said Sally.

Janice felt a little warm glow inside. 'I mean, this is hardly your Range Rover, is it?'

'Thank God,' said Sally, 'that Range Rover was ridiculous. I always felt like a knob driving it into Leatherhead—' Sally stopped. 'Hang on a minute. Janice, would you mind turning the van round? We need to go back the Chobham way. Is that OK?'

Janice slowed the van down and started to put it into reverse. Anything for her friend.

Bronwen Llewellyn spent a lot of the time now with her eyes closed. She looked even tinier than usual in her bed, its sheets and covers kept spotless by friends and neighbours looking after her. She would occasionally wake up and take a sip of water or tea, and sometimes she would wink and whisper, 'I'll have a little sharpener, I will,' and then whoever was attending the bedside would brush her lips with brandy.

Her hair was bright white, and her skin was now translucent and very papery. She had to be handled with the utmost care for fear of tearing her. When her eyes were open, the beady percentage still outweighed the non-beady percentage, and when she'd had a good rest she would speak, completely compos mentis.

'Has he called yet?' she asked her neighbour Gwyneth, who was sitting reading *Take a Break* magazine. Gwyneth shook her head slowly.

There was a thoughtful silence in the room,

'What a prannock,' said Bronwen hoarsely. 'Grade A prannock.'

Gwyneth nodded her silvery head in agreement, although she didn't move her eyes from the article she was reading about Fern Britton.

*

Sally was relieved to find the Range Rover still parked up in the lay-by, exactly where she'd abandoned it that fateful night she'd driven home from Gatwick airport. It felt strange to be at its wheel once again. Janice always had a spare petrol can in her boot, and it would be enough to get her to the Range Rover dealership where Sally and Frank had an excellent relationship with the manager.

Sally checked in her rear-view mirror; Janice was still following behind her. She smiled. How nice it was to have a true and proper friend. Her only real adult friend in the world was Frank, and it was good to double the numbers. Or was Frank a friend any more? Sally frowned. She was so angry with him. Why had she trusted him? How had she ever believed in his bluster?

She indicated left, turned into the Range Rover dealership and parked up in front of the showroom. Within minutes she was at the manager's desk, doing a deal on the Range Rover. For cash.

She emerged light of foot and smiling from ear to ear.

'Ha!' she announced to Janice. 'It's not just my husband that cuts the deals round here! I've got two grand, Janice, please take us straight back to Mr Aziz.'

Janice put the key in the ignition and merry banter filled the van once again. Sally felt great with a wad of cash in her back pocket.

'Do you know what, Janice? I'm the bill payer now in this family! I can't tell you how good that feels after so many years accepting handouts from my husband.'

Sally looked at the money in her hand.

'If Frank had this money in his hand right now, he'd be trying to work out ways of doubling it, trebling it,' she said quietly, 'and often enough he did.'

'Well, just make sure he doesn't get his hands on it!' said Janice jokingly.

Sally looked wistful all of a sudden.

'It makes me think of Trevor,' Sally said.

'Trevor?' said Janice.

'Trevor was Frank's faithful driver for many years. Gave Frank two grand a while ago to invest for him. And Frank's lost it all.' Sally shook her head. 'I wonder how many other Trevors there are out there who trusted him?'

There was a silence in the van.

'Janice, I'm so sorry. I'm going to have to ask you to reverse the van again. We need to go to Epsom. I need to go to Trevor's house immediately.'

Frank Parker hadn't hitchhiked since the age of seventeen, but was amazed at how quickly the skill came back to him. He found that it was manageable, even with narcolepsy; the key thing was to try and do it sitting down. He'd got a piece of cardboard from a kind petrol-pump attendant and had scrawled 'NORTH WALES' on it in black marker pen. And here he was, dropped off on the edge of the M25 at Cobham Services by Geoff Turton.

'Thank you for everything, Geoff,' Frank said as the two men stood face to face in the car park. 'You know it was nothing personal, that burglary fiasco. I just wanted to try and make it up to Sally.'

'I understand, Frank,' said Geoff, a portly man in his sixties who was no stranger to black hair dye. 'Listen, if I thought I was going to lose my Marilyn I'd rob the Bank of England to get her back.'

'Once I'm back on my feet I'll come and see you in the shop, and then I'll be able to buy that ring properly,' promised Frank.

Geoff thought for a moment, and then looked at Frank steadily with his jeweller's eye, the one that used the black monocle to inspect the gems more closely.

'Frank, what colour was the ring that you were trying to steal for Sally?'

Frank thought hard, and looked blank.

'Green? I think?'

'Describe it to me.'

Frank found Geoff confusing, but in the circumstances felt he'd better humour the jeweller.

'Well, it looked very much like a ring, Geoff. Probably had a bit of sparkle to it. Gold, was it? Yeah, it was a gold sparkly blingy thing with green.'

Geoff looked sagely at Frank.

'The ring you stole, Frank, was a large blue sapphire of a square shape, worked all round with tiny white diamonds, sixteen of them altogether, with two larger diamonds on each end. It's set in platinum, giving it a light silvery appearance.'

Frank looked at him and smiled blankly. 'Oh,' was all he could say.

'It seems to me that the ring doesn't really mean anything whatsoever to you, Frank, it has made no impression on your heart or indeed your memory, and to give something so meaningless to Sally is like giving her an empty promise. I don't think she'd want that ring at all. I think you're better off giving her something that means something to you. And therefore to her.'

A person might pop in to Cobham Services off the M25 for a cheese and pickle sandwich, a grainy coffee or a slash; philosophy would be the last thing you'd expect to find there. But Frank found it there that afternoon, and it gave him much to think about.

Before leaving him, Geoff found an old deck chair in the boot of his car, which he insisted Frank sit on while waiting for his ride.

'Good luck, Frank. I hope you get to Snowdonia in one piece,' said Geoff, holding out his hand.

Frank ignored the hand, went in for a hug, then looked Geoff in the eyes.

'I think I've been giving Sally empty promises for most of our marriage, Geoff. I'm going to have to go back to square one. If she'll have me.'

'Going back to square one is good, Frank. Everything is progress from square one,' said Geoff, slipping on his driving gloves and walking towards his Aston Martin.

For the first time, Frank didn't look at the Aston Martin, but at the man driving it. A man from Great Bookham with a bad dye job, even worse slacks and some patent beige slip-on shoes had shown him the path to enlightenment. Frank felt something akin to love for Geoff Turton, and it warmed his heart.

Back at the pool house, Sally sat with Janice over a well-earned cup of tea.

'Well, that two grand disappeared pretty damn fast!' said Sally cheerfully.

'You did the right thing, Sally,' said Janice earnestly, 'you're a good woman. There's not many in your position that would give all that money away. You're a lovely person, Sally, and an inspiration to me . . . to us . . . all of us,' she stumbled, blushing now.

Sally rested her hand on Janice's leg which made Janice blush more deeply.

'I love you, Janice Dawes. You make me feel so, so good!'

Janice took a sip of tea and promptly choked into the cup.

'But I'm back to square one, Janice! I had the money and now it's gone again! How am I going to pay Aziz?

I feel like the sorcerer's apprentice. The more I try and empty the buckets, the more of those bloody brooms appear to pour more water in from their bloody buckets.'

At that moment Mikey and Kyle burst through the door, Mikey breathless with news.

'Dad's gone to Snowdonia!'

Sally was not thinking of Frank at this point but was focused solely on the cash in her daughter's hands.

'So no bail payment? Thank God. I need some cash, Mikey, how much have you got here?' and she grabbed and counted notes out of her daughter's hands.

'But Mum, what about Dad?' Mikey asked quietly.

Sally gave her youngest a hug.

'It's just business, darling. We've got to sort this out before we can think of Dad.'

Mikey unlaced herself from her mother's hug and went into the other room, head hung low. Sally sighed as she watched her daughter go.

'What did I tell you, Janice? The sorcerer's flipping apprentice!'

'I don't want you going into that man's office again, Sal,' said Janice, standing up with authority. 'Give me the cash. I'll spark up the van,' and she left the pool house with something heroic in her gait.

'I love that woman,' said Sally, turning to the family. 'Right, let's finish packing everybody, we've got to ship out.'

The Parker chattels were packed up once more, and thanks again to the majestic force that was Janice Dawes, the Paws Fur Thought van was ready and waiting to take them to their next home. As was Kyle's Allegro.

'Will we be able to cook there?' was Stephen's immediate question.

'Bring the camping stove,' ordered Sally, 'it'll be a movable feast.'

'Do you reckon I might be able to have eight hundred pounds for the netball tour?' asked Emily, taking her nose out of her geography textbook.

'Em,' Sally sighed, 'we need that money for food and petrol. I'm sorry, but we're all making sacrifices.'

'I'm sixteen. I can divorce you, you know,' said Emily.

Sally ruffled her hair. 'You just try! You may find me very difficult to get rid of.'

'Do I look OK?' asked Cleo, who'd emerged from the shower room in a denim jumpsuit, trainers, jacket, and hair tied up in a topknot. Her make-up was subtle, and she had the biggest grin on her face that her mum had ever seen. Sally tried to speak but found that something was catching in her throat. Stephen spoke for her.

'You actually look great, Cleo.'

'Yeah, it's a relief to not see your boobs hanging out,' added Mikey.

'You're beautiful, love,' said Sally, coming up to hug her daughter.

'Thanks Mum. I'm not going to lie, I know we've lost everything, including Dad, but I don't think I've ever been this happy in my life.'

And the two of them stood there hugging for a good fifteen seconds. Sally could have stayed there for ever but Cleo released herself from her mum's clasp.

'I'm not going to lie, Mum, you're going to have to let me go now.'

'Don't be too late, Cleo. And don't drink too much.'

'All right, Mum, do you want to ID me as well?' said Cleo, heading towards the door.

'And Cleo,' Sally struggled to find the words to say this, 'just go easy on Amir, you know? He probably hasn't watched as much *Love Island* as you have. He might not be as . . . experienced in these matters as you.'

Cleo cringed and pulled a face. Everyone was laughing; the fact did not escape Sally that here they were, able to relax and enjoy themselves without Frank's presence. They could have a good time without the ringmaster.

At the door Cleo stopped. 'Oh, I almost forgot. Where are you all going to be tonight?'

All eyes turned to Sally expectantly.

'The Golf Club,' she announced casually.

21

Frank Parker had been a major donor to Leatherhead Golf Club's huge refurbishment project five years ago, and had pretty much single-handedly paid for the new building which housed golf buggies, equipment, spare irons and so forth. As a long-term and trusted member of the Club, and a keystone donor, Frank had been given an honorary set of keys allowing him access to most parts of the complex. It was his favourite thing to give new HNB clients the guided tour, and then whip out his set of keys and unexpectedly open up a door: 'And here, my friends, is the Frank Parker buggy snug!' or 'Voilà the Frank Parker Larder!' in typical showman style.

Sitting around the dinner table in the clubhouse, Sally allowed this image of Frank to rest briefly on her brain, but was interrupted by Mikey.

'Mum, don't you think we should go to Snowdonia to find Dad?'

Sally put down the dinner menu she'd been fiddling with.

'I think we'll leave your dad to stew in his own juices, Mikey.'

'But I miss him. What if he needs us?' Mikey implored.

'He's a grown man. He can look after himself,' Sally sniffed.

'No, he can't,' said Emily. 'He's the most emotionally

immature man I've ever met, and he's shown himself incapable of looking after a) his family and b) himself.'

There was a silence round the table at this little outburst.

'He's still our dad,' said Mikey mournfully.

'Not mine, luckily,' said Emily, as a lady of a certain age, broad of beam, approached the table to take their food order. She looked at Sally with pity in her eyes.

'We've all heard what's happened, Sally. You don't need to say a word. You poor lost lambs,' she added, looking around the table. 'Now I would love to get you all a soft drink on the house. It's the least I can do. Wouldn't that be nice? Something cool and fizzy for the kids? You poor homeless creatures.' She leaned down more closely to Sally. 'You know that I volunteer at the food bank on a Wednesday? I can have a wee word—'

Sally straightened up in her chair and looked the waitress firmly in the eye.

'The offer of soft drinks is very kind, Maureen. I know for one that I would love something fizzy. How about a bottle of champagne, everyone?'

'Mum,' said Mikey with alarm, 'we've only got – ooow!'

Sally had kicked her swiftly on the shin under the table.

'A bottle of house champagne, please, Maureen.'

'And a triple vodka tonic for yours truly,' chipped in Kyle, 'with some roasted peanuts and maybe a little lager chaser, my darling.'

'And we'll order some dinner too,' said Sally jovially, 'it's ages since we've celebrated anything!'

Sally's children looked at each other worriedly.

'It's a bit weird to be celebrating without Dad here, isn't it?' asked Mikey.

Maureen's interest was piqued.

'Yes, what are we celebrating, Sally?'

Sally thought for a moment.

'Freedom, Maureen,' she replied, and she looked around the table one by one at her family and Janice as she spoke, 'and chefs. Great friends. Young love. And fierce girls!' Kyle sought her eye expectantly. Sally sighed. 'Oh yes, and travellers,' she finished, letting her eye rest pointedly on her brother-in-law, 'who travel back to their own homes.'

Maureen had never quite got the measure of Sally Parker, and now realised she never would.

'Right, everyone, let's order!' said Sally.

'Sally, are you sure this is a good idea?' said Emily. 'I've had to forego the Hong Kong netball tour—'

'Go mad! Order WHATEVER you want!' said Sally loudly for Maureen's benefit.

Everyone looked at each other, and then there was a loud gaggle of voices speaking all at once.

James Livesy was not wont to stay in his surgery a moment longer than necessary, but of late he had nowhere else to go, and increasingly found himself alone with his thoughts. A lot of the furniture had already been taken away from his office; all that remained was an armchair, filing cabinet and his skeleton from medical school.

He sat in the dark in his armchair, the streetlamp casting a liverish hue on his gills. His skeleton seemed to be grinning at him from the corner of the room. It was unnerving, so Livesy looked out over Sloane Street and watched his fellow Londoners; some on their way home from work, legal types jumping on the 137 bus, posh ladies walking their dogs in little fur-trimmed jackets, rich Europeans with designer stubble and Armani coats, chinless *Country Life* readers in pink cords and Barbour jackets. All of life was here, if life comprised an income over £120,000 per annum. James Livesy was filled with a deep hatred of every last one of these entitled douche-bags with their safe lives, country piles in the Cotswolds, bouncy luxuriant-haired children at boarding schools who made their parents proud at Speech Day, and pots and pots of cash sitting in Coutts. He turned the brass letter opener over and over in his febrile hands, and wondered for a moment what it would be like to plunge it into his heart. Nobody would hear his cries; this block of villas was made up entirely of offices. And even if somebody were to hear him, not a soul would want to come to the rescue of a disgraced man who could now no longer put 'Doctor' before his name, let alone 'Professor'.

His thoughts turned to Frank Parker. The fool. The night that they'd run into each other in that crapulent hospital had marked the start of Livesy's downfall. If Frank hadn't revealed Livesy's phoney professorship in the ward, none of this would have happened. Livesy was sane enough to know that at some point later he would have been found out, but if Parker hadn't blabbed . . .

He and Parker weren't so different from each other really. Both of them were chancers, out of their league; loners who believed they could survive in this world on ambition and charm alone. As Livesy looked out of the window and surveyed his lost kingdom, he knew that he was going to need a lot more than ambition and charm to survive the next chapter. He reached into the top drawer of his desk and fished out his passport. He turned it over thoughtfully in his hands.

He turned to the skeleton.

'You must have been very unloved, you creepy shitbag of bones. Nobody gave you a decent burial, did they?' He laughed a hollow laugh. 'It seems we may have much in common.' And his hands continued their solitary game, moving from passport back to letter opener as his glassy eyes continued to look out over Sloane Street.

'And that'll be four hundred and thirty-six pounds, please, Sally. As I said the soft drinks were on the house. But I did charge you for the fizz.'

Mikey lifted her head from where she'd been slumped on the table, pretty much asleep. It was after ten thirty. Emily was deep into her Greek homework and Sally and Janice had polished off most of the champagne between the two of them.

'Mum,' Stephen prodded Sally, who was in the middle of roaring with laughter at a story Janice was telling about a dog that pooed on its mistress's wedding dress. 'Mum,' he said more urgently, 'what's the plan?'

Sally looked at him lovingly and ruffled his hair. 'I love you Ste, you are the bestest son ever. And Em and Mikey you are the bestest girls—'

'Mum. You're pissed. Sober up and tell us the plan,' Stephen urged.

'Sssssssssh! I need lossof money, Mikey. What did she say, the old bag?' and Sally now began to speak in a monstrously loud stage whisper. 'Four hundred and thirty-six THOUSAND POUNDS, was it?'

'Mikey's already paid the bill, Mum,' said Stephen, 'and we all want to go to bed now.'

Janice helped up Sally, who was wobbly on her pins and still very giggly, and the tribe left the Golf Club dining area with many goodbyes to Maureen.

'If there's anything . . . anything at all that I can do for you, Sally,' said Maureen earnestly, 'all you have to do is lift the phone.'

'Actually, Maureen, there is one liddlething you could do for me?' said Sally, radically misjudging the distance between her and Maureen's face.

'Couldyou lend Frank about sisssty million pounds?'

Maureen was lost for words. Stephen and Janice took an armpit each and manhandled Sally, now shrieking with laughter, out of the restaurant.

Once outside, Sally motioned for them all to keep quiet, and they snuck round the back. After much fumbling of keys, Sally found the right one to open the door to Frank's outbuilding. They entered the sports hall-like structure where they'd left all of their sleepover stuff with the golf buggies.

'It's going to be so FUN!' said Sally, doing a little dance. 'Like the most exciting sleepover you've ever had!'

'Looks like someone's already started,' said Janice pointing at Mikey, who was snoring on the sleeping bags.

'Sally,' said Emily tersely, 'it's nearly eleven p.m. I won't get my requisite nine hours, you know.'

'Sssssssssshhh,' said Sally giggling. 'We jus' wait here till they've CLOSED the restaurant, then we sneak BACK IN with our sleeping bags, geddit?'

'You mean we're going to sleep the night in the clubhouse restaurant, Mum?' asked Stephen wearily.

'YESSSSSSS!' said his mother elatedly. 'SO FUN!!!'

Stephen and Emily looked grumpily at Sally. Kyle was yawning and going the same way as Mikey. Only Janice was enthusiastic about the idea.

'I'll unsheathe the sleeping bags,' she offered in her can-do manner.

A loud rap at the window made everyone jump out of their skin.

'Busted,' said Emily.

The door opened. Janice braced herself for whichever Golf Club jobsworth happened to be on night-time patrol. A familiar face popped his head round the door, and Amerjit Singh said chirpily,

'Room for one more?'

At six twenty the next morning, Mikey crept out of her sleeping bag, lowering the zip with all the care of a bomb-disposal expert. She needn't have bothered; Kyle's bison levels of snoring were loud enough to mask the opening of all the tombs in Christendom. Mikey counted out the left-over money carefully and divided it into two piles, keeping two thirds of it. She figured that Amerjit would have cash, so the family wouldn't be destitute. She left the other £130.67 on the table under which her mum and Janice Dawes were currently sleeping like dormice. They looked very sweet there together, bag next to bag. Janice had a look of bliss on her face, and Sally slept in the curve of Janice's body, protected by the dog groomer's windbreaker frame.

Mikey layered up with tights, trousers, vest, fleece and jacket, plus hat and gloves. She wanted to be prepared for whatever the elements might throw at her. She had a little rucksack with torch, spare underwear and some flapjacks that Ste had made. She was on a mission and travelling light; she felt focused and totally alert.

She tiptoed out of the clubhouse and checked her watch and her phone. Six twenty-four a.m. She got her BMX from behind a bush, and scooted off into the pitch-black morning.

It was another hour before the rest of the family started to rouse themselves. Kyle was slithering out of his sleeping bag like a snake shedding its skin, when Sally stopped him just in time.

'For God's sake, Kyle, no! Nobody needs to see that!'

'You know I always sleep nude!'

'You know what, Kyle, I didn't. Luckily.'

'For the love of God, please just put some clothes on, Uncle Kyle,' murmured Stephen from his bag, eyes still shut.

'You know there's a saying in Colombia,' said Kyle loudly, '"he who sleeps with an extra skin shall have no descendants".'

'Yet another reason for you to wear pyjamas in bed, Kyle,' mumbled Sally.

'When were you actually in Colombia, Uncle Kyle?' asked Stephen.

There was a pause as Kyle lay in his bag, as if trying to do the maths.

'Er . . . it's got to be about a year ago, man and boy,' he answered vaguely.

Emily, already up and about and folding her sleeping bag, looked thoughtful.

'I don't think you can use that expression for a time-line, Kyle.'

'Listen, bookworm, when you've travelled the world as much as I have, you'll discover that the rules of grammar-learning don't always apply. They're put there by the crackpots and the lizards running the West, to confuse us. Listen to the wind, Emily!'

'I have been all night, Uncle Kyle. My sleeping bag was very close to yours.'

And with that, she made her way to the clubhouse kitchen to get into her school uniform.

Sally's hangover was kicking in. She still had yesterday's clothes on and was feeling sweaty, sick, old, dehydrated and low. She wasn't sure how her grand idea of living in the clubhouse was going to pan out. It had seemed so workable in her head; by day, everyone inside the clubhouse, totally above board because of their Life Membership. They could stay there till eleven p.m., then they would leave as if to go home, but would wait in the outhouse building and sneak back into the clubhouse using Frank's special keys, when everybody had left for the night. What she hadn't factored into the equation was Maureen, the watchful gorgon, and a four-hundred-pound dinner bill every night. Her plan needed fine-tuning.

Amerjit yawned fulsomely and sat up in his bag; he was glad to be out of Hayes. He felt that he could breathe fresh air into his lungs again. Laura would be so proud of him if she only knew how manfully he was grasping his own destiny.

Kyle was making a meal of slithering towards the clubhouse kitchen in his sleeping bag, trying to show off as little flesh as possible.

'Hey, Kyle,' shouted Amerjit, 'that's a good caterpillar action you've got there, my man!'

Kyle laughed, pleased to have an ally in the group at last.

'All you have to do is lose the sleeping bag, then you can hit the dancefloor with that!' Amerjit added.

'NO, DON'T LOSE THE BLOODY SLEEPING BAG!' barked Sally urgently.

Sally gave Janice an imploring look as the two men roared with laughter. She missed Frank. The old Frank would have swept in here, made everyone laugh, charmed the pants off all the clubhouse staff and then driven the family off on some crazy day out. Who was she trying to kid? It was a weekday; the old Frank wouldn't be here, he'd be in the City all day, tweaking his bollocks in that annoying way of his when he was on the phone, and wheedling cash out of yet more clients.

Sally tried to rationalise it all in her befuddled head: so if Old Frank wasn't here because of work, and the new version, Tired Frank, wasn't here because he'd be asleep, then the big question was, which Frank could she actually rely on to be here in this crisis? She couldn't picture that Frank. Not the old one or the new one. This made her upper lip sweat.

She felt itchy in her sleeping bag and had a sudden desire to throw up. This big question was like the start of a hole in a jumper. Once you pull at the hole, it starts to unravel into a crinkly line of wool and then suddenly you don't have a jumper. Sally decided she wasn't going to miss Frank any more. It was too confusing to miss him. And yet. And yet. The years they'd had together, those wonderful years before he got so rich; they'd married too young, that was the problem. If only they'd waited till they were in their thirties. Maybe they'd never have got married at all. But then the children? The children might not have happened.

She looked over at Ste's form, like a Jurassic tortoise in his sleeping bag, and felt an overpowering love for him. And Emily, dressed so smartly in her uniform and ready to go to school; nothing could stop that girl. And Cleo all grown up now. She looked around the clubhouse and could see no Cleo. She made a mental note to find out where Cleo was. And Mikey, the hero. Her sleeping bag was there, folded up. But where was Mikey?

'Guys,' she stood up in her bag and addressed the clubroom, panic making her voice quiver, 'we're two down! Mikey and Cleo aren't here!'

'I wouldn't worry, Mum,' said Stephen's voice from somewhere deep inside his bag. 'Cleo'll be shacked up with lover boy up at Cedar Vale, and Mikey's feral. Don't stress about her; she's like a cockroach, she can survive anything. And she's got a working phone.'

A loud female scream interrupted their conversation, coming from the kitchen, and a clubhouse employee, still dressed in her coat and scarf, came running into the room.

'There's a naked man in the kitchen!' she screamed.

And Kyle stepped out into the clubhouse dining area, nuddy as a newborn babe. But a lot saggier. His scrotum looked about a hundred and fifty years old.

'Oh God,' said Sally, shielding her eyes.

'You're right,' said Janice, turning away. 'Nobody needs to see that.'

'Sally, can I have a word?' Emily asked her aunt, heading for the door with her head down.

'Of course, love,' said Sally. Negotiating a sleeping bag zip with a hangover was proving tricky.

'I'll meet you in the Frank Parker Buggy Suite,' said Emily dryly. 'My sports bag's in there.'

'Oi oi!' shouted Amerjit in Kyle's direction. 'Off to the Tower of London are you, mate? They'll definitely let you in with THOSE crown jewels!' and the two men roared with laughter again. Sally could sense a pattern emerging here, and her heart filled with dread.

She turned to the traumatised kitchen worker, who'd now calmed down and was looking around the clubhouse with a dazed expression.

'I'm so sorry,' said Sally, 'we didn't think anyone would be here till opening time. Are you OK?'

The girl nodded. 'I need to talk to Maureen, my manager.'

Sally's heart sank into her boots. This great clubhouse idea of hers was collapsing like a sandcastle. What could she do? What would Frank do? She had a lightbulb moment.

'Do you know what – sorry, I don't know your name?'

'Jessie.'

'Jessie, hi, lovely to meet you. I'm Sally. Do you know what, Jessie, maybe in exchange for –' and Sally spotted the cash Mikey had left on the table – 'this! You could maybe forget to tell Maureen about the nakedness, us staying over in the clubhouse . . . ?'

Jessie fingered the money thoughtfully.

'That's bribery,' she answered.

'Yes, Jessie, and it's kind of how the world works,' said Sally bluntly.

Jessie thought for a moment while she did some sums in her head.

'I'll do it. But in instalments. Eighty pounds a month for my silence.'

Sally counted out the notes and gave them to Jessie.

'Agreed,' she said and the two women shook hands on it. First the Range Rover, now this. She was becoming quite the wheeler dealer. Frank would be proud of her.

Jessie looked round at the motley bunch. The naked man had thankfully placed a napkin over the strategic area. She retreated back into the kitchen swiftly.

'OK. Where's the rest of the cash?' said Sally.

'That's all there is, Mum,' said Stephen flatly.

'What, fifty pounds sixty-seven?' said Sally. 'There should be a few more hundred?'

Stephen held up a bit of paper.

'Mikey left me a note. She says not to worry, she's gone to find Dad. And she's taken two-thirds of the money.'

'The little thief!' Sally blurted out.

'To be fair, Mum, it was Mikey's money in the first place,' said Stephen reasonably, 'and at least she hasn't used hers to bribe people.'

He looked so disappointed.

'Don't look at me like that, Ste. I had to do what I had to do,' said Sally desperately.

'I didn't think you were like that, Mum. I thought that was more Dad's domain,' and he walked away from his mother.

Sally had no time to process this – there was a frantic knocking at the clubhouse door. Everyone looked over to see Rashida and Yusuf Jamal peering through the glass, in a state of panic.

'Oh no, what now?' said Sally, a light migraine playing over her right eyebrow. Janice let the Jamals in and Sally introduced Amerjit.

'Everything OK up at Cedar Vale?' said Sally, trying to sound breezy. 'You look as if something terrible has happened.'

'It's worse than terrible,' said Yusuf, 'our car has gone.'

'I'm sorry to hear that,' said Sally. 'Have you tried the police?'

'There's no need,' said Yusuf. 'We know that our son took it, the scoundrel.'

Sally paused, and smiled kindly.

'Well I'm sure he'll bring it back,' she said, soothingly.

'He won't. They've gone. Amir and Cleo. They left us a voicemail at around midnight, sounding very giggly I have to say, to tell us that they were leaving. To get married. Either in Afghanistan or Snowdonia. Whichever was the cheaper option.'

Sally's smile faded. There was silence in the room. Stephen sat up in his sleeping bag. She collected her thoughts, which were starting to race out of control.

'I hope to God it's not Afghanistan,' said Sally.

'Me too,' agreed Yusuf.

'I've heard it's pretty heavy out there, isn't it, dude?' said Kyle, approaching with the napkin still held over his privates.

'It's not that,' said Yusuf sharply, 'it's the cost of the long-stay car park at Heathrow. It'll be a bloody fortune!'

Sally sat down, no breath in her lungs. She could not believe what she was hearing. Janice put a reassuring hand on her shoulder, and squeezed it.

'Let me get this straight,' said Sally. 'Amir and Cleo have gone either to Kabul or Snowdonia. Frank's gone to Snowdonia. Mikey's gone to Snowdonia. We have fifty pounds and sixty-seven pence. I don't think we'll get to Afghanistan on that, but we've got a chance with Snowdonia. Start packing, everyone.'

'We will meet you in Snowdonia too,' said Rashida. 'This village, Llanfairfechan, they said in the message? Is it hard to find?'

'I have no idea,' said Sally. 'How will you get there with no car?'

'We'll get an Uber,' said Rashida.

Emily was waiting patiently for her aunt in the outhouse that Frank built. She'd found a pile of stiff cushions for outdoor chairs and sat neatly and compactly on top of them. That was her niece all over, thought Sally as she approached her, always in charge and always ready. Sally, on the other hand, with her hair on end and mascara down her cheeks, felt out of control, like some ageing rocker who was falling, in slow motion, out of a nightclub.

'I will never drink again, Emily, as long as I live,' she announced. 'We haven't got long to chat. We need to pack immediately, OK?'

Emily looked down at her sports kit.

'I've been thinking over what we talked about before, Sally. The scholarship and everything.'

Sally's heart missed a beat. She braced herself.

Emily continued.

'I can't live like this, Sally. I'm not sleeping properly, I'm not eating properly, and my grades are going to suffer. And with things with Frank the way they are and everything . . .' she tailed off uncertainly.

'So, what are you thinking, Em?'

'My friend Joan's asked her mum and dad, and they'd love to have me. She's an only child and she's really nice.'

Sally felt as if her entire body had taken a hit from an enormous wrecking ball ploughing into her chest. She felt her eyes fill with tears. No words came out of her mouth. She was winded.

'I'm sure we can all stay really close, whatever happens,' said Emily, getting down from the cushions. 'I just think it's for the best, that's all. I'm sure my mum will agree. When I can get hold of her.'

'Of course,' whispered Sally. 'Of course.'

'I'm going to go to Joan's tonight if that's OK with you. She's cleared out a wardrobe for me and her mum's cooking me a special welcome dinner.'

'Great,' croaked Sally, 'how lovely.'

'I'd better go, I don't want to be late for physics,' and Emily ran from the outhouse, tears starting to thicken her voice.

Sally stood in the cold, echoing chamber that Frank had paid for, and howled like an animal.

22

The lady in the ticket office at Leatherhead station looked Mikey over as she asked her for a single child ticket to Llanfairfechan. Mikey smiled winningly and explained it was a geography field trip.

She waited on the platform for twenty minutes before boarding the London train. She was going to Victoria, then across town to Euston to make a connection to Crewe. From Crewe she'd make the final leg of her journey to Llanfairfechan. All being well, she'd walk through the door at her great-grandmother's house in the early afternoon. She'd eaten two of Ste's flapjacks and was feeling fortified and ready for action.

Mikey looked out of the train window as the Surrey landscape slipped quickly into the more cluttered, urban landscape of London. She felt excited; she was going to make her dad very proud.

Frank was so exhausted he would have found even summoning pride too physically demanding right now. Everything was a Herculean effort for him, and thank God for Geoff Turton's deck chair. Without that he'd have lain down in the car park and given up long ago. Lifts had been sparse out of Cobham so a very sleepy Frank hit the hay in the Ramada for the night, thanks to the fifty quid given to him by Geoff. He slept fitfully, his dreams alive with Sally. In each dream, he'd present her with an increasingly lavish gift, but at every one she would shake her head silently. Then Geoff Turton would appear behind Sally in the shining white robes of a prophet, contrasting alarmingly with his jet-black tresses, and he would intone in a bass voice full of portent, 'ANOTHER EMPTY PROMISE, FRANK PARKER!'

Frank reckoned he must have gone through about fifty empty promises in his dreams that night, and woke up drenched in sweat. He figured that if he could get to the M40, then that would be a good start. He sat down in his deck chair in Cobham Services car park around eight thirty, the 'NORTH WALES' sign in his lap, and watched the drivers come in and out of the petrol station. It became hypnotic, enough to send Frank off to sleep, which happened after one minute and eight seconds.

Janice, Sally and Stephen had their heads down in the clubhouse, hard at work, packing and tidying up before somebody came to open up for the day. The mood was sombre. Janice noticed that Sally's eyes were red and her cheeks mascara-stained. She was determined to keep an extra vigilant eye on her.

Sally was in no mood to chat, even though Janice had opened up some light conversation about lungworm in dogs and the need for good vitamin supplements for certain types of bichon frise. Liesl and Kurt had been remarkably good-humoured, considering all the uprooting and decamping they'd been put through. Sally and Frank had not shared a bed since Cedar Vale, so she was well used to having Liesl and Kurt to snuggle up with at night. In fact, they were better bedfellows than Frank, who tended to hog the entire duvet, then snore like a boar.

The rest of the Von Trapp dogs had settled in well at Paws Fur Thought under the loving tutelage of Lucy, Janice's faithful assistant. People were offering to rehome the dogs; Janice would have to broach the subject with Sally another time.

Kyle and Amerjit were taking five, chewing the cud while the hive of activity went on around them. The Hayes boys knew each other of old, but Amerjit had only ever thought of Kyle as Frank's brother, not as a proper friend of his own.

'So that's how I ended up in The Chantry,' said Amerjit, finishing his yarn.

'Bad scene, bro,' said Kyle.

'You're joking. Fabulous kip, great food, and I got to talk about myself for two weeks,' said Amerjit. 'It was paradise.'

'And the wife?' asked Kyle, narrowing his eyes like a detective.

Amerjit exhaled.

'It's hard. She's a great woman, Laura, but she doesn't suffer fools –' Amerjit looked wistful – 'and once she thinks you're a fool. That's it. You're dead to her.'

'So *you're* buggered,' said Kyle, smiling. 'In my experience of the fairer sex, and that's encompassing four continents of them,' he continued, settling himself deeper into the leather banquette, 'a woman, be she in eleventh-century Barcelona banged up in some convent, or a ladette in Georgian times working as a lady of the night, right up to our females now with their feminist ways and their "equality this" and "let's burn our bras" that, only wants one thing.'

Amerjit felt put on the spot.

'Equal pay?' he hazarded.

Kyle looked blank.

'No, friend,' he said wisely, 'they want a man who's going to go "grrr" for them, you know, show a bit of muscle and fight for them.'

'Really?' said Amerjit. 'I always thought Laura was perfectly capable of doing that on her own. To be honest, her grrr is what attracted me to her in the first place.'

'Trust me, amigo,' said Kyle, 'if you don't fight for a woman, you might as well consign yourself to the manure heap. In some outer reaches of Guatemala that is literally what happens.'

'What about Sal?' said Amerjit, looking over at the slight, silent figure in camo trousers, trying to get a sleeping bag to fit into a condom-sized plastic sock.

'You see with Sal, here's the problem. Frank's out of fight,' said Kyle, leaning into Amerjit earnestly, 'and out of fight is out of mind.' Kyle was pleased with that, and let it hang in the air for a moment while Amerjit nodded sagely. Kyle continued, 'But the two of us hombres have still got some lead in our pencils. Haven't we? Eh? We can step up to the plate?' Kyle prodded Amerjit's arm. 'Mate, I've got an idea,' and he winked at his new best friend.

Amerjit tried to wink back, but he wasn't very good at winking, another thing which had annoyed Laura, who was an excellent winker.

Amerjit could only wink with both eyes at the same time, so he gave Kyle a very affirmative blink instead.

Mikey was heading down into Victoria Underground station, high on the buzz of rush-hour London, when she heard a familiar voice.

'Mikey? What on earth are you doing here? Is it a D of E expedition or something?'

She turned around to see Tim Daly-Jones in his suit and tie, carrying a briefcase, ready for a day's work in the City.

'I'm off to Snowdonia,' Mikey told him proudly. 'Dad's gone AWOL, we're camping out in the Golf Club and we've got no money. Apart from that,' she said breezily, 'business as usual!'

Tim looked at her, slack-jawed.

'Look,' Mikey continued, 'I'd better run, I've got a connection at Euston to hit,' and she set off. She turned round and called jauntily, 'Don't let the buggers get you down, Tim!' as she bounced down the steps into the Underground.

Tim Daly-Jones looked at the space that Mikey had just filled, with a vacant look, shook his head and then phoned his wife immediately to relay the gossip.

They parked the car as close to the bins as they could, and, feeling like Starsky and Hutch, Kyle and Amerjit leapt out of the orange Austin Allegro. This tight seventies cop choreography was only slightly marred by Kyle having to do a deep lunge by the side of the car to check he hadn't strained his groin. Amerjit felt sweet adrenaline course through his body; he hadn't felt this pumped in a long time, not since Laura had given him the Red Letter Day voucher for his birthday that entitled him to skydive out of an RAF plane. Unfortunately Laura had a last-minute meeting and couldn't accompany Amerjit to the jump site; Amerjit was forced to high-five himself when he'd completed the jump and landed on terra firma.

The weather was crisp and Kyle was in military mode.

'This is the plan, OK? We approach the bins, we keep it three-sixty at all times, and when the time is as ripe as a Colombian papaya, we pounce,' and when he said the word 'pounce' he accompanied it with a little action, like a cat going for a ball of wool.

'We pounce on the bins?' checked Amerjit.

'Affirmative. This reminds me of a raid we pulled off outside Bogota. Hostile country, lots of FARC about, only dusk to help us . . .'

Amerjit looked a tad confused.

'This was a bin raid? In Colombia?' asked Amerjit.

Kyle gave an almost imperceptible sigh.

'There are no refuse facilities in the jungle, Amerjit. Let's just say it was a "person raid" and leave it at that,' and he tapped his nose confidentially. 'We need to get in the zone, amigo. Ready?'

'Check,' said Amerjit.

The Waitrose car park was practically empty, with a couple of yummy mummies pushing their buggies towards the store. There was not a member of staff in sight, not even somebody in a hi-viz vest corralling trollies. The two men strolled nonchalantly towards the bin area until Kyle made a sudden 180 degree turn and adopted a Tai chi stance. Amerjit was taken aback.

'You cool, Kyle?' he asked nervously.

'Seventh sense, Amerjit, seventh sense.' Kyle continued silently towards the bins. Amerjit followed him two paces behind. Both men walked and turned full-circle at the same time, like a pair of spinning tops.

When they were up close to the bins, Kyle fired out the orders in a barked whisper.

'We recce the target, we assess, we raid. Makes sense?'

'It makes seventh sense,' Amerjit whispered back.

Kyle went down quite low, almost to his haunches like a Cossack dancer, and did a circling movement around the bins. Amerjit tried to emulate this, but found it stressful on the hamstrings.

'Assess!' hissed Kyle, as he performed a turkey-like manoeuvre with his head towards the bin. They made several assessments until Kyle issued the order to raid.

The military nature of their operation was forgotten here, as the two men scrambled around the bins, fishing out stuff and trying to grab anything as quickly as possible without being spotted. It was all over in seconds, as Kyle's eagle eye spotted a small child hurtling towards them on a scooter.

'Feds at three o'clock!' barked Kyle. 'Abort! Abort!'

And the two men ran back to the Allegro clutching their wares. Kyle performed a seventeen-point turn out of the parking space before they managed to squeal away from the car park. Both men were buzzing with adrenaline.

After a piece of luck with a game granny in a Mini Metro who talked about her various varicose vein operations, Frank was dropped off at the M40 services at Beaconsfield. She gave him several Mr Kipling French Fancies to keep him going.

Frank set up his deck chair again, got out the North Wales placard, and waited. Beaconsfield was a busy service station with plenty of lorries rumbling past. Frank was just thinking about the possibility of a little twenty winks when a juggernaut stopped beside him with an agonised chorus of brakes. Its jovial-looking driver towered above Frank in his cab, and wound down the window.

'You going to Wales, are you?' he said in the broadest of Welsh accents.

'Yes!' replied Frank, sounding apologetically English. 'Any chance of a lift?'

'Hop in. I'm going home, I am, you can keep me company!'

Frank folded up his deck chair and hoisted himself, plus chair, into the spacious cab of the Welsh lorry driver.

'Stevo,' said the driver, extending a heavily tattooed forearm out to Frank.

'Frank,' said Frank, responding with his rather puny English hand.

'Two out-of-date packs of brie, a box of After Eights, and some nappies?' said Sally, surveying the booty which Kyle and Amerjit had brought to the table.

Kyle put his hand up and Amerjit high-fived it. He couldn't help grinning; it felt novel and life-affirming to share a high-five with somebody else.

'It's an eclectic mix of booty, but in a raid situation, Sal, beggars can't be choosers,' explained Kyle. 'So I think you'll agree that any hunter-gathering activities can now be taken care of by the KA collective, which stands for Kyle and Amerjit,' and Kyle lifted his fist for Amerjit to bump him back.

Sally looked drained. Her face showed none of its usual twinkle or empathy. She looked pinched and tired and was in no mood for banter from Stan and Ollie here.

'Stephen's actually just been to Lidl and bought a really sensible lot of food to match his meal plans,' said Sally curtly, motioning to the four bags by the clubhouse door, 'but thank you, guys, it'll be nice to have a beyond-sell-by-date cheese board in the mix, and if any babies get left on our doorstep . . .'

Sally stopped here and bit her lip. She looked as if she were about to cry. 'What was I saying? Yes, if a baby happens to be dropped on to our doorstep then we'll have a packet of six-to-nine-month nappies. Very useful.'

And then she looked away.

'Mum, what's wrong?' asked Ste, clocking Sally's pale face.

Her lips and jaw trembled, and she looked down at her hands. She took time to get her words together.

'Emily's not coming with us to Snowdonia, Ste,' she said.

There was a silence as everybody took this in.

'How come?'

'She wants to concentrate on her studies, love, and we're not really leading the kind of life which is conducive to that.'

'So, she'll come and join us in a bit, then?' asked Ste. 'In a few days or something?'

Sally looked at her son, with his anxious face and fringe flopping down over his brown eyes. He was wearing his school uniform trousers, but on top he wore his own Droids in The Hood sweatshirt. This mishmash of school and home clothes somehow made Sally want to start blubbing and never stop.

'I can't answer that, Ste,' said Sally slowly. 'She's staying with her friend Joan.'

'Joan Flynn?'

'Yes,' said his mum, 'and her lovely functional parents.'

Stephen looked crestfallen.

'Oh,' was all he managed to say, 'she never said goodbye.'

Janice patted Stephen on the shoulder and then gave Sally an encouraging look.

'Goodbye is often the hardest word to say, Ste,' said Kyle earnestly. 'It's nigh on impossible in the native Ecuadorian language. I could never get my tongue round it.'

'If there's anything we can do, Sal,' said Amerjit gently, 'just ask.'

Sally looked at them all with flashing eyes.

'I'm fine, guys. I'm absolutely fine. Do you know what, I don't think I've ever felt so fine in all of my life. I've never been fricking finer! Cleo's flown off to Kabul,

Emily's abandoned us for a better family and Mikey? Well, we don't even know where she is. She's eleven and she's disappeared. I just COULDN'T BE BETTER!'

Sally sat at a table with her head in her hands. An awkward silence hung in the air like a fart. Stephen broke the ice.

'I think all this is hard for you, Mum, because you've never had to do a day's work in your life.'

The silence after this got a whole five levels more awkward. Stephen shifted from foot to foot and Kyle mimed an 'ouch' with his face.

'What did you say, Ste?' whispered his mum, head still in hands.

'I said, Mum,' and Ste coughed nervously, 'that you've never had to do a day's work in your life. Somebody's always given you money and maybe that's why this is all so hard for you. Just a thought, really.'

Sally released her head from her hands and looked up at the four pairs of eyes on her.

'My mother always said I'd come to nothing, you know.'

The conversation was interrupted by Maureen's brisk approach.

'You can't keep away from this place, can you, Sally?' she said. Sally noticed Jessie the kitchen girl wiping a nearby table and shot her a meaningful look. Sally wondered if Jessie had spilled the beans about the hush money.

'This place is a bit like a home from home for you, isn't it?' continued Maureen breezily, holding up a pair of grubby tie-dye Y-fronts. 'I don't suppose these are anything to do with you lot, are they? They were found hanging off the food-processor this morning.'

The Parker tribe held one another's gazes in an uneasy silence. Maureen stared at Sally.

'Is there a skid mark in the gusset?' Sally inquired dryly. 'If there is, they're Kyle's.'

Maureen looked horrified but couldn't help inspecting, and immediately flung the pants at the nearest men in the room.

Sally stood up purposefully.

'Maureen, I did a terrible thing this morning. I offered to pay one of your clubhouse employees money in return for her silence. My son pointed out the error of my ways and I thank him for that.' She looked squarely at the kitchen girl. 'Jessie, the deal's off.'

Sally picked up her beanie hat. 'Time to move. Snowdonia or bust.'

Stephen looked at his mum, his eyes shining with pride.

Mikey was enjoying the rural part of her journey. The cityscape had long given way to windswept hill country, and the train rattled along in its comforting clackety-clack way. All the flapjacks were finished; Mikey had shared them out with a bunch of university students heading to Bangor. They'd started a game of poker and had just invited her to join.

Mikey was weighing up the possibilities here. She analysed the company carefully, and worked out that there was an eighty-five per cent chance of her winning. She put away a third of the cash into her rucksack, leaving two thirds to play with. The students thought it was hilarious that an eleven year old was playing too. Mikey was happy to be friendly but she was in this game to win; she didn't want to muddy the waters with too much emotional baggage. She put on her poker face, which made her look even younger.

Stevo drove his lorry into the HGV section of the service station; Frank had never been into an HGV section before and felt honoured. This was like being allowed exclusive VIP access. The journey thus far had been pleasant and uneventful. Frank felt comfortable enough in Stevo's cab to nod off occasionally, and during waking hours he and Stevo chumbled away and chatted about life in general. Frank didn't disclose too much information about his own personal circumstances, but was happy to talk to Stevo about life on the road. It was lunchtime and both men were hungry. Frank felt chuffed to be led away from the general public's café area, and into the realm of the truck drivers' secret canteen.

'This is where the proper food is, Frank. None of that overpriced, packaged to buggery, microwave nonsense. You'll get a good plate of hot food in your belly here for less than a fiver.'

The shepherd's pie aroma was deeply inviting and Frank found himself salivating as he and Stevo queued at the counter. Stevo was obviously well known in this café and Frank felt that under his wing he was being given special attention too, with everyone calling him 'love' and 'sweetheart'.

For the first time in a long time, Frank felt appreciated. As he shook pepper over his shepherd's pie, he looked around at his fellow diners and felt that he was Frank again. He was almost moved to tears as a burly man with a tattoo of Theresa May's face on his impossibly wide bicep offered to collect his tray for him. He wished that Sally were here with him now, eating this hearty fayre, and yet it was good to be in the company of men, all with somewhere to go and a mission to accomplish.

'Steady on there,' said Stevo with a chuckle as his companion hunched over his plate and started shovelling in the shepherd's pie. 'I don't want you guffing in my cab, man. Give your digestion a chance!'

'This is the best food I've ever eaten,' said Frank, dispatching the mash and mince down the purple lane, 'except perhaps for Le Manoir aux Quat'Saisons outside Oxford. Orgasmic food; it's got Michelin stars coming out of its arse!'

'I'm not familiar with that one,' said Stevo wryly. 'Is it part of the Little Chef chain?'

Frank laughed.

Stevo looked at Frank carefully and asked, 'So you're used to the finer things of life are you, Frank?'

Frank couldn't reply immediately because he'd just put another big mouthful of shepherd's pie into his mouth, but he was aware that Stevo seemed a little tense. His expression had lost its crinkly, smiling quality and the lines on his face stood out starkly under the harsh strip-lighting of the trucker canteen. There was a disconcerting blue vein pulsing on his forehead, and his neck looked flushed.

Frank smiled with hamster cheeks full of mash and did something that he hadn't done since the early eighties; he put both thumbs up together, like a cheeky children's TV presenter. It was meant as a gesture of levity and good will, a bit of 'we're all in this together' sort of bonhomie. But judging by Stevo's dead-eyed reaction to Frank Parker's perky thumbs, it had not been read that way. Frank's thumbs wilted like two water-starved asparagi, and he didn't know where to put them. He decided it was better just to keep the head down and carry on eating. The fuller his mouth was then the less ability he had to formulate sentences, and that had to work in his favour.

'Fucking Tories,' Stevo muttered under his breath as he picked up his plate aggressively, causing the cutlery to clatter. 'Come on Frank, time to hit the road,' he said, stalking off.

A question flitted through Frank's mind; might he be

better off staying in this lovely warm trucker canteen with its red plastic chairs and steamed-up windows, and maybe just falling asleep for a few hours? Or should he go and share a confined space with a riled-up truck driver who might well have anger-management issues when it came to the more right-leaning end of the political spectrum? Then Frank thought of his grandmother. No, he had to push on to Llanfairfechan. He stood up, wobbled somewhat, and headed out to the truck. He would face an army of lefty Welshmen for Bronwen; he would surmount any challenge at all if it lessened the miles between himself and Llanfairfechan.

Emily sat next to Joan Flynn in maths and listened to her chatting animatedly about what it was going to be like having Emily living with them. She came from a family of three, her and her parents, Linda and Paul.

'We've got a cat, I hope you're not allergic, Em.'

'Not at all, I've been living with seven dogs most of my life,' said Emily with a smile.

'I usually study for three hours every evening,' said Joan, 'from five till six p.m. then after dinner from eight till ten p.m.'

'Music to my ears!' was Emily's response.

'Oh yes! We can practise our music together!' said Joan excitedly.

'Great!' said Emily.

'It's going to be so wonderful having you live with us,' said Joan with her eyes shining. 'We can play board games at the weekend or even go out for a walk sometimes?'

Emily thought of weekends at home, with Cleo getting ready for some mad party, Mikey coming home with tales of her wheeling and dealing, and Ste bringing them all snacks to share in front of some stupid, deeply unsuitable movie. She thought of all of them laughing on the beanbag together until they were nearly sick.

'We can watch *Friends* together, Em! I've seen nearly all the episodes. My favourite character's definitely Phoebe. She's SO funny. Who's yours?'

Emily looked wistfully out of the window,

'Yes. Phoebe's really funny,' she said blankly.

In the first-class carriage of the Crewe-bound train, all was dandy for Mikey Parker. She'd cleaned the students out of most of their cash and had left the game on top, as any wise poker player should. She'd used her winnings to upgrade so that she could take advantage of the free food and onboard waitress service. One of the guards looked at her suspiciously as he checked and double-checked her ticket.

'Are you travelling with someone?' he asked her.

'No, but I'm going to my great-granny's.'

'Shouldn't you be in school?'

'I'm homeschooled,' Mikey said without hesitation, 'it's all the rage in Surrey where I live. I'm just about to do a maths session, actually. I'm self-educating. It's very fluid.'

The guard didn't really know what to say to this, so moved on to the next traveller, leaving Mikey to hug her knees with glee.

She was only half-lying about the maths because counting out her spoils was definitely good for her adding-up skills. She had forty-two pounds left post-upgrade, and couldn't wait to give her dad a blow-by-blow account of her victory.

Frank tried to thaw the chill that had settled in the cab of Stevo's truck. He thought he would start up some nice light chat, nothing too emotional that might ignite Stevo's blue touch-paper, just something banal and neutral.

'I think Thatcher's policies on the free market have been misunderstood, Stevo, especially by the Welsh.'

Stevo's top lip, with a life of its own, flipped back and upwards to reveal his impressive canine teeth. It remained curled while he glared at Frank, and said:

'Don't patronise me, you entitled piece of English scum. You know nothing of Wales, you sorry Surrey twat. I thought you were a decent man of the road when I picked you up, but it turns out you're just another shitty corporate cog in the proto-fascist imperialist capitalist machine.'

Frank coughed lightly.

'You know what, Stevo, if there's a convenient bit of hard shoulder, why not just drop me off and I can make my own way from there? Unless of course you want to get out too, cosh me over the head, dig a deep ditch and bury my proto-fascist imperialist capitalist corpse in it?' Frank laughed a little too long after he'd said this. Stevo's eyes blazed at him coldly.

'I won't be dictated to, Frank. We'll stop when I say.'

'Absolutely, sure, yes of course, you're the boss,' said Frank, who up to till now had never realised he was a soprano.

23

It was nearly five o'clock and the convoy of two vehicles pushed onwards. Kyle's Austin Allegro tailed Janice's Paws Fur Thought van as they left the bright orange world of the motorway and turned off into the dark unknown of Wales. Kyle filled his lungs deeply. He was in a philosophical mood.

'This is what it's all about. The open road; car and Nature in perfect harmony. It's weird how this four-wheeled gas-guzzler can still be painted so perfectly into Nature's mighty canvas. Take two human hearts beating out a Celtic rhythm from aeons gone by, and mix liberally with a 1982 Austin Allegro!'

Amerjit nodded his head slowly and thoughtfully.

'It's hardly a Celtic rhythm from aeons gone by, Kyle,' he said from the back seat. 'We've just passed a Carpet Right and a drive-thru Costa. We're on a dual carriageway heading for Conwy.'

Kyle looked at his buddy in the rear-view mirror and winked. Amerjit was a nervous passenger, which had always peeved Laura, being a bit of a joyrider herself at the steering wheel.

'All right, Mister Shat Nav,' joshed Kyle, 'I suppose you know how many miles away from Conwy we are as well?'

'Sixty-two,' said Amerjit, 'and with an average speed of

366

seventy-eight miles an hour that means our ETA should be around seventeen fifty-six.'

'You OK back there, bud?' said Kyle.

'I'm fine as long as you keep your eyes on the road,' said Amerjit tersely.

'Listen, mate, I'm parched. Lob us a drink from my bag, will you?'

Amerjit sighed, picked up Kyle's less-than-salubrious stripy Guatemalan hold-all and tentatively put his hand inside its murky interior. He fished out an ancient tube of Deep Heat, lots of used tissues, Kyle's passport, an out-of-date Argos catalogue, and three bottles.

'There's nothing to drink, Kyle. It's just beer in here.'

'Nothing to drink?' Kyle snorted with laughter. 'The only drink worthy of a man on the road, amigo, is beer! How do you think those Mexican bus drivers survive? They don't drink Quosh, I'm telling you!'

Kyle chuckled loudly, Amerjit laughed along uncertainly. Kyle shouted towards the back seat,

'Come on Amerjit, you fortysomething fogey! Pass Uncle Kyle his beer! I promise you I drive much better when I've had a couple.'

Amerjit reluctantly passed the rucksack forward, but kept hold of the Argos catalogue and the passport for something, frankly anything to distract and calm himself.

Kyle opened a bottle of beer with his teeth, sluiced some into the back of his throat and belched theatrically.

'Amerjit, music, *por favor*! Lob me the Marillion cassettes, buddy! They're down by your feet!'

The needle on Stevo's speedometer was twitching around the seventy miles per hour mark, which concerned Frank. His eyeballs were scratchy and he was desperate to put the passenger seat into a reclining position, but was too scared to drop off with this maniac at the wheel. Frank had a slick of sweat underneath each eye, and his beanie hat was now warm enough to slow cook a lamb shank in.

'Stevo, you're driving this juggernaut at quite a pace,' he said tentatively, trying to compete with the engine noise.

Stevo shot him a snide look.

'I expect you like fast cars, don't you, Frank? Got a big garage at home for the Maserati, Porsche, Lamborghini, fricking Jag, have you?'

Frank looked nervously at Stevo's forearms which, to his worn-out brain, suddenly seemed double their normal size.

'Just the lawnmowers, actually, Stevo,' he said as subtly as he could.

'Aaaah, the lawnmowers! How very la-di-da!' said Stevo, imitating Frank's English accent. 'The lawnmowers, plural! How many have you got, Frank?'

'Thirty-two,' said Frank without thinking.

'THIRTY-TWO BY CHRIST!' bellowed Stevo as he pressed the accelerator with his boot-clad foot. The speedometer needle travelled up to seventy-three. 'THIRTY-TWO!!! WHO OWNS THIRTY-TWO COCKING LAWNMOWERS? I'll tell you who owns thirty-two lawnmowers, a PRICK owns thirty-two lawnmowers. A rich, capitalist, cock of a man who's leeching off the land, the workers and the poor. WHO THE COCK NEEDS THIRTY-TWO LAWNMOWERS?'

Frank felt similarly to how he had when HNB Capital Management went for a bonding day at Alton Towers and he'd been forced to go on the Nemesis ride; he wondered if he should start self-administering the last rites. He had to get out of this lorry. Whatever and however, he had to get out of it and fast.

'YOU GOT A STATELY FRICKING HOME,

FRANK? WHAT IS IT, ONE LAWNMOWER FOR THE WEST WING, ONE FOR THE COCKING EAST WING, ONE FOR THE NORTH WING? AND WHERE ARE THE OTHER TWENTY-NINE? IN THE PRICKING SERVANTS' QUARTERS, ARE THEY? DOWNTON COCKING ABBEY IS IT, FRANK?'

Stevo's accent had now gone from Welsh to uber-Welsh.

'I don't have the lawnmowers any more, Stevo,' Frank's voice was almost pleading now, 'the Revenue took everything away. I don't have any lawnmowers, I don't have any lawns and I don't have any house. Nothing. It's all been taken away.'

The speedometer calmed down to sixty-five, and Frank allowed himself a shallow breath. The vein in Stevo's neck appeared to be throbbing less angrily. Frank sensed he was on safer ground,

'I'm not even sure if I've got a family any more, Stevo.'

The lorry slowed down to a comfortable sixty, and Stevo rolled his neck and shoulders and breathed out.

'These inequalities get to me, Frank.'

'I can see that, Stevo.'

'It's not right,' Stevo continued, 'that there are four million children living below the poverty line in this country, Frank, four fricking million.'

Frank was silent. He knew nothing about statistics of this kind. The only news he ever read was either to do with the FTSE or the golf.

'That is appalling,' said Frank quietly.

'And these fat cats, these shits that get richer while the poor get poorer, should all be hung, drawn and quartered and their scrotal sacs paraded on pikes and then fed to the cats.'

'What, fed to the fat cats?' asked Frank.

'No, real cats. Real domestic cats,' explained Stevo.

Frank nodded, but was frantically looking for a services sign out of the window; he noticed one saying two miles.

'Stevo,' he said calmly, 'I reckon you must be gagging for a cup of tea, and I'm desperate for a slash. How about we pull over at the next services?'

Stevo nodded. Frank unclenched his buttocks and allowed himself to breathe again.

Mikey's train hadn't moved an inch in over an hour. After changing at Crewe with time to spare and a considerable weight in free biscuits, bread rolls and cans of Sprite tucked into her bag, she'd had to readjust to standard class for the final leg. She'd taken full advantage of the complimentary all-day breakfast options while she could, though, putting away two Continental options and the cooked version thanks to a nice Onboard Leisure Service Executive called Donna.

Mikey sighed. She was bored and desperate to get to Llanfairfechan; she'd seen all the countryside she wanted and had counted her winnings twenty times over.

A nasal voice came over the Tannoy.

'Once again, we do apologise for this unforeseen delay to your service today. Due to signalling problems we will be stopping at the next station, where this train will terminate.'

The train proceeded to grind on infinitesimally slowly, accompanied by the sound effects of relentless Dantesque machinery. Mikey gathered her money into her rucksack and stood up. She was going to have to look lively.

The Paws Fur Thought van reached the outskirts of Conwy at around the six p.m. mark, under a dusky Welsh sky.

'We're about twenty minutes from Llanfairfechan now,'

said Janice, expertly parking the van one-handedly into quite a tight space just off the High Street. She liked to stretch her idle left arm out along the top of the seat, behind both Sally and Stephen who were riding up front with her. Janice hoped that Sally felt secure with her arm placed there. There were no seats in the back of Janice's van, only various meshed sections for transporting dogs.

'I don't know about you chaps, but I'm desperate for a comfort break,' Janice said as she turned off the ignition.

'Let's stretch our legs,' Sally agreed, 'and Liesl and Kurt need a wee too. Plus it'll give the others a chance to catch up with us. We seem to have lost them.'

They found a nice café on the High Street and settled in for coffees and snacks. Sally noticed there was a rail of handmade knits and some hippy dresses.

'Right, I've got a plan. Give me the keys to the van, Jan.'

Janice loved that Sally was now calling her Jan. Every time the word came out of Sally's mouth, it gave her a glow inside her body warmer. Sally chuckled.

'This wo-man got a van plan, Jan!' said Sally, with accompanying bum wiggle.

The women guffawed with laughter; Stephen remained silent.

The moment Sally left the café, Stephen spoke to Janice across the table.

'You know my mum's married, Janice.'

Janice reddened.

'To Frank. Your dad. I'm well aware of that,' she replied.

'I'm worried you're getting too attached, and that you're going to end up getting hurt,' said Stephen, fiddling with a sachet of sugar.

Janice blew out her cheeks before speaking.

'I'm very fond of your mum, Stephen, we're good

friends, but I'm not in any way shape or form attached to her. No, no. No, no, no, no, no, no, no. If anything, I'm detached. Or semi-detached. To her.'

Stephen raised his eyebrows quizzically.

'You've been very kind to us since all of this mess started,' he said, 'and my mum relies on you so much. I just hope she's not taking advantage of you, that's all.'

'I want to be taken advantage of . . .' stammered Janice, 'what I mean is, I want her to rely on me. I want to be her rock, her touchstone. I want her to feel that she can touch me. No, what I mean is, I want her to feel that I am stone and she can touch—'

She was interrupted by Sally, now carrying the bundle of designer clothes she'd rescued from Francesca's house.

'Come on, you two!' said Sally forcefully. 'Why so down? We're on a big adventure, it's like the sequel to *Thelma and Louise*. It's Thelma and Louise and Stephen! And this, my friends,' she held up the bundle of clothes, 'is our next lot of petrol money to take us to Cleo and Mikey.'

'And to Dad,' added Stephen. There was a slight pause. 'But away from Emily,' he added mournfully.

Sally dropped the clothes on the table and slumped into a chair.

'Sally,' said Janice softly, reaching out a hand to take her friend's, while Stephen watched, eagle-eyed, 'it's going to be OK, Sal. You did the right thing. So did Emily.'

'I always knew it was bloody difficult being a mum. But I never realised how horrendous being an aunt was going to be.'

The three sat in thoughtful silence for some moments.

'OK,' said Sally, gearing up, 'time to do business with the lady behind the counter. Time to channel the Frank Parker art of bullshit,' she added grimly.

Janice and Stephen were left with nothing to say, so they watched Sally chatting to the café owner.

'Rocks and touchstones can be replaced, you know, Ste,' said Janice meaningfully. Stephen thought about this, scooped out the last bit of cappuccino foam from his cup, and let it settle on his tongue before swallowing it.

'My dad's a pretty big rock, Janice,' said Stephen deadly serious. 'I don't think he'll shift that easily.'

Janice looked into her flat white.

'The seas have battered and beaten the rock that is Frank Parker, Stephen, and I wonder if he's an igneous rock or a sedimentary rock? I happen to believe that he's the latter, and if that's the case then he's got big problems.'

Stephen now had no idea what Janice was talking about and simply stared at her.

Janice continued. 'Leaky. Porous,' she said knowingly, 'likely to crumble away into nothing and end up as sand on some very faraway beach.'

Janice had fire in her eyes now, and Stephen lowered his for fear of burning up in her gaze.

He was saved by Sally's return to the table.

'Success!' Sally announced. 'She's taken them all! Now that feels like a day's work to me. What do you think, Ste?'

'Dad bought all those clothes for you, Mum,' he said grumpily and stalked off and out of the café.

'Can I do NOTHING right, Jan?' said Sally, throwing her arms up in despair.

'You do everything right, Sal,' said Janice softly. 'You don't know how right.'

The café owner was already in the corner, starting to put the designer clothes on to hangers.

'How much did you get for them?' asked Janice. Sally took the opportunity to ignore this question and look out of the window to inspect the passing cars.

'It's not the amount that counts, Jan, it's the investment—'

Sally was cut short by a wailing police siren. An orange car sped past the café window, followed by the cops in hot pursuit.

'Conwy's lively, isn't it,' mused Sally.

Janice sat bolt upright, her nose aloft like a bloodhound on a scent,

'I'd know that Allegro anywhere,' she said. 'Dicky carburettor, front left lamp out. It's Kyle.'

They raced to the café window to see that, further down the road, Kyle's car had been pulled over by the police. In the flashing blue light, two figures were huddled on the pavement, Kyle gesturing lavishly with his arms. They could hear his protests all the way down the High Street.

'I'm not breathing into that thing, man,' he was shouting, 'that's a violation of my human rights. You could get my DNA off of that and send it to the FBI, for all I know. My spittle is my data, and my data is my soul!'

'Sir, I'm going to have to ask you again to breathe into this breathalyser please. We have reason to believe that you're over the alcohol limit.'

'I can confirm that, officer,' said Amerjit, crossing his arms.

'What?' said Kyle, turning to look at his friend. '*Et tu*, Amerjit?'

'He's drunk three beers, officer,' Amerjit stated, and turned to Kyle sheepishly. 'It was dicey in there, buddy. I'm only doing this to protect you, the other passenger in your car, and the good citizens of Wales.'

'Right, sir,' announced the officer, 'you're coming into the station and that car will be impounded. It's not fit for the road, and neither are you. Let's go.'

Kyle was bundled into the police car calling, 'And

thrice the cock crew! Thrice the cock crew!' He flicked a V-sign at Amerjit, and the door was shut firmly on him.

Sally looked at her watch.

'Oh God. Where the hell is my Mikey?'

'Difficult to know, Mum,' said Stephen, 'since none of us have got working phones. Unlike her. I've kept trying her phone on your friend Janice's phone but it just goes to voicemail.'

'She's our friend, Ste. Not just my friend,' Sally said gently.

Stephen made no response to this.

'I suppose if I did a day's work, Stephen, I could buy my own phone,' said Sally in a loaded tone.

Stephen sighed guiltily.

'Mikey'll be fine, she's probably sitting by a roaring fire in Bronwen's cottage as we speak, eating crumpets.'

'You sure about that, Ste?' asked Sally anxiously.

'Positive,' he replied, crossing his fingers behind his back.

Mikey couldn't have been further from toasted crumpets. She was pacing up and down the dark, windswept platform of Penmaenmawr station, trying not to cry. Gone was the usual Mikey Parker bluster and confidence; her trainers felt flimsy and the layers that had seemed so warm at Euston station were now as effective as crepe paper. She watched the poker-playing students go off in a group together, but felt she couldn't ask for help because she'd stripped them of all their cash. Neither did she want to talk to the railway staff for fear of being grilled about her age.

This was her quest and hers alone. What would her dad think if she were to bail out now and play the weeping eleven-year-old card? Mikey checked her phone. No

375

reception. The sky looked a heavy and menacing grey, like an elephant about to charge down on her. She looked around at the darkened hills. Why hadn't she worn her walking boots?

She took a deep breath and dug her nails into her clenched fists to stop any chance of tears. She approached a group of middle-aged women chatting by a window box.

'I'm sorry to interrupt,' Mikey said politely. 'I'm on my advanced Guides orienteering course and I need to get to Llanfairfechan. To get my badge, I need to get there before nine o'clock tonight, on my own. I'm not allowed to use maps or a phone.' She flashed them a broad, electric Frank Parker smile. 'Any of you lovely ladies happen to know where it is?'

Stephen tried unsuccessfully to fold himself into one of the dog enclosures in the back of the Paws Fur Thought van. With Kyle's Allegro now *hors de combat*, and Amerjit travelling with his mum and Janice, there was no room for Stephen up front. He had to make do with crouching with Liesl and Kurt in a metal crate. The atmosphere was depressed.

'I am my parents' only son,' Stephen observed loudly, 'and here I am being transported like a dog. And I'm hungry.'

'Ferret around in the bags of shopping, Ste, see if there's anything to snack on.'

'There's flour, dried rice, lentils and pasta. Anyone else care for a dried staple snack?'

'I'd do some dried pasta,' said Amerjit.

'It'll give you worms,' said Janice. 'Mrs Teasle gets worms when she eats dried pasta.'

'She's a dog,' said Stephen sourly.

376

Pasta was passed around.

'Who'd have thought we'd be reduced to eating dried pasta,' mused Stephen in the back.

'Stephen, that's enough,' Sally barked at him, 'we're all struggling, OK? We're all in this together as a family.'

'Yeah, a family with three of its four children missing, and also its father,' said Stephen coldly.

'I am trying,' said Sally loudly, 'I AM TRYING, OK? And I will carry on trying—'

She was interrupted by the familiar sound of a wailing police siren.

'FUCKSAKE!' yelled Sally, hitting the dashboard with her fist.

'It's like Downtown LA,' said Amerjit. 'The place is riddled with feds.'

Janice pulled the van over to the side of the road and they waited for the inevitable figure to appear at the driver's window and do the winding-down-the-window mime. It turned out to be the same guy who'd booked Kyle back in Conwy.

'I actually knew this was going to happen,' the officer said with a smile playing on his lips.

'What?' asked Janice.

'All four of you getting into a van which is purposed for the carriage of dogs. This is a three-person vehicle, madam,' and he stretched up his neck to make himself taller.

'My question to you, officer, is why you couldn't have just told us that BEFORE WE DROVE OFF?' shouted Sally.

The officer leaned in closer to the driver's window,

'To be honest, there's not a lot happens round here, see, and I didn't want to forego the opportunity of getting the nee-naw on again. I haven't had it on in months, and today I've had it on twice! That's got to be some kind of record!'

The drizzle that started in Conwy had now developed into proper wet rain.

'Raincoats on, everybody,' ordered Sally. 'Officer Jobsworth, two people will travel in this van, and two of us will walk. OK? Amerjit, we're going on foot. Stephen, you jump up front with Jan.'

Stephen looked grumpy at the prospect of sitting next to his nemesis.

The officer couldn't help but be impressed by this can-do slip of a woman, jumping out and into a downpour in the pitch dark.

'Oh, Jan,' said Sally, 'I almost forgot. Here's fifty quid for petrol money.'

'Was that all you got for that designer gear, Mum? It was worth thousands,' moaned Stephen.

'Worth can only be measured by need, Ste. What use is a silk Chanel kimono out in the pouring rain in Wales? Less than fifty pence, I'd say. You could rip it up into strips and use it to wipe your bottom, I suppose. Drive carefully, Jan. Officer, how many miles to Llanfairfechan?'

'As the crow flies, about five miles that way,' he said, pointing out some fairly robust hills.

'I'm going to find Mikey,' said Sally. 'Be safe every-body, and look after Jan. She's our most precious asset.'

'Great,' said Stephen under his breath.

'Wow,' said Janice slowly, 'I've never been called an "asset" before.'

Sally blew a general kiss into the van and started off down the road without waiting for Amerjit. She passed the officer's car and could hear Kyle's voice in the back, ranting on about miscarriages of justice.

'. . . and I never knew there was a Judas in our midst. Who knew? Enemy Numero Uno against the Christian church, and in this case I am that church. Unbe-frigging-lievable!'

'He's always like this when he's drunk,' said Sally to the officer who'd caught up with her. 'Actually, he's like this when he's sober. Good luck.'

Sally was aware of Amerjit chasing after her, clutching his thin coat around him and slipping on the wet road.

'Ammers, is that the only coat you've got?' asked Sally. 'And look at those shoes. Those aren't going to get you up any Welsh hills.'

He was wearing a pair of pointed shiny brown winkle-pickers and a fashion mackintosh with no hood.

'I came to the Golf Club in my civvies, Sal. All this was kind of unexpected.'

'Here, you can borrow my umbrella,' said the officer. 'Just mind you drop it back to me at the Llandudno Police Station, yes?'

Amerjit took the umbrella gratefully, as Sally started to move off in a general hillwards direction.

'Come on, Amerjit, we want to try and get there before midnight.'

Amerjit used all of his available hands to either lift his collar up around his face, or to hang on to the umbrella, which was now doing battle with the wind.

They hadn't progressed far when a car overtook them and stopped a few metres ahead. Out of the back hopped Yusuf Jamal, swiftly followed by his wife Rashida.

'Fancy bumping into you here, Sally Parker,' said Yusuf, having to speak loudly now that the rain was properly coming down. 'Jump into our Uber – you're soaking.'

'Come, get in quickly,' said Rashida. 'It's a dirty night. Hello again, Amerjit.'

379

'Hi Rashida,' said Amerjit.

The four of them bundled into the Uber and they started off on the final leg to Llanfairfechan.

'Not exactly wedding weather!' said Yusuf.

'I don't think there's any chance of a wedding,' said Sally swiftly.

'You never know,' said Rashida mischievously. 'Two teenage lovebirds that can't keep their hands off each other!'

'Not that again,' said Sally crossly. 'Don't be ridiculous, my daughter's seventeen and isn't getting married to anyone.'

'She's almost the same age you were, Sal,' said Amerjit. 'I remember. I was there!'

'Exactly, Amerjit,' Sally turned on him, 'and look what happened to my fairytale marriage. Listen, Cleo and Amir have known each other less than two weeks, Mrs Jamal. Subject closed.'

'Well, we married young and our marriage has been a great success!' said Rashida a tad smugly, looking at her husband.

'Are you saying that our son isn't good enough for your daughter?' said Yusuf, with less twinkle now.

'No, I'm just saying they're too young,' replied Sally evenly.

'I think Cleo's very lucky to have found somebody like Amir,' said Rashida with a sniff. 'A lot of girls would give anything to marry him.'

'I think he's the lucky one,' said Sally, bristling. 'A gorgeous English rose like her.'

'Hardly an English rose, Mrs Parker,' said Rashida with eyes of granite. 'She has fake hair, a pierced nipple and no dowry. Not exactly a catch on the marriage market.'

'Right,' said Sally leaning forward to the driver, 'stop the car. We're getting out.'

'Sal, no!' pleaded Amerjit. 'It's tipping out there. I won't be able to get any sort of grip on the hillside wearing these shoes.'

'You're very welcome to stay here in the car, Amerjit,' announced Sally, 'but I'm going on foot. I'll see you in Llanfairfechan.'

'Sal, it's so warm in here—'

And with that she slammed the car door in Amerjit's face.

After Frank and Stevo had drunk their cups of tea, Frank excused himself. Once in the calm of the urinals, he had to think fast. How was he going to escape? He scanned the area and saw an open window above the sink. He would have to dig deep, deeper than he had ever dug, to haul himself up to the ledge and through that window. He thought of Sally; for her he'd carry out this act of madness. Like Cathy and Heathcliff, he tried to visualise her on the other side of the window, all passionate eyes willing him on.

He hoicked one foot up on to the sink with a grunt, and then, with a multitude of huffings and puffings, he managed to pull the other foot up. He stood in the sink for a minute or two to gird his loins. The next bit would require some upper body strength that had abandoned him of late. He closed his eyes and hauled himself up to the window with a Biblical roar; he was Samson to Sally's Delilah. The roar came out more like a gargle. All he had to do now was manoeuvre his body through the window, and to freedom. As he made slow, painful progress, he was pleased to see a large bush to act as buffer between him and the cold, hard ground, though he'd happily break a few bones to get away from Stevo. He gave himself to the bush and lay suspended, laughing like a maniac to himself, half-tangled in the foliage and thanking his lucky stars.

Once he'd lowered himself gingerly to terra firma, he decided to sneak round the building to check on Stevo's lorry, which was only a few metres away. He hugged the wall and sidestepped along it carefully. He took a discreet peek, just in time to see Stevo's backside disappearing through the cab door before he shut it and drove off. He couldn't believe it. The bastard was actually abandoning him.

Frank stood for a while in disbelief. He had given every last morsel of his power to get through that gents' window. For absolutely nothing.

Frank trudged off to find somebody with a mobile phone. In a situation like this, there was only one person worth phoning; his messiah, his saviour, his own Holy Trinity of Turton.

Mikey stumbled around on the dark hillside for a good two hours. She was freezing, soaking and really scared now. She could be headed for Llanfairfechan or Gdansk, she was too tired to care. All of a sudden, she spotted the hulking shadow of a barn up ahead, a disused animal byre of some sort. She summoned up her courage and managed a half-jog towards it. There wasn't much in the way of comfort inside, just an old mattress with rusty springs jumping out of it like a jack-in-a-box, but at least it had a roof. She curled up on a corner of the mattress, pulled her fleece and coat around her, nibbled a bread roll, and gave herself over to proper tears. She was eleven, exhausted and all she wanted was her mum and dad.

Sally, soaked to the skin, was shouting into the rain and wind.

'Mikey! MIKEEEEEEEEEY!' she yelled, but the rain and wind absorbed her cries. She changed tack and tried some rousing songs from the eighties. 'Don't you, forget about me . . .' but she trailed off. She really was alone, and not dancing. She was suddenly caught by the memory of leaping around with Frank to that song as teenagers in a Hayes pub lock-in one night. Sally had gone up to the bar to buy their fifth round, and she remembered the wonderful feeling of Frank standing behind her and placing his hands round her waist. He had her back, literally. In the din of that grotty Hayes pub, he promised her he'd make it his life's work to have her back for ever.

Sally stopped and let the rain lash down her face.

'FRAAAAAAAAAAAAAAAAAAANK PAAAAAA-AAAAAARKEEEEEEER!' she raged at the elements.

Sally blundered onwards through bracken and started bellowing the greatest hits of ABC into the rain, as if she didn't already know who had broken her heart.

Sally remembered how she and Frank had danced to these very songs at Cedar Vale when Sally was heavily pregnant with Cleo. It was early summer and the house was just a shell, empty of furniture and full of promise. Frank opened up some champagne and they'd swung through those empty rooms yelling their heads off to that song.

'MIKEEEEEEEEEEEEEEEEEY!' she tried again. 'MIKEEEEEEEEEEEY!'

It seemed that the gods above were looking down on Sally Parker with kind eyes at this exact moment, thinking, 'This sodden woman with poor vocal tuning and inappropriate outdoor footwear needs a break,' because over the brow of a hill she spied the shape of a farm building. As she walked towards it, she shouted and wept all at the same time. She fell into the barn, looking like a drowned vole, her voice hoarse and cracking; it felt good to get under a roof and feel dryness around her at last.

In the shadowy corner she could make out a huddle of something. Sally was frayed, hungry and just wanted to lie down. She didn't care what she lay on, as long as she could take off some wet layers and stretch herself out. On all fours, she padded her hands in front of her in the dark, and felt something warm and alive. She patted harder until she heard,

'Ouch! That was my head!' piercing the dark.

Sally stepped back in alarm but then her heart beat fast.

'Mikey?' she shouted into the darkness.

'Mum?' came the sweet familiar voice back to her.

Sally fell on her daughter and buried her nose into her like a dog with a pup. Mikey burst into tears as her soaking mum kissed and hugged her.

'Hey, that's enough, Mum! Eeeeeurgh! You're all wet, Mum, get off me!'

Sally was half-laughing and half-crying. Mikey yawned and let Sally snuggle her, spoons-style, under her fleece and coat, and the two of them clung to each other in the darkness as the Welsh skies continued to weep.

'I can't believe I've found you, Mikey,' Sally repeated for the tenth time. 'How did you end up here?'

'Mum, could you actually hug me less tightly? I'm feeling a bit faint,' implored her daughter. 'Right, you're not going to believe this, Mum.'

'I will! After today I'll believe absolutely anything!' Sally laughed into her daughter's ear.

'And that's actually quite loud down my ear, Mum. So. I actually travelled first class on the train and won a game of poker!' she told her mum proudly in the dark.

Mikey wouldn't have seen it, but Sally's face was a mix of horror and also pride at this point.

'Mikey Parker, you are just like your father!' said Sally.

'So tomorrow,' said Mikey, 'I reckon we should just get a cab to Bronwen's? I'm flush at the moment, Mum, so it won't be a problem.'

Sally laughed and nuzzled her daughter's hair, which smelled very like one of the Von Trapps.

'Mikey, I'm sticking right by your side because you, my love, are a survivor.'

A pause.

'Thanks, Mum.'

24

The next day brought more clement weather with it. The relentless rain and grinding wind had dissipated, leaving a cold bright day in its place. All was still at Bronwen's cottage. Called Ymyl Y Byd, which translates roughly as 'The Edge of the World', it was a compact little building, parked on a promontory with the expanse of endless navy-blue sea as its back lawn. The plain and sturdy cottage didn't push itself forward in a 'look at me' way, but had dug its hobnailed boots into the land, bent on staying for the duration.

The only arrivals at the cottage so far were not related in any way to Bronwen Llewellyn, so rather than invade her home in the middle of the night, the party had holed up in a local B & B. Bronwen's old friend Gwyneth was chuckling about this as she served them tea in the kitchen.

'Here you all are and Bronwen dying, and none of you are even related to her! She'd love the irony of that!'

Amerjit, Yusuf and Rashida laughed politely as they sipped their tea.

'I am sure she is a very dignified woman,' said Yusuf.

Gwyneth nodded in agreement.

'Oh yes. Dignified and strong. She won't be flossing on the dance floor anytime soon, mind,' Gwyneth added with a smile. 'Biscuit?'

'Yes please, Gwyneth,' said Amerjit, holding up his plate.

Sally and Mikey were slipping down the mountainside and aiming for a track they could see winding through the valley down below. Both looked somewhat battered after their night of roughing it in the barn, but Mikey had made them a breakfast of First Class shortbread with minuscule cartons of UHT milk.

'I'm the one that should be providing for you, Mikey. I've got nothing to bring to the table,' said Sally thoughtfully as they stopped on some rocks to eat.

'It's no biggy, Mum. I'm one of life's copers. Simple as that. Put me in any situation and I'll deal. Yeah?'

Sally laughed out loud.

'Like father like daughter! Now come on you, we've got to get to Llanfairfeckingfechan.'

Mikey laughed too, and took her mum's hand as they continued their descent.

Back in Leatherhead, Emily was sitting at a rather more refined breakfast table. She hadn't slept a wink and had anxious dark rings around her eyes. Ensconced with the Flynn family, she had a feeling of being under surveillance. An array of breads, pastries, cereals and yoghurts were laid out in her honour on a festive tablecloth. Joan had even reminded her mum Linda to buy maple syrup, Emily's favourite. The three Flynns watched as Emily ate her croissant, and then the three of them smiled as one to see her lick the maple syrup off her spoon.

'You must have been half-starved, love!' said Mrs Flynn in her kind, whispery voice.

Emily considered this for a moment.

'My cousin Stephen's a really good cook actually. He made this wicked polenta stew with some kind of crazy cherry liqueur,' she laughed. The Flynns didn't join in, but smiled politely.

Emily looked at her bowl of luxury granola. She wondered what they were all doing now. She hoped they'd managed to get to Snowdonia. And was Mikey's phone still working?

'Your sports kit's washed, ironed and ready to go, Emily, it's snug as a bug in a rug in the airing cupboard,' said Linda Flynn.

Emily wondered if she was always going to talk in that kind whisper; she had a suspicion she would soon find it grating.

'And Paul's put your music stands up, haven't you, Paul?'

'Yes indeedio!' Paul said cheerfully.

'So they're all ready for practice after school,' Linda said in the kind whispery voice. 'Paul and I thought it might be fun for you girls to play some duets for flute and cello?'

'Then you can really get the benefit of each other's instruments, can't you, girls?' winked Paul cheerily.

Joan looked delighted with this idea. Emily found herself gripping her knees under the table. Did the Flynns smile *all* the time? Did they never grump and laugh out loud and tease and talk shit and compete and swear and shout and annoy the living pants off her but hug her like nobody else could, and make her cack herself with laughter?

She looked up at the tableau of Flynns smiling silently at her in unison.

Luckily the phone rang and Paul went to answer it.

'Linda, love,' he called, 'it's your dad. He wants to talk to you about Frank Parker.'

'Frank?' Emily said, antennae up.

Linda took the receiver from her husband.

Emily strained to hear what was being said on the phone but couldn't catch much, so set about destroying a pain au chocolat.

'Have you seen the episode of *Friends* where Phoebe sings that hilarious song with the guitar?' Joan asked Emily.

Paul started chuckling, 'Oh Emily, it is absolutely the funniest thing, it's about a cat that's very smelly I seem to remember, so left-field!' he added with a twinkle.

Emily smiled at Joan supportively. Linda sat down again at the breakfast table.

'So that was my dad on the phone, Emily. He's a friend of your Uncle Frank – Geoff Turton, you probably know him? Anyway, he's just heard from Frank and is bringing him round. Frank wants to talk to you.'

Emily looked stunned. Then smiled.

'Really?' she said, with eyes shining.

A taxi drew up outside Ymyl Y Byd and two well-preserved ladies got out, lifting two suitcases on wheels from the boot. They talked in lowered voices, paid the driver, and in their heels wheeled the cases over stony ground round to the kitchen door. Tea was in progress around the kitchen table, and Amerjit, Yusuf and Rashida all looked up as the ladies entered, wafting a fragrance of sunshine, tans and duty free in their wake. It was difficult to pin an exact age on them; they could have been anything between sixty and seventy-five.

Gwyneth stood up, in hostess mode.

'Are you ladies from Avon?' she asked pleasantly.

'No, dear, Tenerife,' said one.

'How's Mum?' said the other. 'I'm Bronwen's daughter Julia,' and she extended a burnished arm with plenty of dark sun spots, jingling with a chunky gold charm bracelet.

'She's sleeping at the moment, love,' explained Gwyneth. 'Best to leave her resting for now.'

'You are Frank's mum?' said Rashida, putting the jigsaw together.

'I am indeed,' said Julia, smiling, 'and Kyle's too.'

'And you?' said Yusuf, turning to the other lady. The two ladies looked at each other.

'I'm Jackie, and I'm Frank's parent too,' she said, 'and Kyle's.'

'Two mothers?' asked Yusuf. 'One of you is a step-mother, perhaps?'

'Not exactly,' said Julia.

Yusuf and Rashida started to talk to each other earnestly in Pashto. Jackie turned to Amerjit.

'Hello Amerjit, love. Long time no see.'

'Hi Jack. I mean, Mrs Parker,' said Amerjit awkwardly, 'Mr Parker. I mean Mrs Parker. The other Mrs Parker.'

'Just call me Jackie, love.'

'Hi Jackie,' said Amerjit, unable to take his eyes off her, 'it's extraordinary to see you. You look . . . bloody amazing.'

'I always did look good in lemon. And it's amazing what warm highlights can do for you. Now where are my renegade pair of sons?' said Jackie, taking off a pair of soft leather gloves.

'Well, last heard of, Kyle's in a cell in the local cop shop and Frank's gone AWOL from Epsom Police Station.'

'Two sons, two police stations. I don't think Miriam

Stoppard's going to be giving us a parenting award anytime soon, do you, Ju, love?'

They shared a laugh together.

'Where's dear Sally?' asked Julia.

'Where are the kids?' This was Jackie again.

Amerjit, Yusuf and Rashida exchanged a look.

'I think you'd better sit down and have a cup of tea, ladies,' suggested Amerjit.

Sally and Mikey marched down the farm track, sincerely hoping they were going in the direction of Llanfairfechan. As they walked past a field of rather forlorn, damp ponies, Sally spotted a sign leaning up against the gate.

STABLE HAND NEEDED. CASUAL. ASK WITHIN.

They'd just walked past it, when Sally stopped in her tracks.

'Just one minute, Mikey. What was it Ste said, I've never done a day's work in my life?' She turned to her daughter. 'I've just seen a job vacancy.'

A plane touched down on the tarmac of Tampa Bay airport, in the bright Florida sunshine. Passengers were disembarking from the aircraft. From out of the front exit, with other business-class passengers, stepped a tall, tanned man with still luxuriant but greying hair. He was wearing shades and carried nothing with him but a copy of the London *Times* and his passport.

'Thank you for travelling with us today, sir,' said the orange stewardess who'd put her *Thunderbirds*-esque hat on to say goodbye to the passengers.

'Well, you looked after me very well throughout the flight,' said the tall man, and here he looked at the name badge pinned to her breast, 'Lisa.'

Lisa giggled. She just loved these Brits and their cute accents, it got her all shook up every time. The passenger lowered his shades to give her the full benefit of his wickedly glinting eyes.

'And might I ask, Lisa, what's a chap supposed to do when he lands at Tampa Bay airport?'

She blushed and giggled again. He sounded just like that Hugh Grant.

'Why, sir, I don't know? Y'all just love that Florida sunshine, I guess!'

He laughed.

'Make sure you stay protected in the sunshine, Lisa. We wouldn't want your lovely skin getting damaged, would we?'

And he prolonged eye contact. 'Goodbye, Lisa,' he said meaningfully.

'Goodbye, Professor Livesy. And you enjoy that new job at Tampa University, won't you!'

'Oh, I will,' Livesy smiled. He liked the ring of that word 'Professor' attached to his name again, especially when spoken by a pretty girl. It would be there, written on his door when he arrived for work at the university on Monday morning. He'd made sure of that.

The Paws Fur Thought van rumbled up to Bronwen's cottage, and soon Janice and Stephen were round the table, Ste perched on a piano stool from the front room, and Janice compacted into a small garden chair, Liesl and Kurt on her lap.

Julia and Jackie introduced themselves to Stephen, and explained gently that his great-granny was dying. Julia stroked her grandson's cheek with tears in her eyes as he came in for a comforting hug; they hadn't seen him since his christening.

Stephen couldn't take his eyes off the pair of them. He found them utterly fascinating.

'So, which pronoun do they like to use?' he asked both of them directly. The ladies smiled.

'I am she,' said Julia.

'And I am she,' said Jackie.

'You don't want to use "they"?' said Stephen closely. 'It's OK, you know. You're in a safe space.'

They laughed.

'That's so lovely of you, Ste,' said Julia to her grandson. 'Just use "they" when you're talking about us together. Which is most of the time,' she said, patting Jackie's hand.

'Ste,' explained Jackie gently, 'you know that I used to go by the name of Jack. I was Frank's dad.'

Stephen nodded sagely.

'Jack transitioned, came out as a woman and underwent gender confirmation surgery over thirty years ago,' explained Julia to her grandson.

'I'm glad I've got you to explain the technical bit, love,' said Jackie, smiling. 'Even I put my big foot in it sometimes.'

'She was one of the pioneers,' added Julia proudly.

'Now I am Jackie. And I am still married to my gorgeous wife. And I'm still Frank and Kyle's parent.'

'Cool,' Ste said, 'and what does Dad think of all this?' he added.

There was a silence. Julia and Jackie looked at each other.

'So, wait. You are Cleo's grandfather?' said Yusuf, unable to take his eyes off Jackie and her glamorous silk shirt and boot-cut jeans.

'Well,' said Jackie patiently, 'I am Frank's parent, yes . . .'

Yusuf turned to Rashida and the pair of them chatted in

Pashto again earnestly. They were interrupted as the sound of yet another vehicle drew up outside the cottage.

'It's like Piccadilly Circus in here,' said Gwyneth somewhat wearily. 'We'll have to get a car park attendant!'

Jackie looked out of the small kitchen window to see Frank and a small man with alarmingly black hair getting out of an Aston Martin. She bit her bottom lip. She had known that Frank's arrival would come, but she thought she had a bit more time. There was nowhere to hide.

The two men came through the door and the kitchen now felt like a train carriage in rush hour.

Julia and Jackie both stood up.

'Hello, Frank, love,' said Julia softly.

Frank looked at them both.

'No. No. No, no, no. Not you. No way,' and he turned on his heel and walked straight back out of the door.

There was silence in the kitchen. The small man coughed.

'Hello all. I'm Geoff Turton, Leatherhead's premier jeweller.'

It was nearing four in the afternoon, and Bronwen's nearest and dearest had each spent a short time with her while she slept. Dusk was beginning to creep around the cottage when the sound of a car was heard. Rashida let out a shout of 'Amir' and went running round to the front of the cottage with Yusuf at her heels, and everyone else following.

They stopped in their tracks as they saw it was in fact a police car pulling up, with the now familiar local officer at the wheel. Kyle was inside, looking sobered after a night in the clink. He was wearing purple mirrored sunglasses, a bold choice for an October evening in Wales.

The police officer opened the back door of the car and

Kyle stepped out, waving to his assembled audience like Mick Jagger.

'I'm back from the brink, dudes! Officer Lloyd here,' and Kyle gave Officer Lloyd a theatrical bow as he introduced him, 'knows Bronwen, and told me my gran was dying and I should get on home. So if one of you cats can just sort my fine out, then we're all hunky-dory.'

Julia and Jackie rolled their eyes.

'Hasn't changed much, has he?' Jackie said.

'Hello Kyle, darling, how much do you need?' said his long-suffering mum, reaching for her handbag.

All was quiet in The Oast House on the Chobham Road, and Francesca Daly-Jones was delighted to note that her carpets were now spotless after their deep steam clean. She puffed up a cushion and sat down on her bluebell sofa. She leaned forward and couldn't stop herself tweaking the copy of *Horse & Hound* that was angled slightly wrongly on the coffee table.

She then sat for a bit and looked around her, thinking of absolutely nothing. She could hear Eva sorting out the washing in the utility room. She looked over to the windowsill and reminded herself that she must get those frames touched up in the spring. She had a sudden memory of Sally Parker climbing through that very window and breaking one of her favourite photo frames, the silly cow. If she ever saw her again, which she hoped she never would, she would remind Sally of that and demand reimbursement. And Sally would not be able to pay it. Francesca let out a gleeful chuckle. Comeuppance had been due a long time to those Parkers and it was gratifying to see it being meted out.

She checked her mobile phone. She'd spread the Parker gossip on the dog-walkers' WhatsApp group as soon as Tim had told her. No messages back. Even Francesca Daly-

Jones, who had the skin of a rhino when it came to others' emotions, had noticed that the good ladies of Leatherhead were not quite as chummy to her as they had been prior to that fateful Baboon Rehoming Charity Auction evening. Her calls were returned after a longer period of time had elapsed than usual; she knew that a coffee morning had been arranged without her being invited. She checked her mobile phone again. Still no messages. She looked at the clock. It was nearly four thirty. She'd knock up a Gaysford's salad in a bit. And maybe she might just sneak the telly on and see if there was a property show on?

Her quiet was interrupted by keys in the front door. Tim Daly-Jones came in, dressed in golfing attire.

'SHOES, Tim!' were her first words to her husband.

He bumbled back into the hall.

'Why the hell are you back so early, anyway?' she called out.

He came into the sitting room, shoeless, with an ashen face.

'I fell asleep in the golf buggy, Cesca. That's never happened to me before. Right there, in front of the troops, zonko.'

Francesca felt a nervous chill in her hands and stood up. She rubbed her hands together to warm them. She looked at Tim. He looked craggy, the bags underneath his eyes deeper and darker than usual. Francesca didn't like the look of this one bit.

'I feel tired. I'm going to bed,' he said and left her alone in the room with her newly steam-cleaned carpet. She wondered briefly what Sally Parker was doing now, and hoped that it was something uncomfortable and humiliating.

Sally was engaged in an activity that could be described as both of these things, if you are not a lover of horse manure.

Very different if, of course, you are a fan. Sally had never really encountered horse manure before this day, so couldn't really say if she was a fan or not. At the start of her working day she had found the stuff tough going. But now that she'd had quite a few hours to get used to its steaming brown consistency, she'd pushed through the pain barrier and was spurred on by every hour of labour that she notched up. She was rosy of cheek and determined of jaw, and relished the feeling of satisfaction that each spadeful of shit heaped up in the stable gave her. The spade gave a nice metallic grunt every time it made contact with the concrete floor, and Sally was aware of how much her muscles had to work to achieve her goal. Mikey sat on a bag of horse nuts, watching her mum work.

'You've missed a bit,' she pointed out.

At five o'clock the fourth pot of tea was on the brew in Bronwen's kitchen, as the mistress of the house slept on upstairs. Stephen and Julia were deep in conversation about food. They concocted an idea of building a fire in the back garden, which Janice pounced on eagerly. She was desperate to fill this idle time waiting for Sally to come.

'Do you think we should go and look for Frank?' suggested Jackie.

'No,' said Julia firmly, 'remember what he was like when he was a boy? You had to let him marinate in his own juices. I used to hide in the shed when he was like that, remember?'

'Just like Mr Bennet hiding from his daughters!' said Jackie.

'I wish Cleo, Mikey and Emily were here,' said Stephen sadly.

'Oh shuttlecocks,' said Geoff suddenly, 'that reminds me! I've left something in my car.'

A minute later he came in with Emily, who'd fallen asleep in the back.

'Silly me!' he said. 'I knew I'd forgotten something!'

'Happened to me once in Ecuador,' said Kyle thoughtfully. 'I got left in a car boot for two days.'

Stephen almost knocked Emily over he hugged her so hard. There were introductions and explanations all round, and then everyone trouped out into the little back garden to start gathering wood for the fire.

Half an hour later and the garden was full of chat. Everyone was collecting wood, and Jackie and Julia had donned pristine wellies and matching Barbour jackets.

'You've got a fine pair of legs on you, Dad,' said Kyle appreciatively to Jackie.

'Thank you, son. That's very kind of you to say so,' said Jackie, ruffling her son's hair.

'And you know I'm, like, totally cool with you being an ex-dude, Dad? I've seen some pretty fruity things on my travels, and your swapping of the meat and two veg for something a bit more minimal is absolutely fine by me.'

And as he clasped Jackie in a hug and clapped her back, Stephen shouted out,

'Look! On the beach over there!'

And everybody turned to see two figures walking determinedly up towards the cottage from the sea.

As they came closer, Mikey's grin was clear to see, even in the dusk. She started running to her family, shouting with glee,

'We're here! WE'RE HERE! WE MADE IT! AND I'VE STILL GOT A WORKING PHONE!'

As she ran breathlessly into the garden, she was rugby tackled by Emily and Stephen.

'Where's Dad?' was her first question.

'He's having a bit of time out at the moment, Mikey, love,' said Julia gently, 'he'll be back later. Hello. I'm your granny!'

And then the other figure emerged out of the gloaming. It was a person who could only be described as being covered head to toe in shit: brown, sticky manure in the hair, eyelashes, covering the clothes, everywhere.

Emily stepped forward.

'Sally? Is that you?'

The person smiled and as the teeth and blue eyes shone through, it became clear it was indeed Sally in the flesh.

'Em!' she cried joyously 'Ste! Jackie and Julia! Everybody!' She was standing on tiptoes in excitement, finding it hard to take everyone in all at once.

'Mum's got some big news,' said Mikey proudly.

'She fell in a sewer?' asked Kyle.

'My mum,' announced Mikey, 'has done a full day's work and has earned herself thirty-five quid!'

And Mikey pulled out the notes from her pocket and showed them to everybody. Stephen went up to his mum and embraced her, to warning shouts of 'No, Ste! Eeeurgh! Don't do it! She stinks!'

Janice Dawes came forward and took Sally's hand.

'You look like you could use a shower, Sal. I'll get you a towel and a change of clothes, and we'll fill you in.'

'Thank you, Jan, I'll nip upstairs.'

Sally turned left out of the bathroom and padded, freshly showered and changed, into Bronwen's spartan bedroom, trying not to let the door creak. The walls were bare bar the odd picture of a stern, sepia ancestor staring out.

She found Myfanwy doing Bronwen's bedside shift and reading out loud softly:

'. . . "and even though J.Lo has no plans to tour at the moment, sources close to the star say that she's keeping an open mind."' Myfanwy looked up. 'I'm just reading her an extract out of *Heat* magazine, she finds it very soothing.'

Sally looked at Bronwen's minuscule, wafer-like body, difficult to distinguish now from the white sheet which enveloped it, like a proto-shroud. She felt an almost over-whelming sense of regret, wishing that she'd done more with her, chatted more to her, taken her to places, got to know her better. She sat down on a little stool at the end of the bed and patted Bronwen's feet gently.

'She's gone,' whispered Myfanwy.

Sally's eyes filled with tears. 'So quick . . .'

'Always is,' replied Myfanwy sagely.

'Shall I tell the others?' whispered Sally urgently, trying not to look at Bronwen because she'd never seen a dead body before and was terrified.

'No need,' said Myfanwy.

'What?' said Sally, genuinely confused. 'Everyone will want to come and pay their respects.'

'You make it sound like she's dead already, love!' chuckled Myfanwy.

'You just said "she's gone" . . .'

'To sleep, love! She's gone to sleep! Bronwen's having a kip!'

Myfanwy started to chuckle and rock around in her seat, and then Sally started to laugh too. She couldn't stop now that she'd started, and the more Sally laughed the more Myfanwy did, until the two were lost in a vortex of wracking, weeping laughter accompanied by the odd porcine snort. Myfanwy was wiping her eyes, thinking that she'd got over her latest bout, when she looked at Sally and started all over again.

'I'm going to wee myself, I swear . . .' she gasped.

'Don't you pee on my chair, Myfanwy Williams,' came a cracked low voice from the bed.

Sally stood up, her cheeks still damp from the tears of laughter.

'Bronwen, it's Sally.'

'Where's Frank?' she asked immediately.

There was a silence.

'Oh no,' said Bronwen, 'what's the bellend gone and done now?'

Sally sat down again on the stool. Myfanwy started to flick through *Heat* to make it look like she wasn't listening to the conversation.

There was a pause.

'I think I've lost him, Bronwen,' said Sally, her voice starting to break, 'and I don't even know if I want to find him again.'

There was a long pause.

'I don't think you've lost him, Sally. I think you've found yourself.'

Sally was taken aback; this indomitable ninety-year-old life-force was not renowned for her empathy skills.

'I feel happier than I have done in years, Bronwen,' confessed Sally. 'I feel free.'

'Good girl,' said Bronwen, 'I've been worried about you for ages, stuck in that Barbie house like Mariah flipping Carey.'

'The house has gone,' said Sally.

'Good riddance,' whispered Bronwen, 'all style and no substance.'

'I don't suppose you happened to see last week's *Closer*?' interrupted Myfanwy. 'There was a big article about Beyoncé and Jay Z's LA pad; all the mod-cons and

401

luxury items, and they still look as miserable as sin, don't they?'

Sally stared out of the small window at the infinite dark sea with small crests of white chasing each other across its rolling back. She wished she could be a bit of foam on the sea, chasing, chasing and never settling.

'I don't know,' said Sally sadly, 'we lost ourselves along the way somewhere. What we had was so right, so unmatchable. Unassailable. I just wish we could turn back time...'

'Like Cher,' said Myfanwy gravely, 'and look at the state of her.'

'If we could go back to being sixteen,' continued Sally, 'we could just find each other again, I know we could. Get rid of these hollowed-out people that we've become—'

Sally had more to say on the subject, but was aware of a light rasping sound now emerging from the bed; Bronwen was fast asleep and snoring.

'She's gone,' said Myfanwy, starting to chuckle all over again.

Bronwen continued to sleep peacefully upstairs, under the watchful eye of Myfanwy. She occasionally stirred, and once, when there was a particularly loud shout from the garden, she looked as if she might open her eyes. She smiled faintly, thought the better of it, and carried on sleeping.

They all sat around the fire thoughtfully, watching its flames dance in the dark. Sally wore some of Janice's spare clothes, a pair of trousers and bodywarmer. She looked down at the clothes and caught Janice smiling at her, which made her feel sad for some reason.

'My day went so QUICKLY at the stables,' said Sally, to distract herself. 'It was backbreaking work but I just got on with it, didn't I, Mikey? The farmer said he'd never had such a keen worker and offered me the position full time, didn't he, love?'

'Where's Dad?' said Mikey again. 'Shouldn't we go and look for him?'

'Yes,' said Rashida, 'don't you want to know where your husband is, Sally?'

Sally mulled this question over, shook her head and addressed her family around the fire.

'I've spent my entire marriage saying, "Where's Frank?" Always wondering where he is, what he's doing. Waiting for him. I should have had the words "Where's Frank?" forged into a vast necklace and tied round my neck like a cow's halter. And do you know what? The last two days, despite the shitty rain, the wind, the journey into the unknown, I have felt very light of step, Rashida, like a massive weight has been lifted. So the answer to your question is—' Sally shot up out of her deck chair, 'What the hell is Frank doing climbing through that window?'

The rest of the family stood up and looked up at the far end of the house. There was a familiar shambling silhouette at the top of a ladder, scrambling into Bronwen's bedroom.

25

After recovering from the shock of an intruder coming through the bedroom window, Myfanwy calmed down with a Werther's Original and ushered Frank on to a footstool up near Bronwen's head. Her eyelids were now translucent and her lips a bluish white. Frank sat with his head in his hands. He was out of ideas. Out of conversation. Out of gas.

'You know who was spotted in Carlisle?' Myfanwy asked him, by way of conversation. 'Jason Orange. Remember him? Used to be in Take That. I just read it in the "Spotted" section of *Heat*.'

Frank didn't reply. Myfanwy had an inkling from the way his head hung that he might be crying. There was a tap at the door and Sally popped her head around it.

Frank looked at her briefly and then put his head back into his hands. Sally crept into the room and leaned up against the wall, a couple of metres away from her husband. Neither she nor Frank said a word. A veil of silence hung in the room.

'Your beard's grown,' said Sally after a bit.

Frank shook his head.

'When did Hinge and Bracket turn up?' he said, with tears thickening his voice.

'Frank, don't,' said Sally.

404

'You didn't have to deal with kids in your school spitting in your face and beating you up because your dad wore fricking tan tights and a dress, did you?'

'Times are so different now, Frank.'

'Great. They bloody weren't back then. They were diabolical.'

'The kids are really happy to meet their grandparents properly,' said Sally.

Frank wiped his face furiously with his sleeve.

'Would you like a hanky, dear?' asked Myfanwy kindly.

'Yes please,' said Frank.

She handed him one and he blew his nose loudly into it.

'I've screwed everything up, Sal. Everything. Brett Grover's sitting on a million-pound horse on his ranch in Argentina right now, and I'm sitting on a stool that's too small for a flipping gnome, with no money to my name, in this godforsaken corner of nowheresville. Name me one thing that I haven't screwed up.'

There was a telling pause. Sally opened her mouth as if to say something and closed it again.

Frank continued,

'I was down by the sea. I should have just carried on walking without stopping. Like Virginia Woolf . . .'

'Or that lovely poor chap from Manic Street Preachers,' added Myfanwy. 'I used to love the Manics.'

'It would be better for everyone if I just disappeared into the waves,' he said loudly.

'I kissed Dave Aziz,' said Sally suddenly.

Myfanwy put her hand up to her mouth. This was better than *Heat*. Frank lifted his head very slowly to look at his wife. Sally felt her heart stop and her skin prickle.

'Who in holy hell is Dave Aziz?' came a parched, cracked voice from the bed.

'Bronwen!' said Frank and Sally and Myfanwy, turning to her in unison.

'Quick, tell me or I might die not knowing,' she replied.

'He was our landlord at Cedar Vale,' said Sally, full of shame.

'Where?' asked Frank.

'On the mouth,' replied Sally.

'No. I mean where did it happen?'

'In the woods,' she said.

'Oh,' Frank looked thoughtful for a minute, 'why did you do that?'

Sally breathed out.

'Isn't it bloody obvious?' said Bronwen, short of breath. 'Because Sally's found a new sense of self-esteem and this Dave's a bit of a fitty.'

'It happens to the best,' said Myfanwy, knowingly. 'I give you Jennifer Aniston. I give you Sherrie Hewson.'

'I can't claim anything like female empowerment,' said Sally bitterly. 'I just liked the smell of his expensive cologne and his stupid cashmere coat.'

'I love that Égoïste, I do,' said Myfanwy. 'A man wears that and my pants drop like a yo-yo, I'm telling you.'

The only sound in the room was the distant noise of waves sucking on the shore.

'It's my fault,' said Frank simply, 'I'm so sorry.'

Sally felt her guts tie up in knots.

'I'm sorry for screwing everything up,' he continued, 'for being a total and utter tit. And for making you miserable.'

Sally had never, in all the decades she'd known Frank, heard him apologise for anything. He'd rather die than admit to any failure or fault. Her mouth began to tremble and she felt hot tears begin to tumble down her cheeks.

'I'm the one that should be saying sorry, Frank.'

'No, Sal. I'm serious. I mean, why didn't you just run off with Aziz? He's got a working credit card, a great line in coats, by the sounds of it, and a house.'

'Please don't say that, Frank. That's not the reason I fell for you. All you had when I fell in love with you was a dodgy mullet and a devastating smile.'

Frank smiled briefly.

'I'm so tired, Sal.'

'I know, Frank. And I've ignored it. I haven't been looking after you.'

'I've been a cock, Sal.'

'Yes, you have, to be fair,' interrupted his grandmother from the bed, 'and if you don't mind, you two, I'm gagging for a bit of shuteye. I'm the one that's bloody tired here. I'm dying, you know.'

At the top of the staircase, Sally and Frank sat squashed in next to the Stannah stairlift together and listened to the noise of family floating up from the garden.

'I wish Cleo would come home,' said Sally quietly, 'although it's amazing that Emily came. What a girl, all under her own steam.'

Frank looked at his wife.

'Not under her own steam. I fetched her and brought her with me in Geoff's car.'

There was a stunned silence. Sally was speechless.

'What?'

'I phoned Geoff and explained that I wanted to give you something that really meant something. Not just a shitty sapphire ring from his jewellery shop. And definitely not another empty promise, I've given you enough of those, so we went to get Em from Joan's house. We had good chats in the car, me and Em, ironed out a lot of things, and so here we are at the Edge of the World.'

Frank said all this completely matter-of-factly, unaware that his wife was sat next to him, tears streaming down her face, with a look she hadn't given him for many, many months. She got up and started down the staircase.

When she was nearly at the bottom, Frank called,

'Did you kiss Dave Aziz, like tongue-kiss?'

Lucinda Tennant sat in her fur coat in her freezing kitchen, wondering where Miles was. He'd promised to be back in time to cook supper for her, but was unlikely to show up much before midnight, as was his wont. She sighed and opened the plastic packet of mini pork pies whose sell-by date had been sometime last month.

Her gnarled fingers picked one out and she bit into it with yellowed teeth. The pork inside the pie was very slightly blue. Her jaw clicked as she masticated it around her mouth, and she looked up at the dusty Tennant coat of arms, hanging beside the kitchen clock. She let a slight smile play over her pork-pie jelly lips.

Out in the garden, Sally put a big blanket around Frank's shoulders at around eight p.m., as the Parker tribe ate bowls of soup courtesy of Julia and Stephen. Kyle had found some old wardrobe doors that he added to the fire, causing it to spark and spit like crazy. The fire had the effect it always does, of making the people sitting around it thoughtful and almost dreamlike in its fantastical glow. Frank sat between his wife and Amerjit. Janice sat on the other side of the fire, looking thoughtful, Liesl and Kurt on her lap.

'It feels weird to all be sitting here enjoying ourselves while your granny's up there,' said Amerjit, throwing a concerned look up at Bronwen's window.

'We've all seen her now, and she didn't want us moping around her up there,' said Frank. 'We'll go up when the time's right.'

'The time is definitely right to go and talk to your mum, Frank,' Sally said.

'Which one?' answered Frank curtly. 'I've got so many to choose from.'

'Grow up, Frank, you've ignored them and they're lovely.'

'This reminds me of being back in the Wimpy,' said Amerjit, looking dreamily into the fire, 'with you two. Bickering!'

'Better grub than the Wimpy, though,' said Frank, looking over at Stephen proudly, 'thanks to my talented son. Who knew, eh? Who knew? All that time he spent scoffing the food, and none of us realised that he could actually cook it!'

'Frank!' said Sally again, hitting him on the thigh.

All of them looked into the hypnotic heat of the fire and sat with their thoughts.

'I'm so sorry about Laura, Ammers,' Frank said. 'You must have been devastated, mate.'

'It's not the best,' said Amerjit, 'but thanks for taking me into the bosom like this. And I'm sorry I wasn't there when HNB hit the skids.'

Frank smiled and looked deep into the fire.

'The Hayes Naughty Boys. I don't think a single client of ours ever realised that's what it stood for!' The two men laughed.

Kyle came over with his guitar poised, worryingly ready for action.

'I tell you what, folks, there was a time in the pen back there when I thought, "Shit, this is going to be like Guan-fricking-tanamo, pass me an orange boiler suit, quick!"'

Amerjit slapped his friend on the back.

'I'm sure you could have handled it, Kyle, what with all of your travels in the wilds of South and Central America. Talking of which, I looked through your passport, mate, when we were in the car. It ran out two years ago.' Kyle looked suddenly deeply engrossed in tuning his guitar strings. 'There was no sign of any entry or exit Visa stamps to Colombia, Ecuador, Paraguay, nothing. Nada.'

Kyle coughed and quickly struck up Bob Dylan's 'Idiot Wind' very loudly indeed.

Sally looked at Frank and tried desperately not to laugh.

Stephen looked up at Bronwen's window.

'Do you think she's going to last the night, Mum?' he said with a worried look.

'Gwyneth's going to call us up when the time's ready,' said Sally softly, stroking his hair. She turned to Frank, thinking of how much Cleo was going to miss her great-granny. 'You don't really think Cleo and Amir went to Kabul, do you Frank?'

Frank sighed.'Cleo is capable of anything. I underesti-mated her badly.'

And at that precise moment there was an enormous squeal as Cleo herself and Amir came tumbling into the garden. Everyone got out of their deck chairs at once, even Frank.

'We parked the car down the road, oh yeah, sorry for nicking it, Yusuf, that was legit bad of us. We wanted to creep up here and PRANK YOU ALL!'

There was much shouting and laughter as the final pieces of the Parker family jigsaw were put into place.

Rashida and Yusuf looked as if they would burst with pride at the sight of their beautiful son looking so handsome in the firelight. And Rashida grabbed Cleo's hand as she spotted some sparkle on her wedding finger.

'Look,' she shouted to the assembled throng, 'they've done it! I knew they would!'

Sally's face fell. Please God, not another teenage wedding.

'Oh don't be hashtag sad-face, Mum,' said Cleo with wide eyes. 'Amir and I are really happy, aren't we, darling?'

And she poked him playfully in the ribs.

'We are,' said Amir proudly. 'Cleo, or should I say, Mrs Jamal here, has made me the happiest man from Snowdonia to Kabul!'

A cheer went up around the fire, which neither Sally nor Frank had the heart to join in with.

'Let's see the ring, Cleo,' said Geoff Turton, stepping forward officially, as the only qualified jeweller in the assembled company. He squinted at it, turned Cleo's finger around in the firelight. Cleo started to giggle.

'That's paste,' said Geoff, 'it's good paste, but it's paste.'

There was a pause.

'BECAUSE IT'S FAKE!!!' shouted Cleo, clutching herself like she was about to wee. 'We PRANKED YOU ALL AGAIN! OF COURSE we didn't get married, I've only known Amir for like two weeks and, no offence babe, but I'll probably get a bit bored of you after about three months?'

'No wedding plans at all?' This was Rashida.

'Er . . . NO!?' said Cleo playfully.

Amir looked a bit crestfallen, and Rashida took on a tiger-mother stance, as if she might deck Cleo right there by the fire.

Frank smiled at the teenagers with relief in his eyes.

'Well I'm pleased about that, Cleo, because I don't know how I'd pay for a wedding.'

Mikey piped up suddenly,

'Ooh! I've heard from Dom—'

'Hang on,' interrupted Cleo, 'I'm not going to lie, Mikey, how is it that a) you've still got a working phone, b) it's still charged, and c) it's got reception?'

Mikey just tapped her nose confidentially.

'Anyway, as I was saying, I've heard from Dom and we've got just over two grand for the lawnmower plus a couple more K on our little investment. So, looks like we're afloat again, Dad,' and she looked to Frank with hope and eagerness in her eyes.

Frank looked at Mikey.

'Your kite was up, Mikey. Well done.'

You would have seen the smile that lit up Mikey's face from as far away as Swansea.

'I want to meet this Dom character,' Frank added. 'Maybe the four of us should sit down and talk business together?'

Amerjit nodded his approval.

Mikey paused for a second. 'I'll have to think about it, Dad. What are the terms?'

Emily pulled out her flute and she and Kyle did a bit of improvised noodling; Stephen and Jackie brought out a cake, which was shared amongst everyone. Geoff looked very happy with the situation.

'Coffee and walnut cake. My favourite,' he said enthusiastically.

Janice had a piece of cake in her hand too, and put it down gently on to its plate. She looked over at Sally in the firelight. Sally was stroking Cleo's hair tenderly, as she explained gently to her daughter that Bronwen was dying.

Sally looked serene. She didn't look tired any more. She looked like a phoenix that had just stepped out from that bonfire.

Janice then watched as Frank touched his wife's hair without her noticing and smiled contentedly to himself. Janice nodded, put the dogs down, got up out of her deck chair, and quietly and unseen, went round to the front of the cottage and got into her Paws Fur Thought van. She suddenly realised that she was missing Mrs Teasle and Lucy. She needed to get home. She put the key in the ignition, turned the dial to Mellow Magic, and drove away from the Edge of The World.

The fireside chat was broken by the noise of an old-fashioned telephone ring.

'Bound to be for me,' Kyle coughed, 'I'll get it,' and he shambled off into the house, only to return soon after, calling for Emily.

'Me?' said Emily, stunned.

'Yeah it's for you. Some hot-sounding chick wants to talk to you, Em. Gravelly voice. Nancy.'

Emily's face registered about seven expressions at once.

'What?' she said, looking like she might burst into tears, and running towards the house. 'Are you sure?'

Frank and Sally were about to speak when Gwyneth's voice called out of Bronwen's window.

'It's time. Bronwen's asking for you all. Come now.'

The Parkers squeezed into Bronwen's tiny bedroom and looked soberly at her tiny little body wheezing and crackling intermittently. Her eyes were tight shut.

'Love you, Gran,' said Kyle, 'you were a total fucking legend.'

'I'll thank you not to swear, Kyle Parker,' said Bronwen suddenly and clearly, out of her haze, 'and I'll thank you not to talk about me in the past tense.'

The sombre mood was broken. Bronwen was back in the room.

Myfanwy, Gwyneth, the Jamals, Geoff Turton and Amerjit remained downstairs in the kitchen out of respect, where Myfanwy couldn't resist regaling them all with the red-hot news that Sally had kissed Dave Aziz.

Back in Bronwen's bedroom, the Parkers stood shoulder to shoulder, all holding hands or embracing, except for Frank and Jackie who stood side by side but not touching. Sally broke the silence.

'This is all that matters. The fact that we are here now. A family. Whatever happens, this is all that matters.'

There was a thoughtful pause. Kyle started to sob.

'Well you say that, Sally Parker,' said Bronwen's small but firm voice, 'but this isn't actually about you. It's about me and my grand finale. I'm ready to go now. I'm not sure where I'm going but rest assured, I will be greatly entertained by keeping an eye on you motley lot. I've left the house to Julia, my daughter, Jackie, her wife and you, Frank, and Kyle, my grandsons. What an absolute car crash that's going to be . . .'

Jackie turned to Frank and said quietly,

'Although you may not like how things turned out, Frank, you are still my son. And I love you. I always will.'

Frank looked at Jackie briefly, and then nodded firmly. And then nodded again. He needed to keep nodding so as not to cry. No words came to him. Sally saw this and moved round the circle to Frank. She put her hand on his shoulder.

'. . . and for the love of God, Frank,' said Bronwen with

the little oxygen left in her lungs, 'get rid of that bloody beard. Frank Zappa you are not . . .'

And with that Bronwen Llewellyn left this Earth.

The undertakers would come soon to take her body away. They would then bring the body home to Ymyl Y Byd in her coffin, and she would be laid out in the front parlour for a period of proper, dignified mourning.

Frank reached his hand out and found Sally's. She squeezed his hand back.

'I'm so glad I got hold of Nancy,' he whispered. Sally gave her husband a confused look.

'Hang on, Frank. That was me. I got hold of Nancy,' she whispered back.

'Yeah, but I phoned the number that Kerry gave me,' whispered Frank.

'So did I!' protested Sally. 'I phoned Kerry and got the number off her. I phoned Nancy!'

They looked at each other and smiled. Frank scanned the room, everybody together in a silent circle. This was unheard of in the Parker family, and the like of which would probably never be seen again.

He swallowed hard and gathered his strength.

'Are we all right, Sal?' asked Frank.

Sally didn't answer for a bit.

'Who knows, Frank?' she replied after a while.

Frank nodded. She hadn't let go of his hand. He looked around him. It had been a good day.

Acknowledgements

I need to thank many key people without whom I couldn't have begun to write this book. Ben, Floss and Vita for being the constant compass, anchor and rock of everything. Coky for being the first vital sounding-board for this story. Miko for being a shrewd advisor on everything. My mum and Kasia who always have my back, whichever way the kite is flying. Susie Donkin and Kate Weinberg for their early-doors enthusiasm. Ellie Wood for top thoughts and advice. Samira Higham for her tireless support. Philipp Habsburg for his useful musings on the world of the hedge-fund manager. Neera Sehgal for great thoughts on everything Hayes-related. Paul Stevens for being the most long-suffering literary agent ever. Sherise Hobbs, my brilliant editor at Headline, who saw the potential of the story and was there alongside with supreme patience and upbeat encouragement. Flora Rees for being the most arousingly rigorous copy editor – nobody knows the intricacies of a train route like her. Yeti Lambregts for her superlative artwork. Lou Swannell and Fergus Edmondson at Headline for their commitment and graft, and Mari Evans, Jen Doyle and Becky Bader for championing the book from the earliest stage. I mustn't forget Perks. She didn't have too much to do with the book but she'll be peeved if I don't mention her. Adam Mickiewicz, whom I rather cheekily salute in the first paragraph. Thanks to my local library who put up with me huffing and puffing over the first draft for the whole of winter 2019. And finally, to Leatherhead and all who reside in you. Without you I would be nothing.